Walt Disney

The Return of Snow White and the Seven Dwarfs

Illustrated by
Romano Scarpa

with Luciano Gatto
and Rodolfo Ciminio

Written by
Romano Scarpa
and Guido Martina

FANTAGRAPHICS BOOKS

Seattle

Collector's Note

This is the long-anticipated English-language debut of Disney comics maestro Romano Scarpa's first-ever Snow White tales. Best known for Mickey Mouse and Scrooge McDuck adventures, Romano Scarpa (1927–2005) began his Disney comics career with Disney's original full-length movie princess. These stories, following from Disney's own 1930s and 1940s comics (the Evil Queen's name is Grimhilde, the Seven Dwarfs are brothers), add new witches, wizards, spells, and even a Three Caballeros-inspired parrot to the mix.

Scarpa's enthusiasm and respect for Walt Disney's 1937 masterwork is always evident. And with his loving design of Snow White (inspired by his wife, Sandra Zenardi), the movie's sense of wonder, drama, comedy, and danger bursts from every page.

While lesser hands might have delivered a purely childish take on fairy-tale sequels, Scarpa, building upon a rich legacy, provides a great Disney experience that has taken far too long to reach these shores.

◆

Publisher: Gary Groth • Senior Editor: J. Michael Catron
Designer: Keeli McCarthy • Production: Paul Baresh • Associate Publisher: Eric Reynolds

Fantagraphics Books, Inc. • 7563 Lake City Way NE • Seattle WA 98115 • (800) 657-1100

Visit us at fantagraphics.com. Follow us on Twitter at @fantagraphics
and on Facebook at facebook.com/fantagraphics.

First printing: December 2017 • ISBN 978-1-68396-075-1
Printed in the Republic of Korea • Library of Congress Control Number: 2017944468

The stories in this book were originally published in Italy
and appear here in English for the first time.
"Menace of the Witch's Ruby" ("Biancaneve e verde fiamma") in *Topolino* #78, #79,
and #80, November 10, November 25, and December 10, 1953. (I TL 78-AP)
"Peril of the Witch of Potions" ("Biancaneve, la strega e lo scudiero")
in *Albi D'oro* #54045, November 7, 1954. (I AO 54045-AA)
"The Throne of Diamonds" ("I Sette Nani e il trono di diamanti") in *Topolino* #172
and #173, October 10 and October 25, 1957. (I TL 172-BP)
"The Secret of the Eighth Dwarf" ("I 7 Nani e l'anello di betulla")
in *Topolino* #238, June 19, 1960. (I TL 238-A)

Also available:
Walt Disney's Donald Duck: "Secret of Hondorica"
Walt Disney's Mickey Mouse: "The Mysterious Dr. X"
Walt Disney Uncle Scrooge and Donald Duck: "Escape From Forbidden Valley"

Contents

Cover colors by Keeli McCarthy

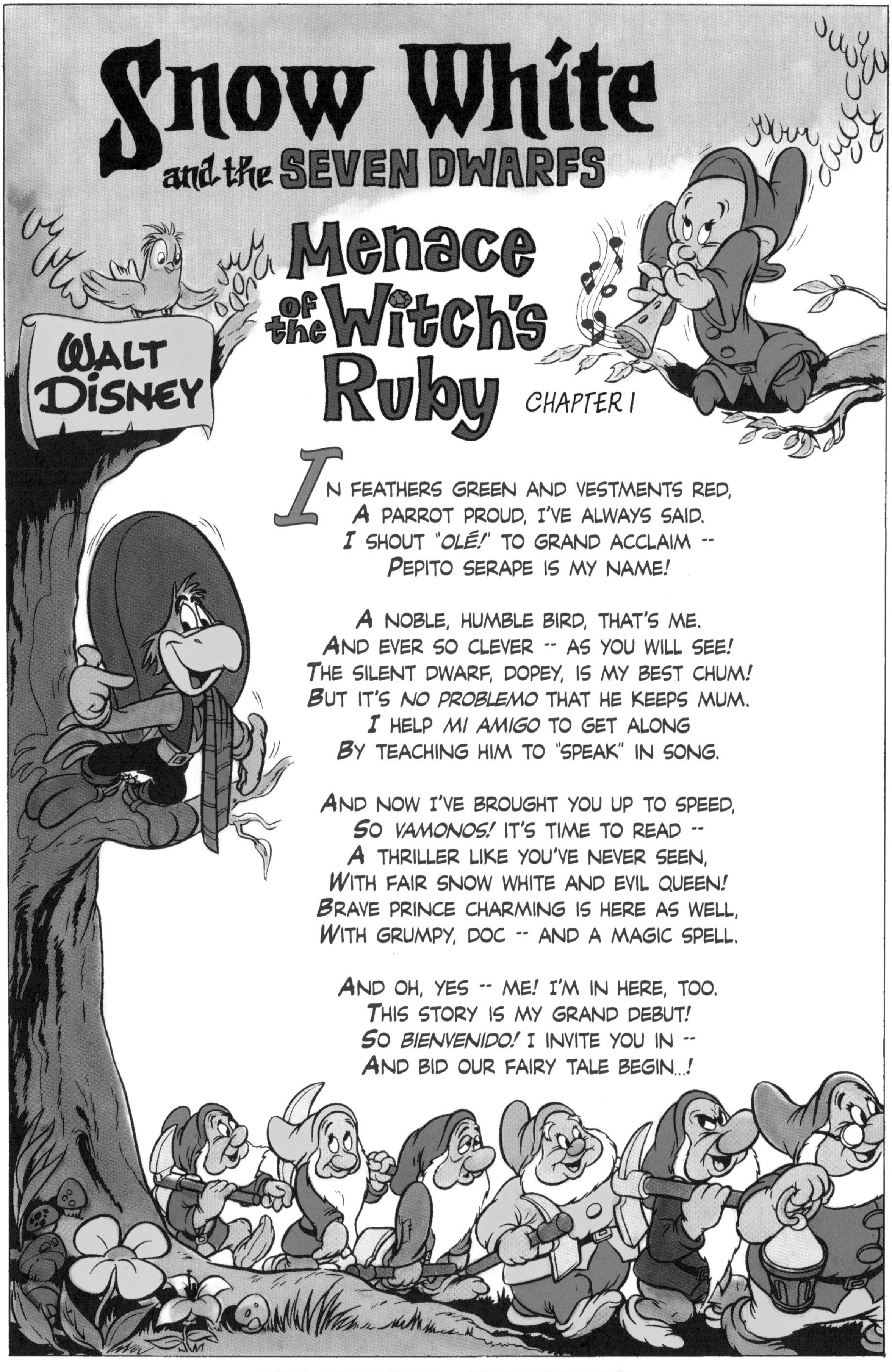
Snow White and the SEVEN DWARFS
Menace of the Witch's Ruby
WALT DISNEY
CHAPTER I
IN FEATHERS GREEN AND VESTMENTS RED,
A PARROT PROUD, I'VE ALWAYS SAID.
I SHOUT "OLÉ!" TO GRAND ACCLAIM --
PEPITO SERAPE IS MY NAME!
A NOBLE, HUMBLE BIRD, THAT'S ME.
AND EVER SO CLEVER -- AS YOU WILL SEE!
THE SILENT DWARF, DOPEY, IS MY BEST CHUM!
BUT IT'S NO PROBLEMO THAT HE KEEPS MUM.
I HELP MI AMIGO TO GET ALONG
BY TEACHING HIM TO "SPEAK" IN SONG.
AND NOW I'VE BROUGHT YOU UP TO SPEED,
SO VAMONOS! IT'S TIME TO READ --
A THRILLER LIKE YOU'VE NEVER SEEN,
WITH FAIR SNOW WHITE AND EVIL QUEEN!
BRAVE PRINCE CHARMING IS HERE AS WELL,
WITH GRUMPY, DOC -- AND A MAGIC SPELL.
AND OH, YES -- ME! I'M IN HERE, TOO.
THIS STORY IS MY GRAND DEBUT!
SO BIENVENIDO! I INVITE YOU IN --
AND BID OUR FAIRY TALE BEGIN...!

STORY: GUIDO MARTINA • ART: ROMANO SCARPA
TRANSLATION: ALBERTO BECATTINI • DIALOG: JONATHAN H. GRAY WITH DAVID GERSTEIN
TITLE LETTERING: KEELI MCCARTHY • EDITING: J. MICHAEL CATRON

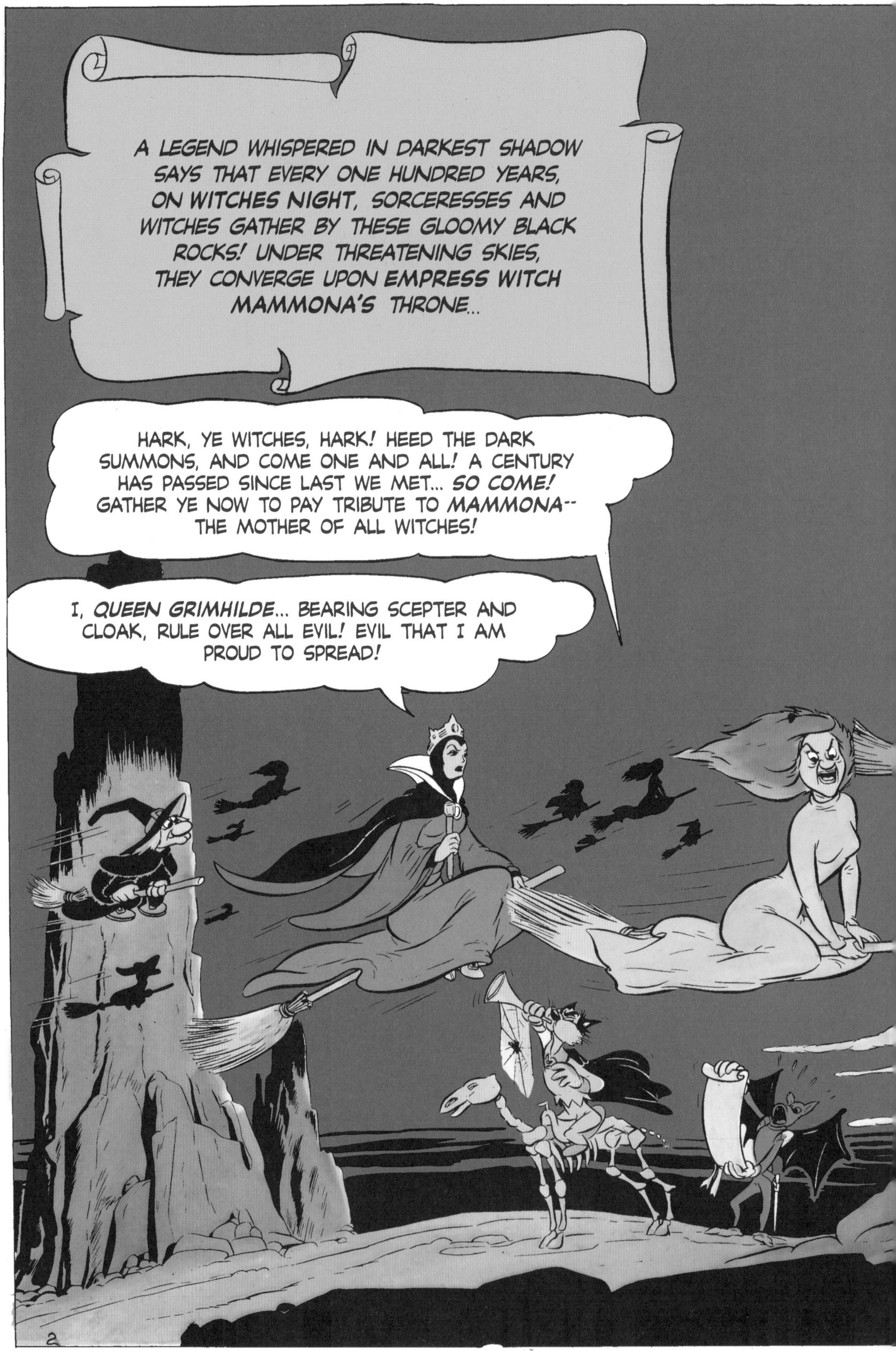
A LEGEND WHISPERED IN DARKEST SHADOW SAYS THAT EVERY ONE HUNDRED YEARS, ON WITCHES NIGHT, SORCERESSES AND WITCHES GATHER BY THESE GLOOMY BLACK ROCKS! UNDER THREATENING SKIES, THEY CONVERGE UPON EMPRESS WITCH MAMMONA'S THRONE...
HARK, YE WITCHES, HARK! HEED THE DARK SUMMONS, AND COME ONE AND ALL! A CENTURY HAS PASSED SINCE LAST WE MET... SO COME! GATHER YE NOW TO PAY TRIBUTE TO MAMMONA-- THE MOTHER OF ALL WITCHES!
I, QUEEN GRIMHILDE... BEARING SCEPTER AND CLOAK, RULE OVER ALL EVIL! EVIL THAT I AM PROUD TO SPREAD!
2

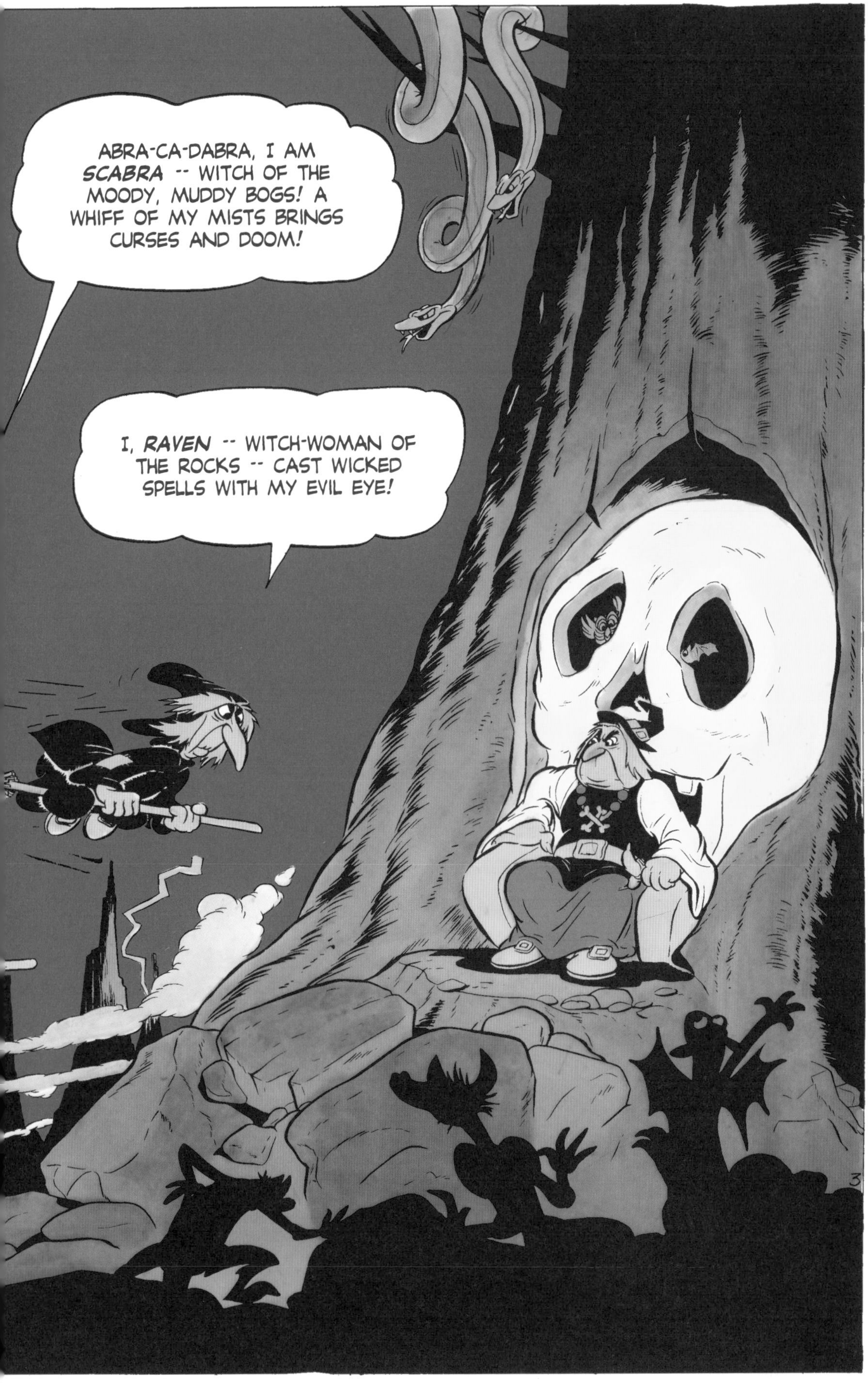
ABRA-CA-DABRA, I AM *SCABRA* -- WITCH OF THE MOODY, MUDDY BOGS! A WHIFF OF MY MISTS BRINGS CURSES AND DOOM!
I, *RAVEN* -- WITCH-WOMAN OF THE ROCKS -- CAST WICKED SPELLS WITH MY EVIL EYE!

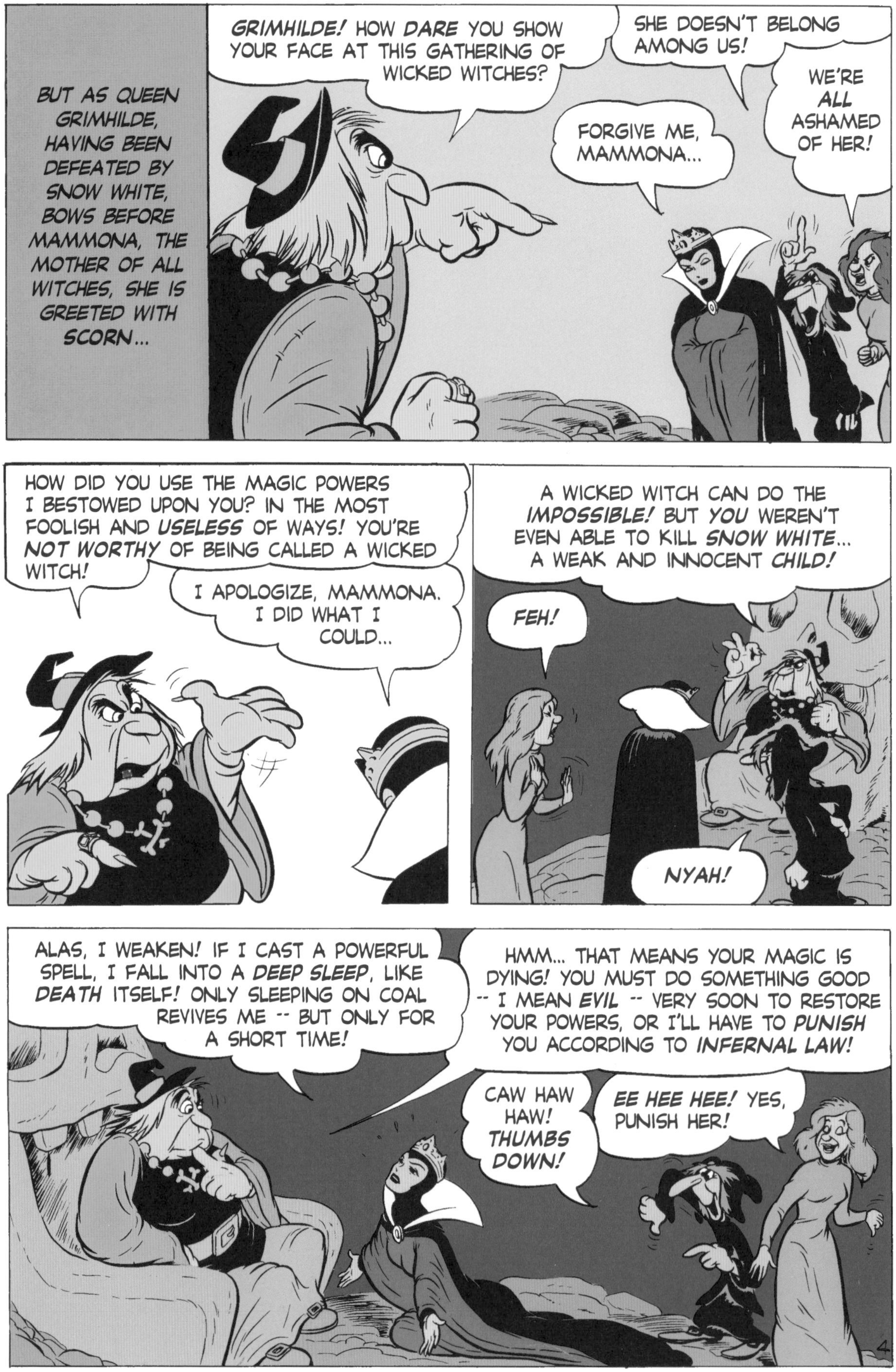
BUT AS QUEEN GRIMHILDE, HAVING BEEN DEFEATED BY SNOW WHITE, BOWS BEFORE MAMMONA, THE MOTHER OF ALL WITCHES, SHE IS GREETED WITH SCORN...
GRIMHILDE! HOW DARE YOU SHOW YOUR FACE AT THIS GATHERING OF WICKED WITCHES?
SHE DOESN'T BELONG AMONG US!
WE'RE ALL ASHAMED OF HER!
FORGIVE ME, MAMMONA...
HOW DID YOU USE THE MAGIC POWERS I BESTOWED UPON YOU? IN THE MOST FOOLISH AND USELESS OF WAYS! YOU'RE NOT WORTHY OF BEING CALLED A WICKED WITCH!
I APOLOGIZE, MAMMONA. I DID WHAT I COULD...
A WICKED WITCH CAN DO THE IMPOSSIBLE! BUT YOU WEREN'T EVEN ABLE TO KILL SNOW WHITE... A WEAK AND INNOCENT CHILD!
FEH!
NYAH!
ALAS, I WEAKEN! IF I CAST A POWERFUL SPELL, I FALL INTO A DEEP SLEEP, LIKE DEATH ITSELF! ONLY SLEEPING ON COAL REVIVES ME -- BUT ONLY FOR A SHORT TIME!
HMM... THAT MEANS YOUR MAGIC IS DYING! YOU MUST DO SOMETHING GOOD -- I MEAN EVIL -- VERY SOON TO RESTORE YOUR POWERS, OR I'LL HAVE TO PUNISH YOU ACCORDING TO INFERNAL LAW!
CAW HAW HAW! THUMBS DOWN!
EE HEE HEE! YES, PUNISH HER!
4

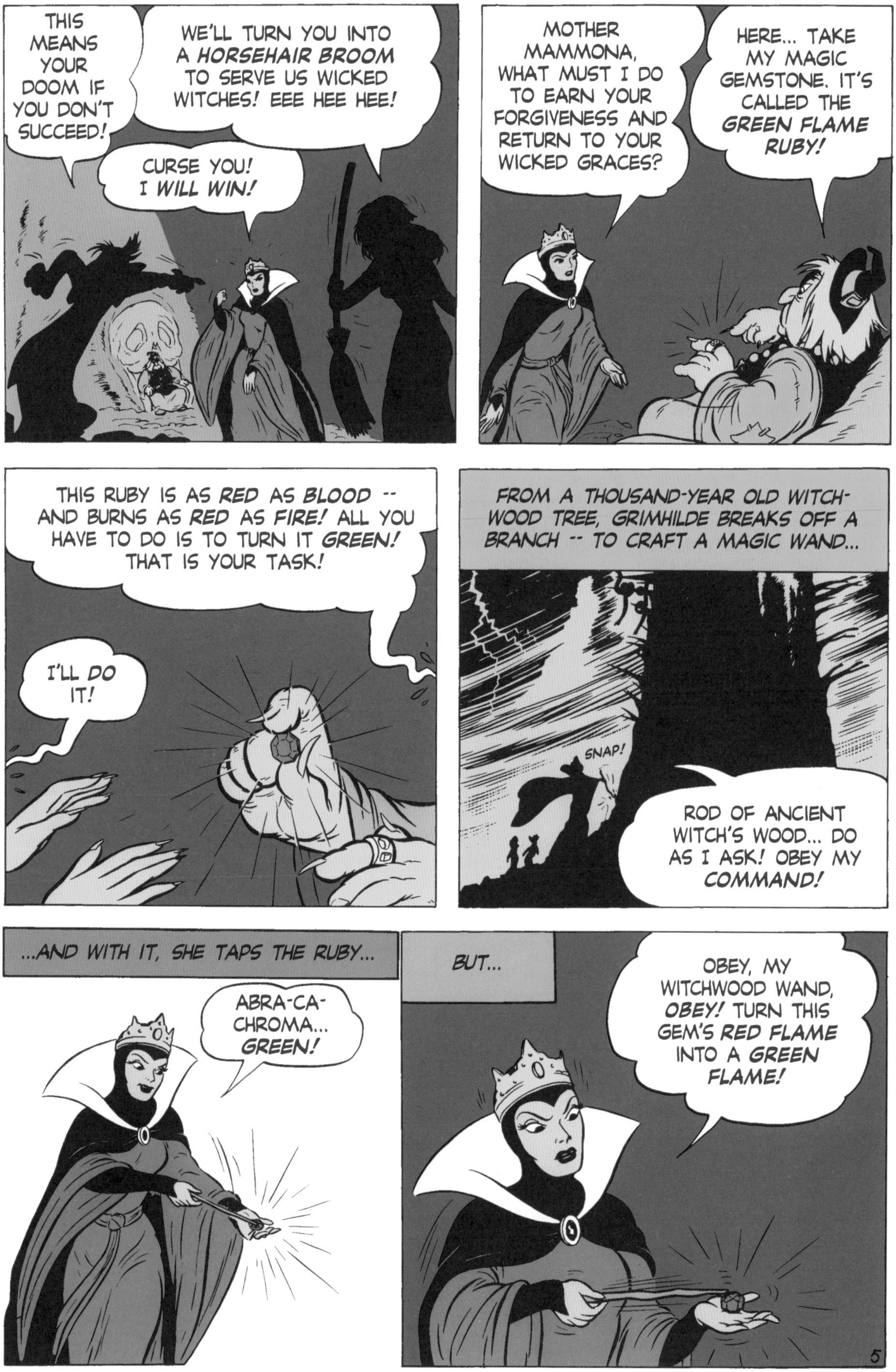
THIS MEANS YOUR DOOM IF YOU DON'T SUCCEED!
WE'LL TURN YOU INTO A HORSEHAIR BROOM TO SERVE US WICKED WITCHES! EEE HEE HEE!
CURSE YOU! I WILL WIN!
MOTHER MAMMONA, WHAT MUST I DO TO EARN YOUR FORGIVENESS AND RETURN TO YOUR WICKED GRACES?
HERE... TAKE MY MAGIC GEMSTONE. IT'S CALLED THE GREEN FLAME RUBY!
THIS RUBY IS AS RED AS BLOOD -- AND BURNS AS RED AS FIRE! ALL YOU HAVE TO DO IS TO TURN IT GREEN! THAT IS YOUR TASK!
I'LL DO IT!
FROM A THOUSAND-YEAR OLD WITCH-WOOD TREE, GRIMHILDE BREAKS OFF A BRANCH -- TO CRAFT A MAGIC WAND...
SNAP!
ROD OF ANCIENT WITCH'S WOOD... DO AS I ASK! OBEY MY COMMAND!
...AND WITH IT, SHE TAPS THE RUBY...
ABRA-CA-CHROMA... GREEN!
BUT...
OBEY, MY WITCHWOOD WAND, OBEY! TURN THIS GEM'S RED FLAME INTO A GREEN FLAME!
5

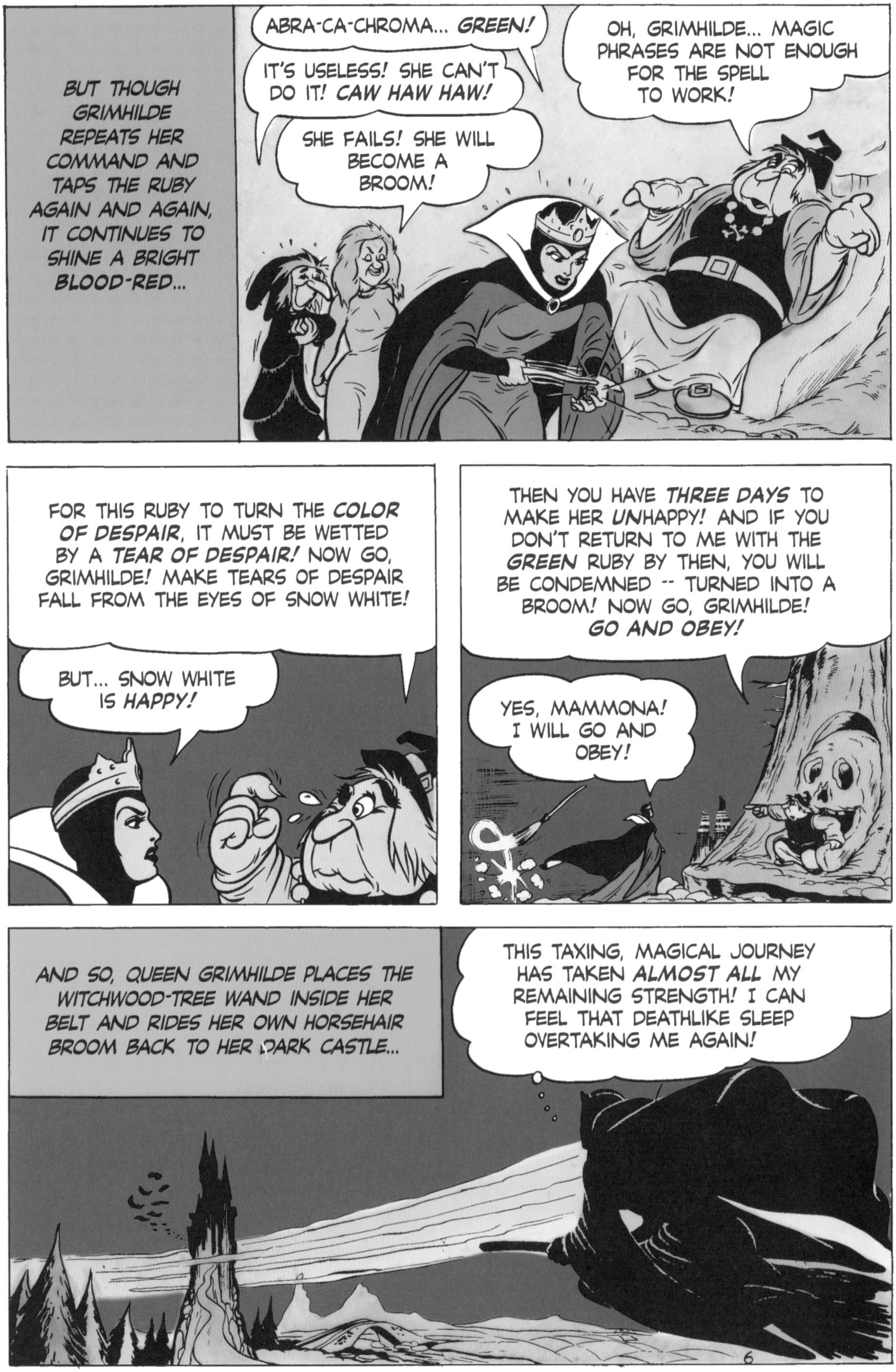

BUT THOUGH GRIMHILDE REPEATS HER COMMAND AND TAPS THE RUBY AGAIN AND AGAIN, IT CONTINUES TO SHINE A BRIGHT BLOOD-RED...
ABRA-CA-CHROMA... GREEN!
IT'S USELESS! SHE CAN'T DO IT! CAW HAW HAW!
SHE FAILS! SHE WILL BECOME A BROOM!
OH, GRIMHILDE... MAGIC PHRASES ARE NOT ENOUGH FOR THE SPELL TO WORK!
FOR THIS RUBY TO TURN THE COLOR OF DESPAIR, IT MUST BE WETTED BY A TEAR OF DESPAIR! NOW GO, GRIMHILDE! MAKE TEARS OF DESPAIR FALL FROM THE EYES OF SNOW WHITE!
BUT... SNOW WHITE IS HAPPY!
THEN YOU HAVE THREE DAYS TO MAKE HER UNHAPPY! AND IF YOU DON'T RETURN TO ME WITH THE GREEN RUBY BY THEN, YOU WILL BE CONDEMNED -- TURNED INTO A BROOM! NOW GO, GRIMHILDE! GO AND OBEY!
YES, MAMMONA! I WILL GO AND OBEY!
AND SO, QUEEN GRIMHILDE PLACES THE WITCHWOOD-TREE WAND INSIDE HER BELT AND RIDES HER OWN HORSEHAIR BROOM BACK TO HER DARK CASTLE...
THIS TAXING, MAGICAL JOURNEY HAS TAKEN ALMOST ALL MY REMAINING STRENGTH! I CAN FEEL THAT DEATHLIKE SLEEP OVERTAKING ME AGAIN!
6

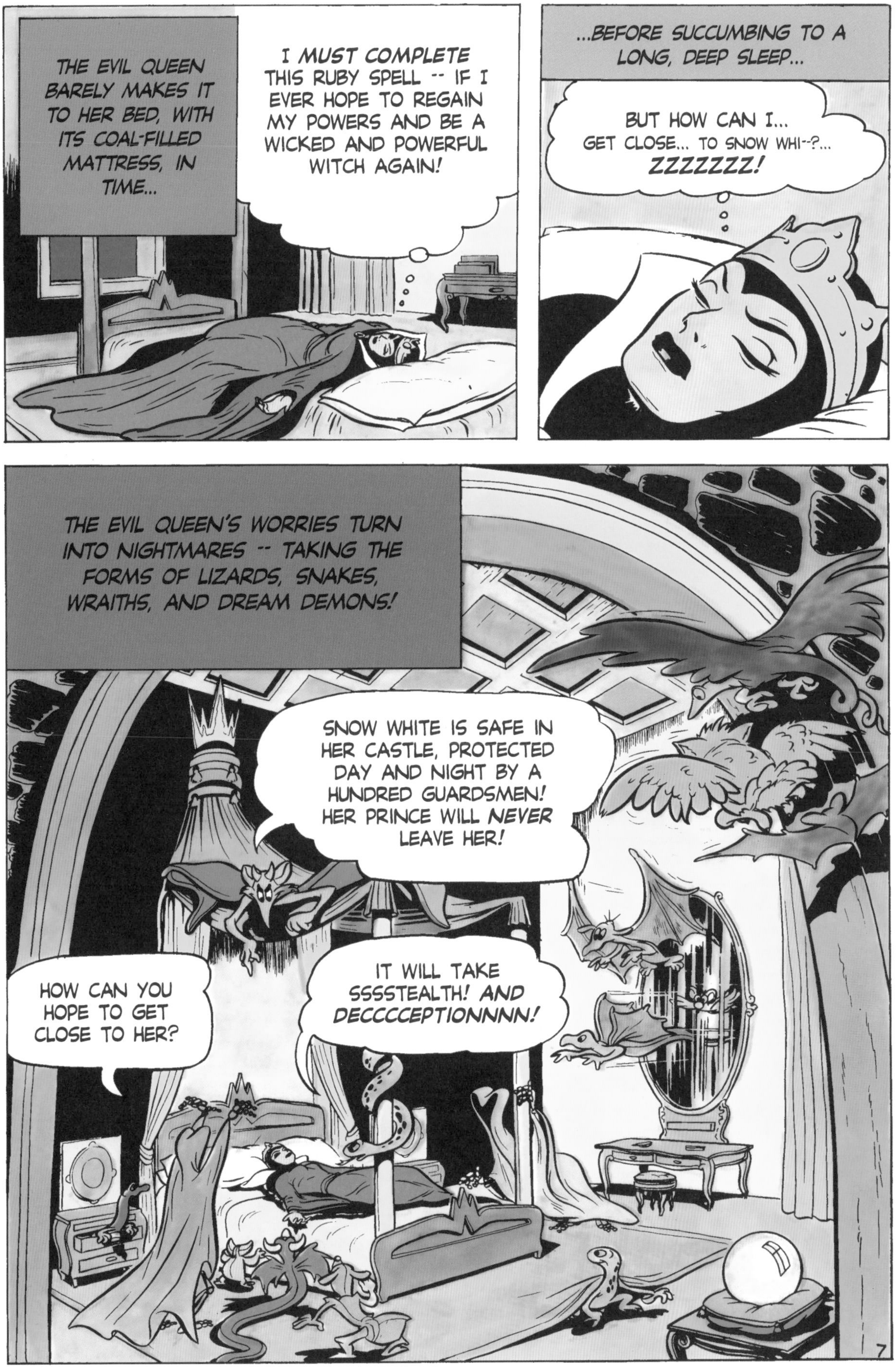
THE EVIL QUEEN BARELY MAKES IT TO HER BED, WITH ITS COAL-FILLED MATTRESS, IN TIME...
I MUST COMPLETE THIS RUBY SPELL -- IF I EVER HOPE TO REGAIN MY POWERS AND BE A WICKED AND POWERFUL WITCH AGAIN!
...BEFORE SUCCUMBING TO A LONG, DEEP SLEEP...
BUT HOW CAN I... GET CLOSE... TO SNOW WHI--?... ZZZZZZZ!
THE EVIL QUEEN'S WORRIES TURN INTO NIGHTMARES -- TAKING THE FORMS OF LIZARDS, SNAKES, WRAITHS, AND DREAM DEMONS!
SNOW WHITE IS SAFE IN HER CASTLE, PROTECTED DAY AND NIGHT BY A HUNDRED GUARDSMEN! HER PRINCE WILL NEVER LEAVE HER!
HOW CAN YOU HOPE TO GET CLOSE TO HER?
IT WILL TAKE SSSSTEALTH! AND DECCCCEPTIONNNN!
7

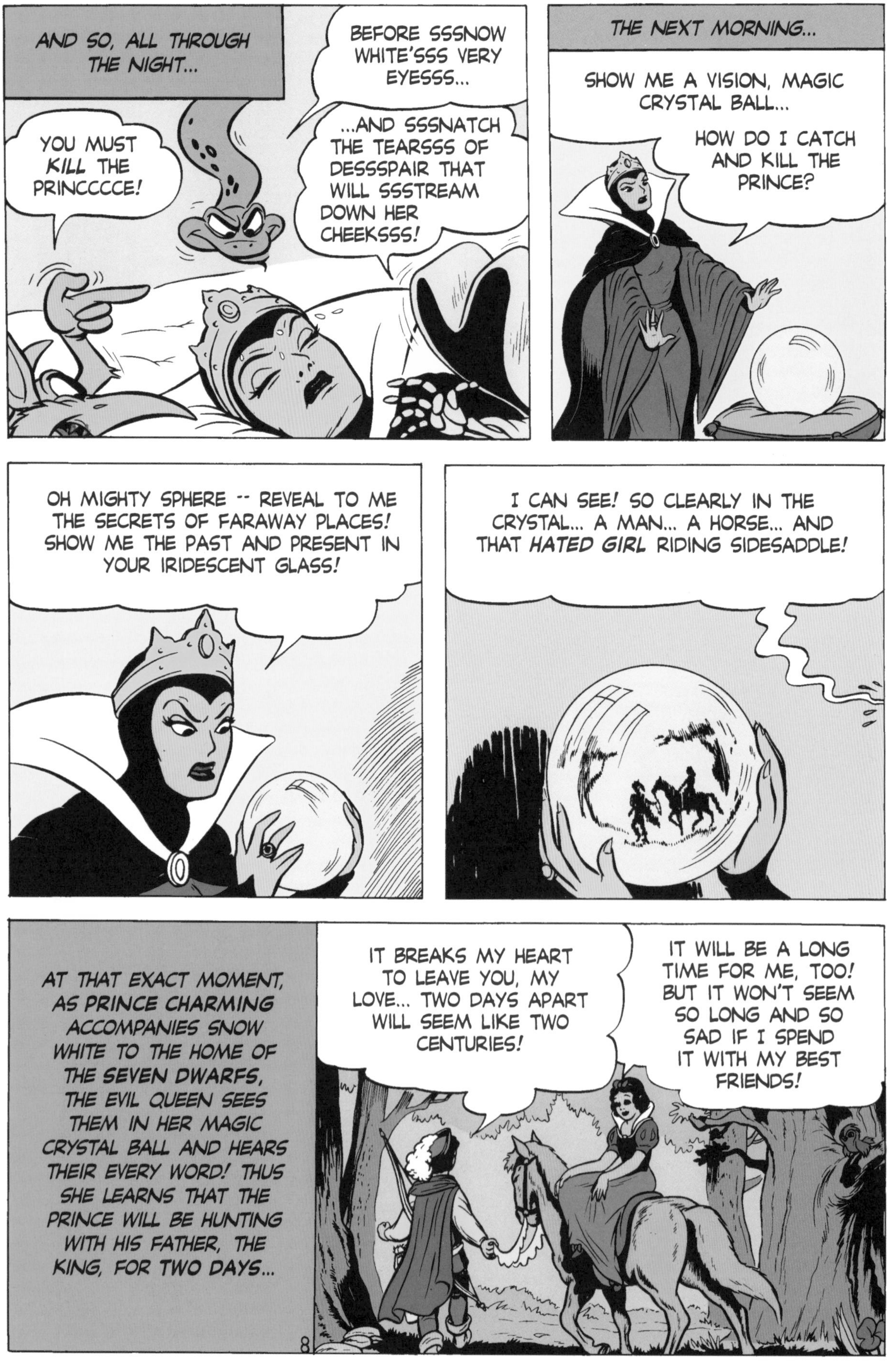
AND SO, ALL THROUGH THE NIGHT...
YOU MUST KILL THE PRINCCCCE!
BEFORE SSSNOW WHITE'SSS VERY EYESSS...
...AND SSSNATCH THE TEARSSS OF DESSSPAIR THAT WILL SSSTREAM DOWN HER CHEEKSSS!
THE NEXT MORNING...
SHOW ME A VISION, MAGIC CRYSTAL BALL...
HOW DO I CATCH AND KILL THE PRINCE?
OH MIGHTY SPHERE -- REVEAL TO ME THE SECRETS OF FARAWAY PLACES! SHOW ME THE PAST AND PRESENT IN YOUR IRIDESCENT GLASS!
I CAN SEE! SO CLEARLY IN THE CRYSTAL... A MAN... A HORSE... AND THAT HATED GIRL RIDING SIDESADDLE!
AT THAT EXACT MOMENT, AS PRINCE CHARMING ACCOMPANIES SNOW WHITE TO THE HOME OF THE SEVEN DWARFS, THE EVIL QUEEN SEES THEM IN HER MAGIC CRYSTAL BALL AND HEARS THEIR EVERY WORD! THUS SHE LEARNS THAT THE PRINCE WILL BE HUNTING WITH HIS FATHER, THE KING, FOR TWO DAYS...
IT BREAKS MY HEART TO LEAVE YOU, MY LOVE... TWO DAYS APART WILL SEEM LIKE TWO CENTURIES!
IT WILL BE A LONG TIME FOR ME, TOO! BUT IT WON'T SEEM SO LONG AND SO SAD IF I SPEND IT WITH MY BEST FRIENDS!
8

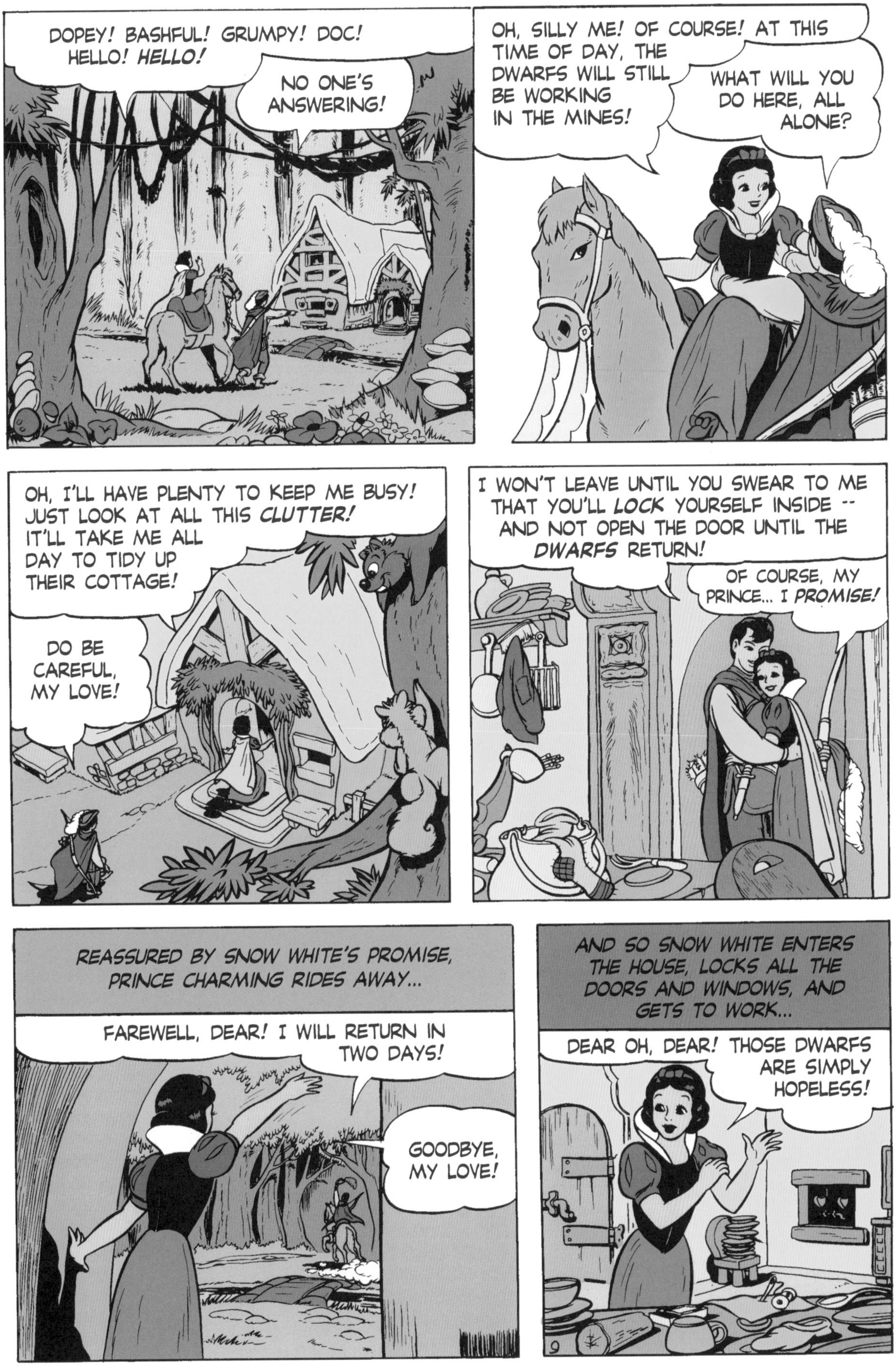
DOPEY! BASHFUL! GRUMPY! DOC! HELLO! HELLO!
NO ONE'S ANSWERING!
OH, SILLY ME! OF COURSE! AT THIS TIME OF DAY, THE DWARFS WILL STILL BE WORKING IN THE MINES!
WHAT WILL YOU DO HERE, ALL ALONE?
OH, I'LL HAVE PLENTY TO KEEP ME BUSY! JUST LOOK AT ALL THIS CLUTTER! IT'LL TAKE ME ALL DAY TO TIDY UP THEIR COTTAGE!
DO BE CAREFUL, MY LOVE!
I WON'T LEAVE UNTIL YOU SWEAR TO ME THAT YOU'LL LOCK YOURSELF INSIDE -- AND NOT OPEN THE DOOR UNTIL THE DWARFS RETURN!
OF COURSE, MY PRINCE... I PROMISE!
REASSURED BY SNOW WHITE'S PROMISE, PRINCE CHARMING RIDES AWAY...
FAREWELL, DEAR! I WILL RETURN IN TWO DAYS!
GOODBYE, MY LOVE!
AND SO SNOW WHITE ENTERS THE HOUSE, LOCKS ALL THE DOORS AND WINDOWS, AND GETS TO WORK...
DEAR OH, DEAR! THOSE DWARFS ARE SIMPLY HOPELESS!

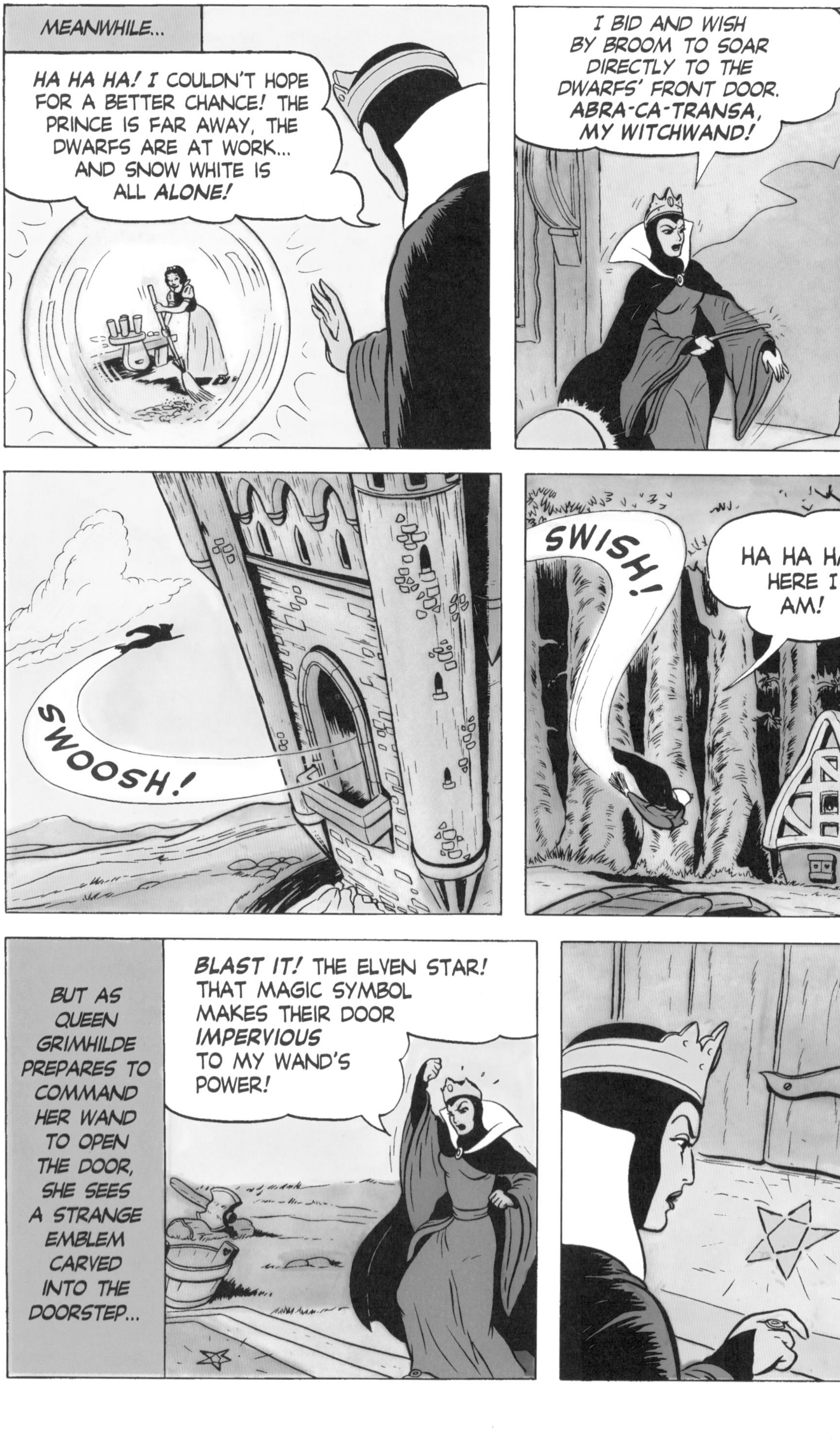
MEANWHILE...
HA HA HA! I COULDN'T HOPE FOR A BETTER CHANCE! THE PRINCE IS FAR AWAY, THE DWARFS ARE AT WORK... AND SNOW WHITE IS ALL ALONE!
I BID AND WISH BY BROOM TO SOAR DIRECTLY TO THE DWARFS' FRONT DOOR. ABRA-CA-TRANSA, MY WITCHWAND!
SWOOSH!
SWISH!
HA HA HA! HERE I AM!
BUT AS QUEEN GRIMHILDE PREPARES TO COMMAND HER WAND TO OPEN THE DOOR, SHE SEES A STRANGE EMBLEM CARVED INTO THE DOORSTEP...
BLAST IT! THE ELVEN STAR! THAT MAGIC SYMBOL MAKES THEIR DOOR IMPERVIOUS TO MY WAND'S POWER!
10

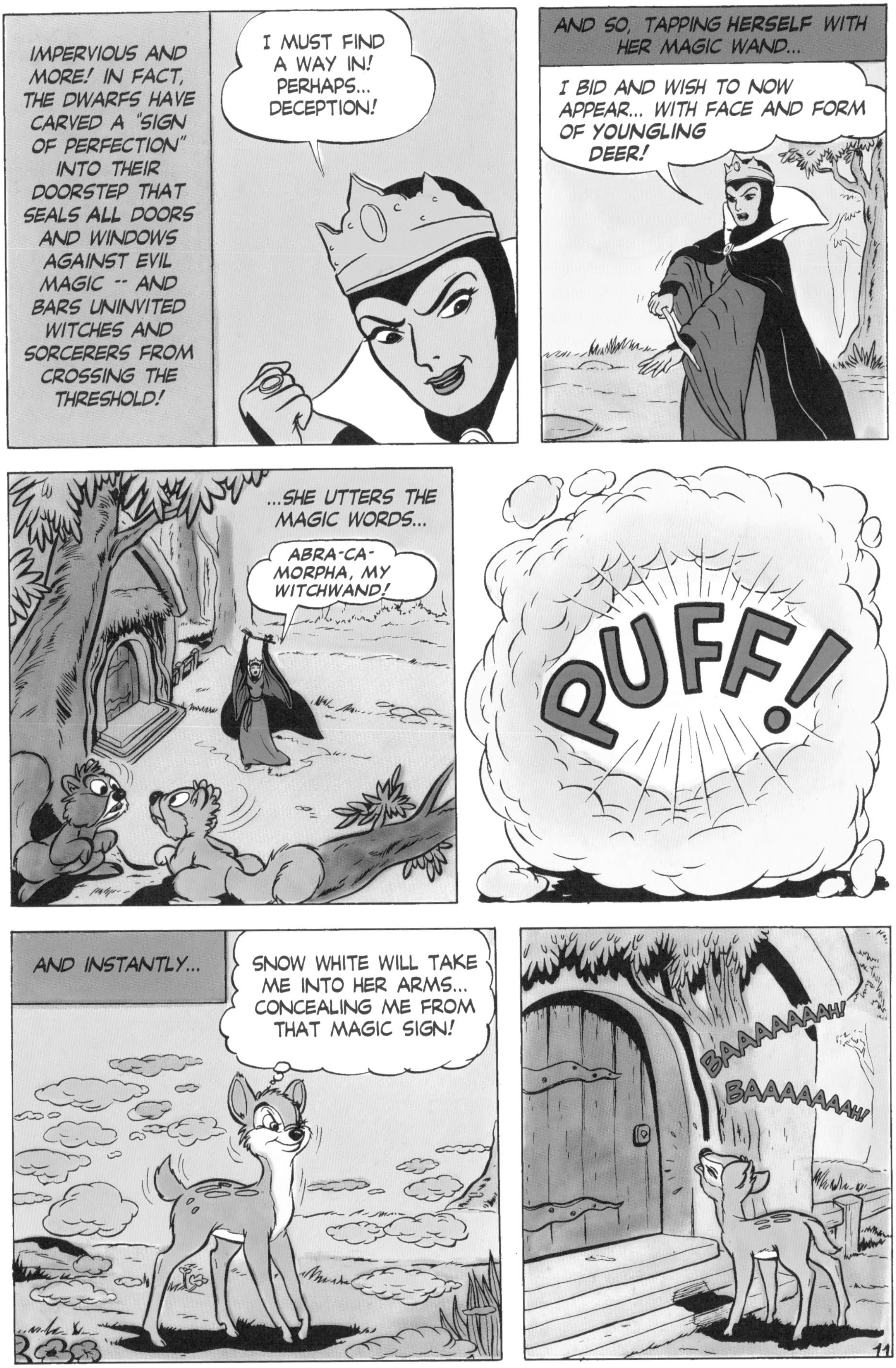
IMPERVIOUS AND MORE! IN FACT, THE DWARFS HAVE CARVED A "SIGN OF PERFECTION" INTO THEIR DOORSTEP THAT SEALS ALL DOORS AND WINDOWS AGAINST EVIL MAGIC -- AND BARS UNINVITED WITCHES AND SORCERERS FROM CROSSING THE THRESHOLD!
I MUST FIND A WAY IN! PERHAPS... DECEPTION!
AND SO, TAPPING HERSELF WITH HER MAGIC WAND...
I BID AND WISH TO NOW APPEAR... WITH FACE AND FORM OF YOUNGLING DEER!
...SHE UTTERS THE MAGIC WORDS...
ABRA-CA-MORPHA, MY WITCHWAND!
PUFF!
AND INSTANTLY...
SNOW WHITE WILL TAKE ME INTO HER ARMS... CONCEALING ME FROM THAT MAGIC SIGN!
BAAAAAAAH!
BAAAAAAAH!
11

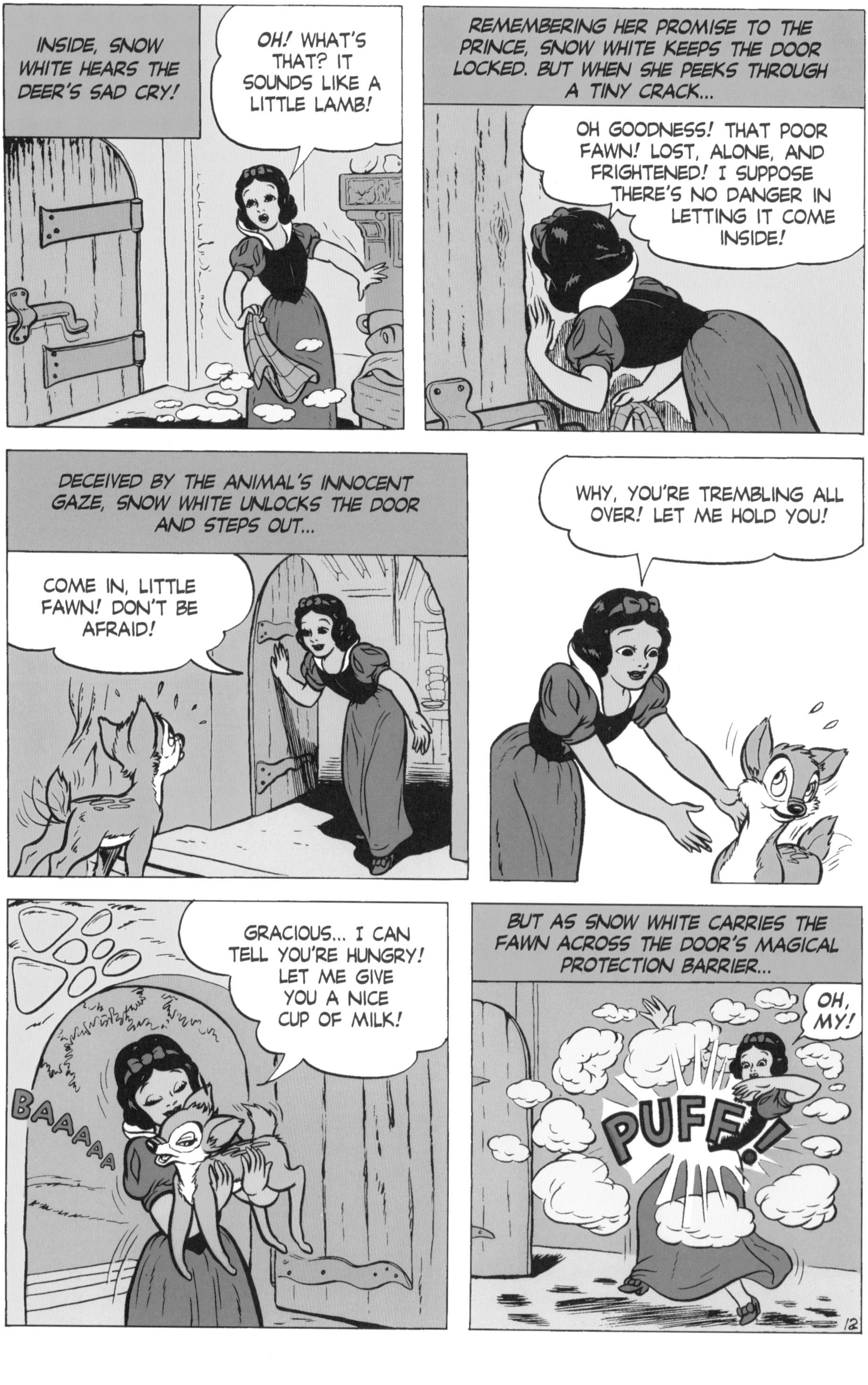
INSIDE, SNOW WHITE HEARS THE DEER'S SAD CRY!
OH! WHAT'S THAT? IT SOUNDS LIKE A LITTLE LAMB!
REMEMBERING HER PROMISE TO THE PRINCE, SNOW WHITE KEEPS THE DOOR LOCKED. BUT WHEN SHE PEEKS THROUGH A TINY CRACK...
OH GOODNESS! THAT POOR FAWN! LOST, ALONE, AND FRIGHTENED! I SUPPOSE THERE'S NO DANGER IN LETTING IT COME INSIDE!
DECEIVED BY THE ANIMAL'S INNOCENT GAZE, SNOW WHITE UNLOCKS THE DOOR AND STEPS OUT...
COME IN, LITTLE FAWN! DON'T BE AFRAID!
WHY, YOU'RE TREMBLING ALL OVER! LET ME HOLD YOU!
GRACIOUS... I CAN TELL YOU'RE HUNGRY! LET ME GIVE YOU A NICE CUP OF MILK!
BAAAAA
BUT AS SNOW WHITE CARRIES THE FAWN ACROSS THE DOOR'S MAGICAL PROTECTION BARRIER...
OH, MY!
PUFF!
12

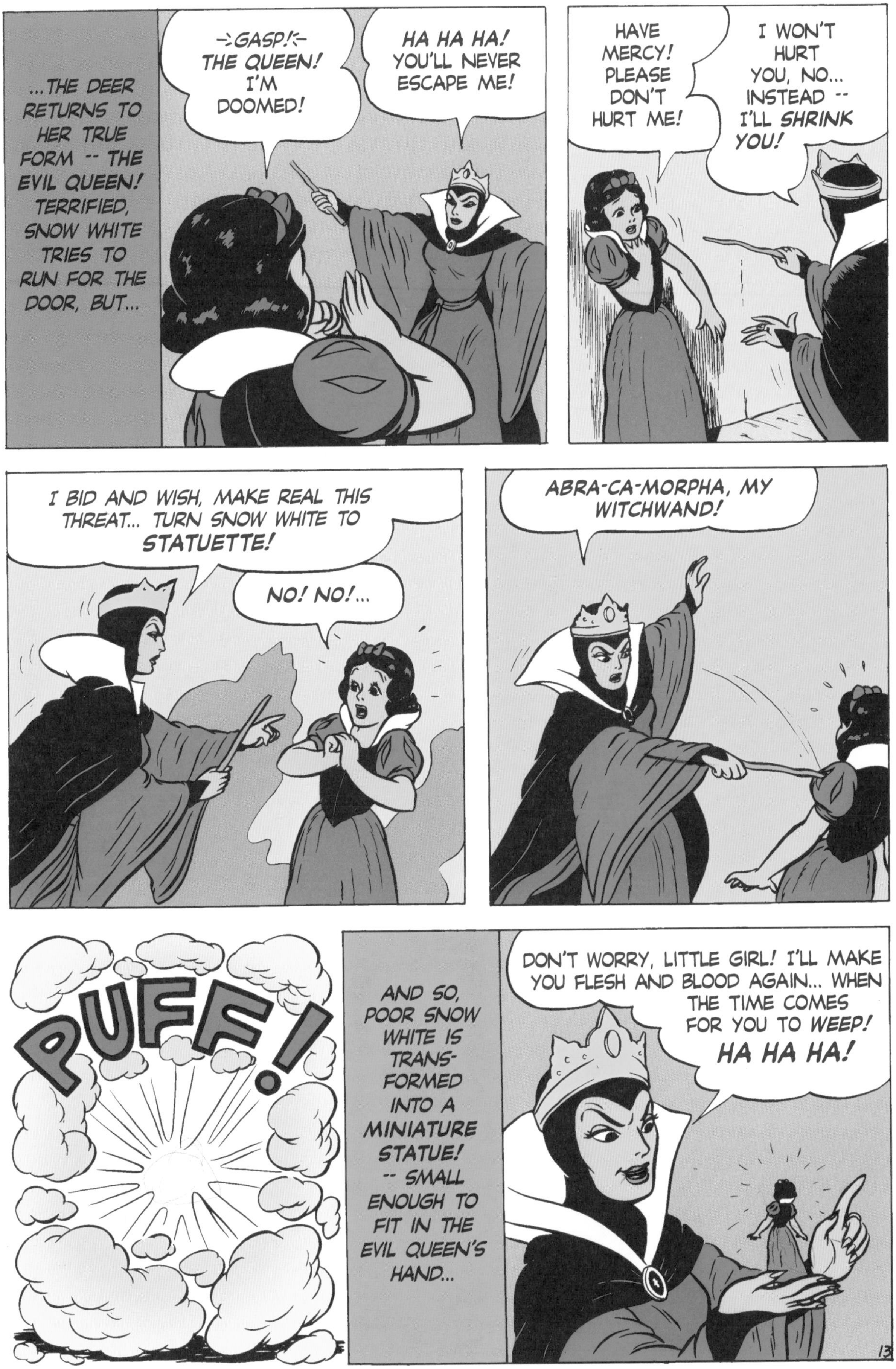
...THE DEER RETURNS TO HER TRUE FORM -- THE EVIL QUEEN! TERRIFIED, SNOW WHITE TRIES TO RUN FOR THE DOOR, BUT...
-GASP!- THE QUEEN! I'M DOOMED!
HA HA HA! YOU'LL NEVER ESCAPE ME!
HAVE MERCY! PLEASE DON'T HURT ME!
I WON'T HURT YOU, NO... INSTEAD -- I'LL SHRINK YOU!
I BID AND WISH, MAKE REAL THIS THREAT... TURN SNOW WHITE TO STATUETTE!
NO! NO!...
ABRA-CA-MORPHA, MY WITCHWAND!
PUFF!
AND SO, POOR SNOW WHITE IS TRANS-FORMED INTO A MINIATURE STATUE! -- SMALL ENOUGH TO FIT IN THE EVIL QUEEN'S HAND...
DON'T WORRY, LITTLE GIRL! I'LL MAKE YOU FLESH AND BLOOD AGAIN... WHEN THE TIME COMES FOR YOU TO WEEP! HA HA HA!
13

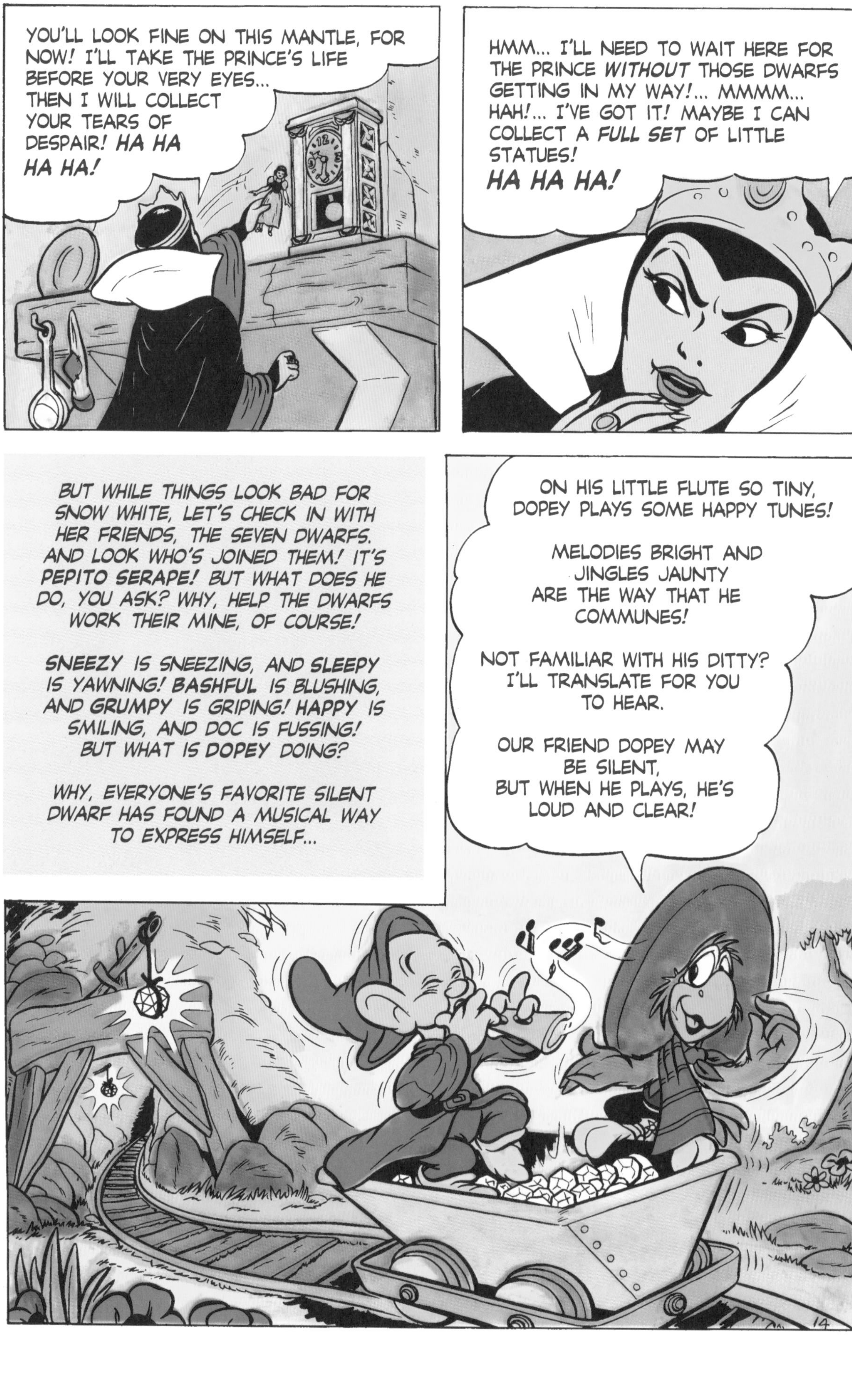

YOU'LL LOOK FINE ON THIS MANTLE, FOR NOW! I'LL TAKE THE PRINCE'S LIFE BEFORE YOUR VERY EYES... THEN I WILL COLLECT YOUR TEARS OF DESPAIR! HA HA HA HA!
HMM... I'LL NEED TO WAIT HERE FOR THE PRINCE WITHOUT THOSE DWARFS GETTING IN MY WAY!... MMMM... HAH!... I'VE GOT IT! MAYBE I CAN COLLECT A FULL SET OF LITTLE STATUES! HA HA HA!
BUT WHILE THINGS LOOK BAD FOR SNOW WHITE, LET'S CHECK IN WITH HER FRIENDS, THE SEVEN DWARFS. AND LOOK WHO'S JOINED THEM! IT'S PEPITO SERAPE! BUT WHAT DOES HE DO, YOU ASK? WHY, HELP THE DWARFS WORK THEIR MINE, OF COURSE!
SNEEZY IS SNEEZING, AND SLEEPY IS YAWNING! BASHFUL IS BLUSHING, AND GRUMPY IS GRIPING! HAPPY IS SMILING, AND DOC IS FUSSING! BUT WHAT IS DOPEY DOING?
WHY, EVERYONE'S FAVORITE SILENT DWARF HAS FOUND A MUSICAL WAY TO EXPRESS HIMSELF...
ON HIS LITTLE FLUTE SO TINY, DOPEY PLAYS SOME HAPPY TUNES!
MELODIES BRIGHT AND JINGLES JAUNTY ARE THE WAY THAT HE COMMUNES!
NOT FAMILIAR WITH HIS DITTY? I'LL TRANSLATE FOR YOU TO HEAR.
OUR FRIEND DOPEY MAY BE SILENT, BUT WHEN HE PLAYS, HE'S LOUD AND CLEAR!
14

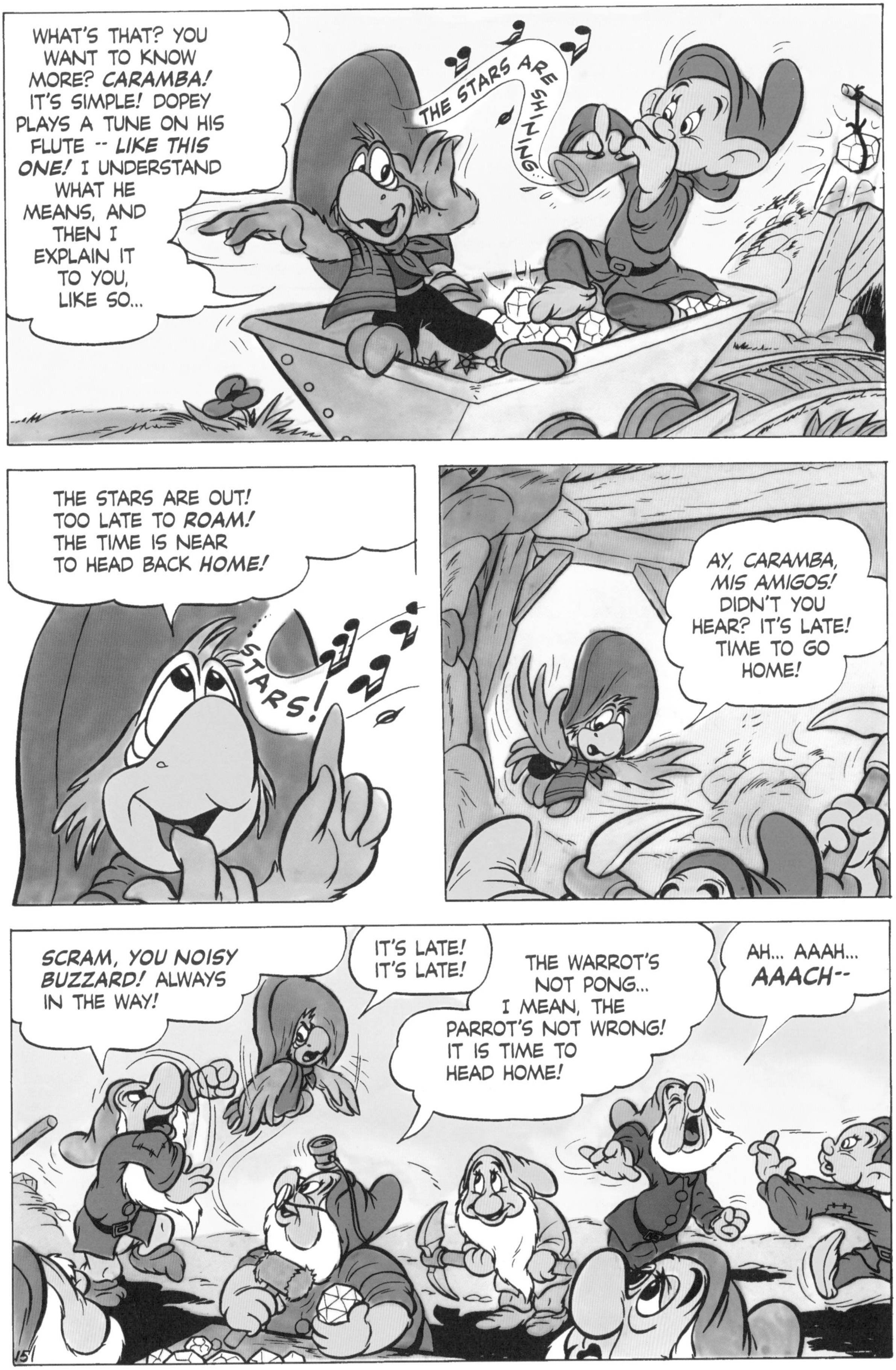
WHAT'S THAT? YOU WANT TO KNOW MORE? CARAMBA! IT'S SIMPLE! DOPEY PLAYS A TUNE ON HIS FLUTE -- LIKE THIS ONE! I UNDERSTAND WHAT HE MEANS, AND THEN I EXPLAIN IT TO YOU, LIKE SO...
THE STARS ARE SHINING...
THE STARS ARE OUT! TOO LATE TO ROAM! THE TIME IS NEAR TO HEAD BACK HOME!
STARS!
AY, CARAMBA, MIS AMIGOS! DIDN'T YOU HEAR? IT'S LATE! TIME TO GO HOME!
SCRAM, YOU NOISY BUZZARD! ALWAYS IN THE WAY!
IT'S LATE! IT'S LATE!
THE WARROT'S NOT PONG... I MEAN, THE PARROT'S NOT WRONG! IT IS TIME TO HEAD HOME!
AH... AAAH... AAACH--
15

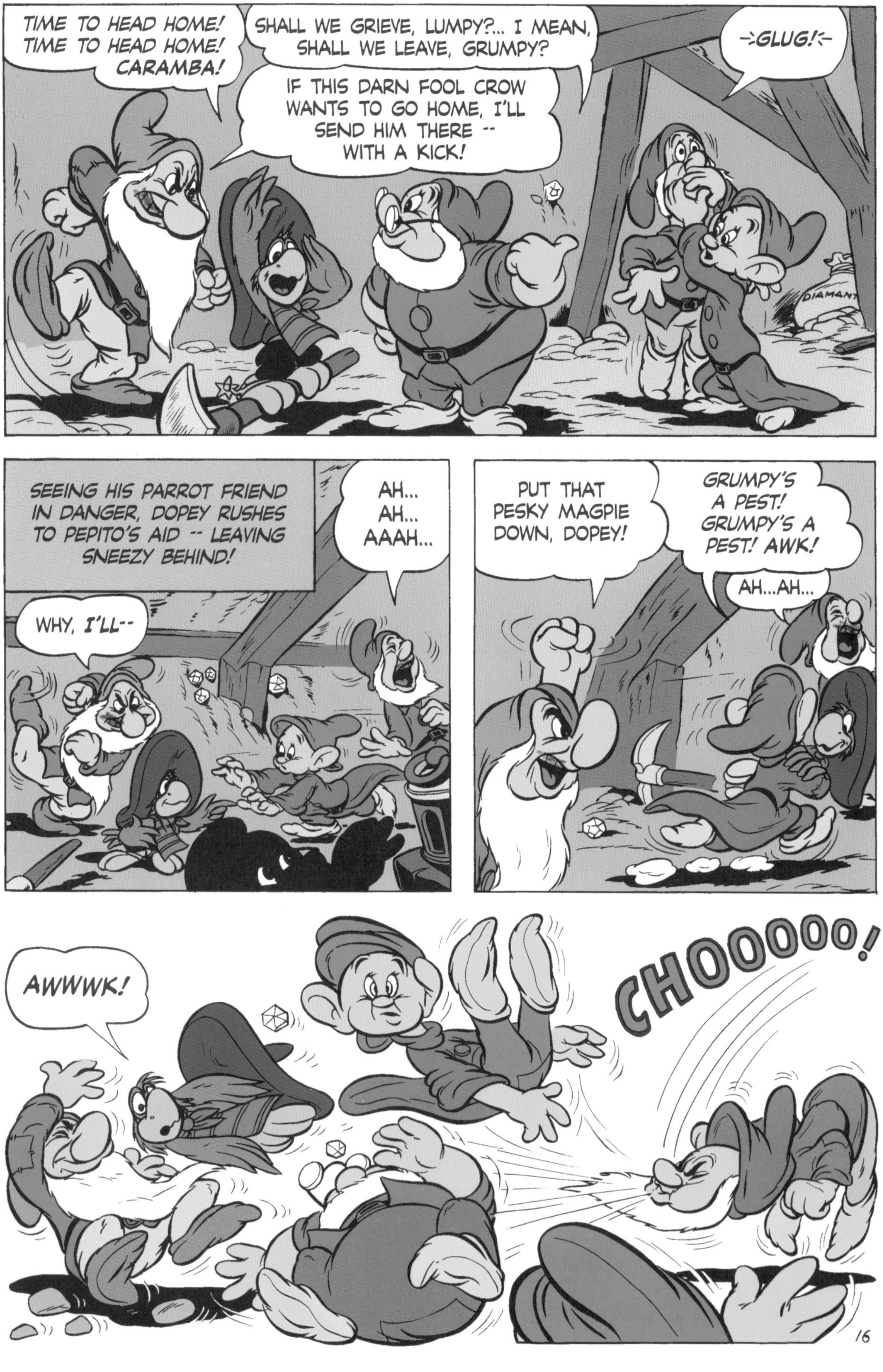

TIME TO HEAD HOME! TIME TO HEAD HOME! CARAMBA!
SHALL WE GRIEVE, LUMPY?... I MEAN, SHALL WE LEAVE, GRUMPY?
IF THIS DARN FOOL CROW WANTS TO GO HOME, I'LL SEND HIM THERE -- WITH A KICK!
-GLUG!-
DIAMANT
SEEING HIS PARROT FRIEND IN DANGER, DOPEY RUSHES TO PEPITO'S AID -- LEAVING SNEEZY BEHIND!
AH... AH... AAAH...
WHY, I'LL--
PUT THAT PESKY MAGPIE DOWN, DOPEY!
GRUMPY'S A PEST! GRUMPY'S A PEST! AWK!
AH...AH...
AWWWK!
CHOOOOOO!
16

AY-YI-YOW!

CARAMBA! I'VE NEVER BEEN SO INSULTED! I'M GOING HOME! ADIOS!

GET BACK HERE, DOPEY! WE AIN'T GOING HOME 'TIL OUR WORK IS DONE!

YOU HAD YOUR FILL O' DANCING AND PLAYING! NOW GET BACK TO WORK!

WHEN DO WE GO HOME?

WHEN THE RIME'S TIGHT... TIME'S RIGHT! NOW YA GOT ME DOIN' IT!

AND SO, PEPITO RETURNS TO THE DWARFS' COTTAGE, HIS PRIDE -- AND BACKSIDE -- BOTH DEEPLY OFFENDED...

OK, HAVE IT YOUR WAY, GRUMPY! YOU'RE RID OF ME! ⇥HMMPF!⇤

17

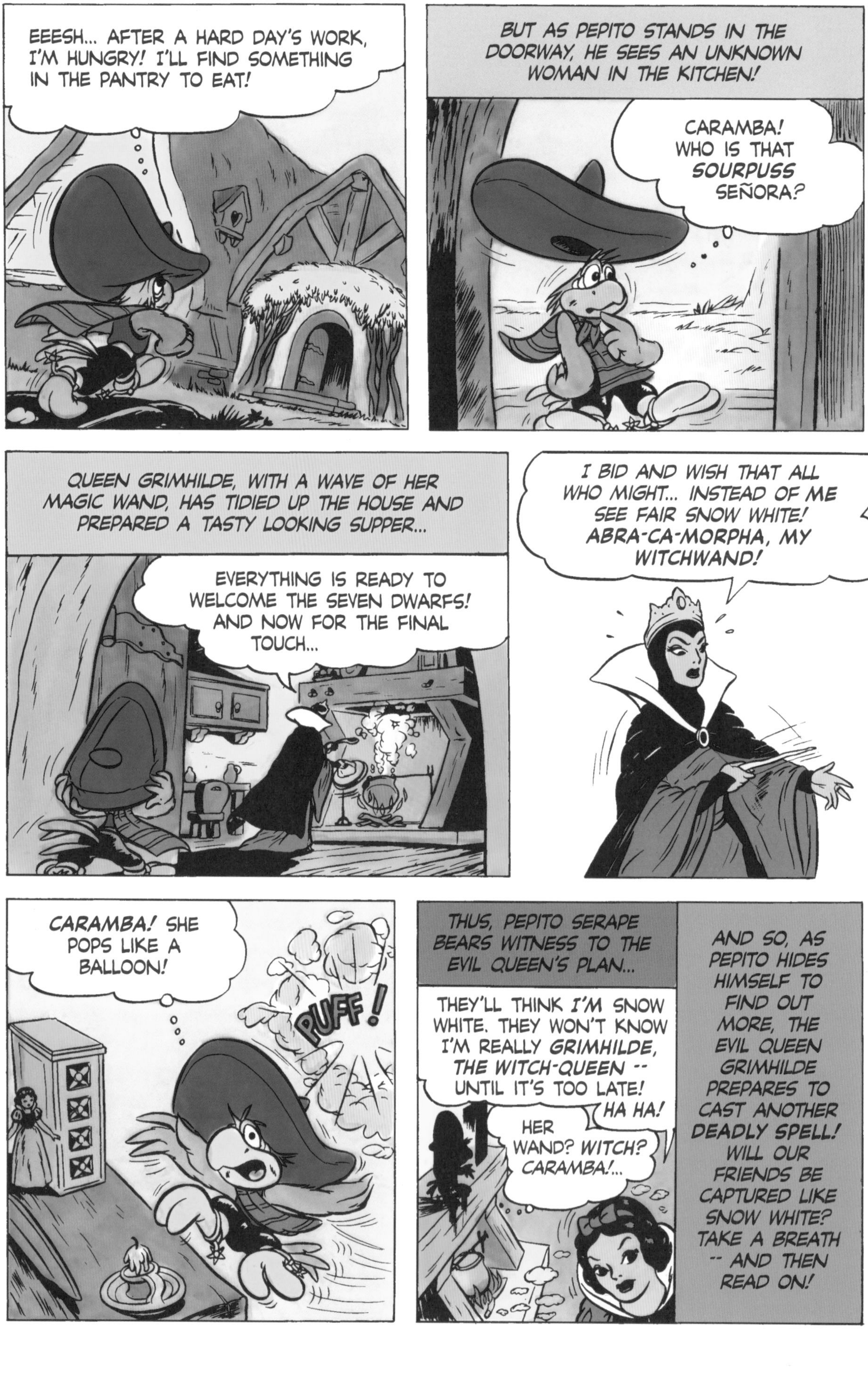

EEESH... AFTER A HARD DAY'S WORK, I'M HUNGRY! I'LL FIND SOMETHING IN THE PANTRY TO EAT!
BUT AS PEPITO STANDS IN THE DOORWAY, HE SEES AN UNKNOWN WOMAN IN THE KITCHEN!
CARAMBA! WHO IS THAT SOURPUSS SEÑORA?
QUEEN GRIMHILDE, WITH A WAVE OF HER MAGIC WAND, HAS TIDIED UP THE HOUSE AND PREPARED A TASTY LOOKING SUPPER...
EVERYTHING IS READY TO WELCOME THE SEVEN DWARFS! AND NOW FOR THE FINAL TOUCH...
I BID AND WISH THAT ALL WHO MIGHT... INSTEAD OF ME SEE FAIR SNOW WHITE! ABRA-CA-MORPHA, MY WITCHWAND!
CARAMBA! SHE POPS LIKE A BALLOON!
PUFF!
THUS, PEPITO SERAPE BEARS WITNESS TO THE EVIL QUEEN'S PLAN...
THEY'LL THINK I'M SNOW WHITE. THEY WON'T KNOW I'M REALLY GRIMHILDE, THE WITCH-QUEEN -- UNTIL IT'S TOO LATE!
HA HA!
HER WAND? WITCH? CARAMBA!...
AND SO, AS PEPITO HIDES HIMSELF TO FIND OUT MORE, THE EVIL QUEEN GRIMHILDE PREPARES TO CAST ANOTHER DEADLY SPELL! WILL OUR FRIENDS BE CAPTURED LIKE SNOW WHITE? TAKE A BREATH -- AND THEN READ ON!

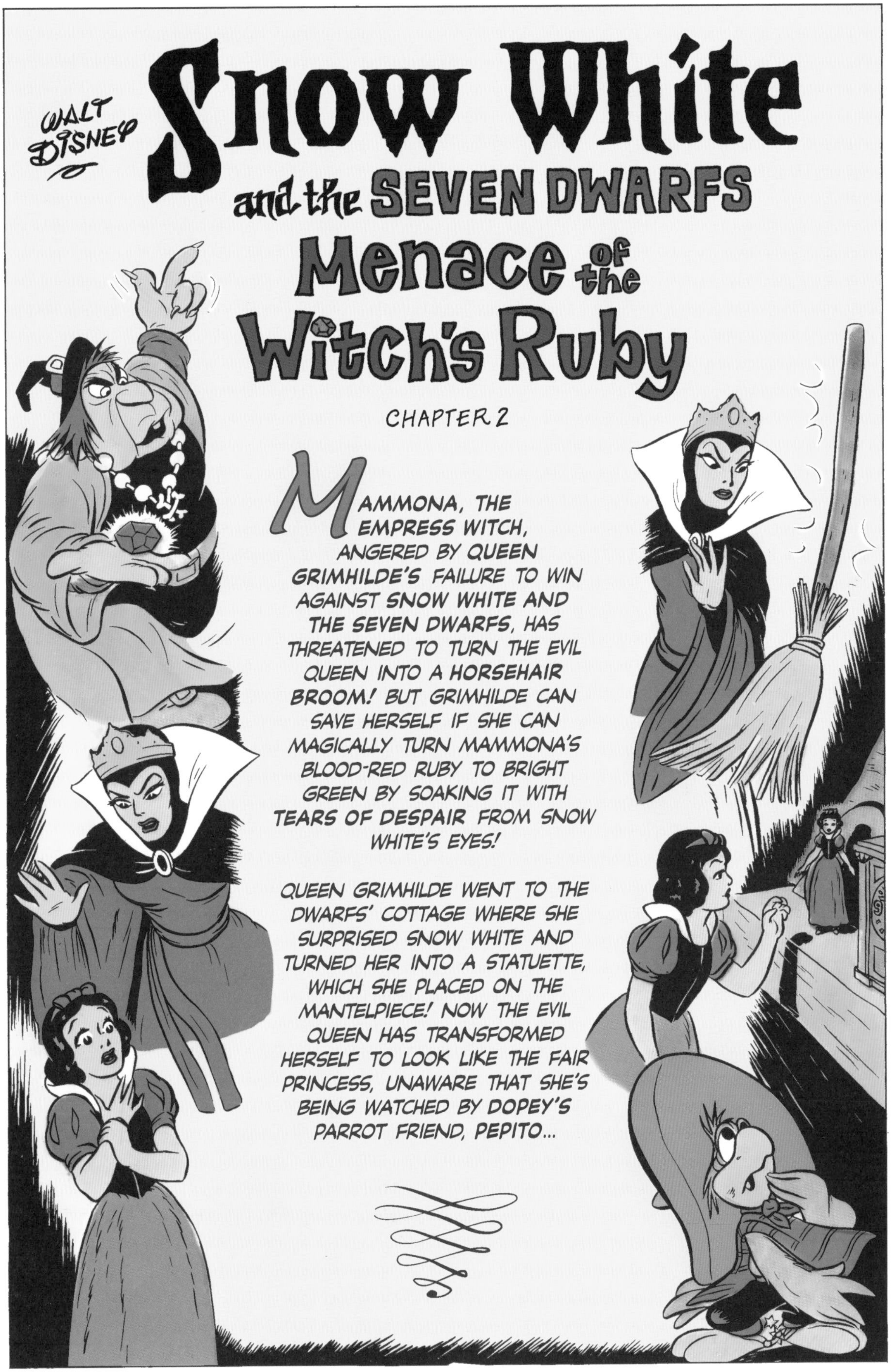

Walt Disney
Snow White and the SEVEN DWARFS
Menace of the Witch's Ruby
CHAPTER 2
MAMMONA, THE EMPRESS WITCH, ANGERED BY QUEEN GRIMHILDE'S FAILURE TO WIN AGAINST SNOW WHITE AND THE SEVEN DWARFS, HAS THREATENED TO TURN THE EVIL QUEEN INTO A HORSEHAIR BROOM! BUT GRIMHILDE CAN SAVE HERSELF IF SHE CAN MAGICALLY TURN MAMMONA'S BLOOD-RED RUBY TO BRIGHT GREEN BY SOAKING IT WITH TEARS OF DESPAIR FROM SNOW WHITE'S EYES!
QUEEN GRIMHILDE WENT TO THE DWARFS' COTTAGE WHERE SHE SURPRISED SNOW WHITE AND TURNED HER INTO A STATUETTE, WHICH SHE PLACED ON THE MANTELPIECE! NOW THE EVIL QUEEN HAS TRANSFORMED HERSELF TO LOOK LIKE THE FAIR PRINCESS, UNAWARE THAT SHE'S BEING WATCHED BY DOPEY'S PARROT FRIEND, PEPITO...

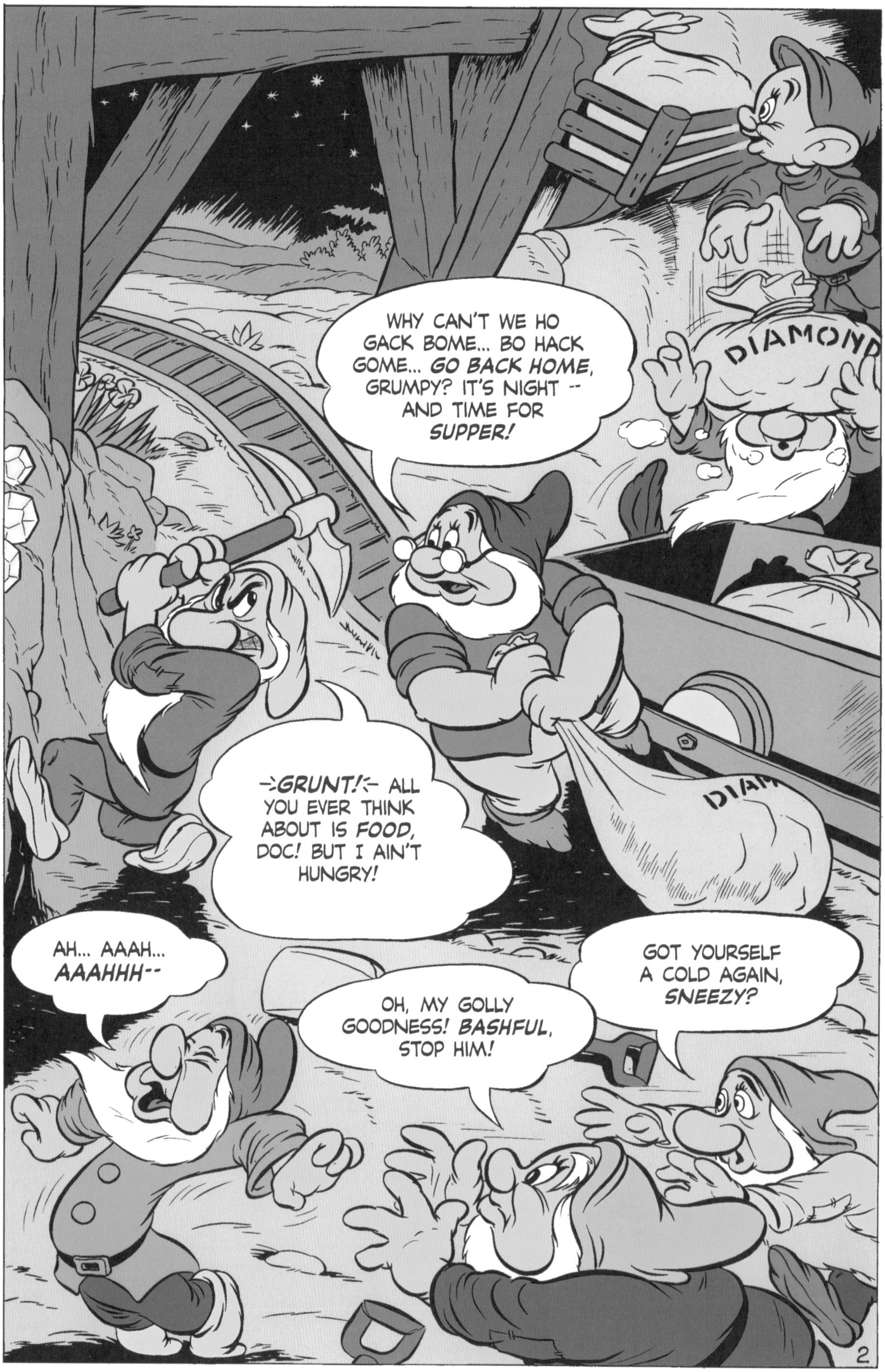
WHY CAN'T WE HO GACK BOME... BO HACK GOME... GO BACK HOME, GRUMPY? IT'S NIGHT -- AND TIME FOR SUPPER!
DIAMOND
DIAM
-GRUNT!- ALL YOU EVER THINK ABOUT IS FOOD, DOC! BUT I AIN'T HUNGRY!
AH... AAAH... AAAHHH--
OH, MY GOLLY GOODNESS! BASHFUL, STOP HIM!
GOT YOURSELF A COLD AGAIN, SNEEZY?
2

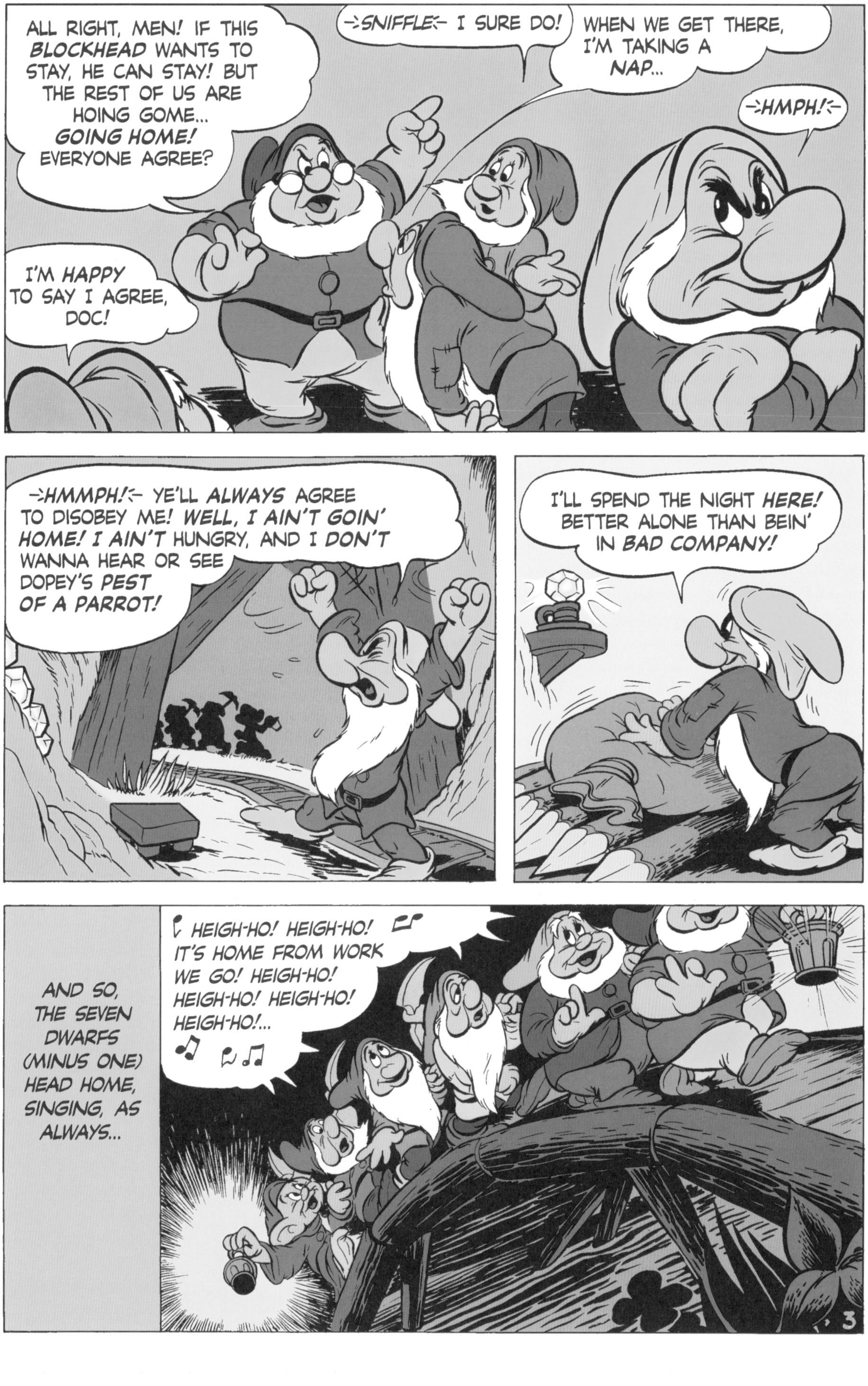
ALL RIGHT, MEN! IF THIS BLOCKHEAD WANTS TO STAY, HE CAN STAY! BUT THE REST OF US ARE HOING GOME... GOING HOME! EVERYONE AGREE?
-SNIFFLE- I SURE DO!
WHEN WE GET THERE, I'M TAKING A NAP...
-HMPH!-
I'M HAPPY TO SAY I AGREE, DOC!
-HMMPH!- YE'LL ALWAYS AGREE TO DISOBEY ME! WELL, I AIN'T GOIN' HOME! I AIN'T HUNGRY, AND I DON'T WANNA HEAR OR SEE DOPEY'S PEST OF A PARROT!
I'LL SPEND THE NIGHT HERE! BETTER ALONE THAN BEIN' IN BAD COMPANY!
AND SO, THE SEVEN DWARFS (MINUS ONE) HEAD HOME, SINGING, AS ALWAYS...
HEIGH-HO! HEIGH-HO! IT'S HOME FROM WORK WE GO! HEIGH-HO! HEIGH-HO! HEIGH-HO! HEIGH-HO!...
3

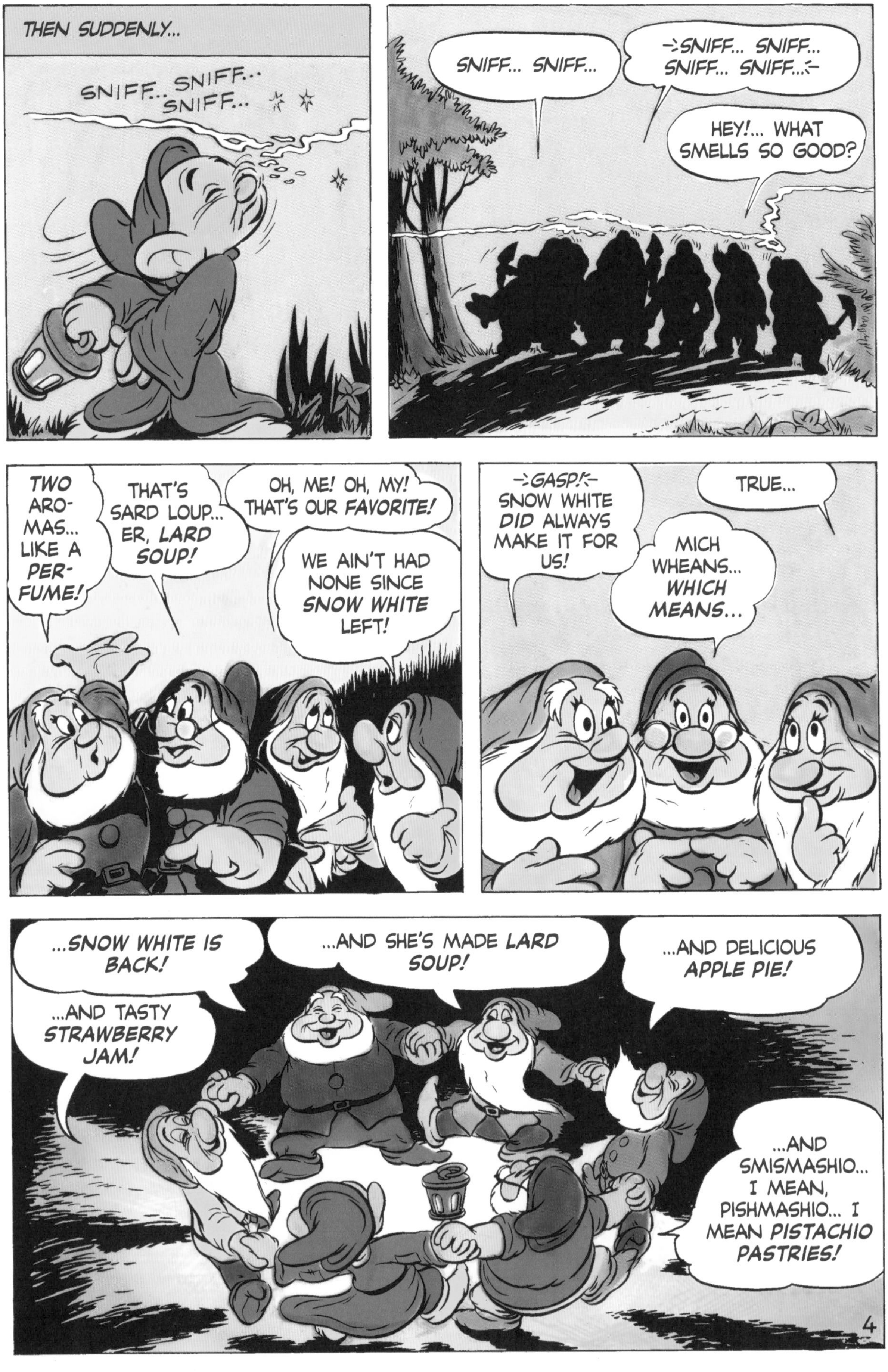
THEN SUDDENLY...
SNIFF... SNIFF... SNIFF...
SNIFF... SNIFF...
SNIFF... SNIFF... SNIFF... SNIFF...
HEY!... WHAT SMELLS SO GOOD?
TWO ARO-MAS... LIKE A PER-FUME!
THAT'S SARD LOUP... ER, LARD SOUP!
OH, ME! OH, MY! THAT'S OUR FAVORITE!
WE AIN'T HAD NONE SINCE SNOW WHITE LEFT!
GASP! SNOW WHITE DID ALWAYS MAKE IT FOR US!
TRUE...
MICH WHEANS... WHICH MEANS...
...SNOW WHITE IS BACK!
...AND SHE'S MADE LARD SOUP!
...AND DELICIOUS APPLE PIE!
...AND TASTY STRAWBERRY JAM!
...AND SMISMASHIO... I MEAN, PISHMASHIO... I MEAN PISTACHIO PASTRIES!
4

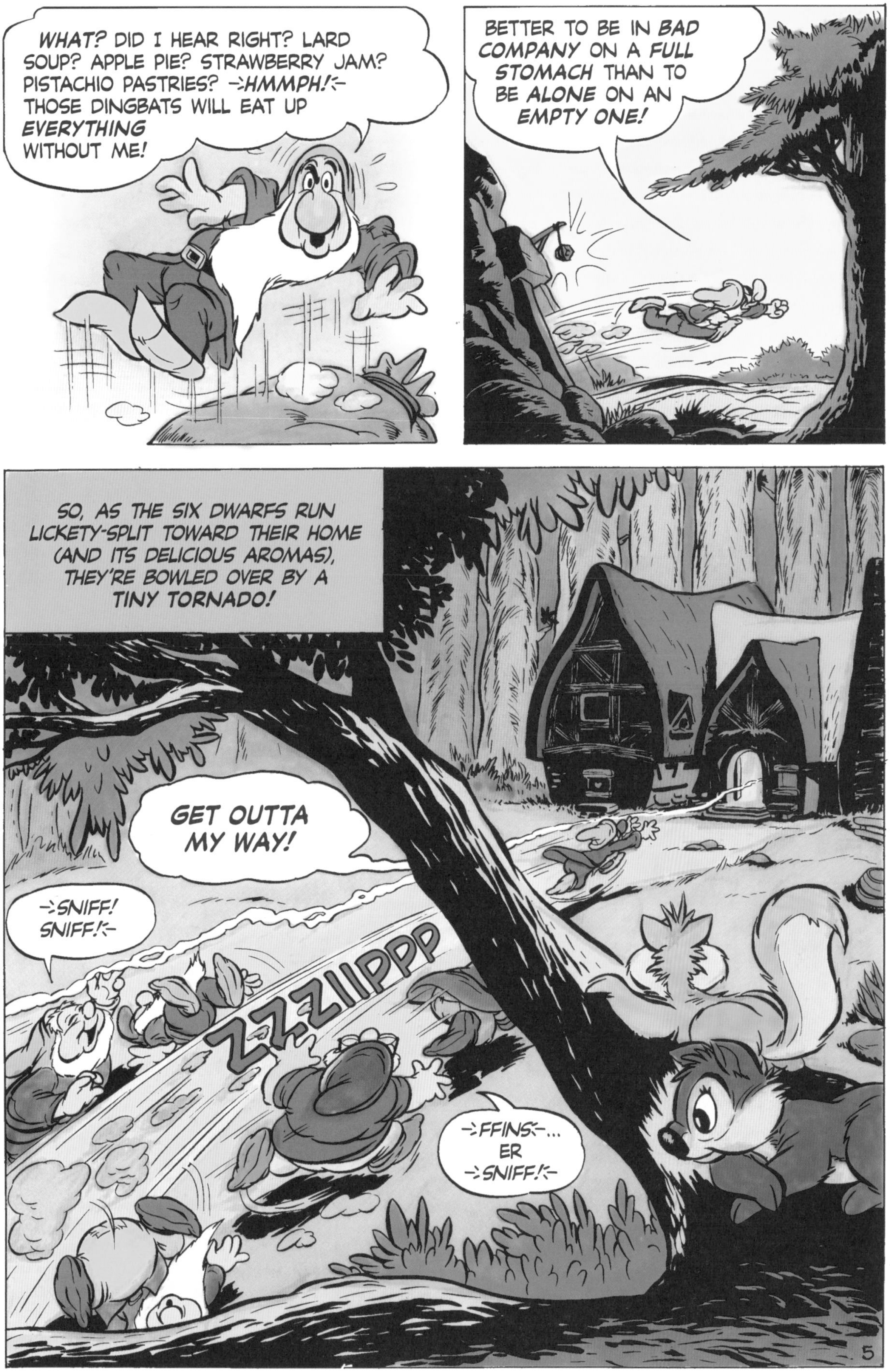
WHAT? DID I HEAR RIGHT? LARD SOUP? APPLE PIE? STRAWBERRY JAM? PISTACHIO PASTRIES? -HMMPH!- THOSE DINGBATS WILL EAT UP EVERYTHING WITHOUT ME!
BETTER TO BE IN BAD COMPANY ON A FULL STOMACH THAN TO BE ALONE ON AN EMPTY ONE!
SO, AS THE SIX DWARFS RUN LICKETY-SPLIT TOWARD THEIR HOME (AND ITS DELICIOUS AROMAS), THEY'RE BOWLED OVER BY A TINY TORNADO!
GET OUTTA MY WAY!
-SNIFF! SNIFF!-
ZZZIIPPP
-FFINS-... ER -SNIFF!-
5

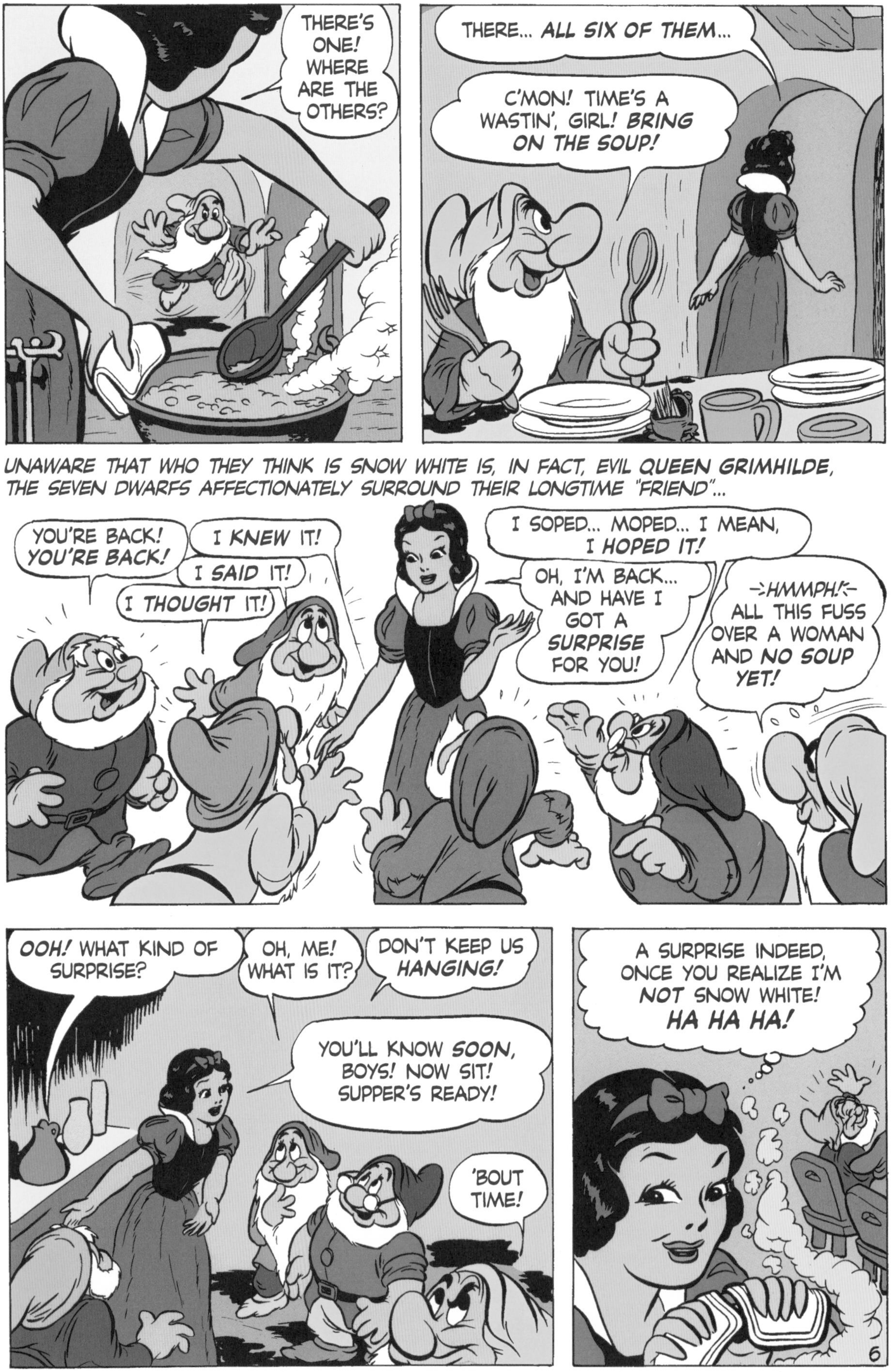
THERE'S ONE! WHERE ARE THE OTHERS?
THERE... ALL SIX OF THEM...
C'MON! TIME'S A WASTIN', GIRL! BRING ON THE SOUP!
UNAWARE THAT WHO THEY THINK IS SNOW WHITE IS, IN FACT, EVIL QUEEN GRIMHILDE, THE SEVEN DWARFS AFFECTIONATELY SURROUND THEIR LONGTIME "FRIEND"...
YOU'RE BACK! YOU'RE BACK!
I KNEW IT!
I SAID IT!
I THOUGHT IT!
I SOPED... MOPED... I MEAN, I HOPED IT!
OH, I'M BACK... AND HAVE I GOT A SURPRISE FOR YOU!
-HMMPH!- ALL THIS FUSS OVER A WOMAN AND NO SOUP YET!
OOH! WHAT KIND OF SURPRISE?
OH, ME! WHAT IS IT?
DON'T KEEP US HANGING!
YOU'LL KNOW SOON, BOYS! NOW SIT! SUPPER'S READY!
'BOUT TIME!
A SURPRISE INDEED, ONCE YOU REALIZE I'M NOT SNOW WHITE! HA HA HA!
6

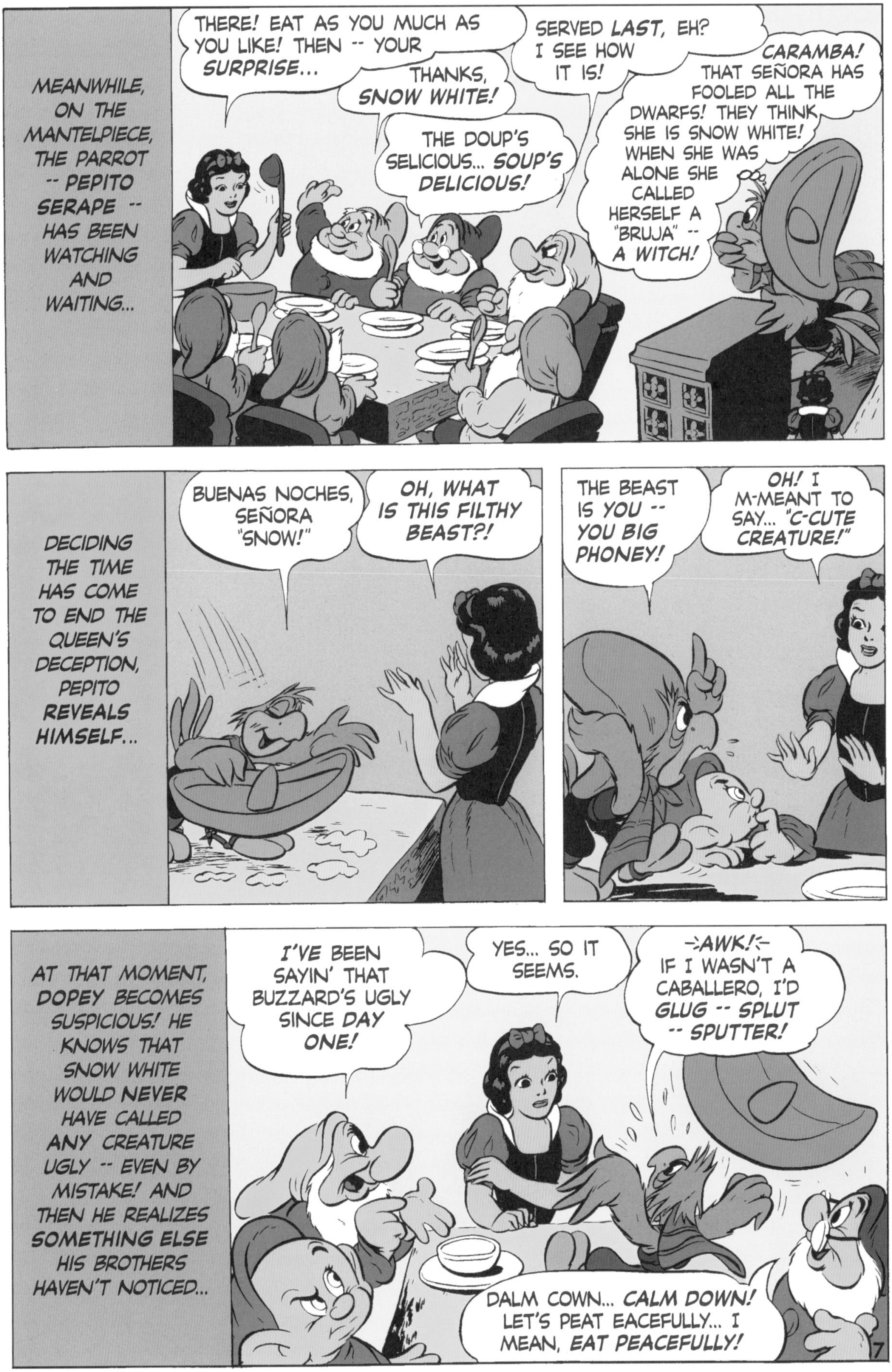
MEANWHILE, ON THE MANTELPIECE, THE PARROT -- PEPITO SERAPE -- HAS BEEN WATCHING AND WAITING...
THERE! EAT AS YOU MUCH AS YOU LIKE! THEN -- YOUR SURPRISE...
THANKS, SNOW WHITE!
THE DOUP'S SELICIOUS... SOUP'S DELICIOUS!
SERVED LAST, EH? I SEE HOW IT IS!
CARAMBA! THAT SEÑORA HAS FOOLED ALL THE DWARFS! THEY THINK SHE IS SNOW WHITE! WHEN SHE WAS ALONE SHE CALLED HERSELF A "BRUJA" -- A WITCH!
DECIDING THE TIME HAS COME TO END THE QUEEN'S DECEPTION, PEPITO REVEALS HIMSELF...
BUENAS NOCHES, SEÑORA "SNOW!"
OH, WHAT IS THIS FILTHY BEAST?!
THE BEAST IS YOU -- YOU BIG PHONEY!
OH! I M-MEANT TO SAY... "C-CUTE CREATURE!"
AT THAT MOMENT, DOPEY BECOMES SUSPICIOUS! HE KNOWS THAT SNOW WHITE WOULD NEVER HAVE CALLED ANY CREATURE UGLY -- EVEN BY MISTAKE! AND THEN HE REALIZES SOMETHING ELSE HIS BROTHERS HAVEN'T NOTICED...
I'VE BEEN SAYIN' THAT BUZZARD'S UGLY SINCE DAY ONE!
YES... SO IT SEEMS.
AWK! IF I WASN'T A CABALLERO, I'D GLUG -- SPLUT -- SPUTTER!
DALM COWN... CALM DOWN! LET'S PEAT EACEFULLY... I MEAN, EAT PEACEFULLY!
7

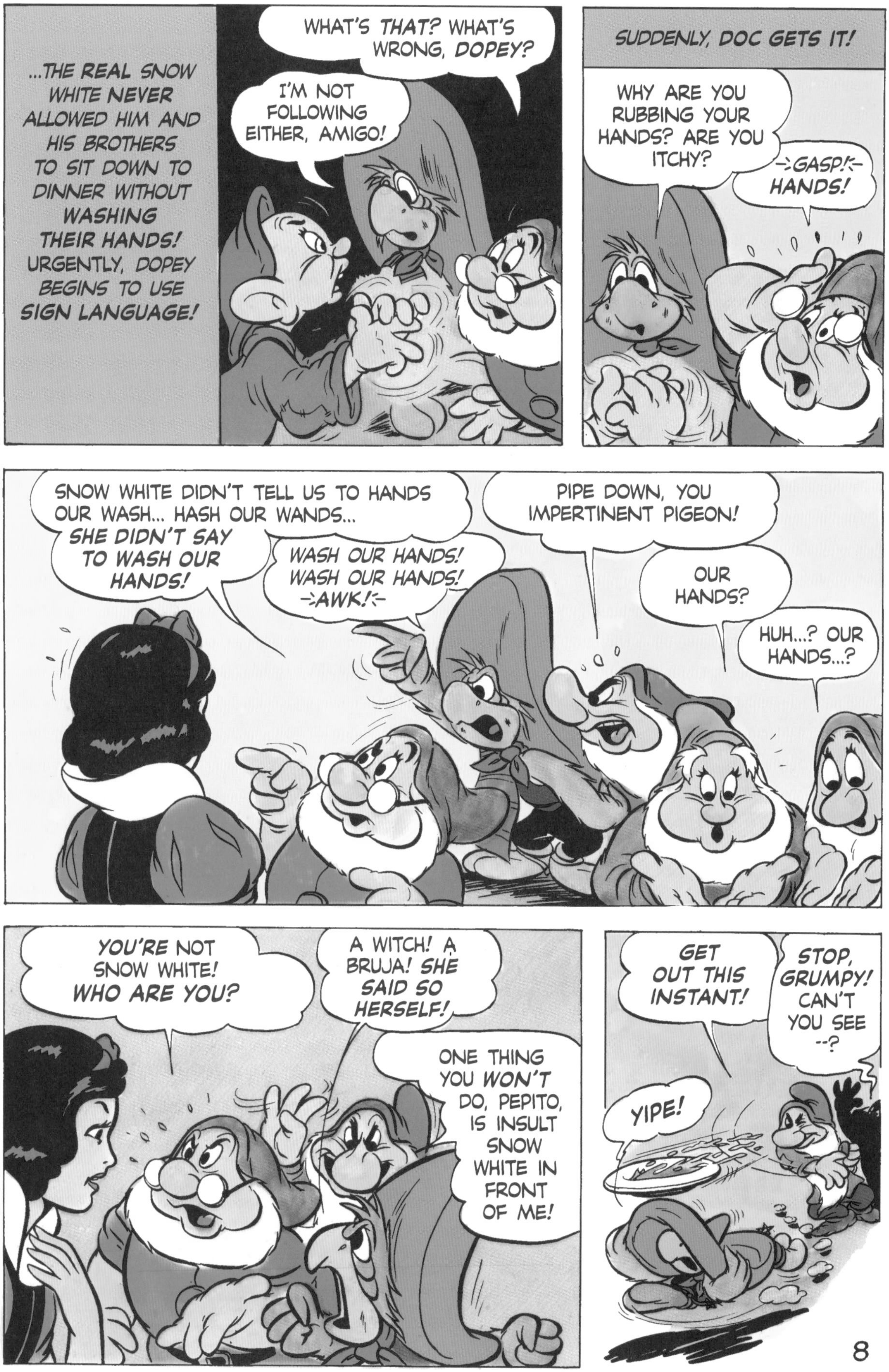
...THE REAL SNOW WHITE NEVER ALLOWED HIM AND HIS BROTHERS TO SIT DOWN TO DINNER WITHOUT WASHING THEIR HANDS! URGENTLY, DOPEY BEGINS TO USE SIGN LANGUAGE!
WHAT'S THAT? WHAT'S WRONG, DOPEY?
I'M NOT FOLLOWING EITHER, AMIGO!
SUDDENLY, DOC GETS IT!
WHY ARE YOU RUBBING YOUR HANDS? ARE YOU ITCHY?
-GASP!- HANDS!
SNOW WHITE DIDN'T TELL US TO HANDS OUR WASH... HASH OUR WANDS... SHE DIDN'T SAY TO WASH OUR HANDS!
WASH OUR HANDS! WASH OUR HANDS! -AWK!-
PIPE DOWN, YOU IMPERTINENT PIGEON!
OUR HANDS?
HUH...? OUR HANDS...?
YOU'RE NOT SNOW WHITE! WHO ARE YOU?
A WITCH! A BRUJA! SHE SAID SO HERSELF!
ONE THING YOU WON'T DO, PEPITO, IS INSULT SNOW WHITE IN FRONT OF ME!
GET OUT THIS INSTANT!
STOP, GRUMPY! CAN'T YOU SEE --?
YIPE!
8

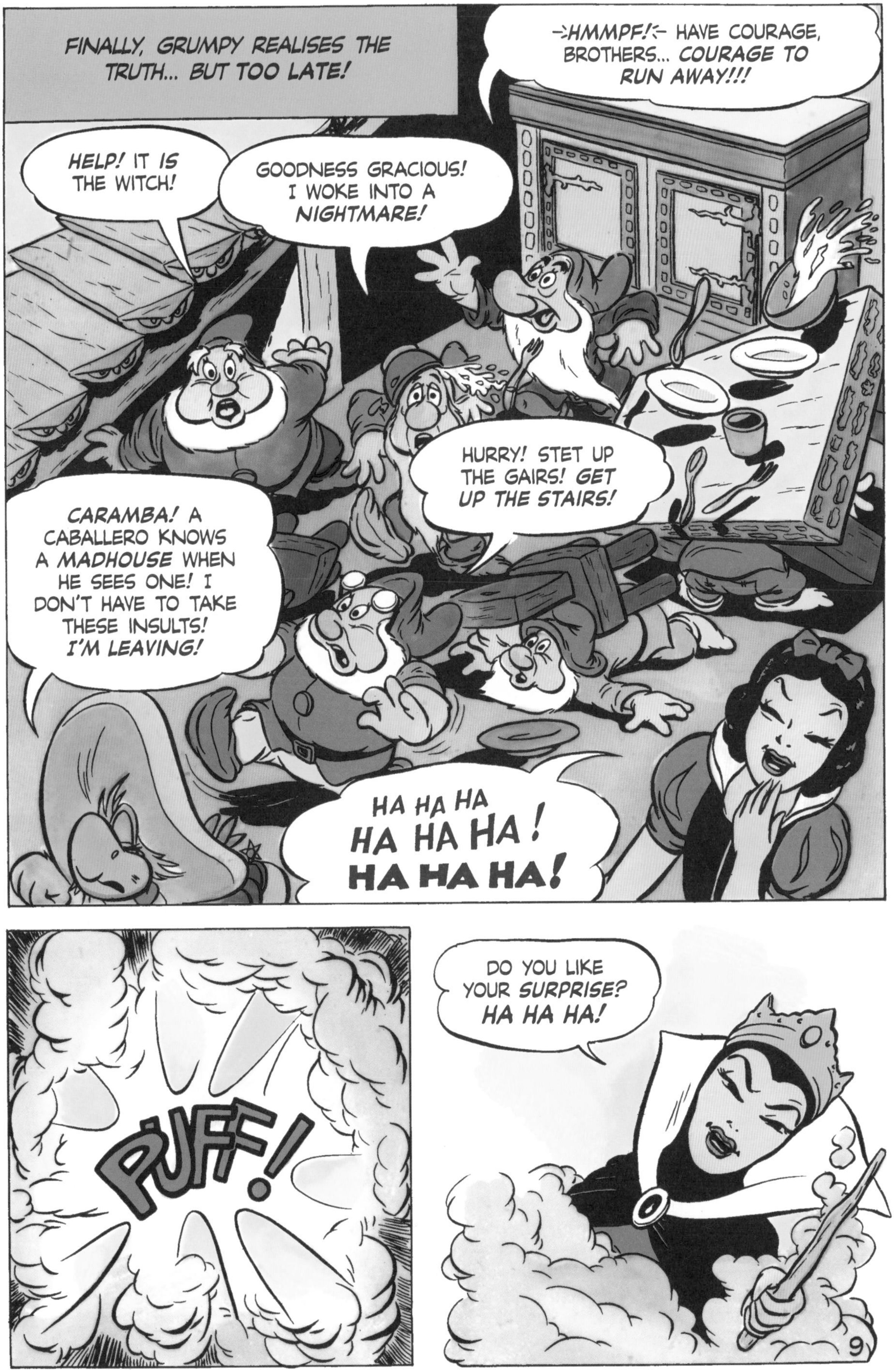
FINALLY, GRUMPY REALISES THE TRUTH... BUT TOO LATE!
–HMMPF!– HAVE COURAGE, BROTHERS... COURAGE TO RUN AWAY!!!
HELP! IT IS THE WITCH!
GOODNESS GRACIOUS! I WOKE INTO A NIGHTMARE!
HURRY! STET UP THE GAIRS! GET UP THE STAIRS!
CARAMBA! A CABALLERO KNOWS A MADHOUSE WHEN HE SEES ONE! I DON'T HAVE TO TAKE THESE INSULTS! I'M LEAVING!
HA HA HA HA HA HA! HA HA HA!
PUFF!
DO YOU LIKE YOUR SURPRISE? HA HA HA!
9

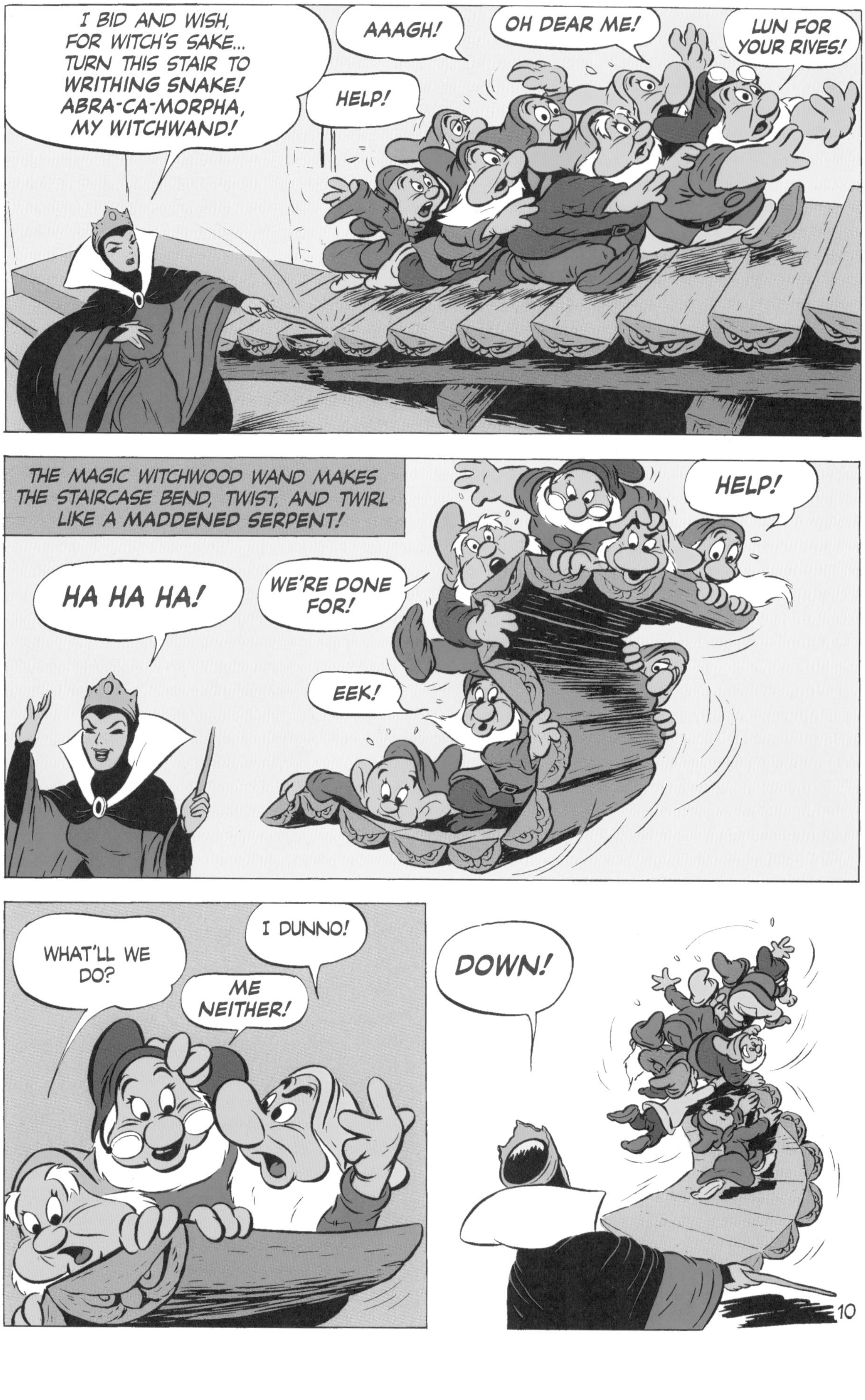
I BID AND WISH, FOR WITCH'S SAKE... TURN THIS STAIR TO WRITHING SNAKE! ABRA-CA-MORPHA, MY WITCHWAND!
AAAGH!
HELP!
OH DEAR ME!
LUN FOR YOUR RIVES!
THE MAGIC WITCHWOOD WAND MAKES THE STAIRCASE BEND, TWIST, AND TWIRL LIKE A MADDENED SERPENT!
HA HA HA!
WE'RE DONE FOR!
HELP!
EEK!
WHAT'LL WE DO?
I DUNNO!
ME NEITHER!
DOWN!
10

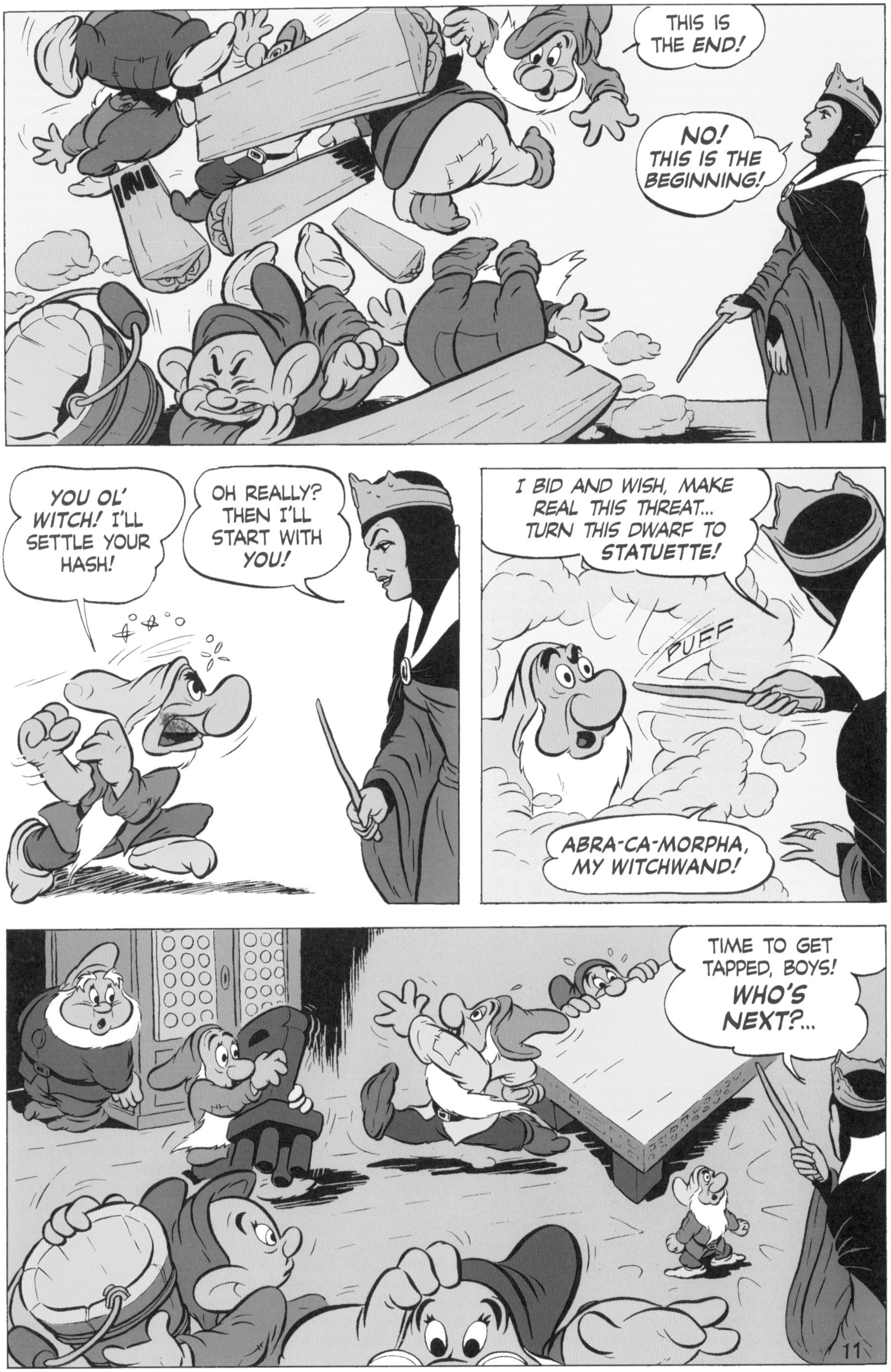
THIS IS THE END!
NO! THIS IS THE BEGINNING!
YOU OL' WITCH! I'LL SETTLE YOUR HASH!
OH REALLY? THEN I'LL START WITH YOU!
I BID AND WISH, MAKE REAL THIS THREAT... TURN THIS DWARF TO STATUETTE!
PUFF
ABRA-CA-MORPHA, MY WITCHWAND!
TIME TO GET TAPPED, BOYS! WHO'S NEXT?...
11

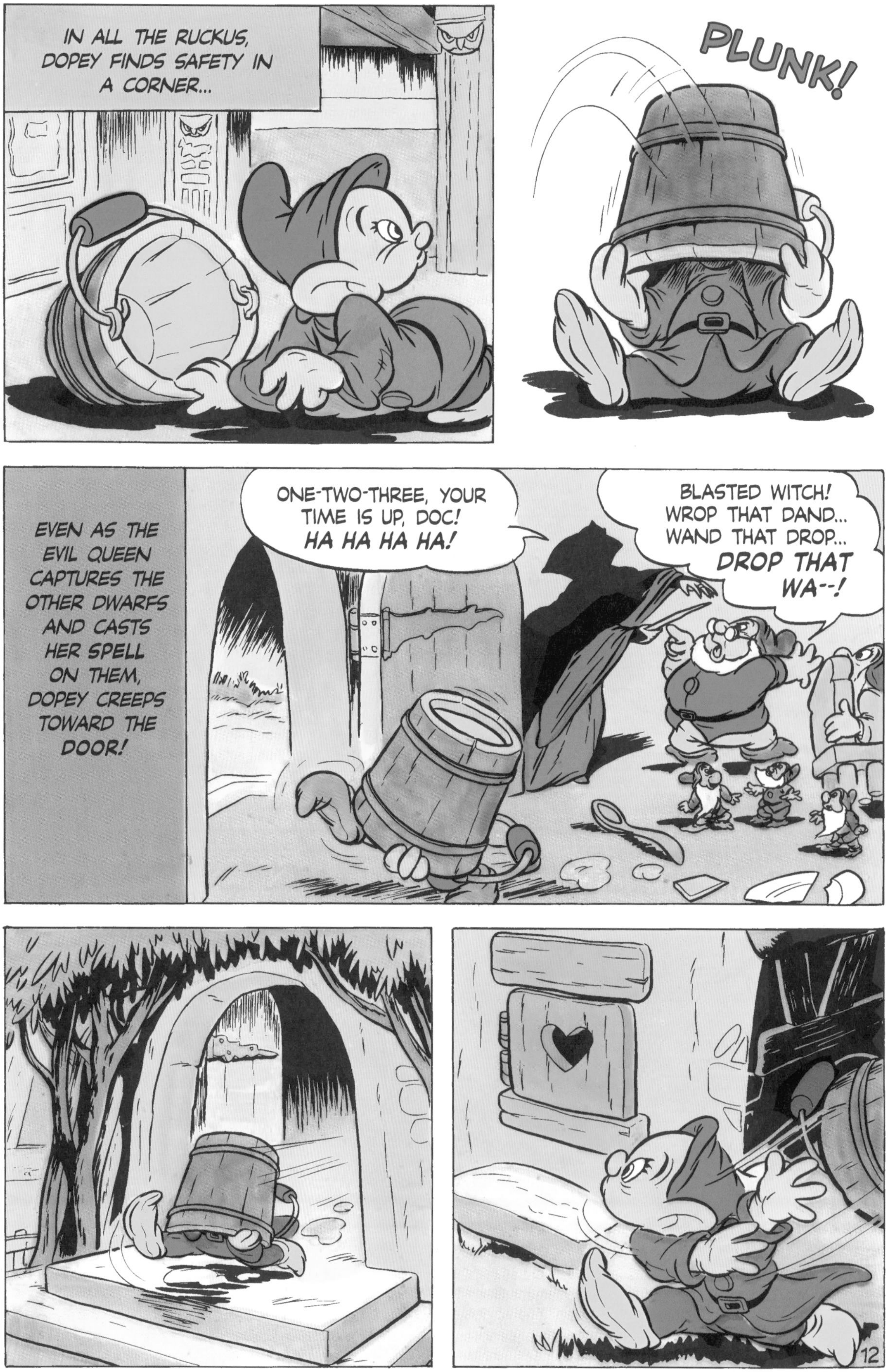
IN ALL THE RUCKUS, DOPEY FINDS SAFETY IN A CORNER...
PLUNK!
EVEN AS THE EVIL QUEEN CAPTURES THE OTHER DWARFS AND CASTS HER SPELL ON THEM, DOPEY CREEPS TOWARD THE DOOR!
ONE-TWO-THREE, YOUR TIME IS UP, DOC! HA HA HA HA!
BLASTED WITCH! WROP THAT DAND... WAND THAT DROP... DROP THAT WA--!
12

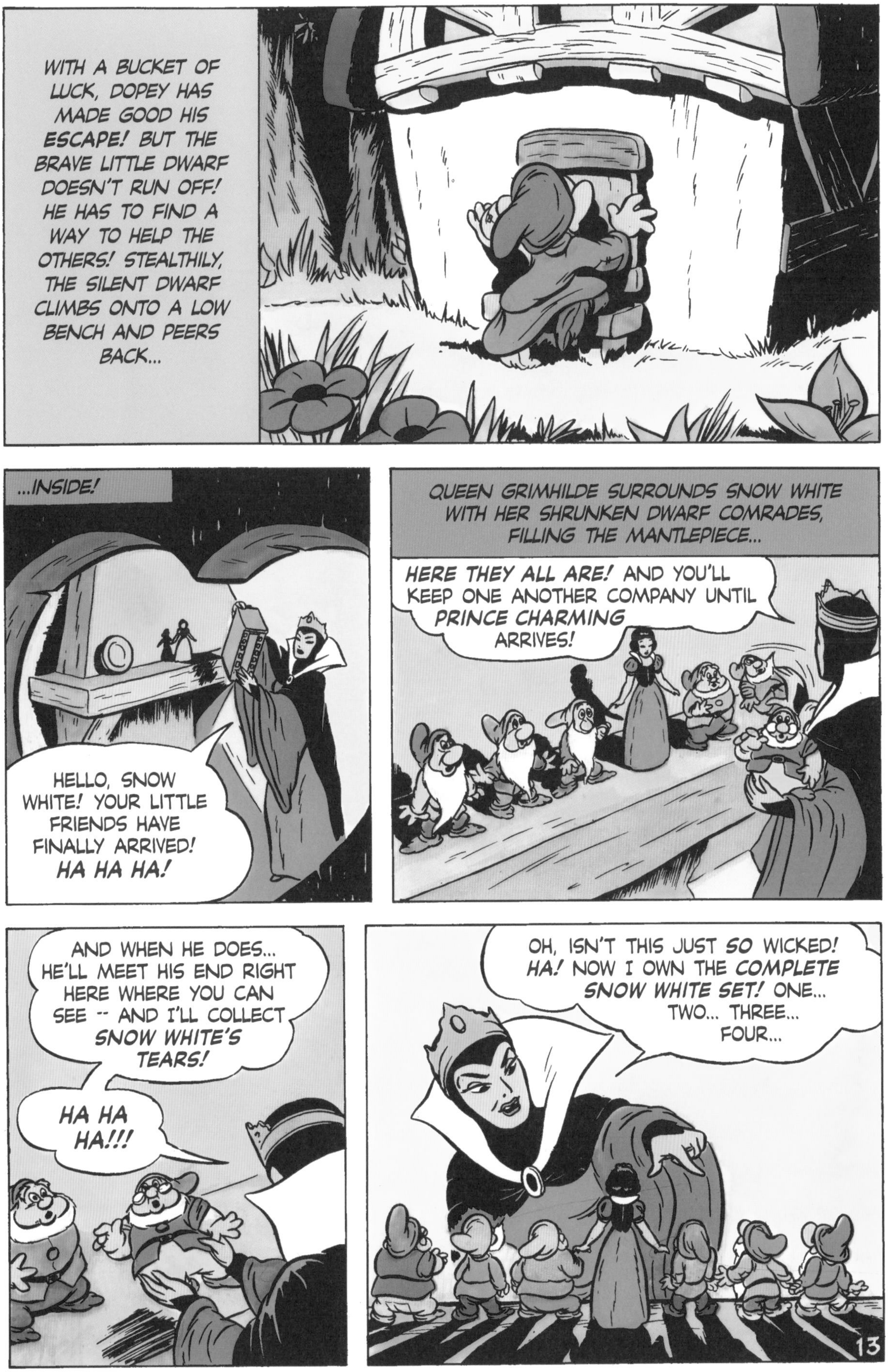
WITH A BUCKET OF LUCK, DOPEY HAS MADE GOOD HIS ESCAPE! BUT THE BRAVE LITTLE DWARF DOESN'T RUN OFF! HE HAS TO FIND A WAY TO HELP THE OTHERS! STEALTHILY, THE SILENT DWARF CLIMBS ONTO A LOW BENCH AND PEERS BACK...
...INSIDE!
HELLO, SNOW WHITE! YOUR LITTLE FRIENDS HAVE FINALLY ARRIVED! HA HA HA!
QUEEN GRIMHILDE SURROUNDS SNOW WHITE WITH HER SHRUNKEN DWARF COMRADES, FILLING THE MANTLEPIECE...
HERE THEY ALL ARE! AND YOU'LL KEEP ONE ANOTHER COMPANY UNTIL PRINCE CHARMING ARRIVES!
AND WHEN HE DOES... HE'LL MEET HIS END RIGHT HERE WHERE YOU CAN SEE -- AND I'LL COLLECT SNOW WHITE'S TEARS!
HA HA HA!!!
OH, ISN'T THIS JUST SO WICKED! HA! NOW I OWN THE COMPLETE SNOW WHITE SET! ONE... TWO... THREE... FOUR...
13

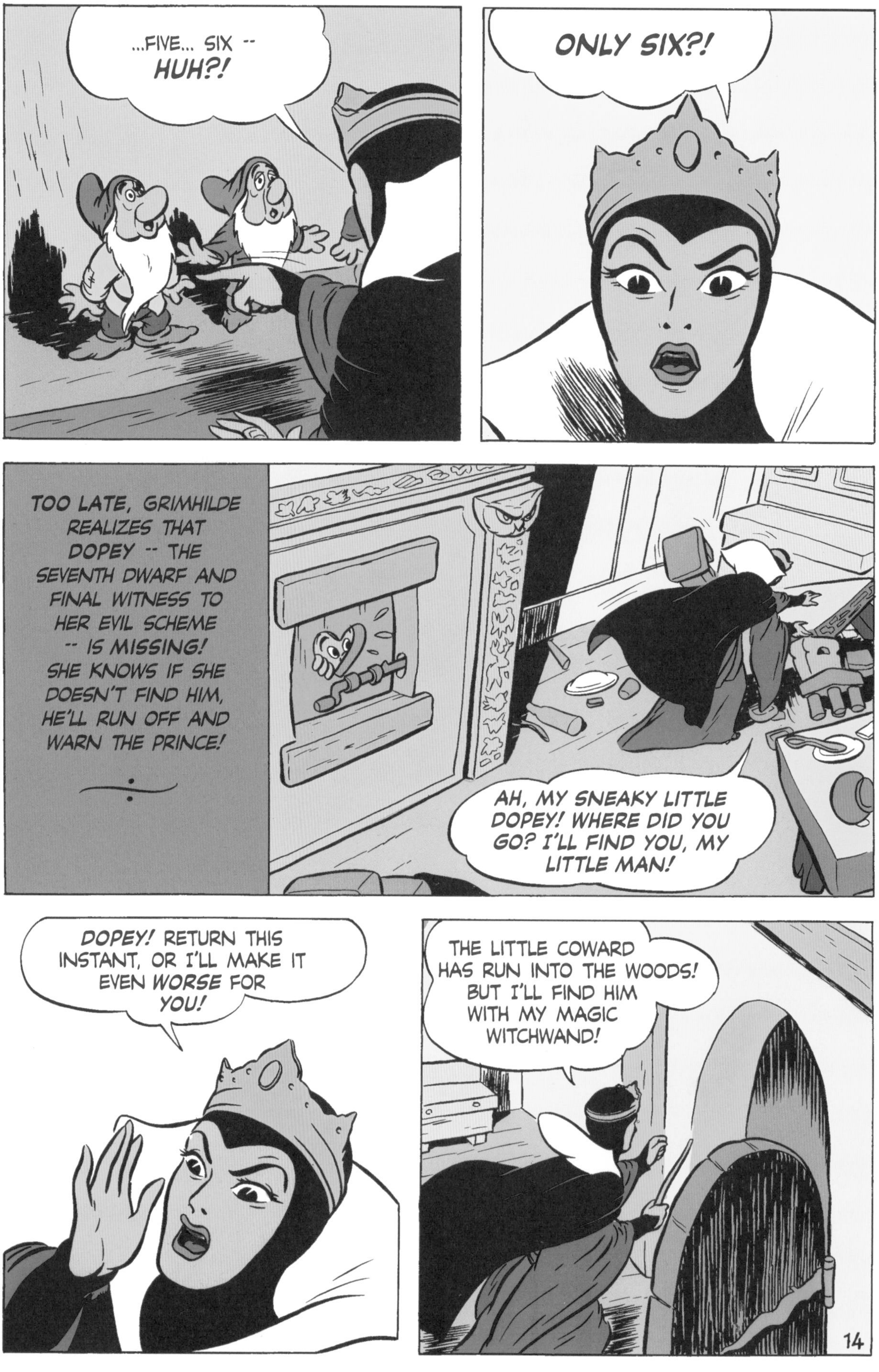

...FIVE... SIX -- HUH?!
ONLY SIX?!
TOO LATE, GRIMHILDE REALIZES THAT DOPEY -- THE SEVENTH DWARF AND FINAL WITNESS TO HER EVIL SCHEME -- IS MISSING! SHE KNOWS IF SHE DOESN'T FIND HIM, HE'LL RUN OFF AND WARN THE PRINCE!
AH, MY SNEAKY LITTLE DOPEY! WHERE DID YOU GO? I'LL FIND YOU, MY LITTLE MAN!
DOPEY! RETURN THIS INSTANT, OR I'LL MAKE IT EVEN WORSE FOR YOU!
THE LITTLE COWARD HAS RUN INTO THE WOODS! BUT I'LL FIND HIM WITH MY MAGIC WITCHWAND!
14

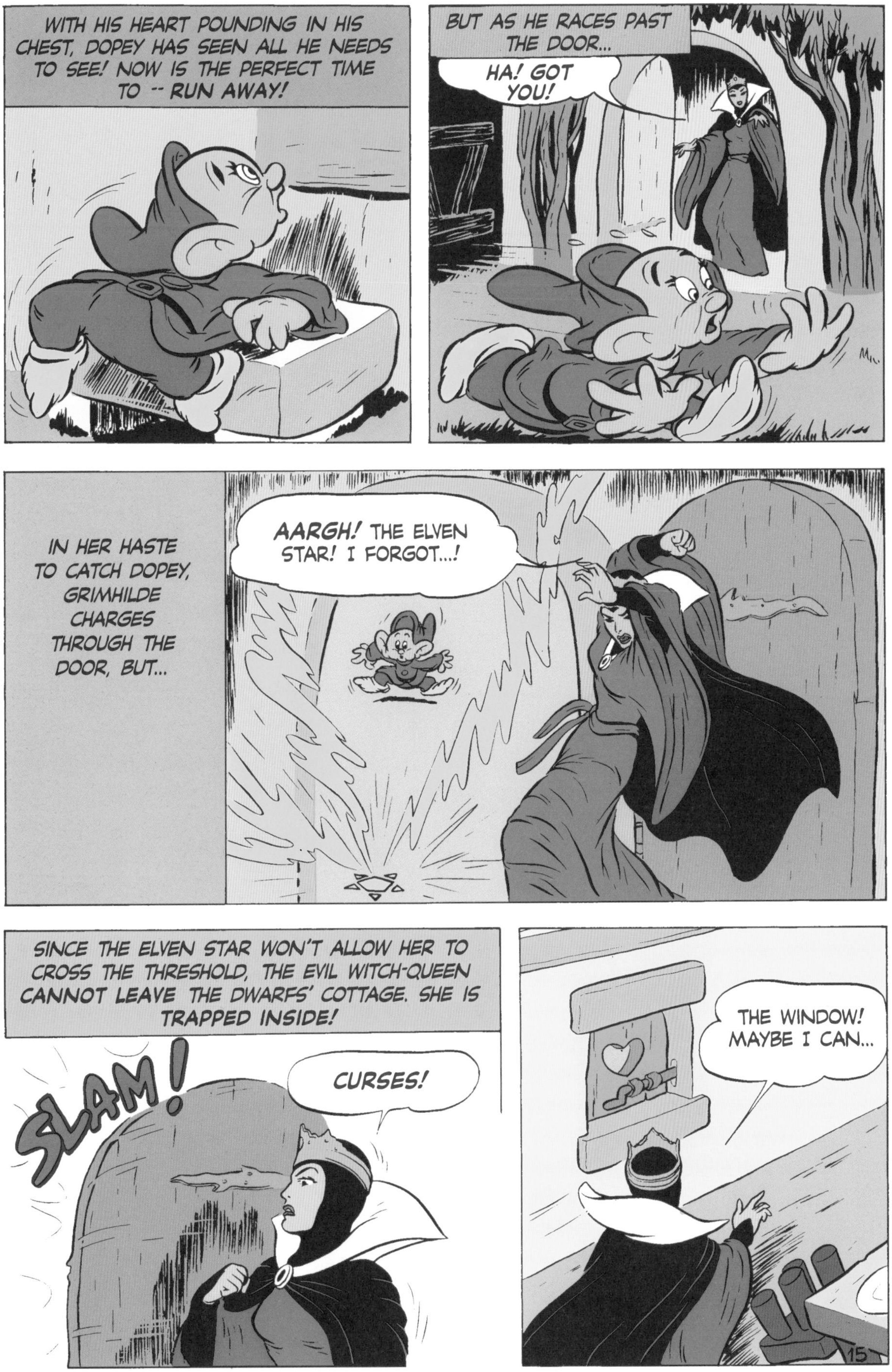
WITH HIS HEART POUNDING IN HIS CHEST, DOPEY HAS SEEN ALL HE NEEDS TO SEE! NOW IS THE PERFECT TIME TO -- RUN AWAY!
BUT AS HE RACES PAST THE DOOR...
HA! GOT YOU!
IN HER HASTE TO CATCH DOPEY, GRIMHILDE CHARGES THROUGH THE DOOR, BUT...
AARGH! THE ELVEN STAR! I FORGOT...!
SINCE THE ELVEN STAR WON'T ALLOW HER TO CROSS THE THRESHOLD, THE EVIL WITCH-QUEEN CANNOT LEAVE THE DWARFS' COTTAGE. SHE IS TRAPPED INSIDE!
SLAM!
CURSES!
THE WINDOW! MAYBE I CAN...
15

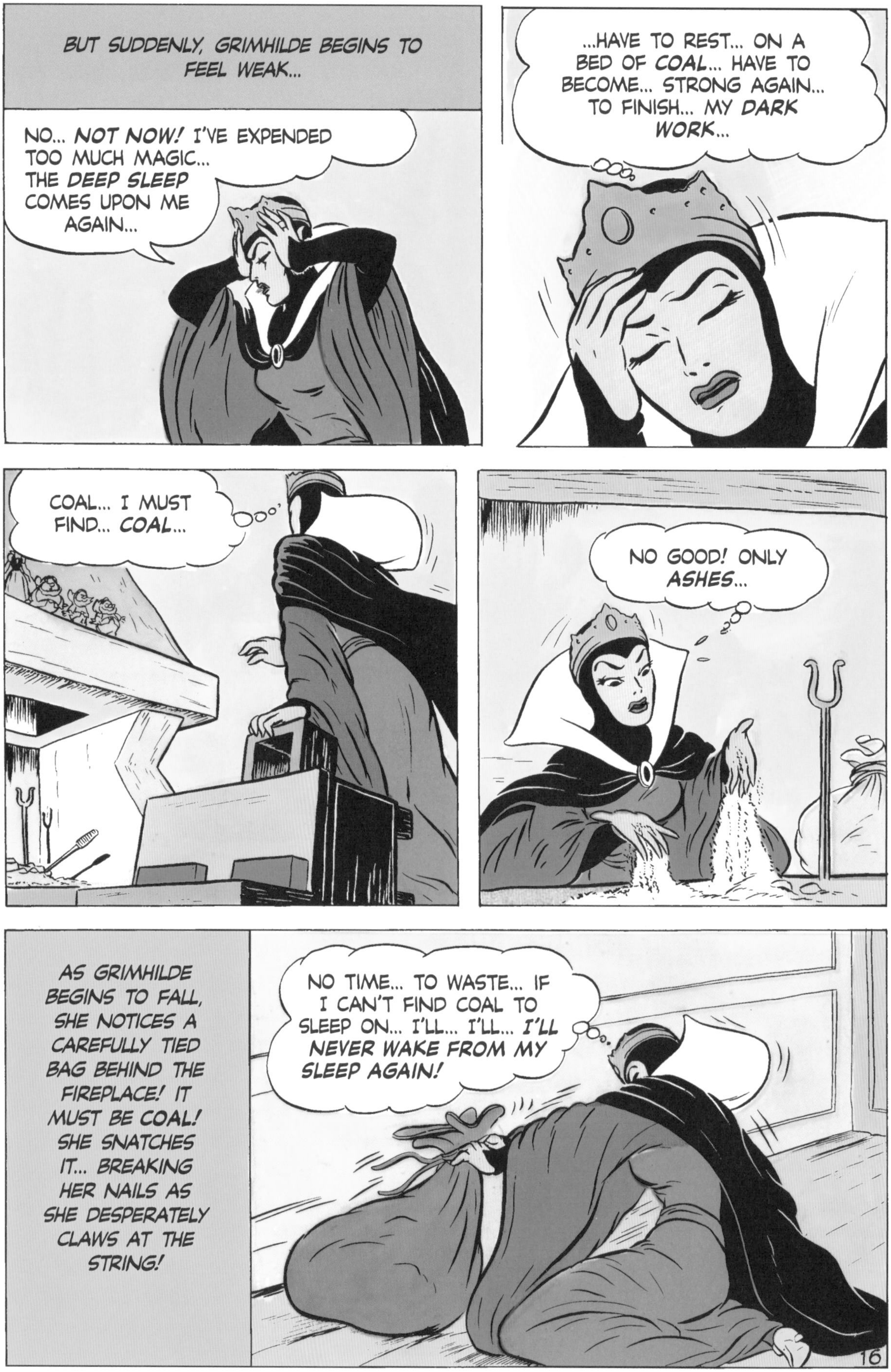
BUT SUDDENLY, GRIMHILDE BEGINS TO FEEL WEAK...
NO... NOT NOW! I'VE EXPENDED TOO MUCH MAGIC... THE DEEP SLEEP COMES UPON ME AGAIN...
...HAVE TO REST... ON A BED OF COAL... HAVE TO BECOME... STRONG AGAIN... TO FINISH... MY DARK WORK...
COAL... I MUST FIND... COAL...
NO GOOD! ONLY ASHES...
AS GRIMHILDE BEGINS TO FALL, SHE NOTICES A CAREFULLY TIED BAG BEHIND THE FIREPLACE! IT MUST BE COAL! SHE SNATCHES IT... BREAKING HER NAILS AS SHE DESPERATELY CLAWS AT THE STRING!
NO TIME... TO WASTE... IF I CAN'T FIND COAL TO SLEEP ON... I'LL... I'LL... I'LL NEVER WAKE FROM MY SLEEP AGAIN!
16

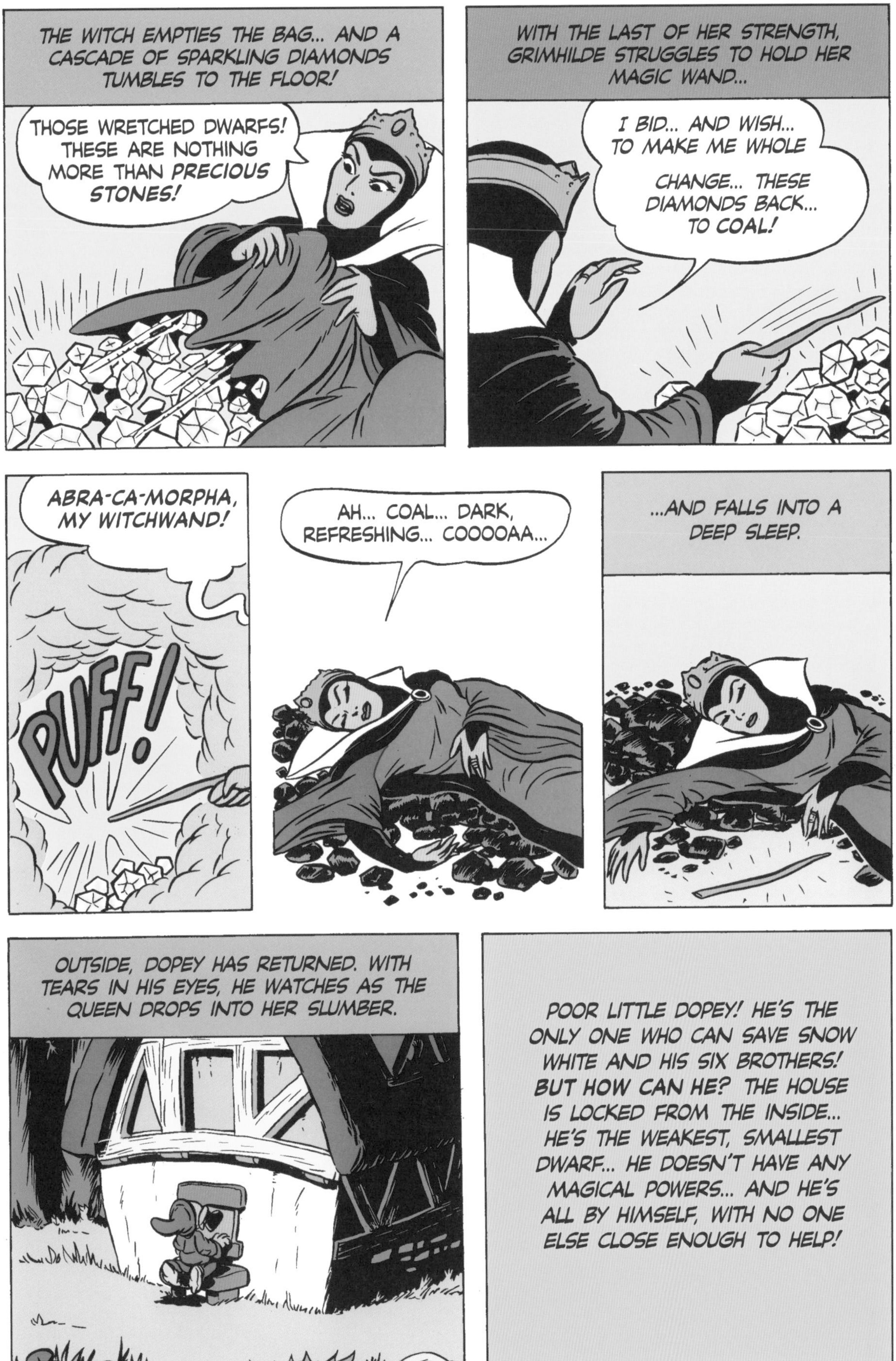

THE WITCH EMPTIES THE BAG... AND A CASCADE OF SPARKLING DIAMONDS TUMBLES TO THE FLOOR!
THOSE WRETCHED DWARFS! THESE ARE NOTHING MORE THAN PRECIOUS STONES!
WITH THE LAST OF HER STRENGTH, GRIMHILDE STRUGGLES TO HOLD HER MAGIC WAND...
I BID... AND WISH... TO MAKE ME WHOLE
CHANGE... THESE DIAMONDS BACK... TO COAL!
ABRA-CA-MORPHA, MY WITCHWAND!
PUFF!
AH... COAL... DARK, REFRESHING... COOOOAA...
...AND FALLS INTO A DEEP SLEEP.
OUTSIDE, DOPEY HAS RETURNED. WITH TEARS IN HIS EYES, HE WATCHES AS THE QUEEN DROPS INTO HER SLUMBER.
POOR LITTLE DOPEY! HE'S THE ONLY ONE WHO CAN SAVE SNOW WHITE AND HIS SIX BROTHERS! BUT HOW CAN HE? THE HOUSE IS LOCKED FROM THE INSIDE... HE'S THE WEAKEST, SMALLEST DWARF... HE DOESN'T HAVE ANY MAGICAL POWERS... AND HE'S ALL BY HIMSELF, WITH NO ONE ELSE CLOSE ENOUGH TO HELP!

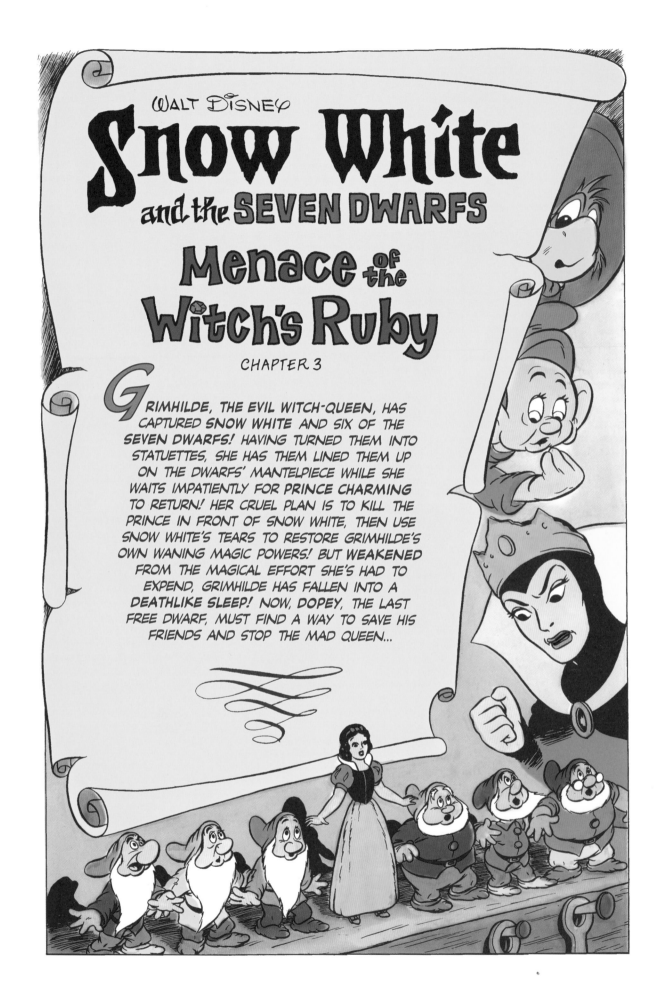

WALT DISNEY

Snow White
and the SEVEN DWARFS
Menace of the Witch's Ruby

CHAPTER 3

Grimhilde, the evil witch-queen, has captured Snow White and six of the seven dwarfs! Having turned them into statuettes, she has them lined them up on the dwarfs' mantelpiece while she waits impatiently for Prince Charming to return! Her cruel plan is to kill the prince in front of Snow White, then use Snow White's tears to restore Grimhilde's own waning magic powers! But weakened from the magical effort she's had to expend, Grimhilde has fallen into a deathlike sleep! Now, Dopey, the last free dwarf, must find a way to save his friends and stop the mad queen...

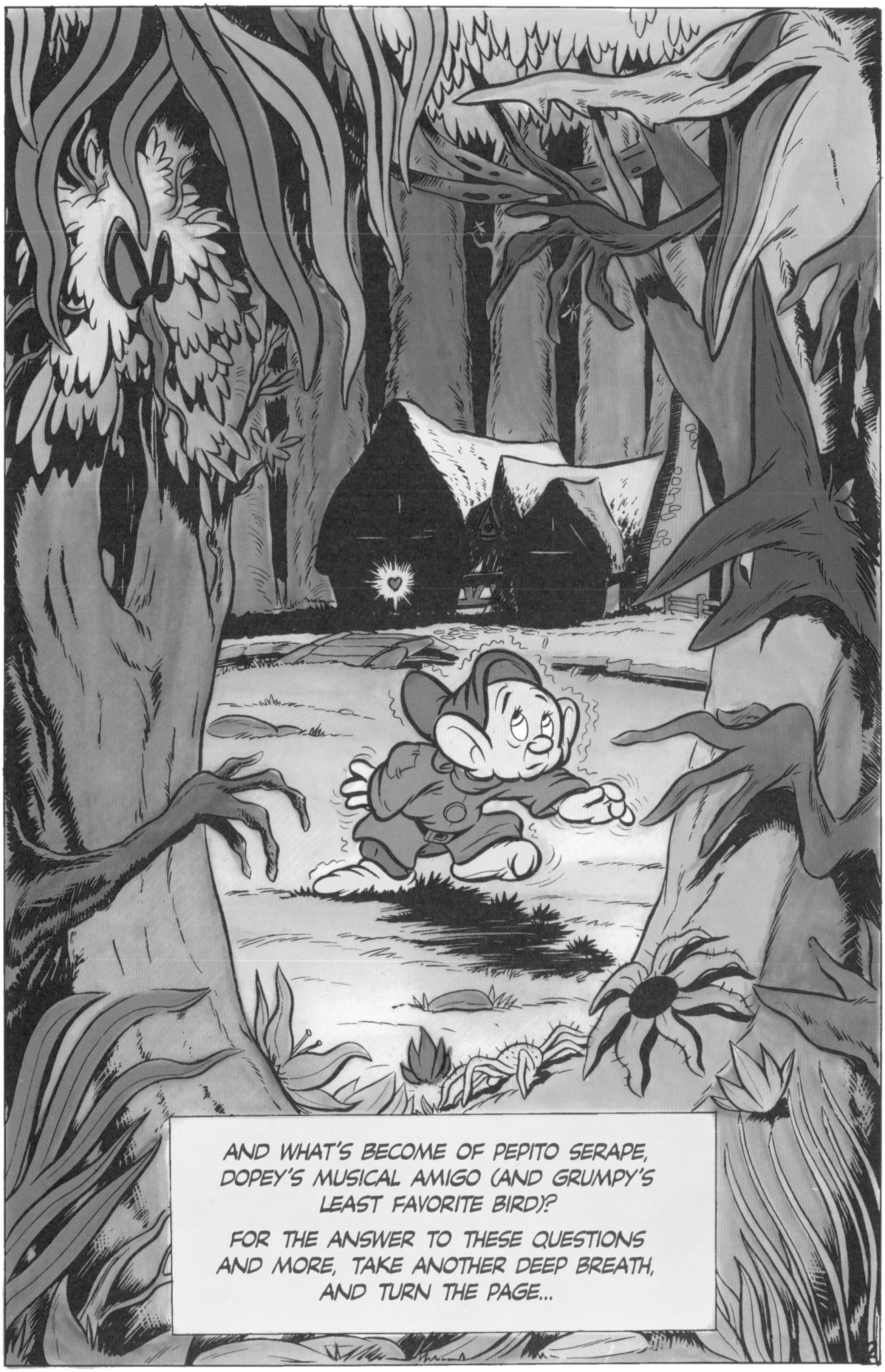
AND WHAT'S BECOME OF PEPITO SERAPE, DOPEY'S MUSICAL AMIGO (AND GRUMPY'S LEAST FAVORITE BIRD)?
FOR THE ANSWER TO THESE QUESTIONS AND MORE, TAKE ANOTHER DEEP BREATH, AND TURN THE PAGE...

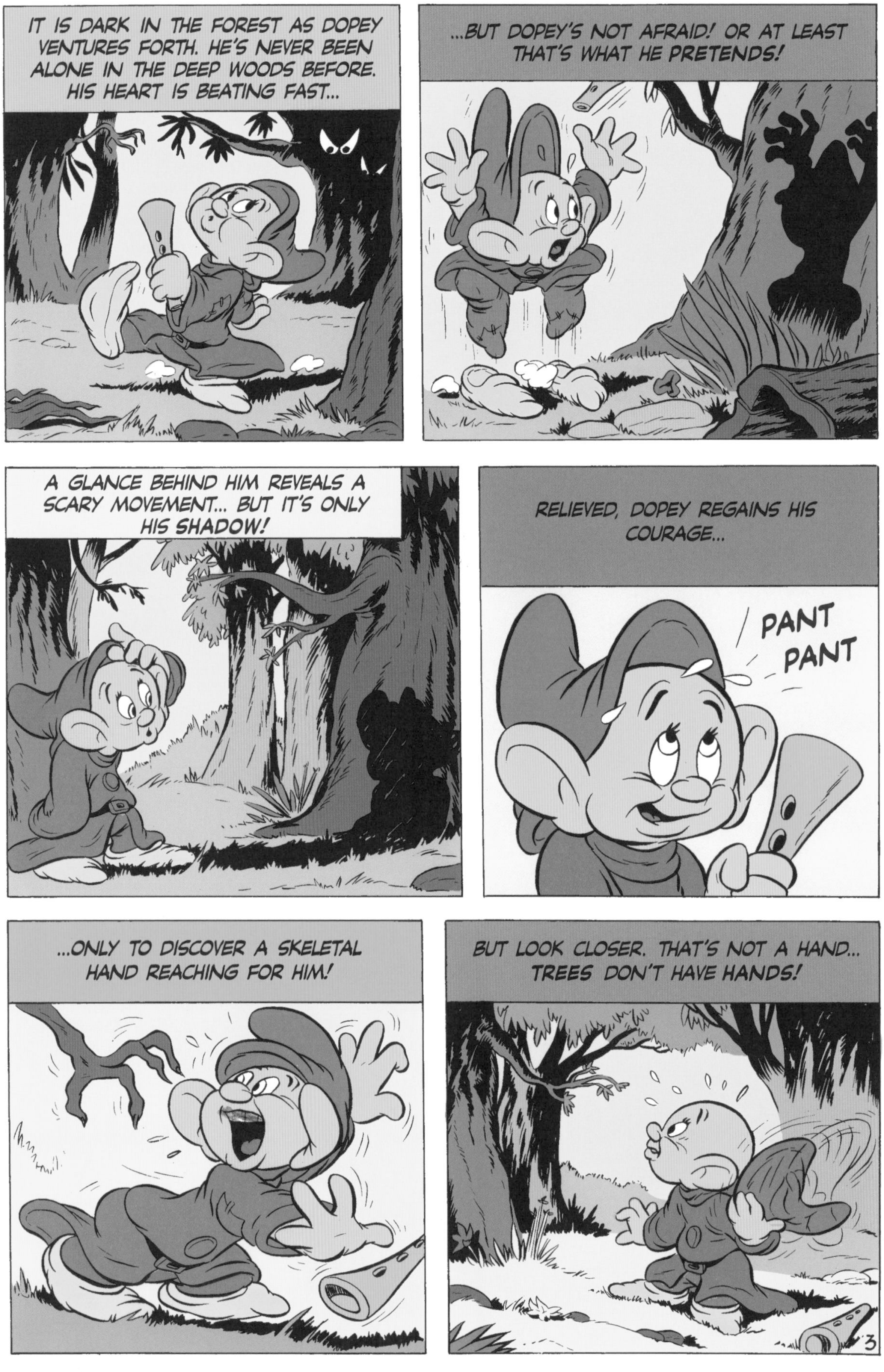
IT IS DARK IN THE FOREST AS DOPEY VENTURES FORTH. HE'S NEVER BEEN ALONE IN THE DEEP WOODS BEFORE. HIS HEART IS BEATING FAST...
...BUT DOPEY'S NOT AFRAID! OR AT LEAST THAT'S WHAT HE PRETENDS!
A GLANCE BEHIND HIM REVEALS A SCARY MOVEMENT... BUT IT'S ONLY HIS SHADOW!
RELIEVED, DOPEY REGAINS HIS COURAGE...
PANT PANT
...ONLY TO DISCOVER A SKELETAL HAND REACHING FOR HIM!
BUT LOOK CLOSER. THAT'S NOT A HAND... TREES DON'T HAVE HANDS!
3

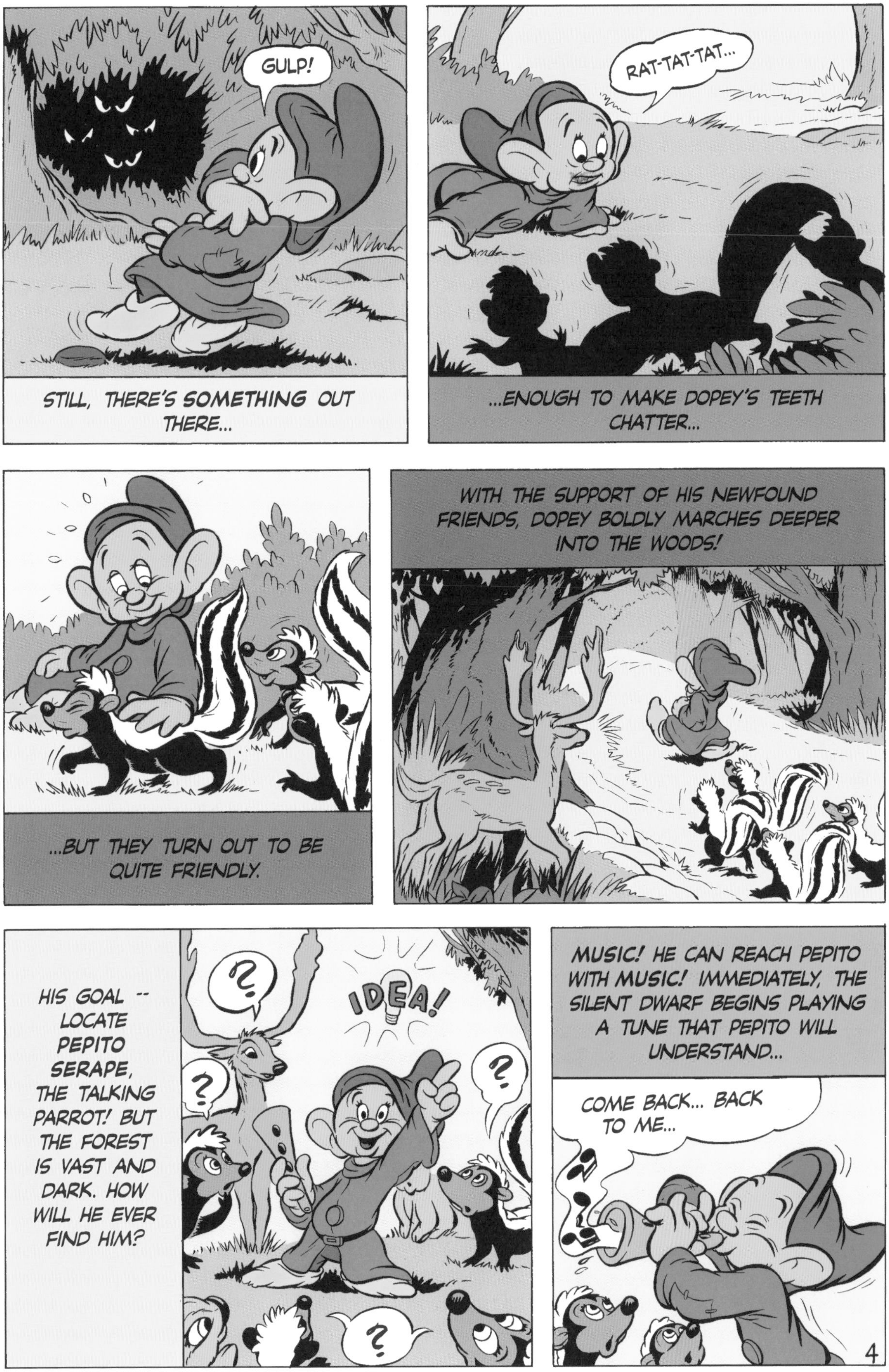
GULP!
STILL, THERE'S SOMETHING OUT THERE...
RAT-TAT-TAT...
...ENOUGH TO MAKE DOPEY'S TEETH CHATTER...
...BUT THEY TURN OUT TO BE QUITE FRIENDLY.
WITH THE SUPPORT OF HIS NEWFOUND FRIENDS, DOPEY BOLDLY MARCHES DEEPER INTO THE WOODS!
HIS GOAL -- LOCATE PEPITO SERAPE, THE TALKING PARROT! BUT THE FOREST IS VAST AND DARK. HOW WILL HE EVER FIND HIM?
?
IDEA!
?
?
?
MUSIC! HE CAN REACH PEPITO WITH MUSIC! IMMEDIATELY, THE SILENT DWARF BEGINS PLAYING A TUNE THAT PEPITO WILL UNDERSTAND...
COME BACK... BACK TO ME...
4

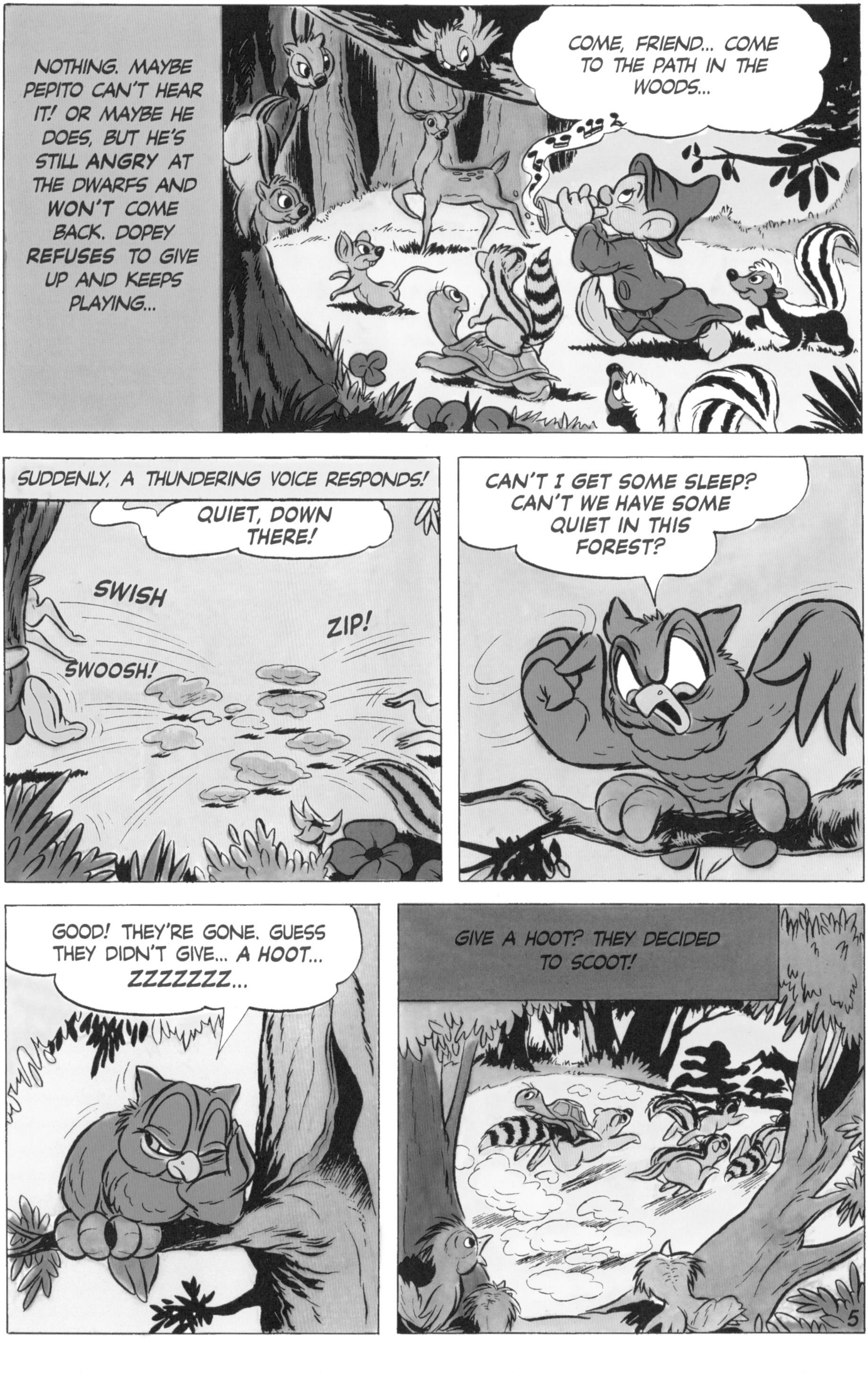

NOTHING. MAYBE PEPITO CAN'T HEAR IT! OR MAYBE HE DOES, BUT HE'S STILL ANGRY AT THE DWARFS AND WON'T COME BACK. DOPEY REFUSES TO GIVE UP AND KEEPS PLAYING...
COME, FRIEND... COME TO THE PATH IN THE WOODS...
SUDDENLY, A THUNDERING VOICE RESPONDS!
QUIET, DOWN THERE!
SWISH
ZIP!
SWOOSH!
CAN'T I GET SOME SLEEP? CAN'T WE HAVE SOME QUIET IN THIS FOREST?
GOOD! THEY'RE GONE. GUESS THEY DIDN'T GIVE... A HOOT... ZZZZZZZ...
GIVE A HOOT? THEY DECIDED TO SCOOT!
5

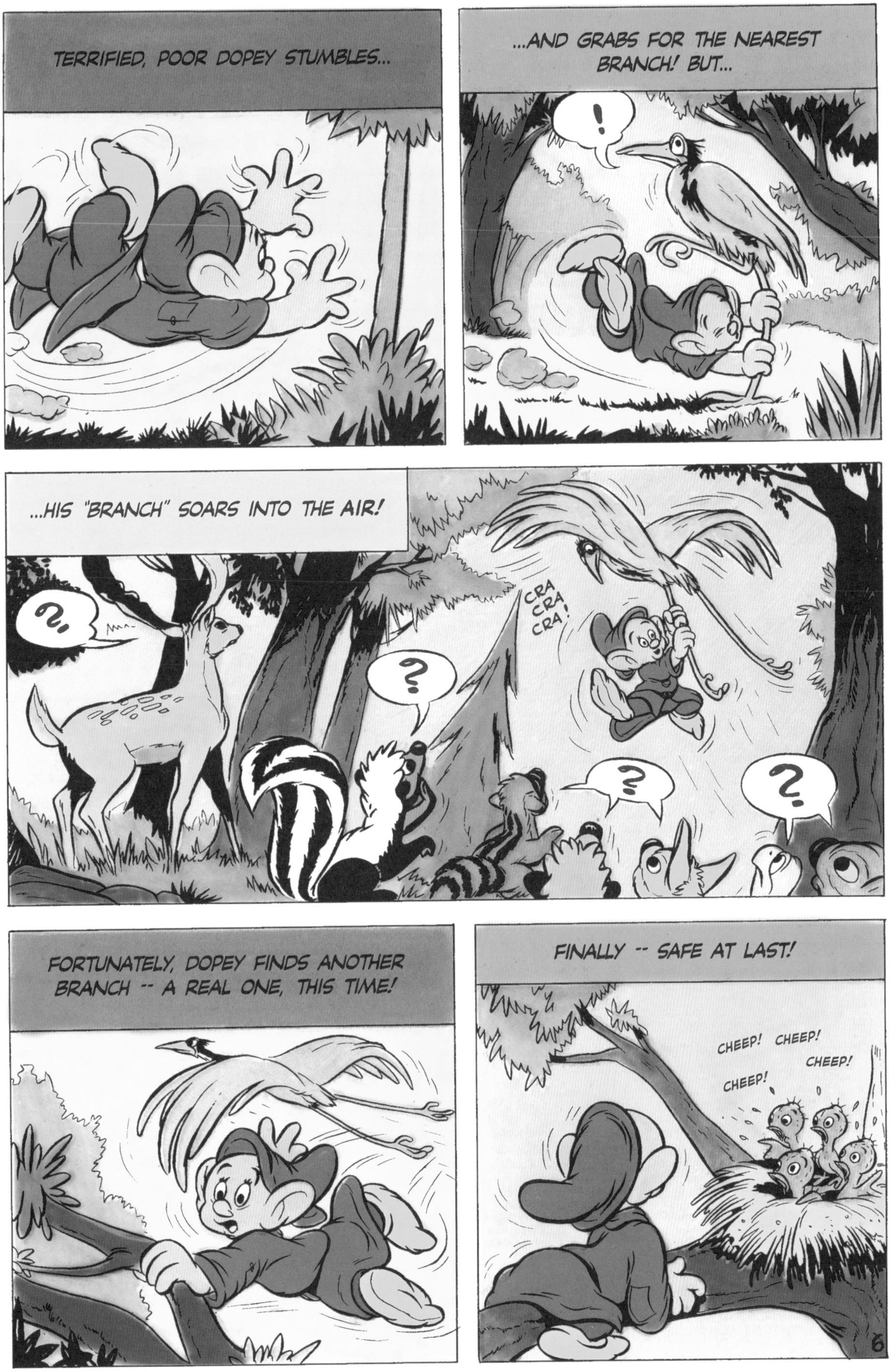
TERRIFIED, POOR DOPEY STUMBLES...
...AND GRABS FOR THE NEAREST BRANCH! BUT...
!
...HIS "BRANCH" SOARS INTO THE AIR!
?
CRA CRA CRA!
?
?
?
FORTUNATELY, DOPEY FINDS ANOTHER BRANCH -- A REAL ONE, THIS TIME!
FINALLY -- SAFE AT LAST!
CHEEP! CHEEP!
CHEEP!
CHEEP!
6

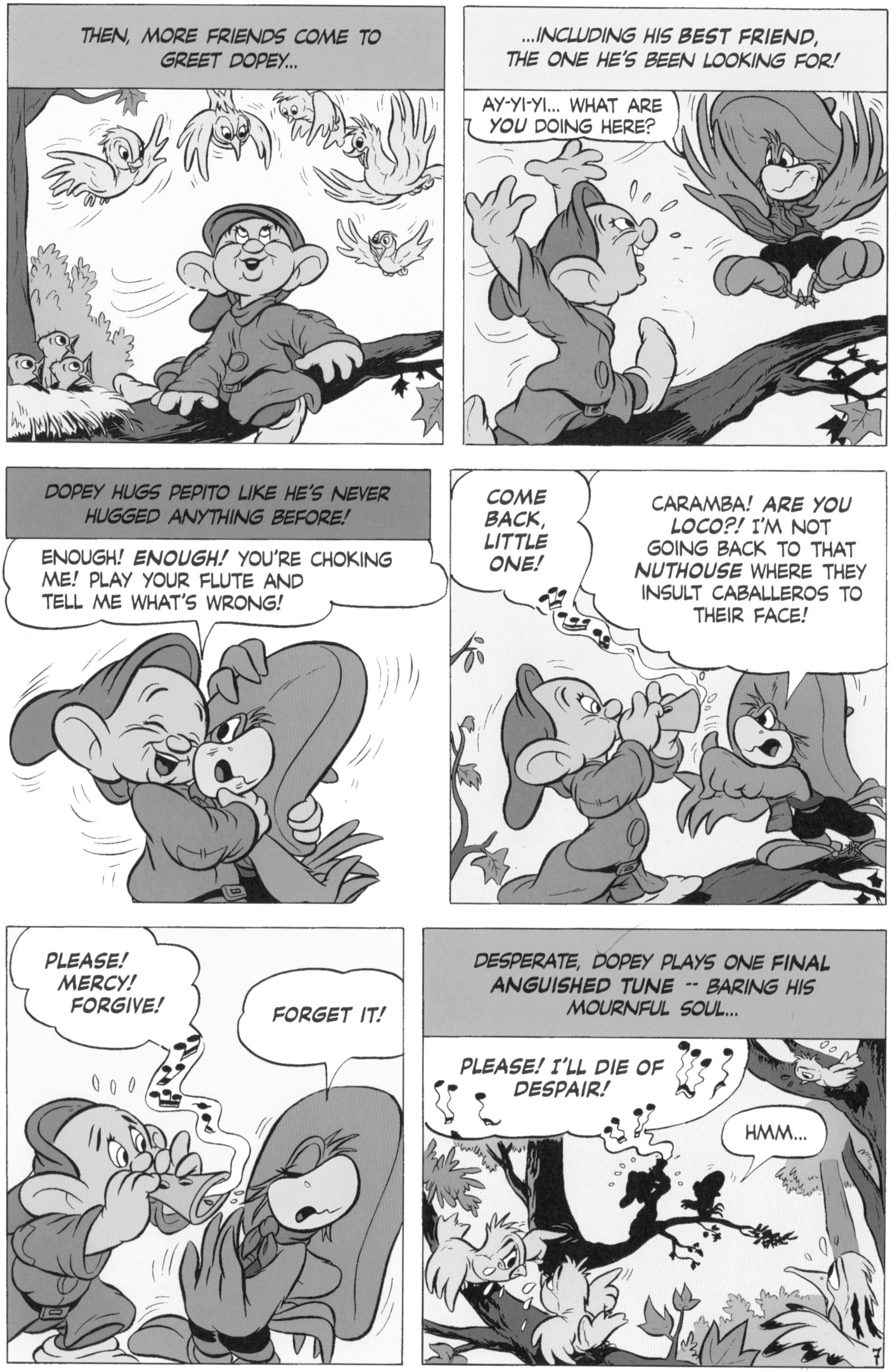
THEN, MORE FRIENDS COME TO GREET DOPEY...
...INCLUDING HIS BEST FRIEND, THE ONE HE'S BEEN LOOKING FOR!
AY-YI-YI... WHAT ARE YOU DOING HERE?
DOPEY HUGS PEPITO LIKE HE'S NEVER HUGGED ANYTHING BEFORE!
ENOUGH! ENOUGH! YOU'RE CHOKING ME! PLAY YOUR FLUTE AND TELL ME WHAT'S WRONG!
COME BACK, LITTLE ONE!
CARAMBA! ARE YOU LOCO?! I'M NOT GOING BACK TO THAT NUTHOUSE WHERE THEY INSULT CABALLEROS TO THEIR FACE!
PLEASE! MERCY! FORGIVE!
FORGET IT!
DESPERATE, DOPEY PLAYS ONE FINAL ANGUISHED TUNE -- BARING HIS MOURNFUL SOUL...
PLEASE! I'LL DIE OF DESPAIR!
HMM...
7

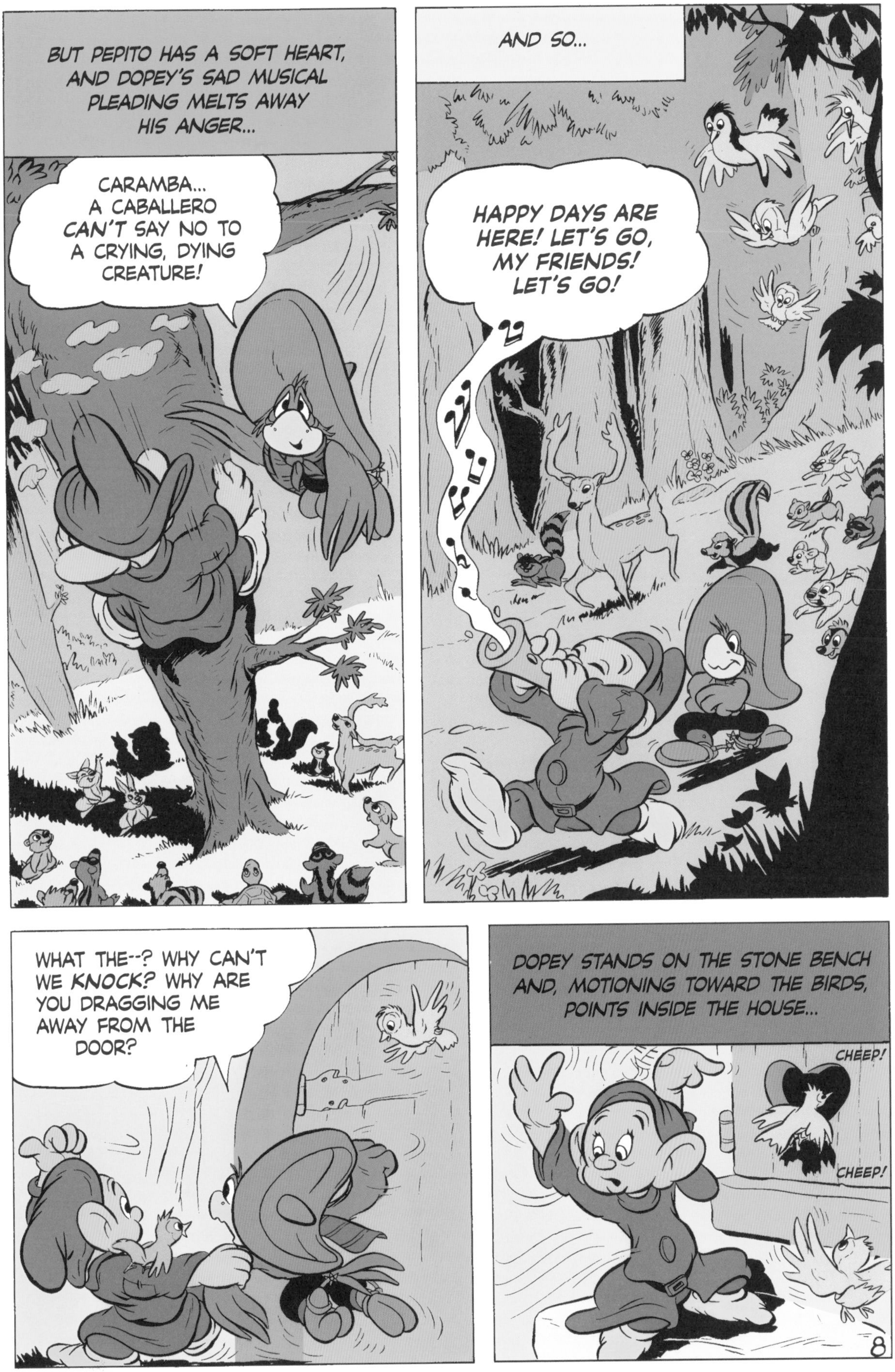
BUT PEPITO HAS A SOFT HEART, AND DOPEY'S SAD MUSICAL PLEADING MELTS AWAY HIS ANGER...
CARAMBA... A CABALLERO CAN'T SAY NO TO A CRYING, DYING CREATURE!
AND SO...
HAPPY DAYS ARE HERE! LET'S GO, MY FRIENDS! LET'S GO!
WHAT THE--? WHY CAN'T WE KNOCK? WHY ARE YOU DRAGGING ME AWAY FROM THE DOOR?
DOPEY STANDS ON THE STONE BENCH AND, MOTIONING TOWARD THE BIRDS, POINTS INSIDE THE HOUSE...
CHEEP!
CHEEP!
8

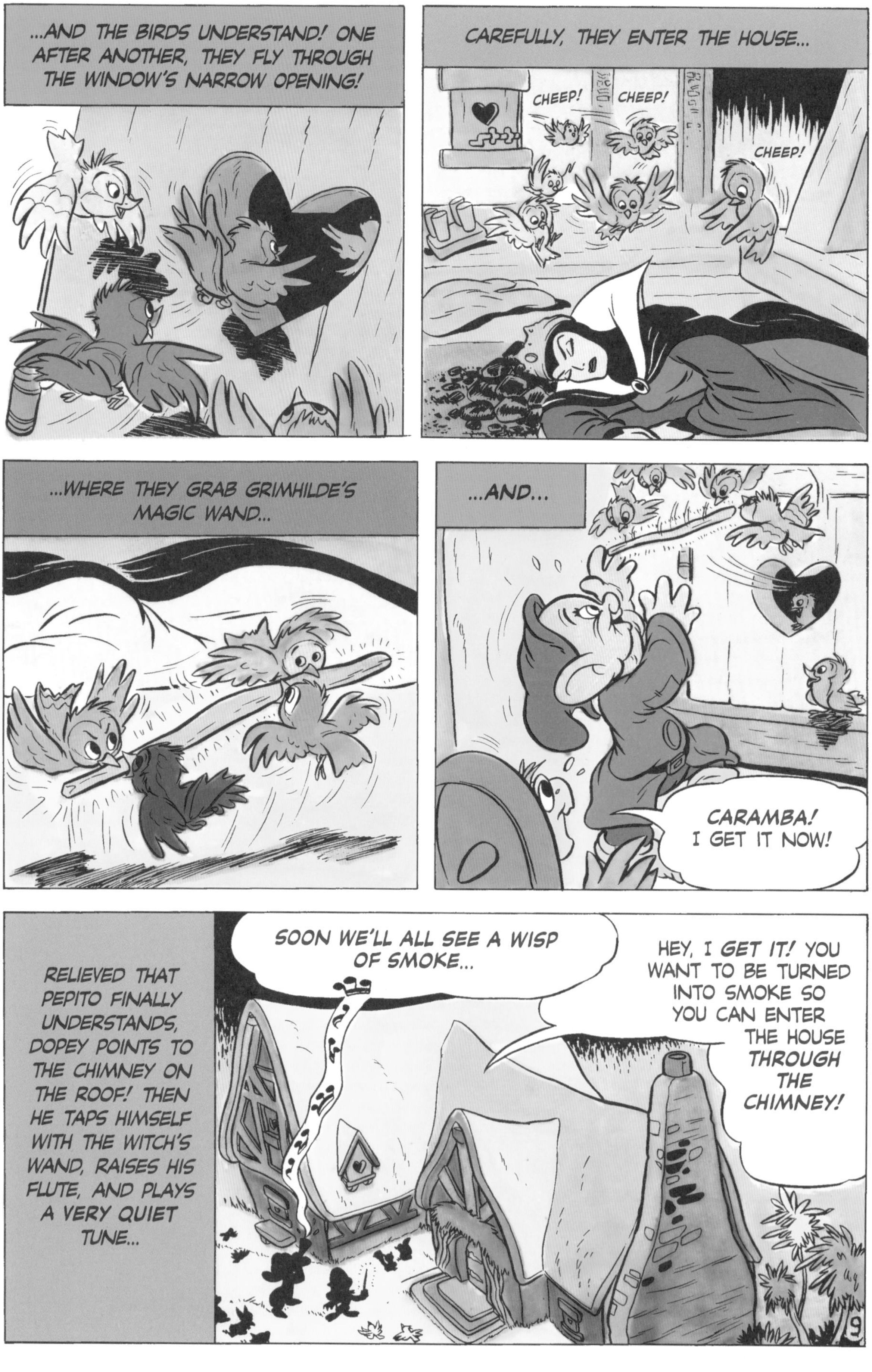

...AND THE BIRDS UNDERSTAND! ONE AFTER ANOTHER, THEY FLY THROUGH THE WINDOW'S NARROW OPENING!
CAREFULLY, THEY ENTER THE HOUSE...
CHEEP!
CHEEP!
CHEEP!
...WHERE THEY GRAB GRIMHILDE'S MAGIC WAND...
...AND...
CARAMBA! I GET IT NOW!
RELIEVED THAT PEPITO FINALLY UNDERSTANDS, DOPEY POINTS TO THE CHIMNEY ON THE ROOF! THEN HE TAPS HIMSELF WITH THE WITCH'S WAND, RAISES HIS FLUTE, AND PLAYS A VERY QUIET TUNE...
SOON WE'LL ALL SEE A WISP OF SMOKE...
HEY, I GET IT! YOU WANT TO BE TURNED INTO SMOKE SO YOU CAN ENTER THE HOUSE THROUGH THE CHIMNEY!
9

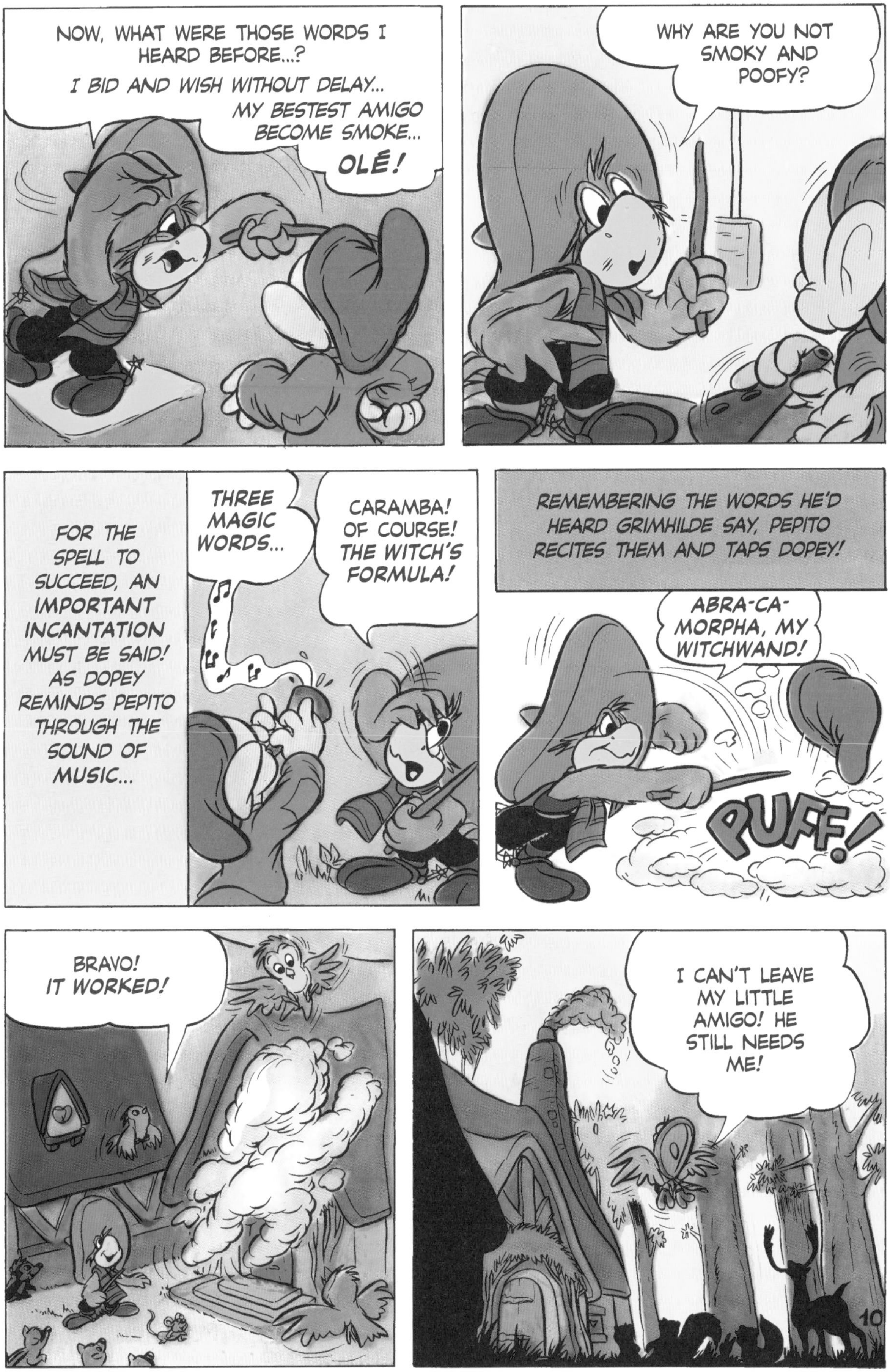
NOW, WHAT WERE THOSE WORDS I HEARD BEFORE...? I BID AND WISH WITHOUT DELAY... MY BESTEST AMIGO BECOME SMOKE... OLÉ!
WHY ARE YOU NOT SMOKY AND POOFY?
FOR THE SPELL TO SUCCEED, AN IMPORTANT INCANTATION MUST BE SAID! AS DOPEY REMINDS PEPITO THROUGH THE SOUND OF MUSIC...
THREE MAGIC WORDS...
CARAMBA! OF COURSE! THE WITCH'S FORMULA!
REMEMBERING THE WORDS HE'D HEARD GRIMHILDE SAY, PEPITO RECITES THEM AND TAPS DOPEY!
ABRA-CA-MORPHA, MY WITCHWAND!
PUFF!
BRAVO! IT WORKED!
I CAN'T LEAVE MY LITTLE AMIGO! HE STILL NEEDS ME!
10

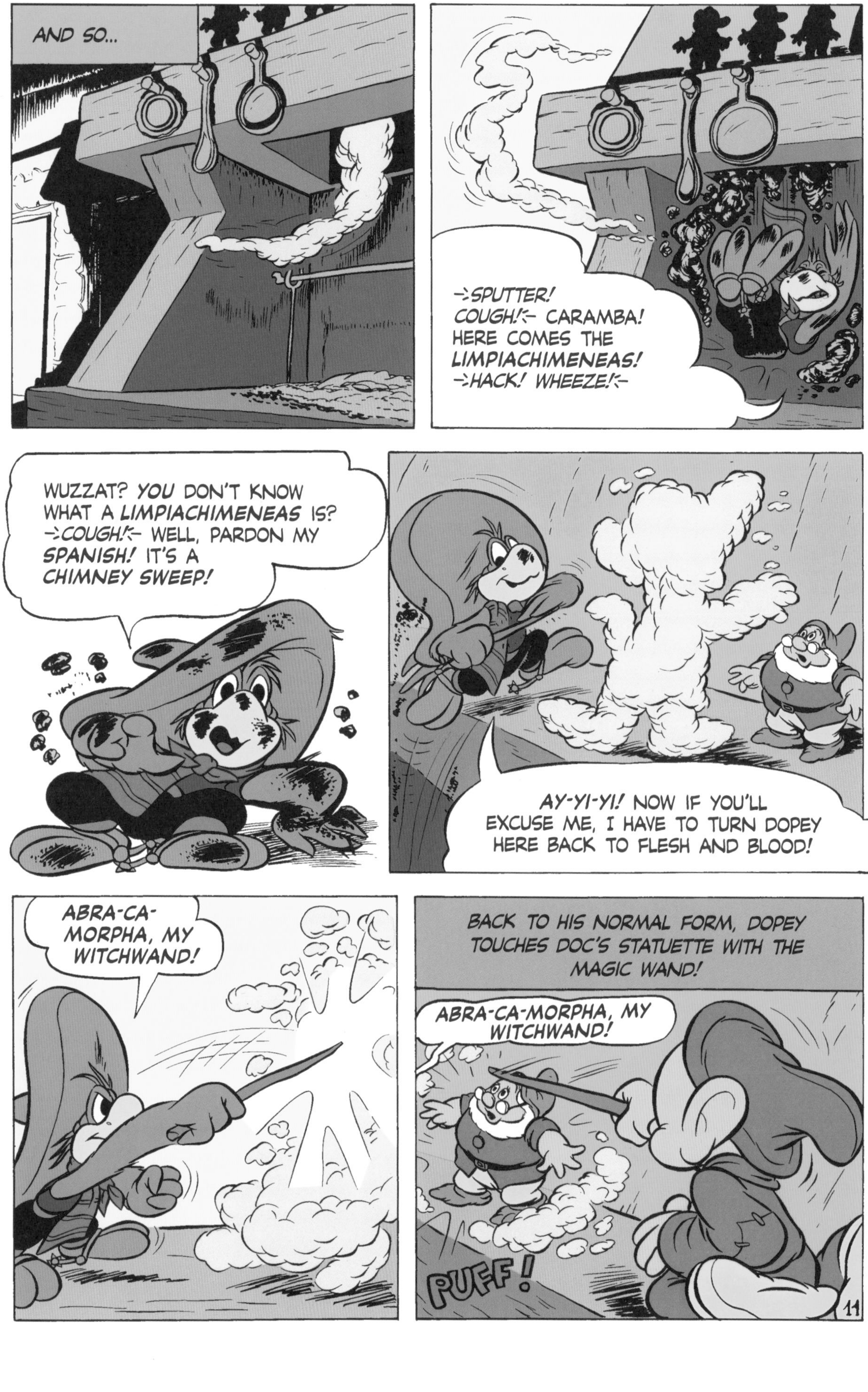
AND SO...
-SPUTTER! COUGH!- CARAMBA! HERE COMES THE LIMPIACHIMENEAS! -HACK! WHEEZE!-
WUZZAT? YOU DON'T KNOW WHAT A LIMPIACHIMENEAS IS? -COUGH!- WELL, PARDON MY SPANISH! IT'S A CHIMNEY SWEEP!
AY-YI-YI! NOW IF YOU'LL EXCUSE ME, I HAVE TO TURN DOPEY HERE BACK TO FLESH AND BLOOD!
ABRA-CA-MORPHA, MY WITCHWAND!
BACK TO HIS NORMAL FORM, DOPEY TOUCHES DOC'S STATUETTE WITH THE MAGIC WAND!
ABRA-CA-MORPHA, MY WITCHWAND!
PUFF!
11

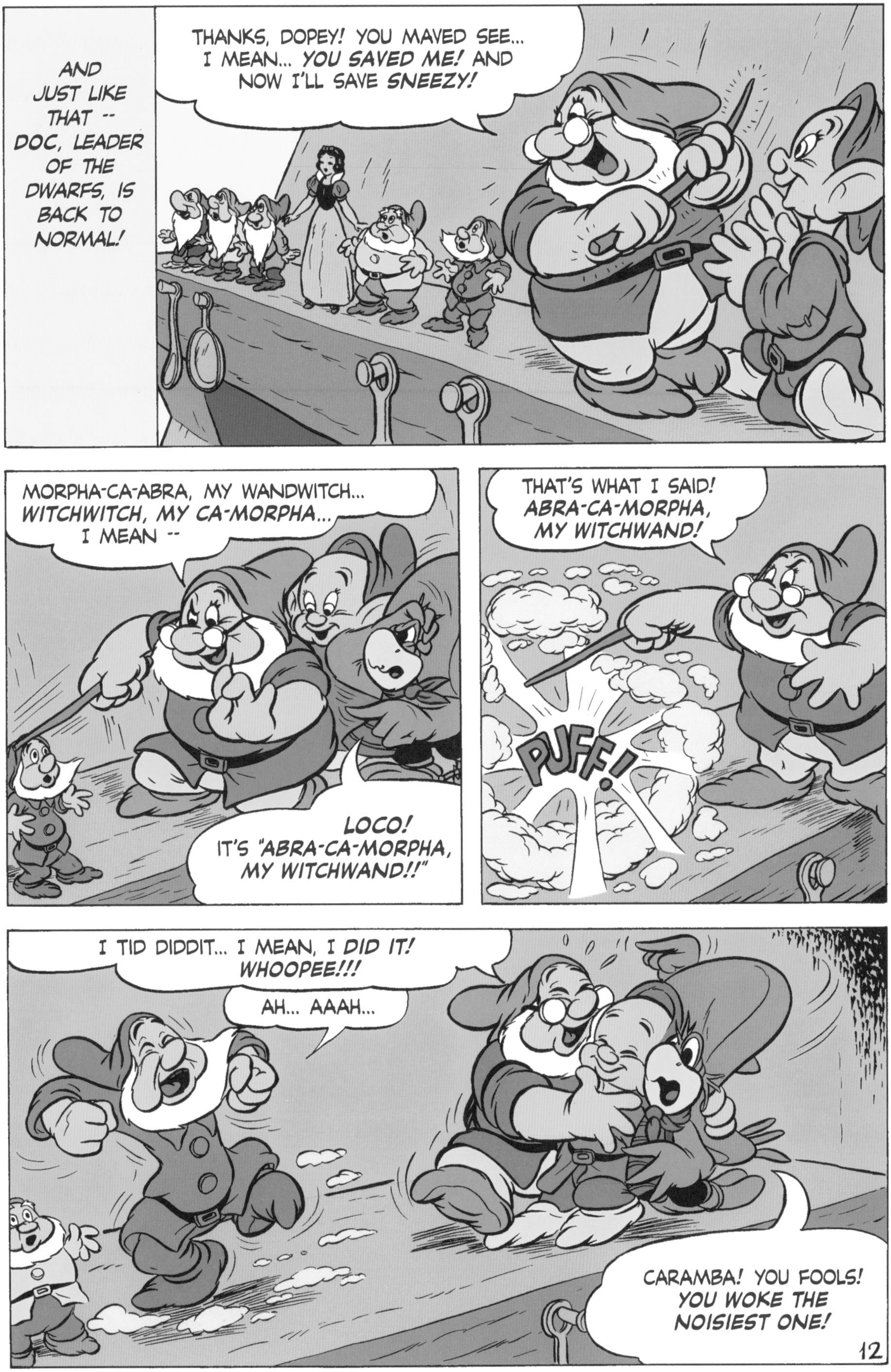
AND JUST LIKE THAT -- DOC, LEADER OF THE DWARFS, IS BACK TO NORMAL!
THANKS, DOPEY! YOU MAVED SEE... I MEAN... YOU SAVED ME! AND NOW I'LL SAVE SNEEZY!
MORPHA-CA-ABRA, MY WANDWITCH... WITCHWITCH, MY CA-MORPHA... I MEAN --
LOCO! IT'S "ABRA-CA-MORPHA, MY WITCHWAND!!"
THAT'S WHAT I SAID! ABRA-CA-MORPHA, MY WITCHWAND!
PUFF!
I TID DIDDIT... I MEAN, I DID IT! WHOOPEE!!!
AH... AAAH...
CARAMBA! YOU FOOLS! YOU WOKE THE NOISIEST ONE!
12

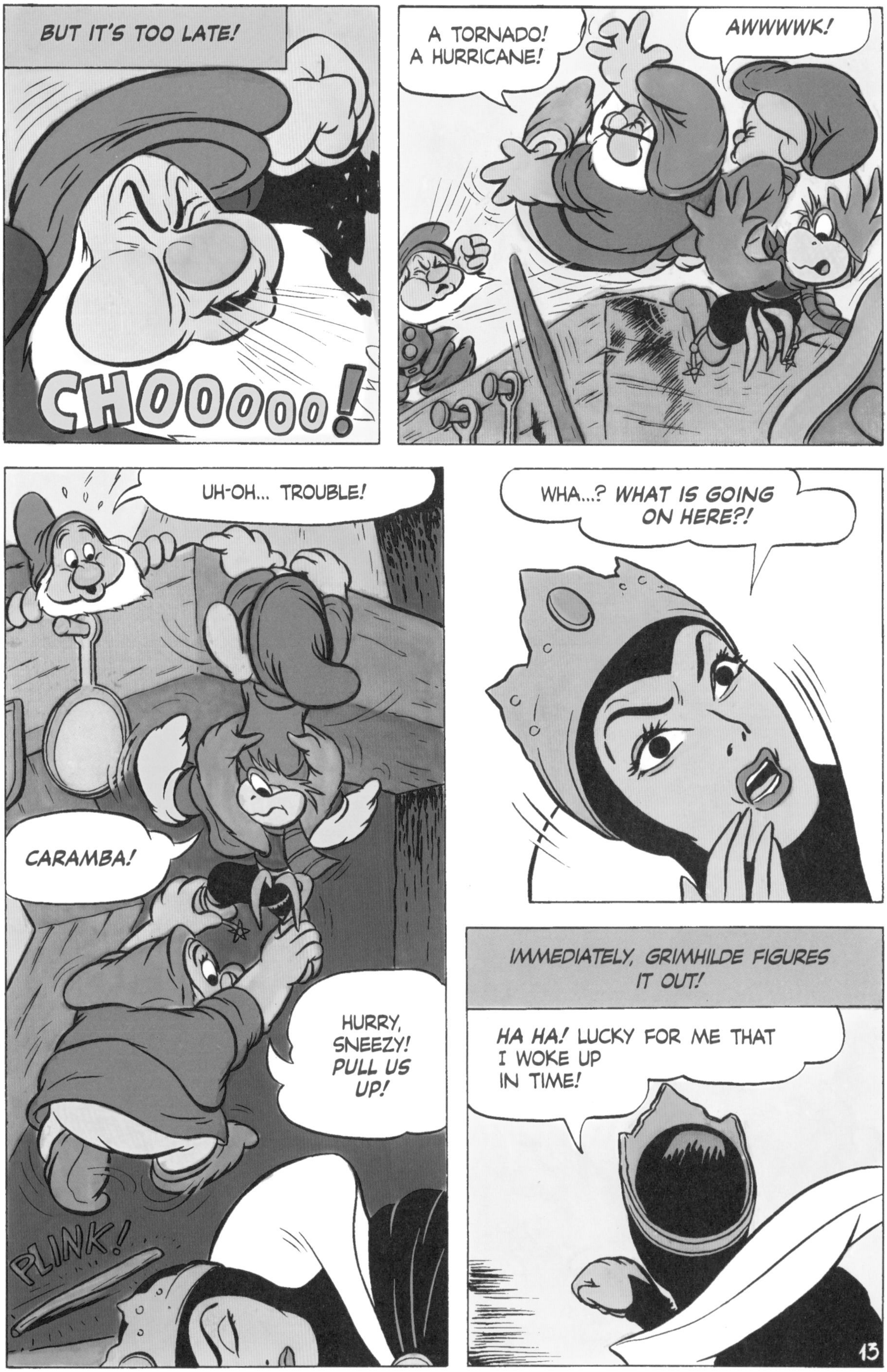
BUT IT'S TOO LATE!
CHOOOOOO!
A TORNADO! A HURRICANE!
AWWWWK!
UH-OH... TROUBLE!
CARAMBA!
HURRY, SNEEZY! PULL US UP!
PLINK!
WHA...? WHAT IS GOING ON HERE?!
IMMEDIATELY, GRIMHILDE FIGURES IT OUT!
HA HA! LUCKY FOR ME THAT I WOKE UP IN TIME!
13

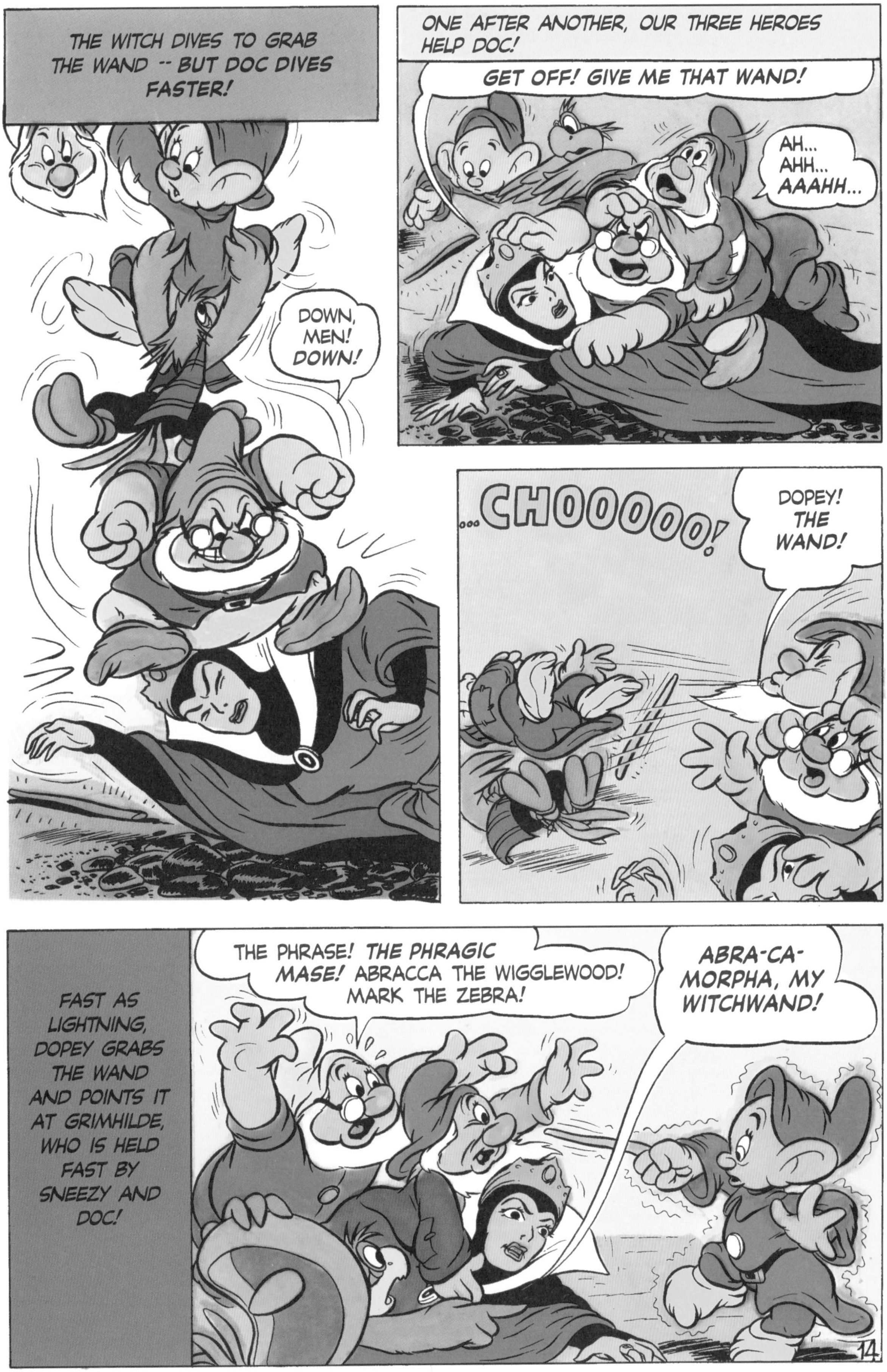
THE WITCH DIVES TO GRAB THE WAND -- BUT DOC DIVES FASTER!
DOWN, MEN! DOWN!
ONE AFTER ANOTHER, OUR THREE HEROES HELP DOC!
GET OFF! GIVE ME THAT WAND!
AH... AHH... AAAHH...
...CHOOOOOO!
DOPEY! THE WAND!
FAST AS LIGHTNING, DOPEY GRABS THE WAND AND POINTS IT AT GRIMHILDE, WHO IS HELD FAST BY SNEEZY AND DOC!
THE PHRASE! THE PHRAGIC MASE! ABRACCA THE WIGGLEWOOD! MARK THE ZEBRA!
ABRA-CA-MORPHA, MY WITCHWAND!
14

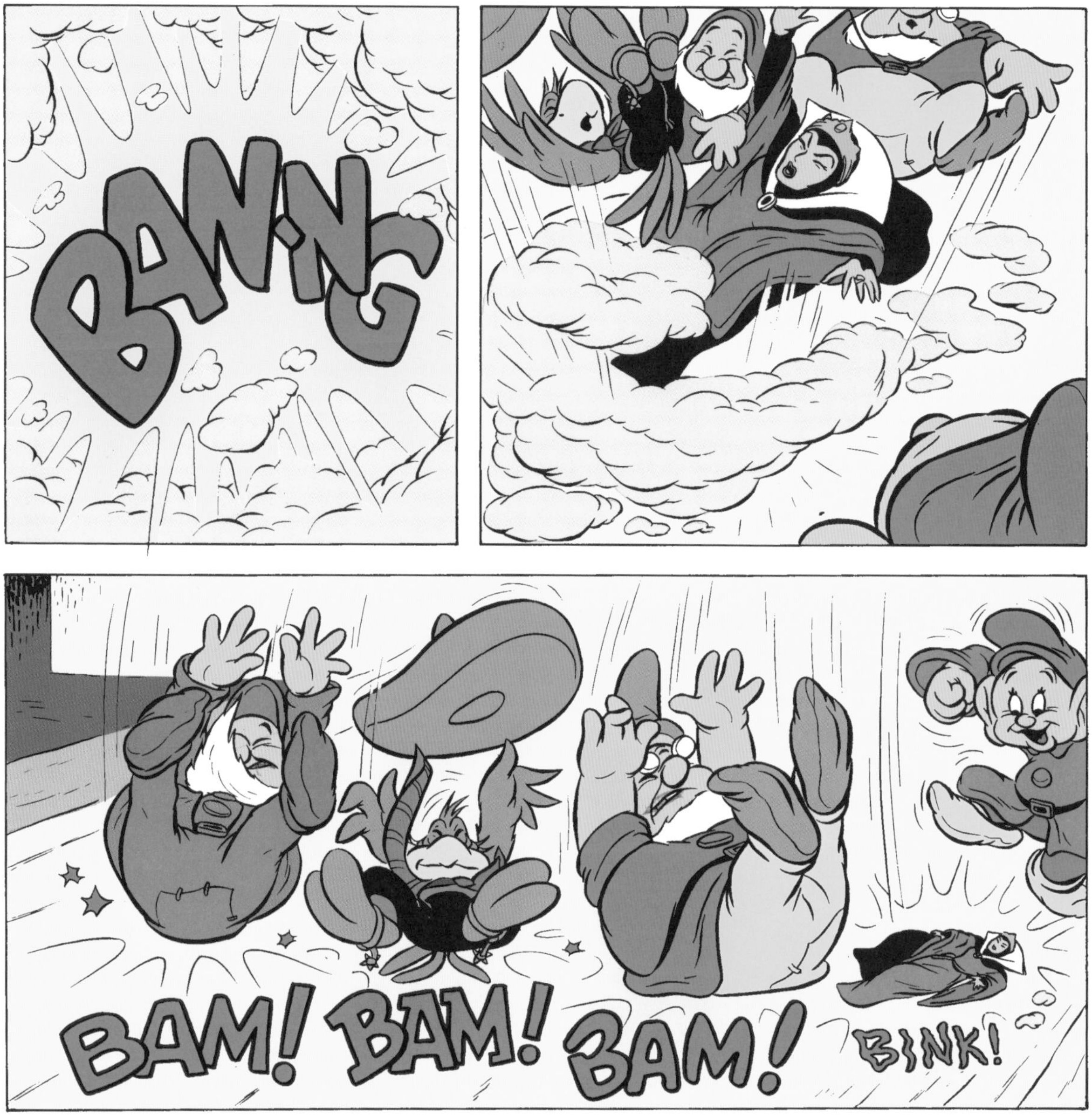
BAN-NG
BAM! BAM! BAM!
BINK!

AY, CARAMABA! SO NOW YOU KNOW HOW OUR ADVENTURE CAME TO AN END! AND I'M PRETTY SURE YOU CAN GUESS THE REST... WITH THE HELP OF THE WITCHWOOD WAND, **SNOW WHITE** AND THE **REMAINING DWARFS** WERE FREED FROM THE SPELL! MEANWHILE, THE EVIL **QUEEN** -- NOW A POCKET-SIZED PUPPET -- WAS HUNG ON A PEG! **PRINCE CHARMING** ARRIVED LATER THAT DAY, AND SNOW WHITE TOLD HIM EVERYTHING!

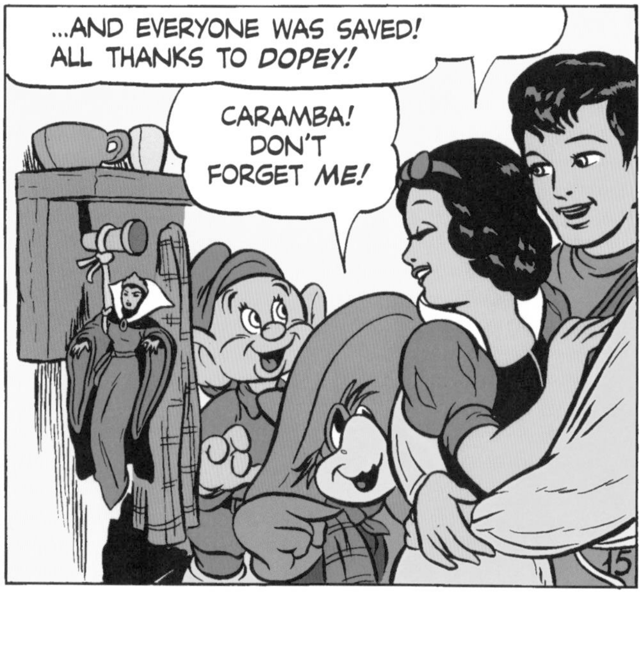
...AND EVERYONE WAS SAVED! ALL THANKS TO DOPEY!
CARAMBA! DON'T FORGET ME!
15

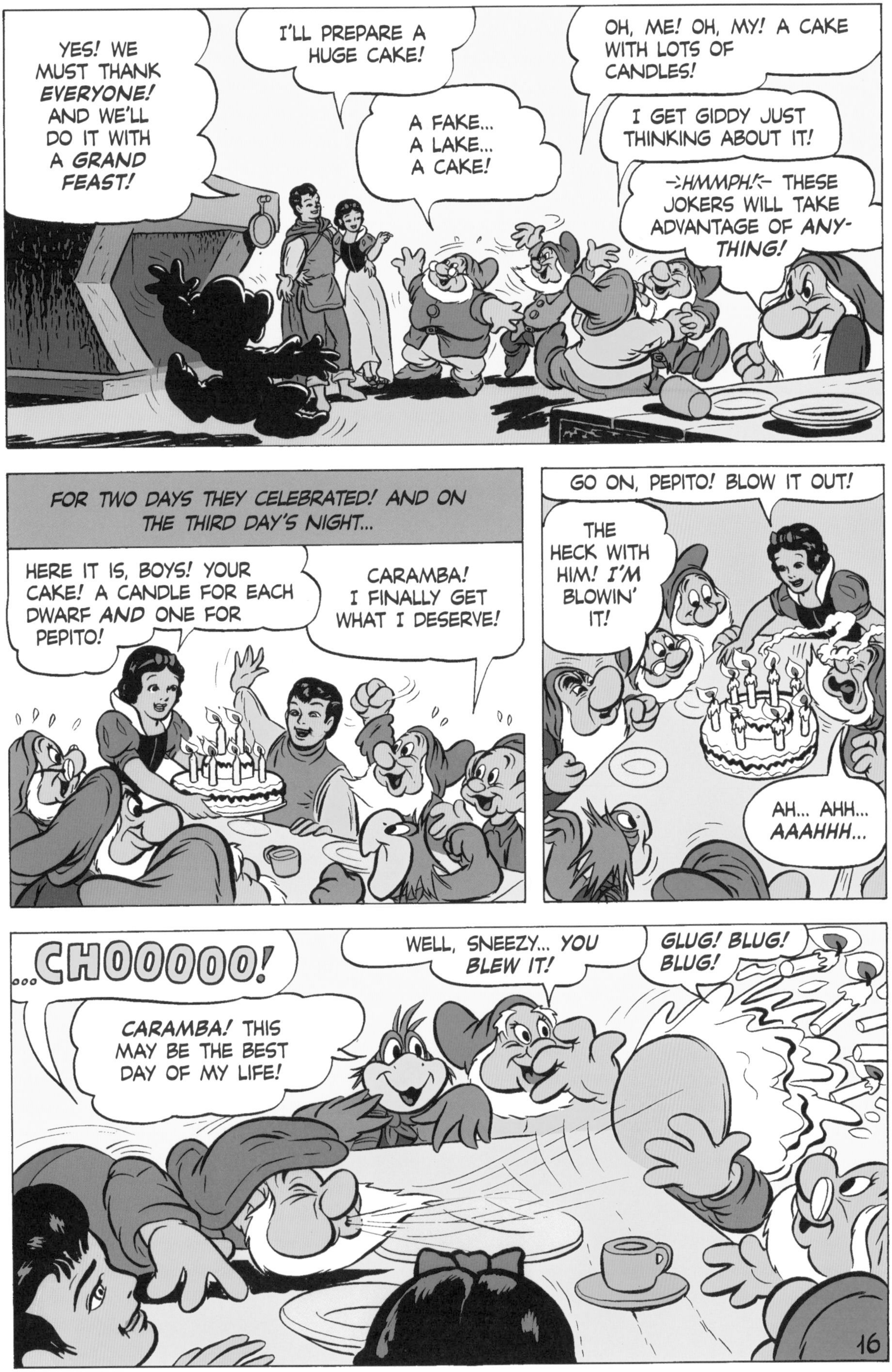
YES! WE MUST THANK EVERYONE! AND WE'LL DO IT WITH A GRAND FEAST!
I'LL PREPARE A HUGE CAKE!
A FAKE... A LAKE... A CAKE!
OH, ME! OH, MY! A CAKE WITH LOTS OF CANDLES!
I GET GIDDY JUST THINKING ABOUT IT!
-HMMPH!- THESE JOKERS WILL TAKE ADVANTAGE OF ANY-THING!
FOR TWO DAYS THEY CELEBRATED! AND ON THE THIRD DAY'S NIGHT...
HERE IT IS, BOYS! YOUR CAKE! A CANDLE FOR EACH DWARF AND ONE FOR PEPITO!
CARAMBA! I FINALLY GET WHAT I DESERVE!
GO ON, PEPITO! BLOW IT OUT!
THE HECK WITH HIM! I'M BLOWIN' IT!
AH... AHH... AAAHHH...
...CHOOOOOO!
CARAMBA! THIS MAY BE THE BEST DAY OF MY LIFE!
WELL, SNEEZY... YOU BLEW IT!
GLUG! BLUG! BLUG!
16

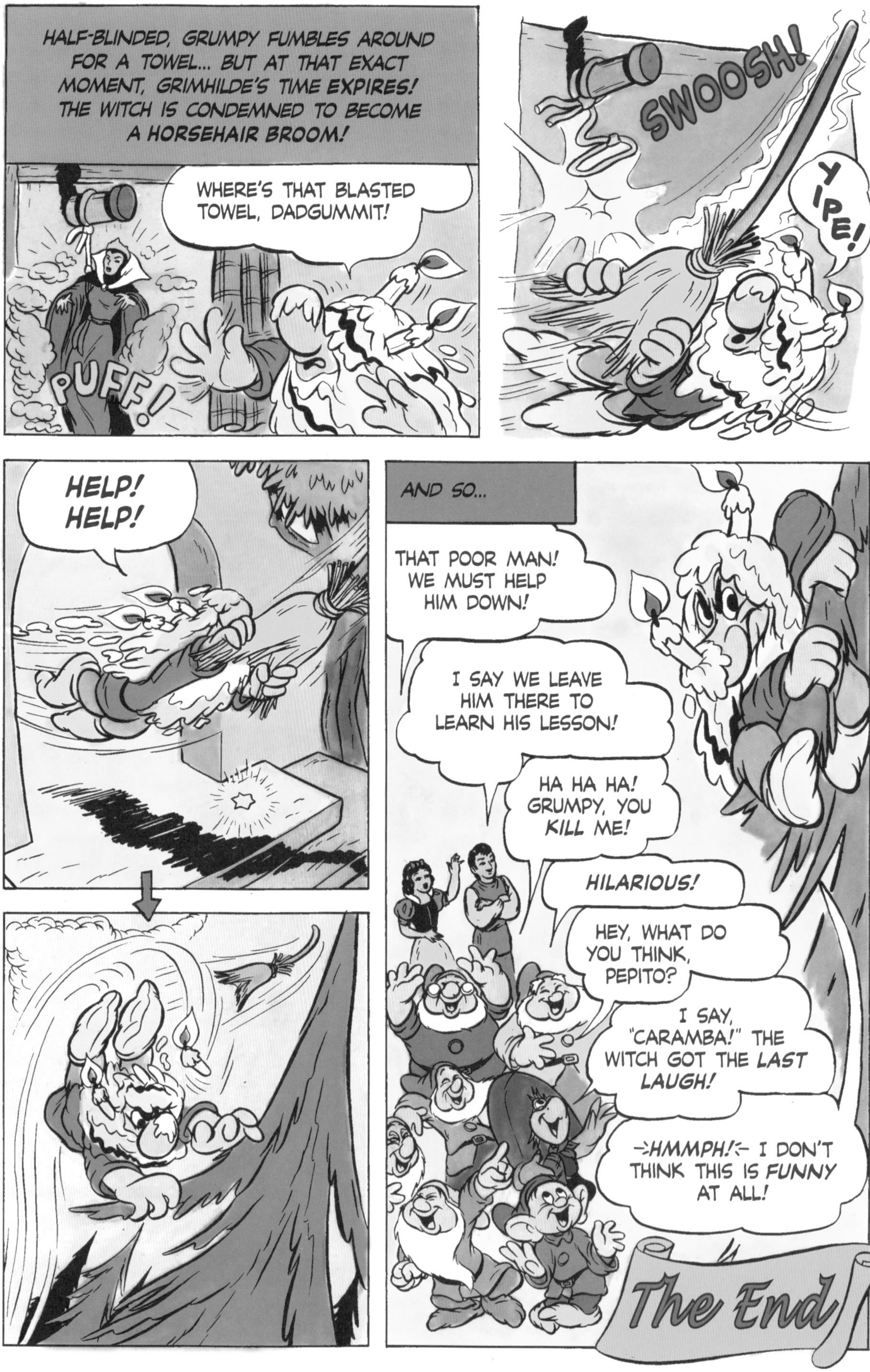
HALF-BLINDED, GRUMPY FUMBLES AROUND FOR A TOWEL... BUT AT THAT EXACT MOMENT, GRIMHILDE'S TIME EXPIRES! THE WITCH IS CONDEMNED TO BECOME A HORSEHAIR BROOM!
WHERE'S THAT BLASTED TOWEL, DADGUMMIT!
PUFF!
SWOOSH!
YIPE!
HELP! HELP!
AND SO...
THAT POOR MAN! WE MUST HELP HIM DOWN!
I SAY WE LEAVE HIM THERE TO LEARN HIS LESSON!
HA HA HA! GRUMPY, YOU KILL ME!
HILARIOUS!
HEY, WHAT DO YOU THINK, PEPITO?
I SAY, "CARAMBA!" THE WITCH GOT THE LAST LAUGH!
HMMPH! I DON'T THINK THIS IS FUNNY AT ALL!
The End

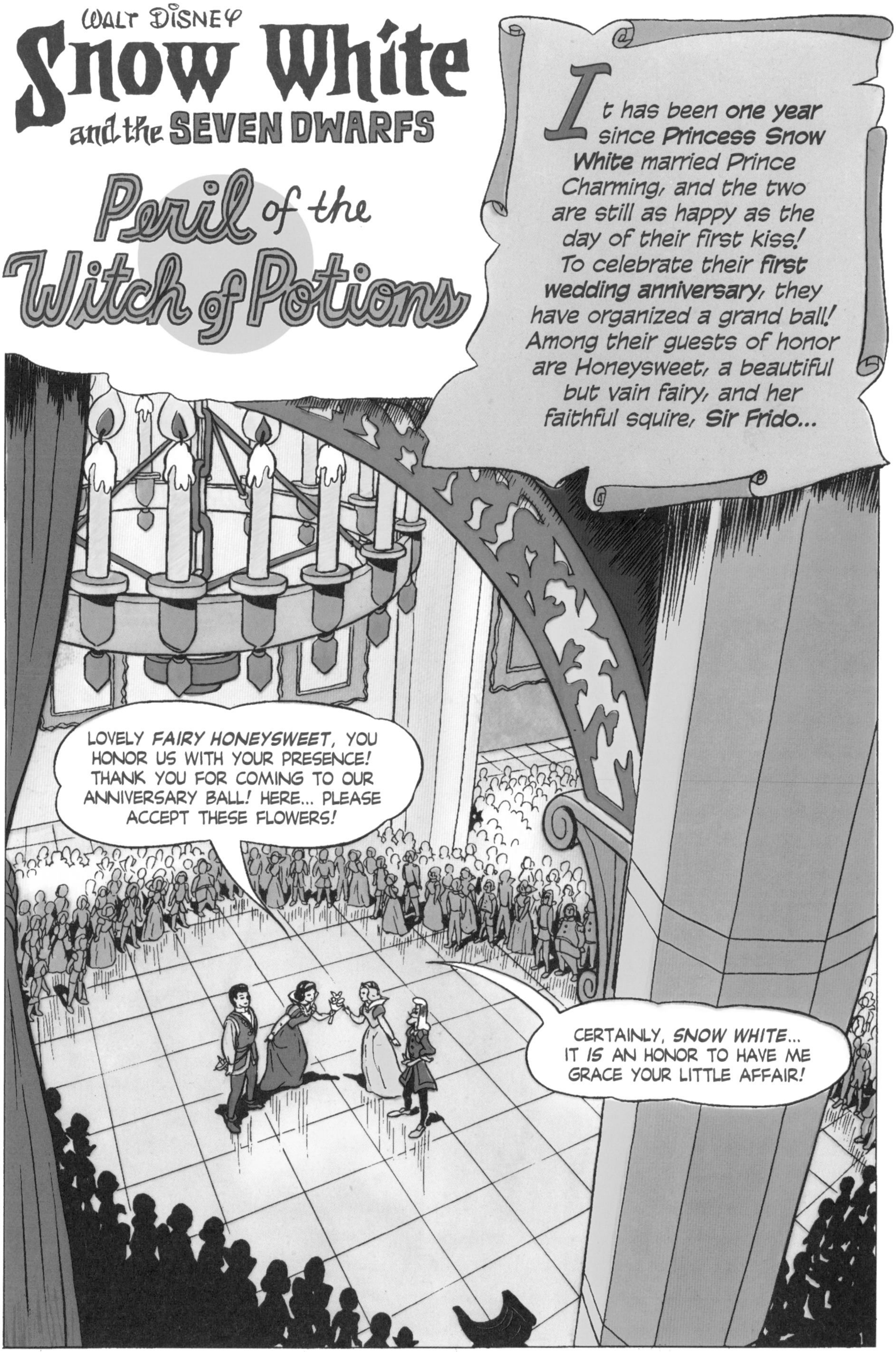
WALT DISNEY
Snow White and the SEVEN DWARFS
Peril of the Witch of Potions
It has been one year since Princess Snow White married Prince Charming, and the two are still as happy as the day of their first kiss! To celebrate their first wedding anniversary, they have organized a grand ball! Among their guests of honor are Honeysweet, a beautiful but vain fairy, and her faithful squire, Sir Frido...
LOVELY FAIRY HONEYSWEET, YOU HONOR US WITH YOUR PRESENCE! THANK YOU FOR COMING TO OUR ANNIVERSARY BALL! HERE... PLEASE ACCEPT THESE FLOWERS!
CERTAINLY, SNOW WHITE... IT IS AN HONOR TO HAVE ME GRACE YOUR LITTLE AFFAIR!

STORY: GUIDO MARTINA • ART: ROMANO SCARPA
TRANSLATION: ALBERTO BECATTINI • DIALOG: JONATHAN H. GRAY WITH DAVID GERSTEIN
TITLE LETTERING: KEELI MCCARTHY • EDITING: J. MICHAEL CATRON

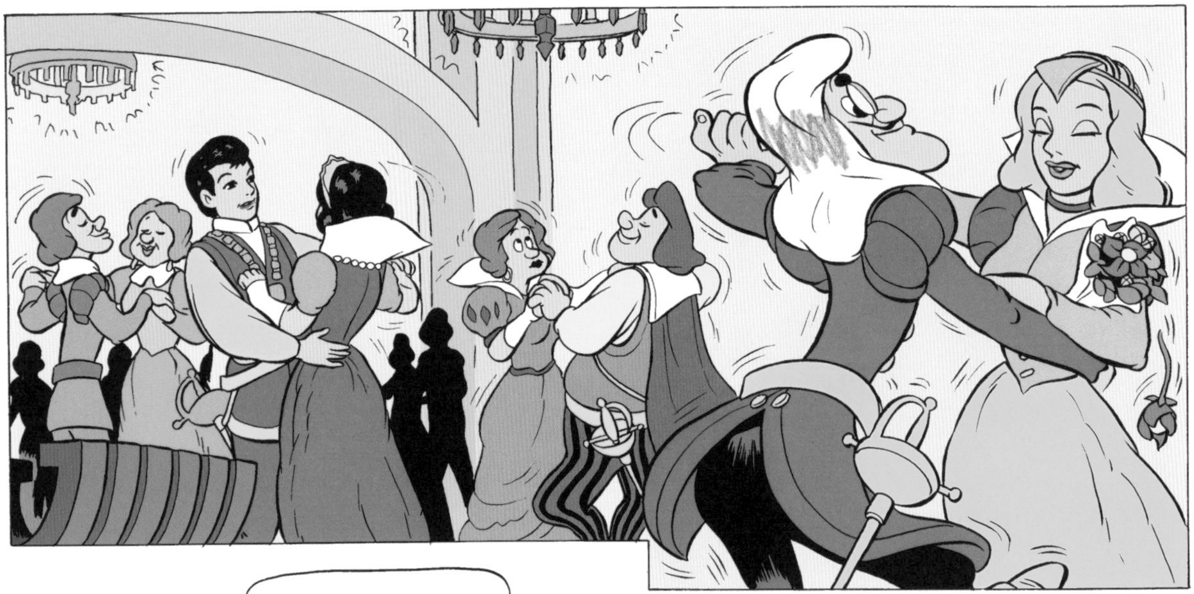

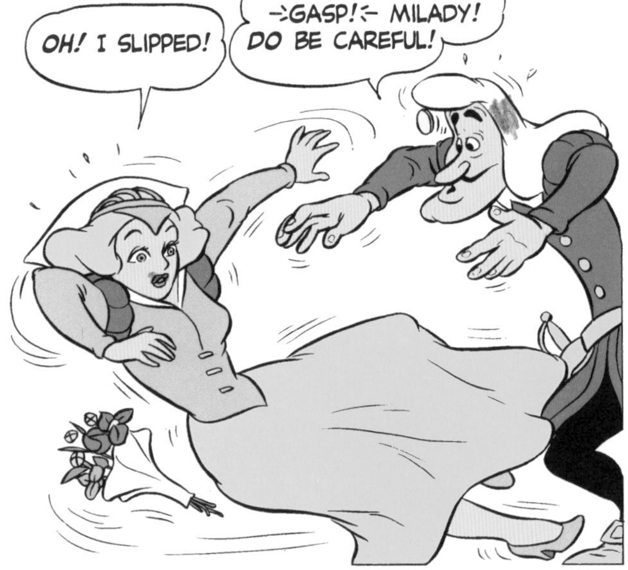
OH! I SLIPPED!
-GASP!- MILADY! DO BE CAREFUL!

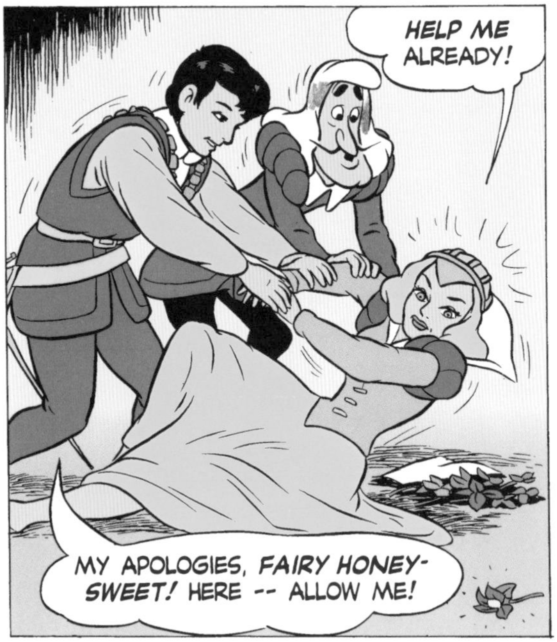
HELP ME ALREADY!
MY APOLOGIES, FAIRY HONEY-SWEET! HERE -- ALLOW ME!

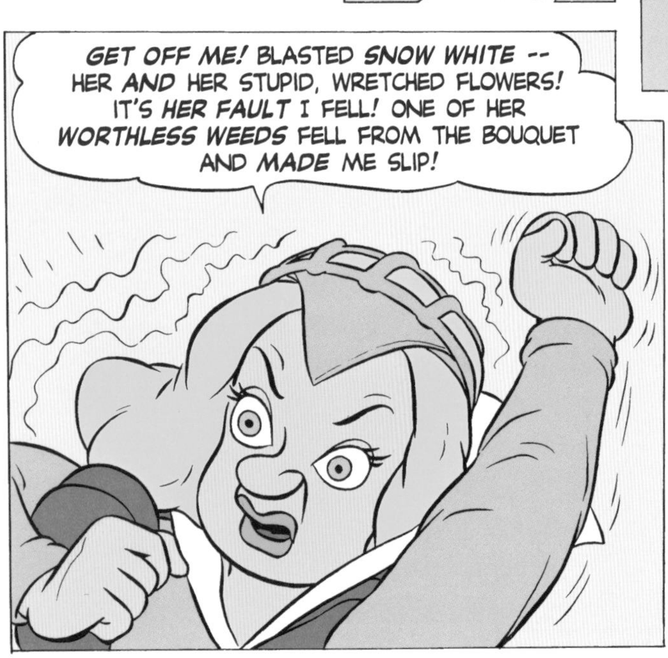
GET OFF ME! BLASTED SNOW WHITE -- HER AND HER STUPID, WRETCHED FLOWERS! IT'S HER FAULT I FELL! ONE OF HER WORTHLESS WEEDS FELL FROM THE BOUQUET AND MADE ME SLIP!

*What the ball's attendees don't know is that "gentle" Honeysweet is really the **Witch of Potions!** She gained her fairy form by stealing the beauty of a **young princess...***

*But the **books of magic** are very clear about how to break a spell of false beauty! Should such a one fall -- and fail to maintain her poise and manners -- she will change back to her true self!*

And so the witch loses her fairy form and reverts to...

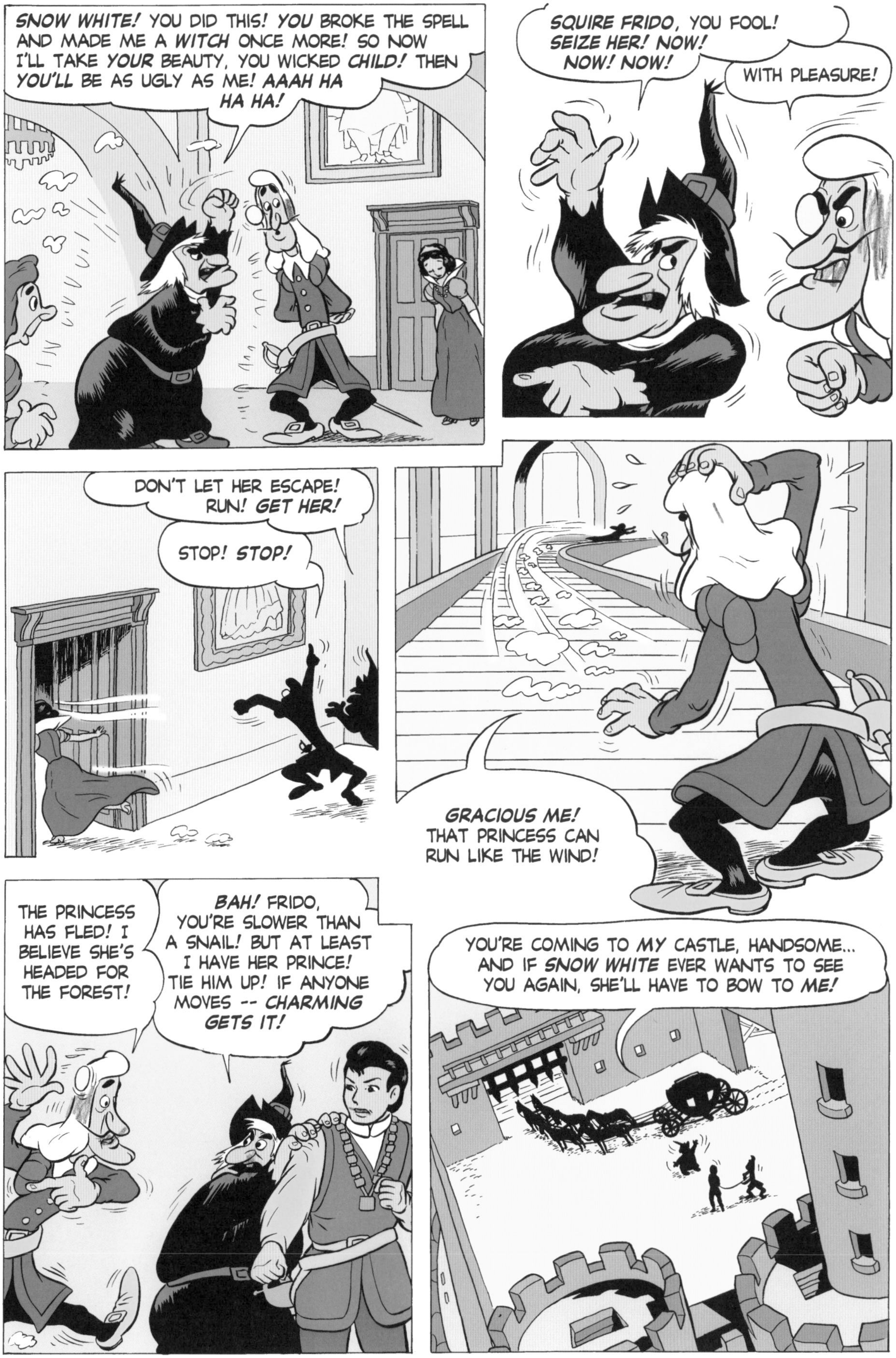
SNOW WHITE! YOU DID THIS! YOU BROKE THE SPELL AND MADE ME A WITCH ONCE MORE! SO NOW I'LL TAKE YOUR BEAUTY, YOU WICKED CHILD! THEN YOU'LL BE AS UGLY AS ME! AAAH HA HA HA!
SQUIRE FRIDO, YOU FOOL! SEIZE HER! NOW! NOW! NOW!
WITH PLEASURE!
DON'T LET HER ESCAPE! RUN! GET HER!
STOP! STOP!
GRACIOUS ME! THAT PRINCESS CAN RUN LIKE THE WIND!
THE PRINCESS HAS FLED! I BELIEVE SHE'S HEADED FOR THE FOREST!
BAH! FRIDO, YOU'RE SLOWER THAN A SNAIL! BUT AT LEAST I HAVE HER PRINCE! TIE HIM UP! IF ANYONE MOVES -- CHARMING GETS IT!
YOU'RE COMING TO MY CASTLE, HANDSOME... AND IF SNOW WHITE EVER WANTS TO SEE YOU AGAIN, SHE'LL HAVE TO BOW TO ME!

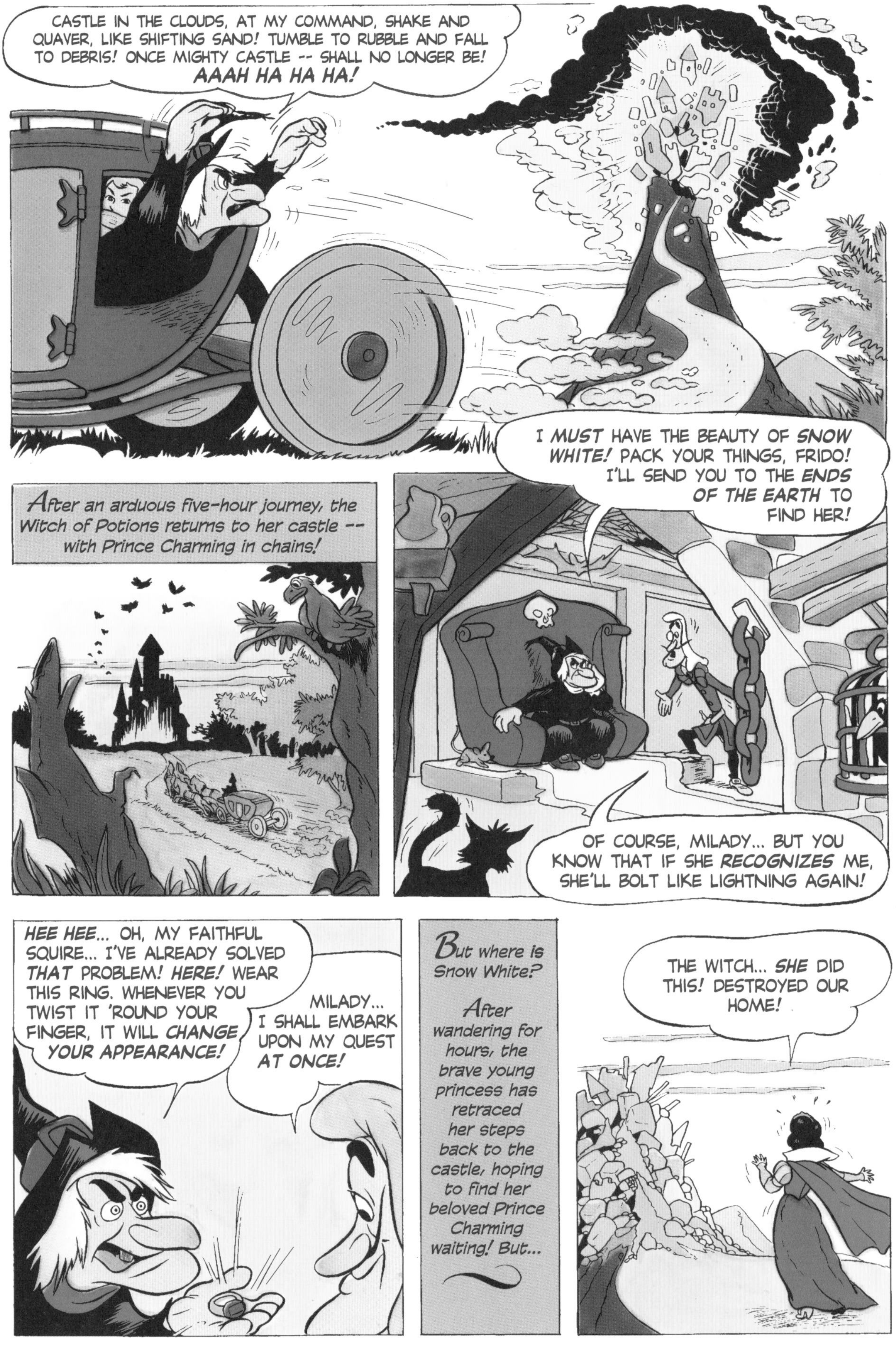
CASTLE IN THE CLOUDS, AT MY COMMAND, SHAKE AND QUAVER, LIKE SHIFTING SAND! TUMBLE TO RUBBLE AND FALL TO DEBRIS! ONCE MIGHTY CASTLE -- SHALL NO LONGER BE! AAAH HA HA HA!
After an arduous five-hour journey, the Witch of Potions returns to her castle -- with Prince Charming in chains!
I MUST HAVE THE BEAUTY OF SNOW WHITE! PACK YOUR THINGS, FRIDO! I'LL SEND YOU TO THE ENDS OF THE EARTH TO FIND HER!
OF COURSE, MILADY... BUT YOU KNOW THAT IF SHE RECOGNIZES ME, SHE'LL BOLT LIKE LIGHTNING AGAIN!
HEE HEE... OH, MY FAITHFUL SQUIRE... I'VE ALREADY SOLVED THAT PROBLEM! HERE! WEAR THIS RING. WHENEVER YOU TWIST IT 'ROUND YOUR FINGER, IT WILL CHANGE YOUR APPEARANCE!
MILADY... I SHALL EMBARK UPON MY QUEST AT ONCE!
But where is Snow White?
After wandering for hours, the brave young princess has retraced her steps back to the castle, hoping to find her beloved Prince Charming waiting! But...
THE WITCH... SHE DID THIS! DESTROYED OUR HOME!

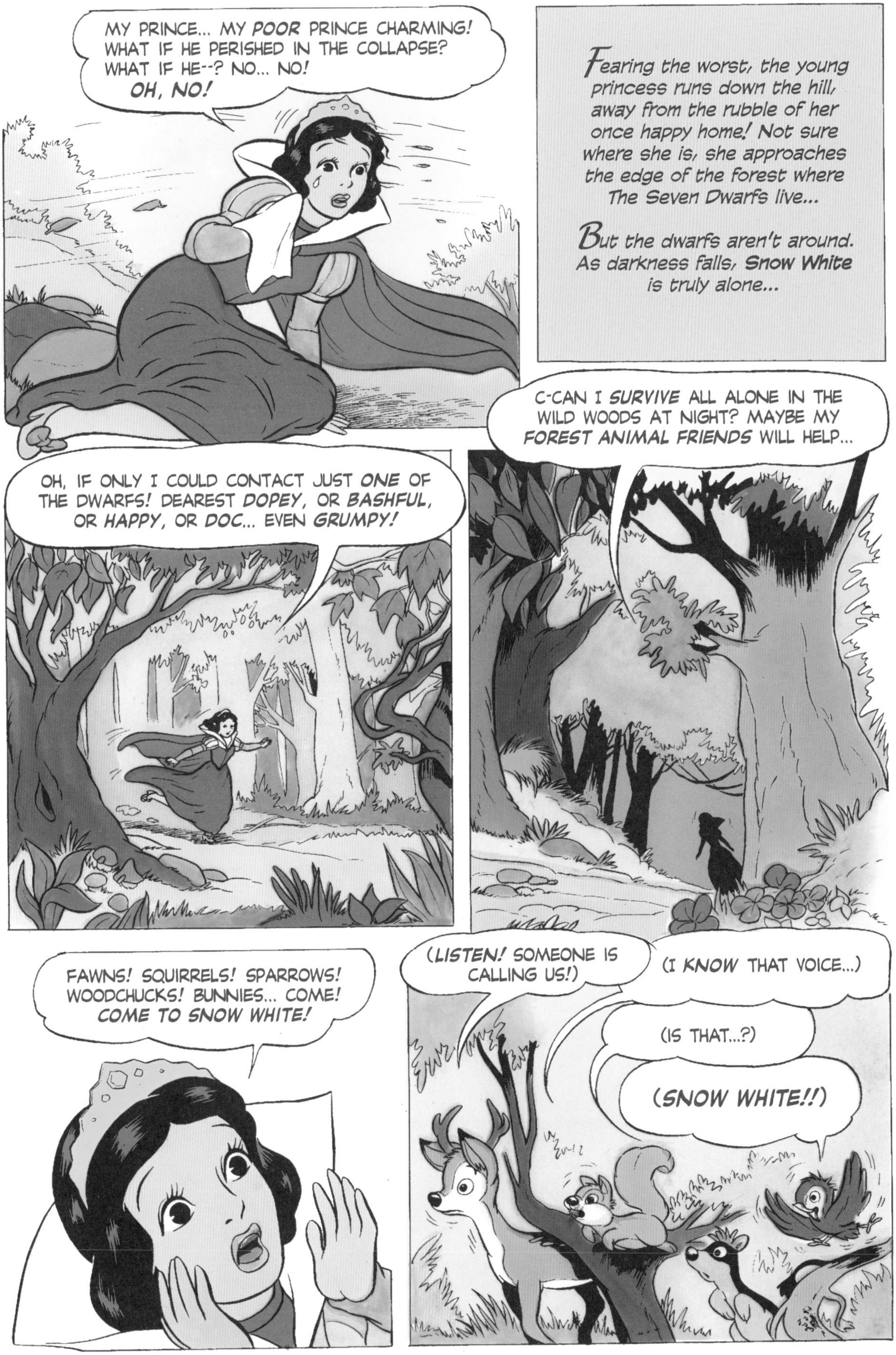
MY PRINCE... MY POOR PRINCE CHARMING! WHAT IF HE PERISHED IN THE COLLAPSE? WHAT IF HE--? NO... NO! OH, NO!
Fearing the worst, the young princess runs down the hill, away from the rubble of her once happy home! Not sure where she is, she approaches the edge of the forest where The Seven Dwarfs live...
But the dwarfs aren't around. As darkness falls, Snow White is truly alone...
OH, IF ONLY I COULD CONTACT JUST ONE OF THE DWARFS! DEAREST DOPEY, OR BASHFUL, OR HAPPY, OR DOC... EVEN GRUMPY!
C-CAN I SURVIVE ALL ALONE IN THE WILD WOODS AT NIGHT? MAYBE MY FOREST ANIMAL FRIENDS WILL HELP...
FAWNS! SQUIRRELS! SPARROWS! WOODCHUCKS! BUNNIES... COME! COME TO SNOW WHITE!
(LISTEN! SOMEONE IS CALLING US!)
(I KNOW THAT VOICE...)
(IS THAT...?)
(SNOW WHITE!!)

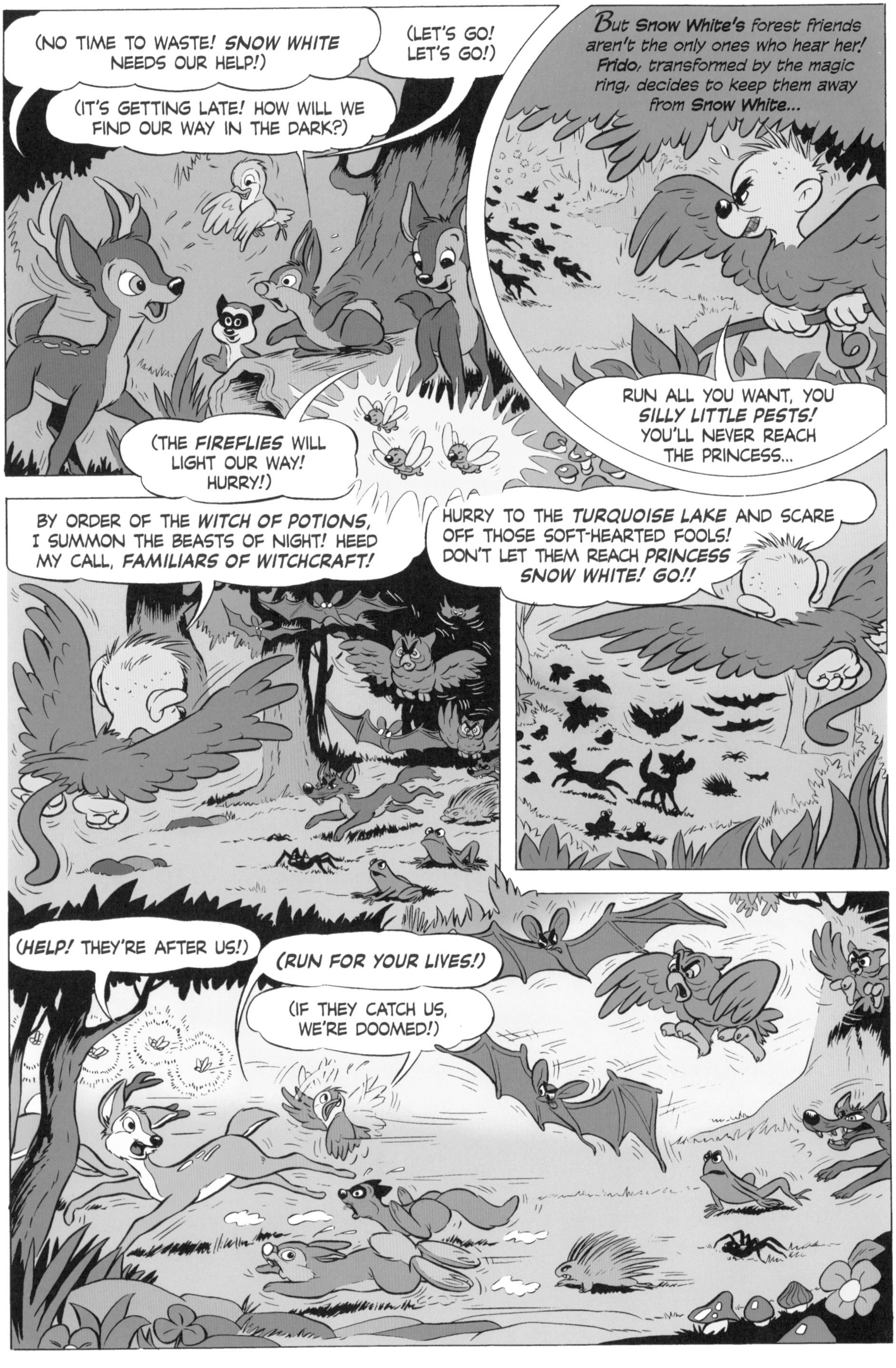

(NO TIME TO WASTE! SNOW WHITE NEEDS OUR HELP!)
(LET'S GO! LET'S GO!)
(IT'S GETTING LATE! HOW WILL WE FIND OUR WAY IN THE DARK?)
(THE FIREFLIES WILL LIGHT OUR WAY! HURRY!)
But Snow White's forest friends aren't the only ones who hear her! Frido, transformed by the magic ring, decides to keep them away from Snow White...
RUN ALL YOU WANT, YOU SILLY LITTLE PESTS! YOU'LL NEVER REACH THE PRINCESS...
BY ORDER OF THE WITCH OF POTIONS, I SUMMON THE BEASTS OF NIGHT! HEED MY CALL, FAMILIARS OF WITCHCRAFT!
HURRY TO THE TURQUOISE LAKE AND SCARE OFF THOSE SOFT-HEARTED FOOLS! DON'T LET THEM REACH PRINCESS SNOW WHITE! GO!!
(HELP! THEY'RE AFTER US!)
(RUN FOR YOUR LIVES!)
(IF THEY CATCH US, WE'RE DOOMED!)

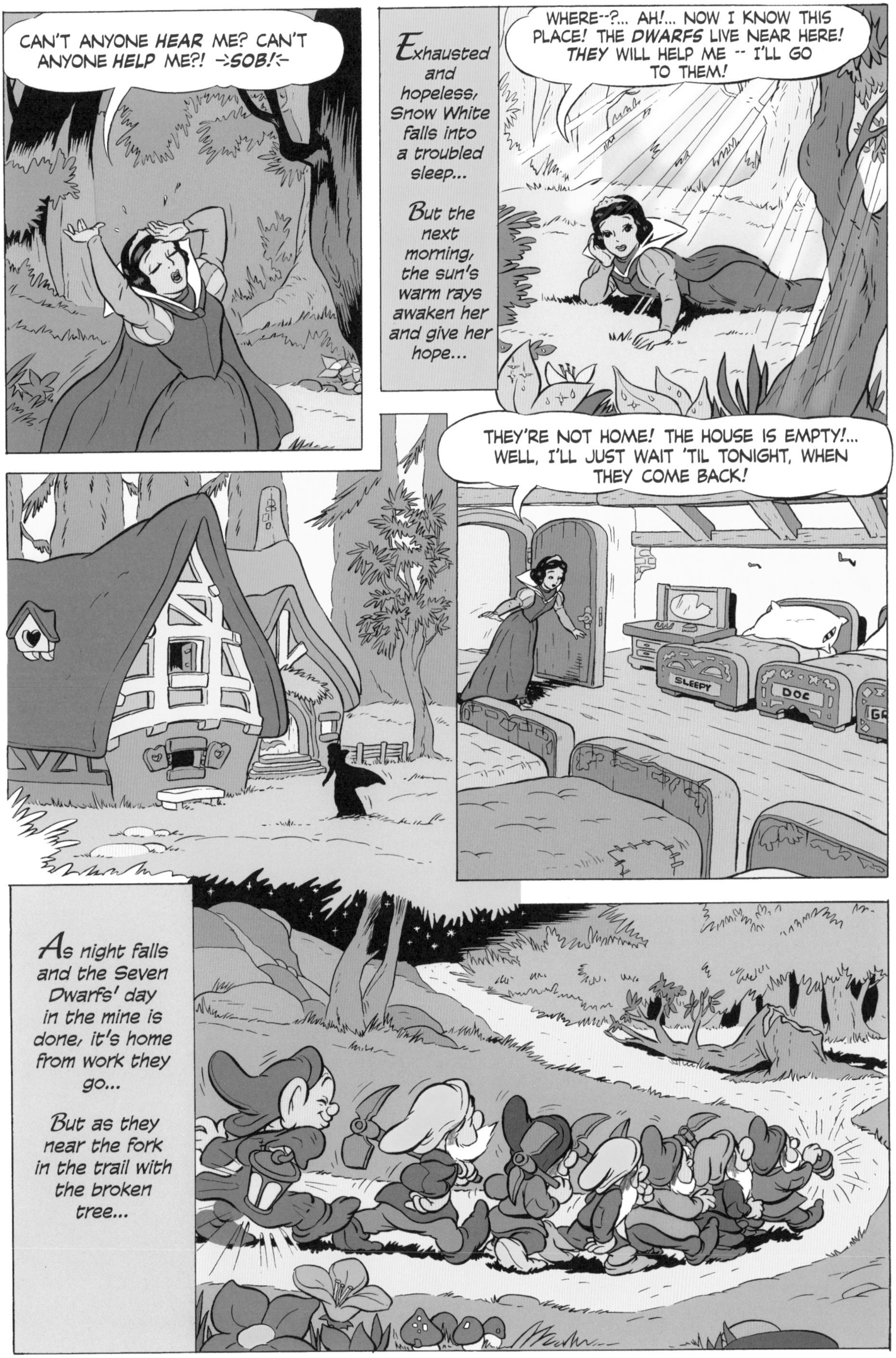
CAN'T ANYONE HEAR ME? CAN'T ANYONE HELP ME?! -SOB!-
Exhausted and hopeless, Snow White falls into a troubled sleep...
But the next morning, the sun's warm rays awaken her and give her hope...
WHERE--?... AH!... NOW I KNOW THIS PLACE! THE DWARFS LIVE NEAR HERE! THEY WILL HELP ME -- I'LL GO TO THEM!
THEY'RE NOT HOME! THE HOUSE IS EMPTY!... WELL, I'LL JUST WAIT 'TIL TONIGHT, WHEN THEY COME BACK!
SLEEPY
DOC
As night falls and the Seven Dwarfs' day in the mine is done, it's home from work they go...
But as they near the fork in the trail with the broken tree...

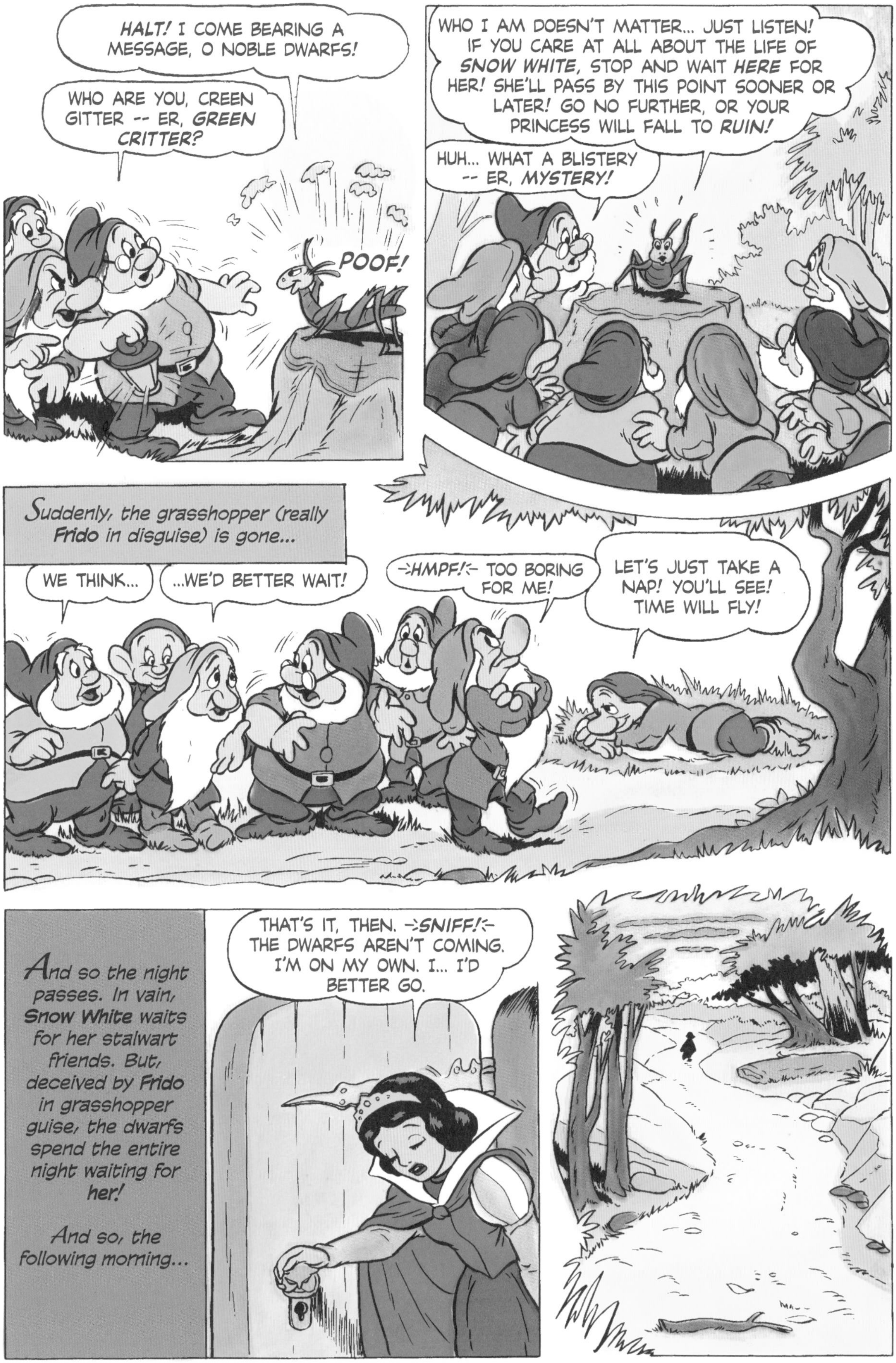
HALT! I COME BEARING A MESSAGE, O NOBLE DWARFS!
WHO ARE YOU, CREEN GITTER -- ER, GREEN CRITTER?
POOF!
WHO I AM DOESN'T MATTER... JUST LISTEN! IF YOU CARE AT ALL ABOUT THE LIFE OF SNOW WHITE, STOP AND WAIT HERE FOR HER! SHE'LL PASS BY THIS POINT SOONER OR LATER! GO NO FURTHER, OR YOUR PRINCESS WILL FALL TO RUIN!
HUH... WHAT A BLISTERY -- ER, MYSTERY!
Suddenly, the grasshopper (really Frido in disguise) is gone...
WE THINK...
...WE'D BETTER WAIT!
HMPF! TOO BORING FOR ME!
LET'S JUST TAKE A NAP! YOU'LL SEE! TIME WILL FLY!
And so the night passes. In vain, Snow White waits for her stalwart friends. But, deceived by Frido in grasshopper guise, the dwarfs spend the entire night waiting for her!
And so, the following morning...
THAT'S IT, THEN. SNIFF! THE DWARFS AREN'T COMING. I'M ON MY OWN. I... I'D BETTER GO.

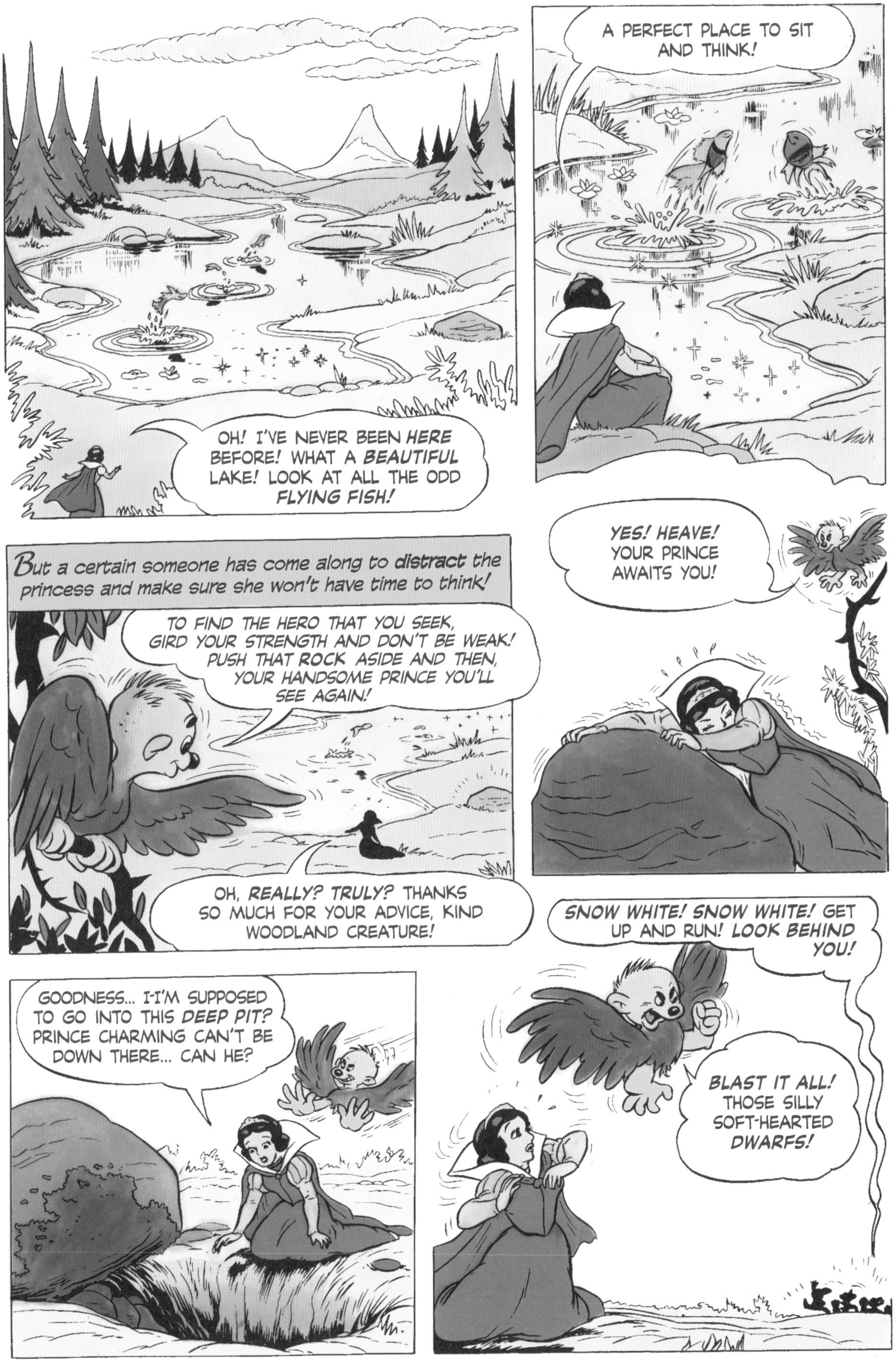
OH! I'VE NEVER BEEN HERE BEFORE! WHAT A BEAUTIFUL LAKE! LOOK AT ALL THE ODD FLYING FISH!
A PERFECT PLACE TO SIT AND THINK!
But a certain someone has come along to distract the princess and make sure she won't have time to think!
TO FIND THE HERO THAT YOU SEEK, GIRD YOUR STRENGTH AND DON'T BE WEAK! PUSH THAT ROCK ASIDE AND THEN, YOUR HANDSOME PRINCE YOU'LL SEE AGAIN!
OH, REALLY? TRULY? THANKS SO MUCH FOR YOUR ADVICE, KIND WOODLAND CREATURE!
YES! HEAVE! YOUR PRINCE AWAITS YOU!
GOODNESS... I-I'M SUPPOSED TO GO INTO THIS DEEP PIT? PRINCE CHARMING CAN'T BE DOWN THERE... CAN HE?
SNOW WHITE! SNOW WHITE! GET UP AND RUN! LOOK BEHIND YOU!
BLAST IT ALL! THOSE SILLY SOFT-HEARTED DWARFS!

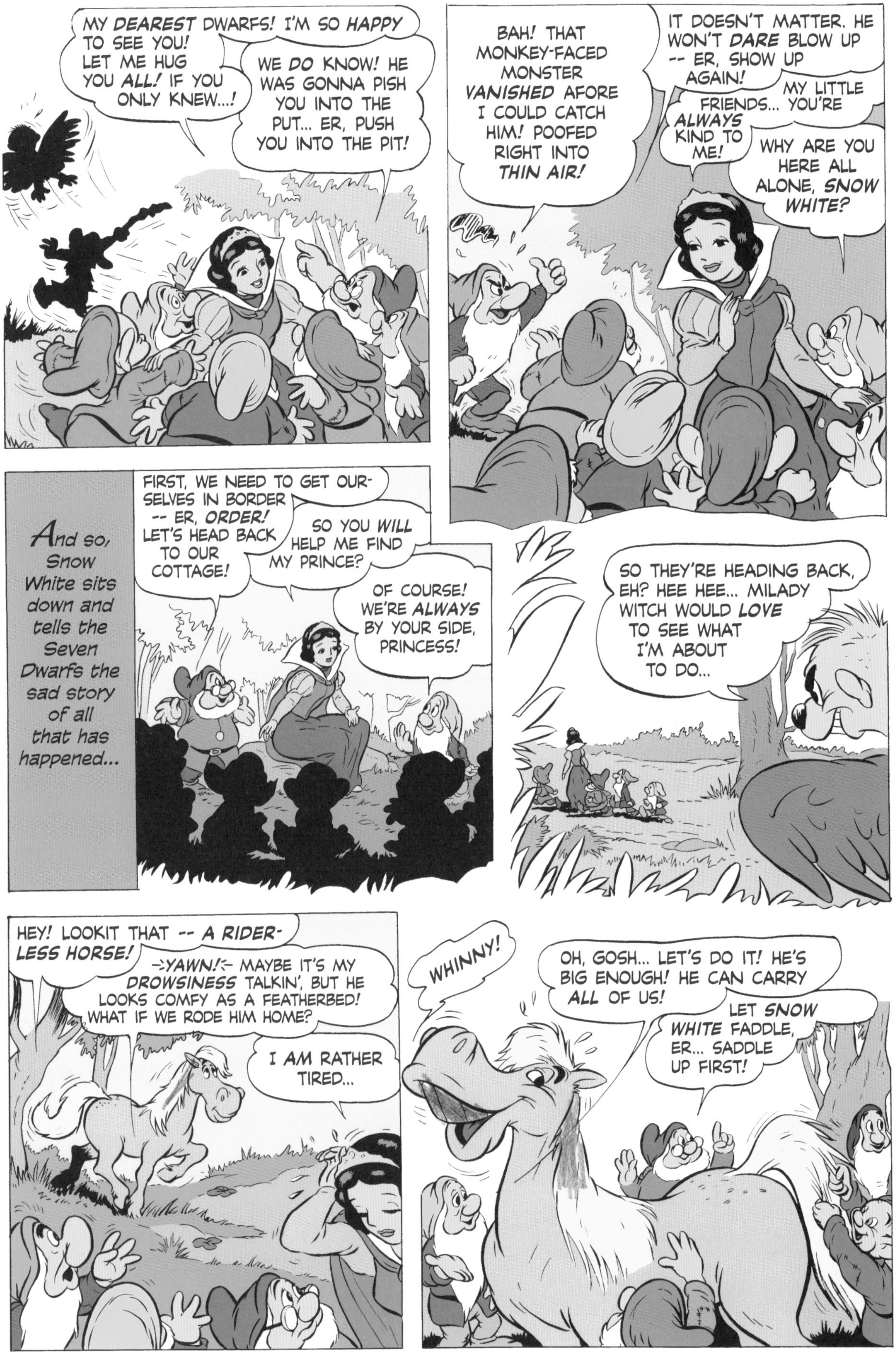
MY DEAREST DWARFS! I'M SO HAPPY TO SEE YOU! LET ME HUG YOU ALL! IF YOU ONLY KNEW...!
WE DO KNOW! HE WAS GONNA PISH YOU INTO THE PUT... ER, PUSH YOU INTO THE PIT!
BAH! THAT MONKEY-FACED MONSTER VANISHED AFORE I COULD CATCH HIM! POOFED RIGHT INTO THIN AIR!
IT DOESN'T MATTER. HE WON'T DARE BLOW UP -- ER, SHOW UP AGAIN!
MY LITTLE FRIENDS... YOU'RE ALWAYS KIND TO ME!
WHY ARE YOU HERE ALL ALONE, SNOW WHITE?
And so, Snow White sits down and tells the Seven Dwarfs the sad story of all that has happened...
FIRST, WE NEED TO GET OURSELVES IN BORDER -- ER, ORDER! LET'S HEAD BACK TO OUR COTTAGE!
SO YOU WILL HELP ME FIND MY PRINCE?
OF COURSE! WE'RE ALWAYS BY YOUR SIDE, PRINCESS!
SO THEY'RE HEADING BACK, EH? HEE HEE... MILADY WITCH WOULD LOVE TO SEE WHAT I'M ABOUT TO DO...
HEY! LOOKIT THAT -- A RIDERLESS HORSE!
⇒YAWN!⇐ MAYBE IT'S MY DROWSINESS TALKIN', BUT HE LOOKS COMFY AS A FEATHERBED! WHAT IF WE RODE HIM HOME?
I AM RATHER TIRED...
WHINNY!
OH, GOSH... LET'S DO IT! HE'S BIG ENOUGH! HE CAN CARRY ALL OF US!
LET SNOW WHITE FADDLE, ER... SADDLE UP FIRST!

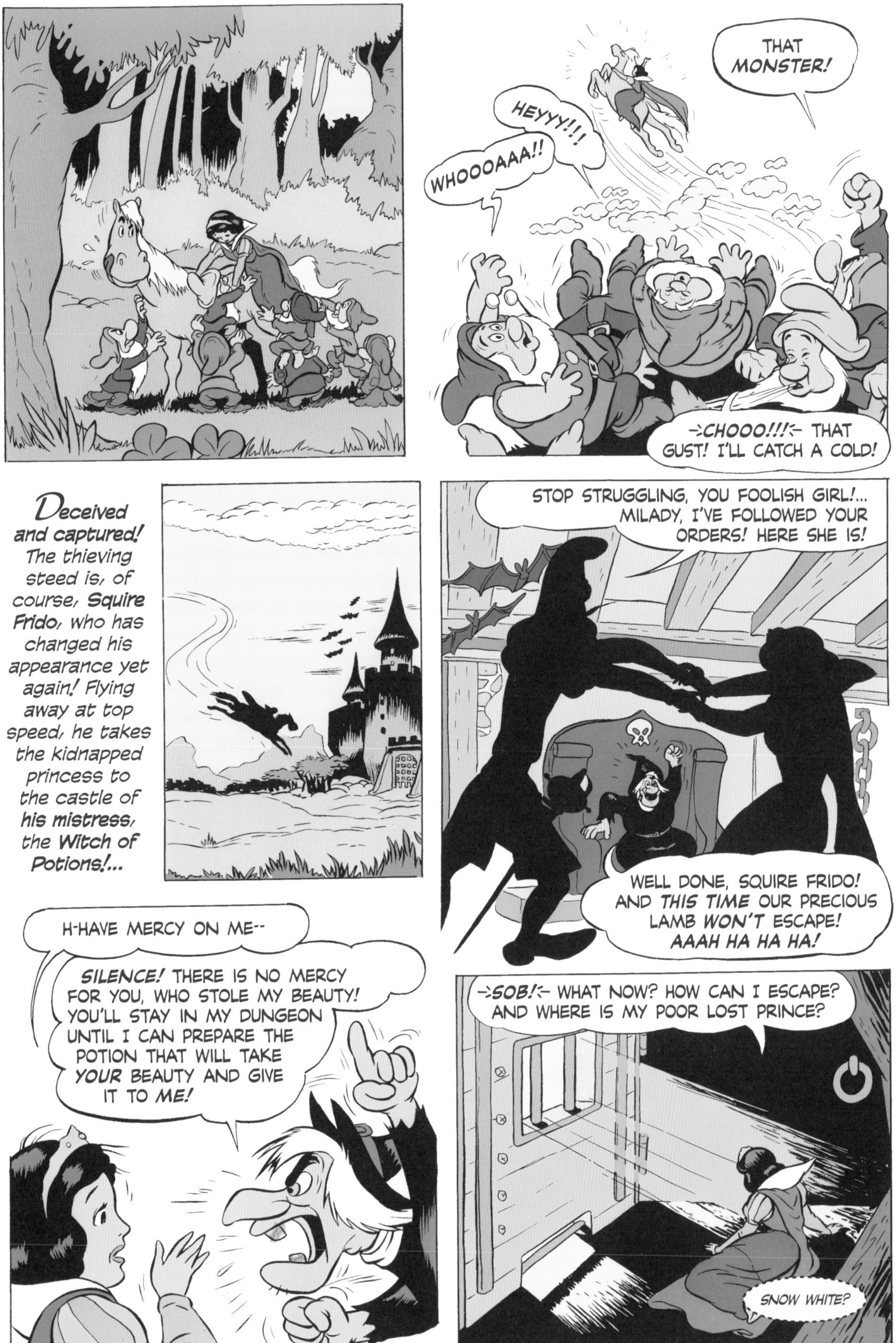

HEYYY!!!
WHOOOAAA!!
THAT MONSTER!
-CHOOO!!!- THAT GUST! I'LL CATCH A COLD!
Deceived and captured! The thieving steed is, of course, Squire Frido, who has changed his appearance yet again! Flying away at top speed, he takes the kidnapped princess to the castle of his mistress, the Witch of Potions!...
STOP STRUGGLING, YOU FOOLISH GIRL!... MILADY, I'VE FOLLOWED YOUR ORDERS! HERE SHE IS!
WELL DONE, SQUIRE FRIDO! AND THIS TIME OUR PRECIOUS LAMB WON'T ESCAPE! AAAH HA HA HA!
H-HAVE MERCY ON ME--
SILENCE! THERE IS NO MERCY FOR YOU, WHO STOLE MY BEAUTY! YOU'LL STAY IN MY DUNGEON UNTIL I CAN PREPARE THE POTION THAT WILL TAKE YOUR BEAUTY AND GIVE IT TO ME!
-SOB!- WHAT NOW? HOW CAN I ESCAPE? AND WHERE IS MY POOR LOST PRINCE?
SNOW WHITE?

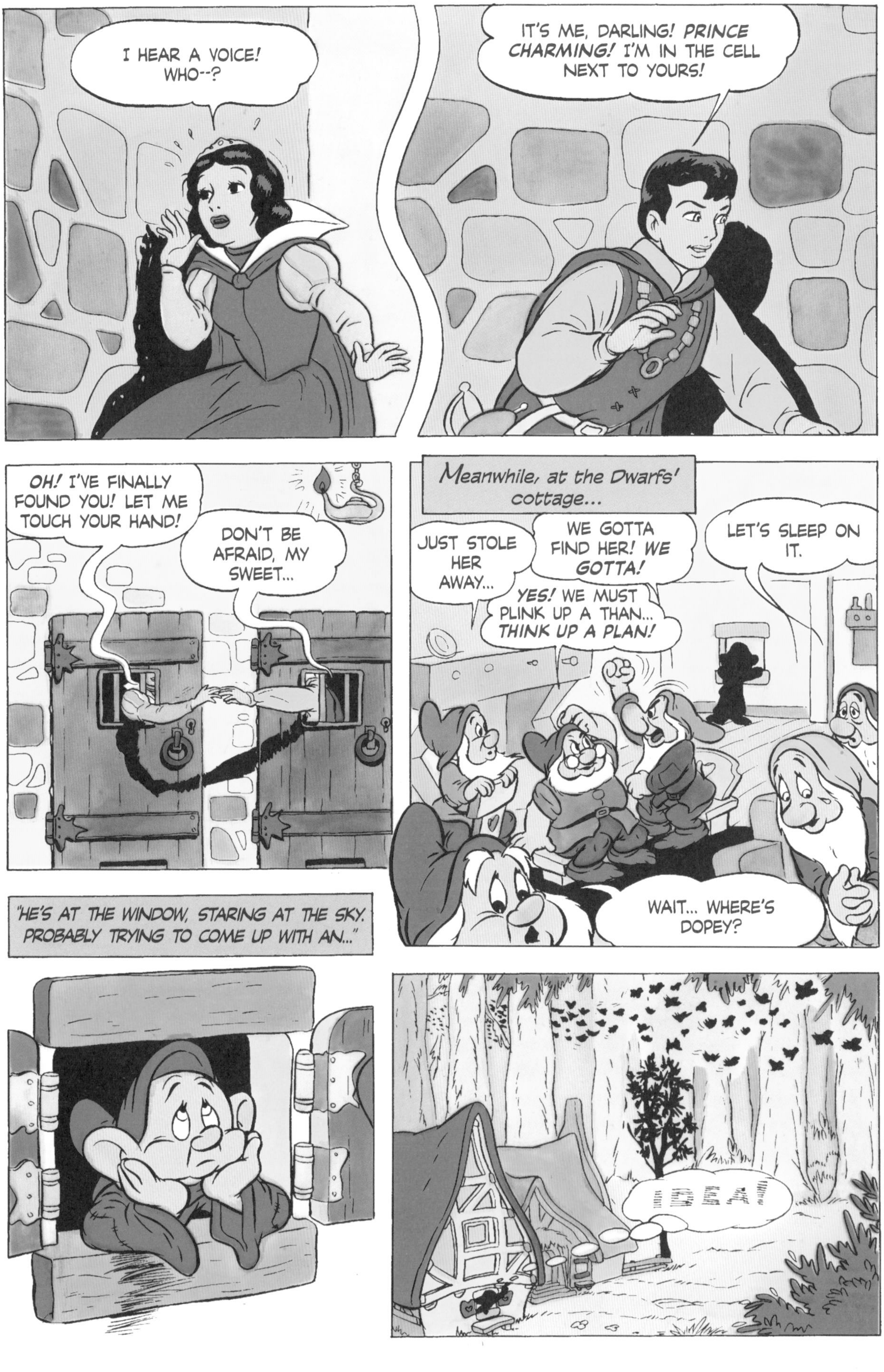

I HEAR A VOICE! WHO--?
IT'S ME, DARLING! PRINCE CHARMING! I'M IN THE CELL NEXT TO YOURS!
OH! I'VE FINALLY FOUND YOU! LET ME TOUCH YOUR HAND!
DON'T BE AFRAID, MY SWEET...
Meanwhile, at the Dwarfs' cottage...
JUST STOLE HER AWAY...
WE GOTTA FIND HER! WE GOTTA!
LET'S SLEEP ON IT.
YES! WE MUST PLINK UP A THAN... THINK UP A PLAN!
WAIT... WHERE'S DOPEY?
"HE'S AT THE WINDOW, STARING AT THE SKY. PROBABLY TRYING TO COME UP WITH AN..."
IDEA!

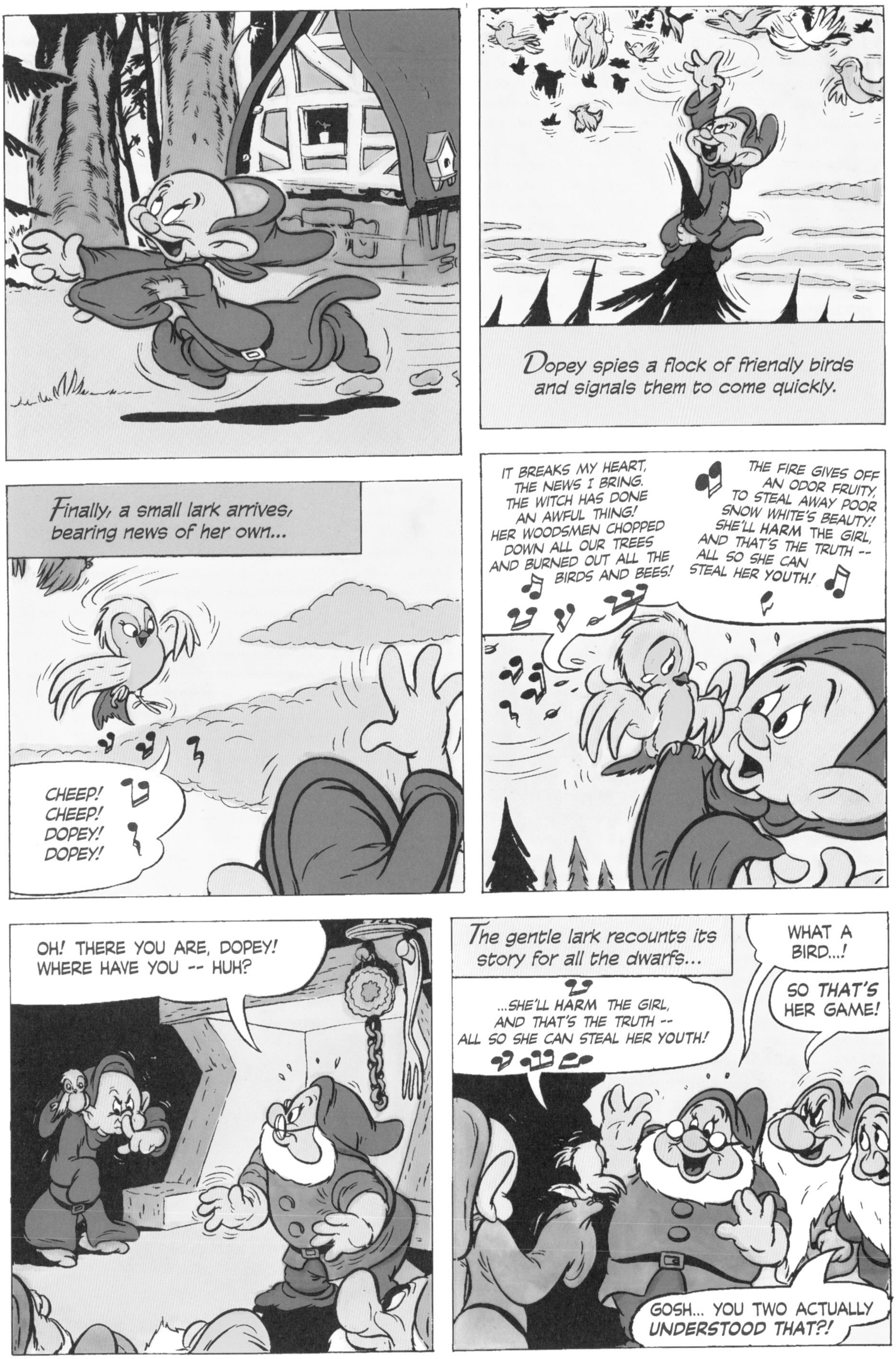
Dopey spies a flock of friendly birds and signals them to come quickly.
Finally, a small lark arrives, bearing news of her own...
CHEEP! CHEEP! DOPEY! DOPEY!
IT BREAKS MY HEART, THE NEWS I BRING. THE WITCH HAS DONE AN AWFUL THING! HER WOODSMEN CHOPPED DOWN ALL OUR TREES AND BURNED OUT ALL THE BIRDS AND BEES!
THE FIRE GIVES OFF AN ODOR FRUITY, TO STEAL AWAY POOR SNOW WHITE'S BEAUTY! SHE'LL HARM THE GIRL, AND THAT'S THE TRUTH -- ALL SO SHE CAN STEAL HER YOUTH!
OH! THERE YOU ARE, DOPEY! WHERE HAVE YOU -- HUH?
The gentle lark recounts its story for all the dwarfs...
...SHE'LL HARM THE GIRL, AND THAT'S THE TRUTH -- ALL SO SHE CAN STEAL HER YOUTH!
WHAT A BIRD...!
SO THAT'S HER GAME!
GOSH... YOU TWO ACTUALLY UNDERSTOOD THAT?!

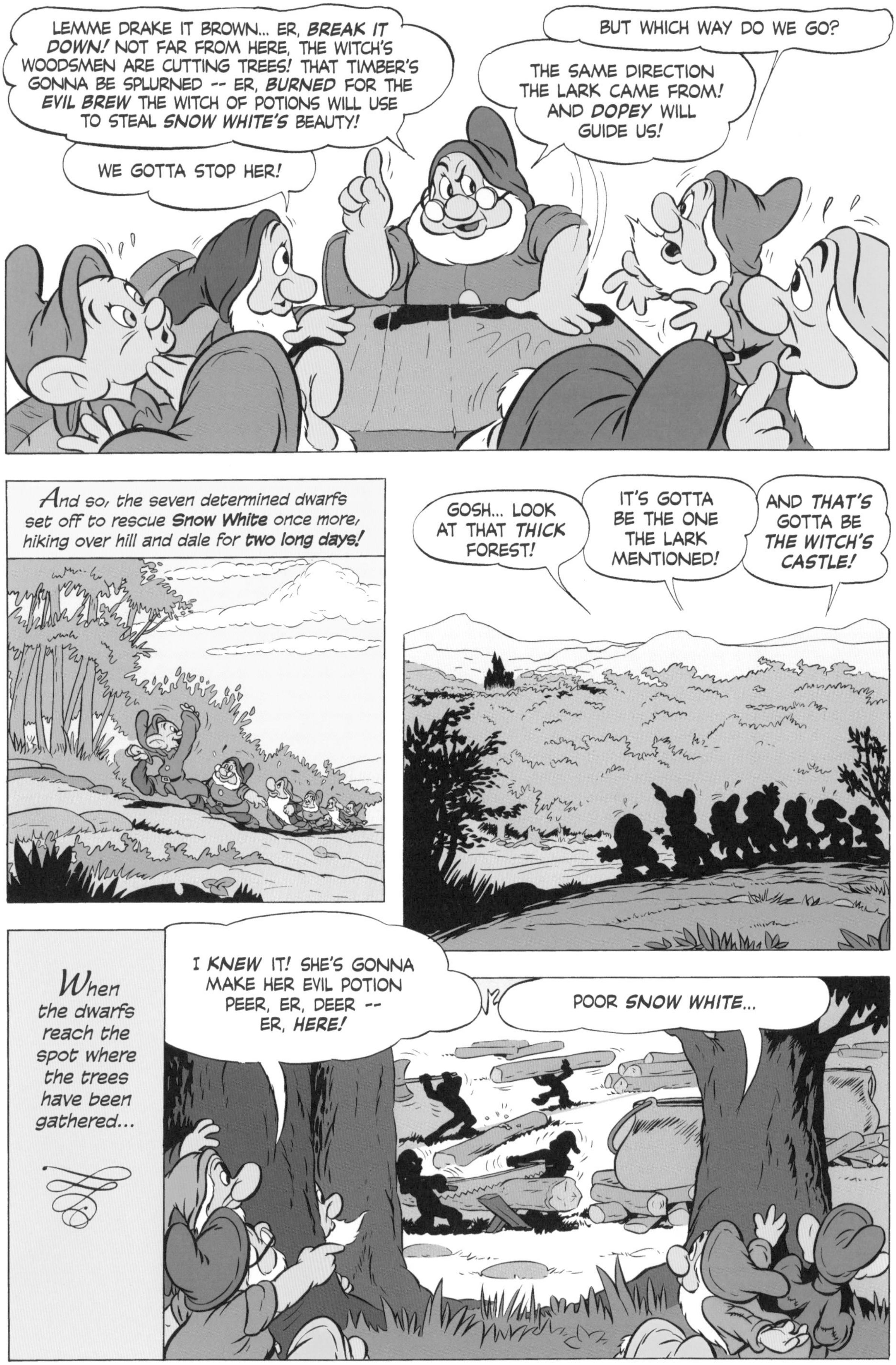
LEMME DRAKE IT BROWN... ER, BREAK IT DOWN! NOT FAR FROM HERE, THE WITCH'S WOODSMEN ARE CUTTING TREES! THAT TIMBER'S GONNA BE SPLURNED -- ER, BURNED FOR THE EVIL BREW THE WITCH OF POTIONS WILL USE TO STEAL SNOW WHITE'S BEAUTY!
WE GOTTA STOP HER!
BUT WHICH WAY DO WE GO?
THE SAME DIRECTION THE LARK CAME FROM! AND DOPEY WILL GUIDE US!
And so, the seven determined dwarfs set off to rescue Snow White once more, hiking over hill and dale for two long days!
GOSH... LOOK AT THAT THICK FOREST!
IT'S GOTTA BE THE ONE THE LARK MENTIONED!
AND THAT'S GOTTA BE THE WITCH'S CASTLE!
When the dwarfs reach the spot where the trees have been gathered...
I KNEW IT! SHE'S GONNA MAKE HER EVIL POTION PEER, ER, DEER -- ER, HERE!
POOR SNOW WHITE...

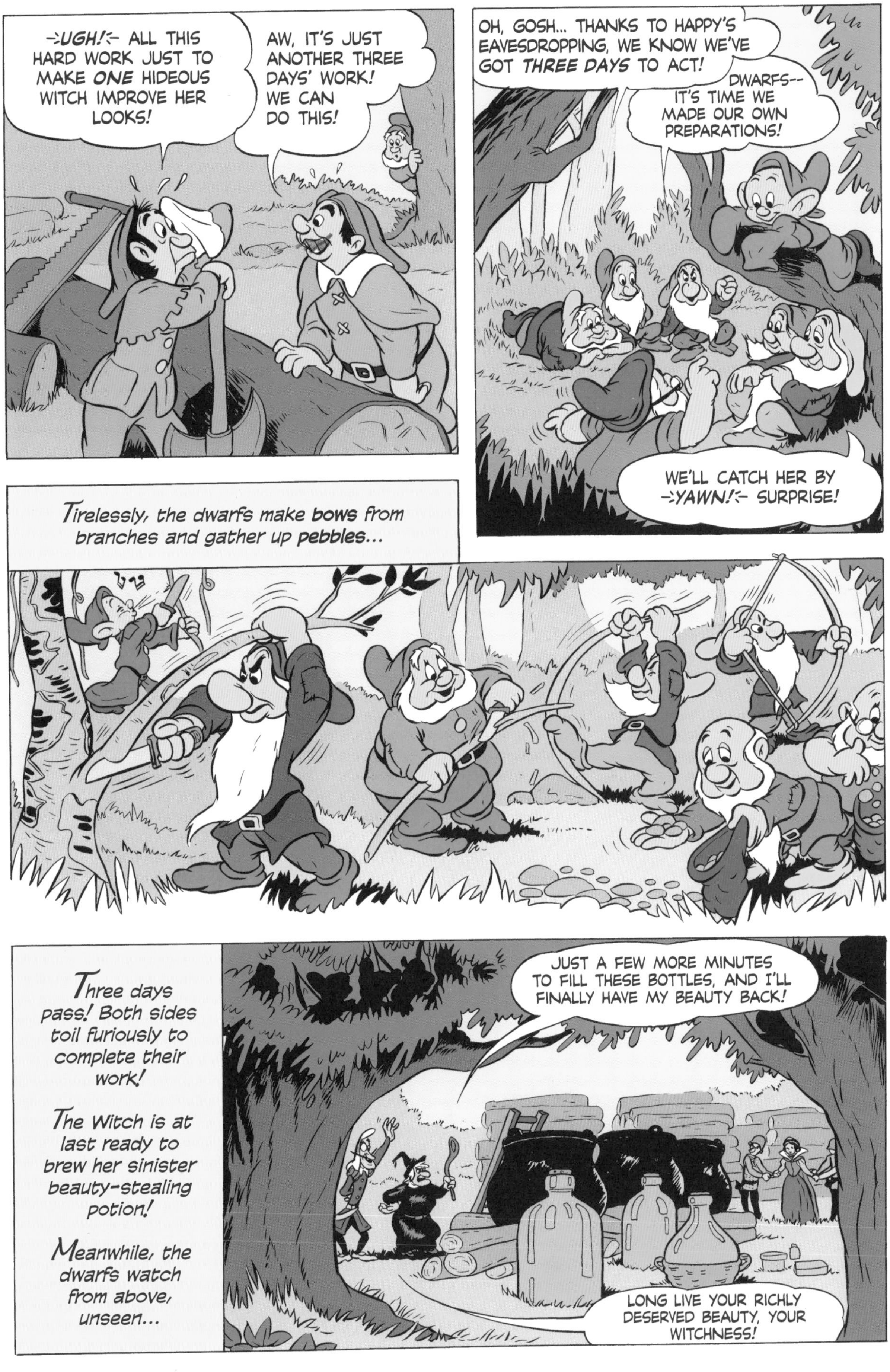

-UGH!- ALL THIS HARD WORK JUST TO MAKE ONE HIDEOUS WITCH IMPROVE HER LOOKS!
AW, IT'S JUST ANOTHER THREE DAYS' WORK! WE CAN DO THIS!
OH, GOSH... THANKS TO HAPPY'S EAVESDROPPING, WE KNOW WE'VE GOT THREE DAYS TO ACT!
DWARFS-- IT'S TIME WE MADE OUR OWN PREPARATIONS!
WE'LL CATCH HER BY -YAWN!- SURPRISE!
Tirelessly, the dwarfs make bows from branches and gather up pebbles...
Three days pass! Both sides toil furiously to complete their work!
The Witch is at last ready to brew her sinister beauty-stealing potion!
Meanwhile, the dwarfs watch from above, unseen...
JUST A FEW MORE MINUTES TO FILL THESE BOTTLES, AND I'LL FINALLY HAVE MY BEAUTY BACK!
LONG LIVE YOUR RICHLY DESERVED BEAUTY, YOUR WITCHNESS!

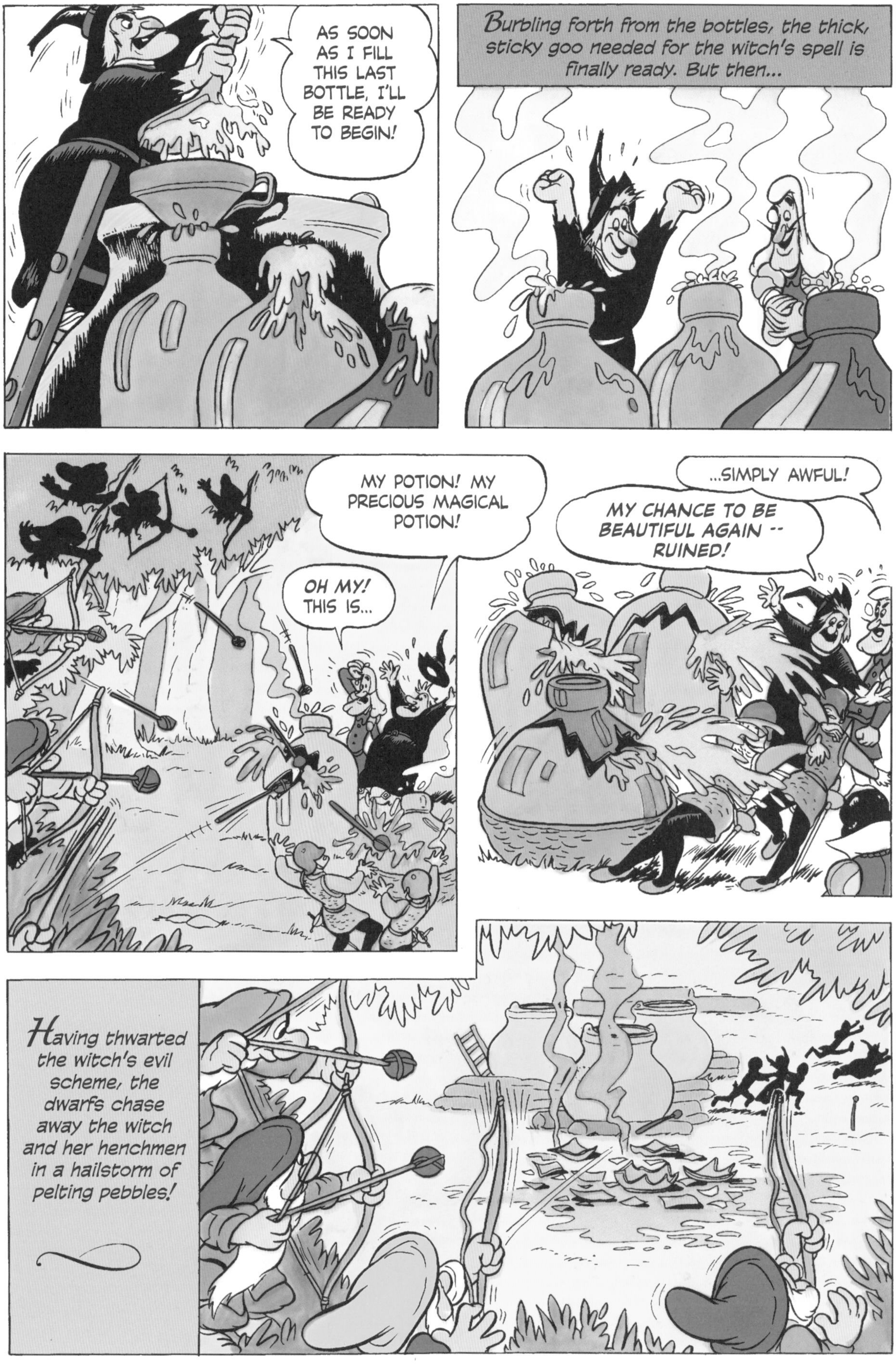
AS SOON AS I FILL THIS LAST BOTTLE, I'LL BE READY TO BEGIN!
Burbling forth from the bottles, the thick, sticky goo needed for the witch's spell is finally ready. But then...
MY POTION! MY PRECIOUS MAGICAL POTION!
OH MY! THIS IS...
...SIMPLY AWFUL!
MY CHANCE TO BE BEAUTIFUL AGAIN -- RUINED!
Having thwarted the witch's evil scheme, the dwarfs chase away the witch and her henchmen in a hailstorm of pelting pebbles!

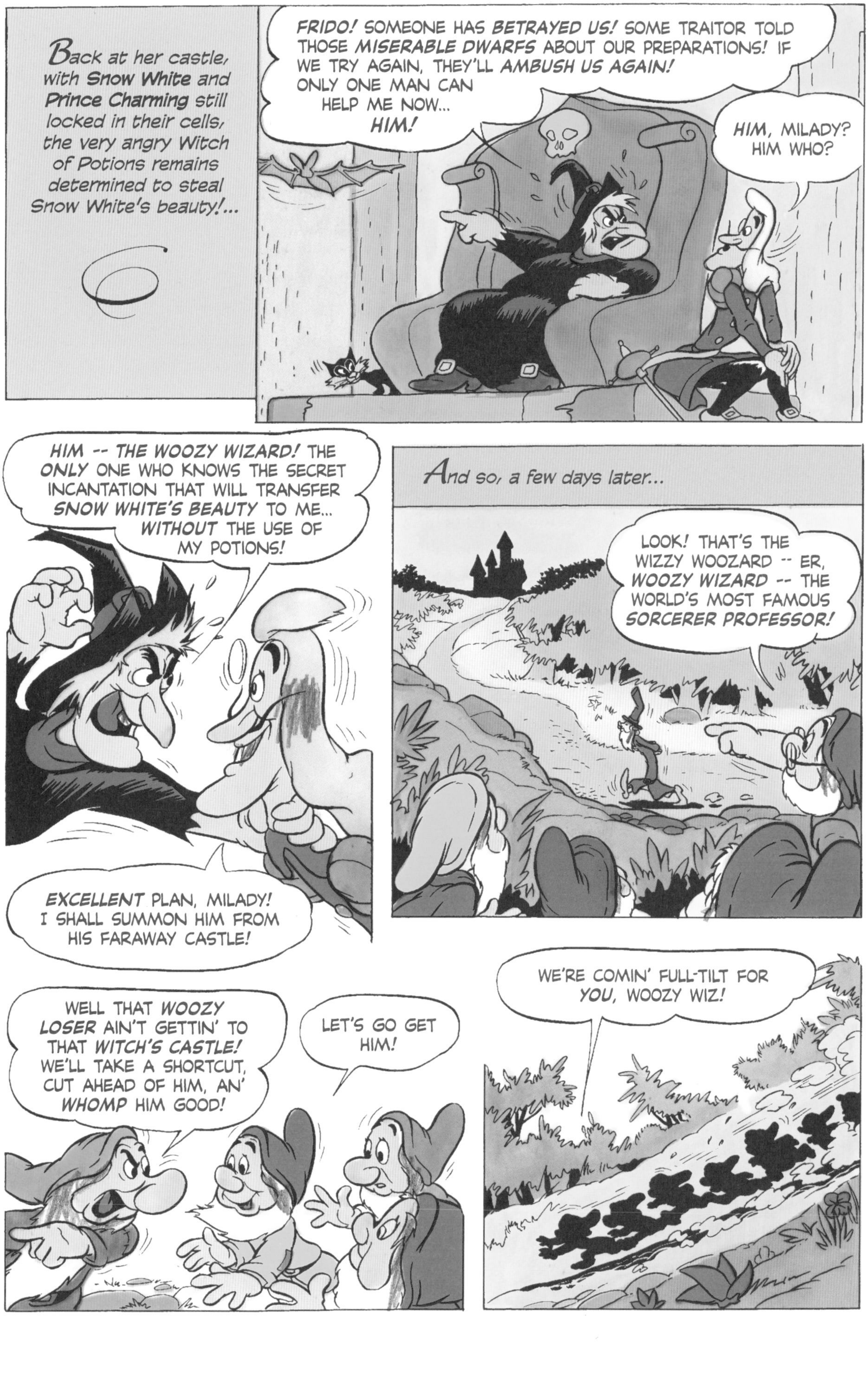

Back at her castle, with Snow White and Prince Charming still locked in their cells, the very angry Witch of Potions remains determined to steal Snow White's beauty!...
FRIDO! SOMEONE HAS BETRAYED US! SOME TRAITOR TOLD THOSE MISERABLE DWARFS ABOUT OUR PREPARATIONS! IF WE TRY AGAIN, THEY'LL AMBUSH US AGAIN! ONLY ONE MAN CAN HELP ME NOW... HIM!
HIM, MILADY? HIM WHO?
HIM -- THE WOOZY WIZARD! THE ONLY ONE WHO KNOWS THE SECRET INCANTATION THAT WILL TRANSFER SNOW WHITE'S BEAUTY TO ME... WITHOUT THE USE OF MY POTIONS!
EXCELLENT PLAN, MILADY! I SHALL SUMMON HIM FROM HIS FARAWAY CASTLE!
And so, a few days later...
LOOK! THAT'S THE WIZZY WOOZARD -- ER, WOOZY WIZARD -- THE WORLD'S MOST FAMOUS SORCERER PROFESSOR!
WELL THAT WOOZY LOSER AIN'T GETTIN' TO THAT WITCH'S CASTLE! WE'LL TAKE A SHORTCUT, CUT AHEAD OF HIM, AN' WHOMP HIM GOOD!
LET'S GO GET HIM!
WE'RE COMIN' FULL-TILT FOR YOU, WOOZY WIZ!

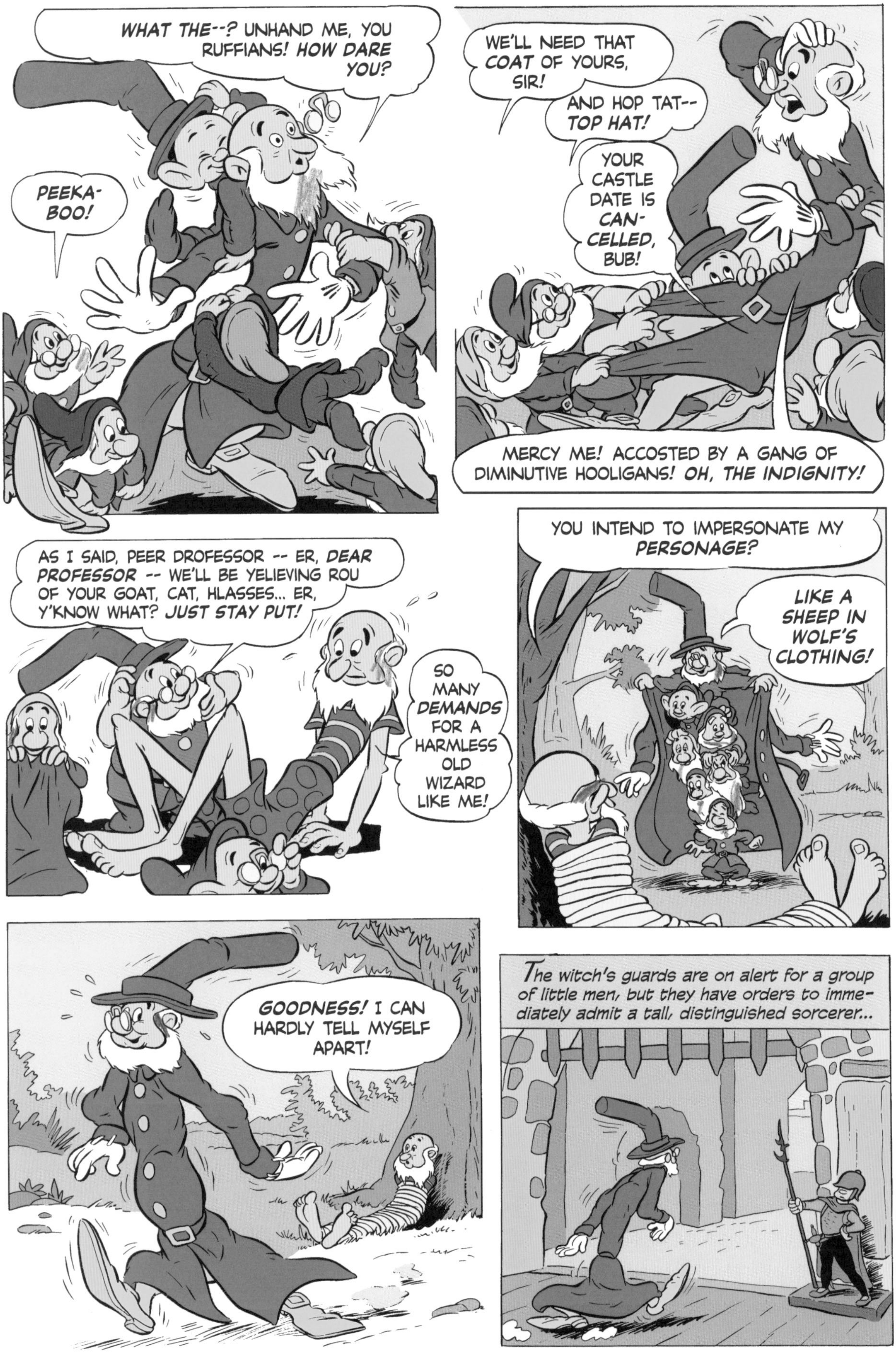

WHAT THE--? UNHAND ME, YOU RUFFIANS! HOW DARE YOU?
PEEKA-BOO!
WE'LL NEED THAT COAT OF YOURS, SIR!
AND HOP TAT-- TOP HAT!
YOUR CASTLE DATE IS CAN-CELLED, BUB!
MERCY ME! ACCOSTED BY A GANG OF DIMINUTIVE HOOLIGANS! OH, THE INDIGNITY!
AS I SAID, PEER DROFESSOR -- ER, DEAR PROFESSOR -- WE'LL BE YELIEVING ROU OF YOUR GOAT, CAT, HLASSES... ER, Y'KNOW WHAT? JUST STAY PUT!
SO MANY DEMANDS FOR A HARMLESS OLD WIZARD LIKE ME!
YOU INTEND TO IMPERSONATE MY PERSONAGE?
LIKE A SHEEP IN WOLF'S CLOTHING!
GOODNESS! I CAN HARDLY TELL MYSELF APART!
The witch's guards are on alert for a group of little men, but they have orders to immediately admit a tall, distinguished sorcerer...

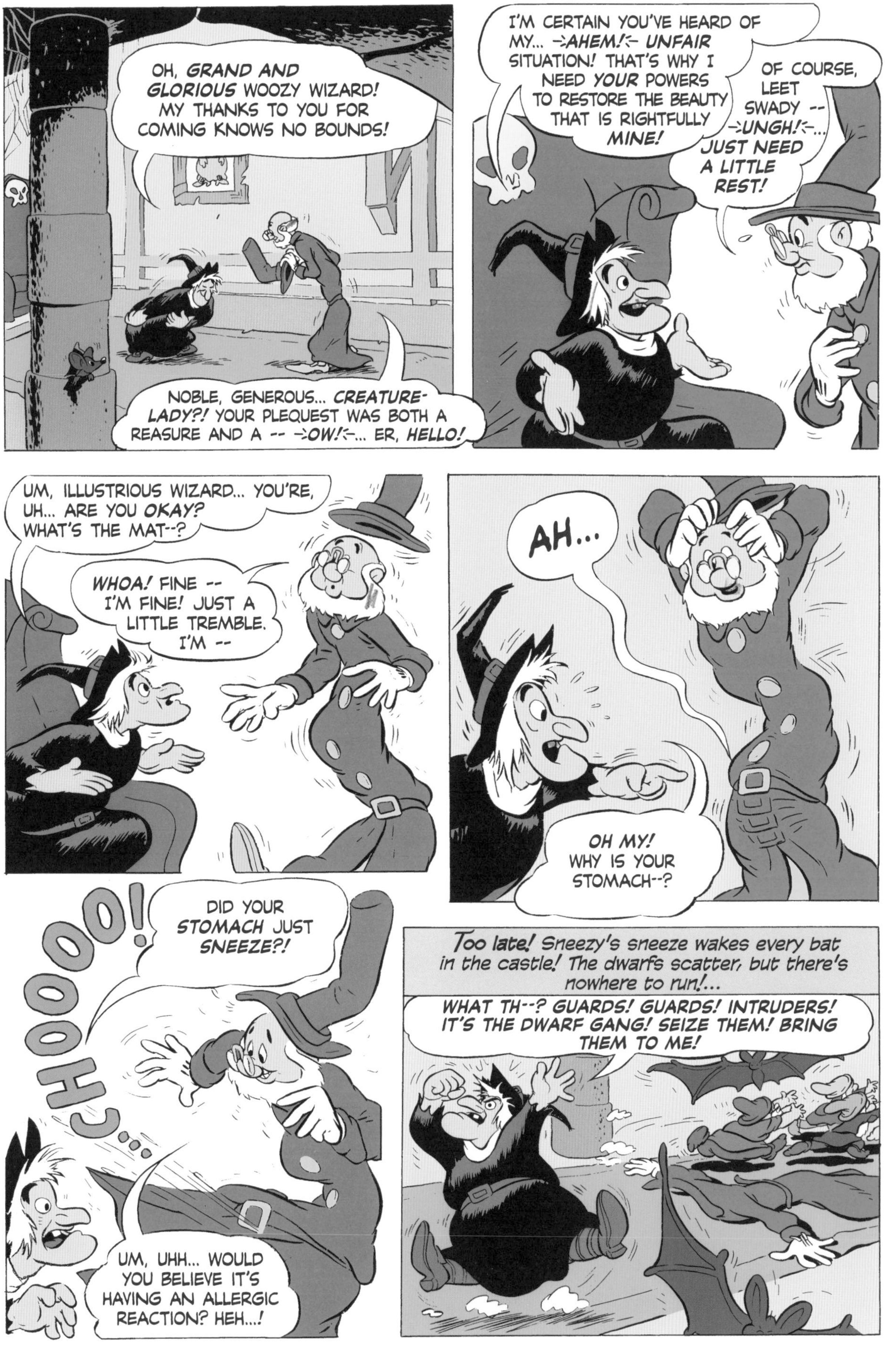
OH, GRAND AND GLORIOUS WOOZY WIZARD! MY THANKS TO YOU FOR COMING KNOWS NO BOUNDS!
NOBLE, GENEROUS... CREATURE-LADY?! YOUR PLEQUEST WAS BOTH A REASURE AND A -- OW!... ER, HELLO!
I'M CERTAIN YOU'VE HEARD OF MY... AHEM! UNFAIR SITUATION! THAT'S WHY I NEED YOUR POWERS TO RESTORE THE BEAUTY THAT IS RIGHTFULLY MINE!
OF COURSE, LEET SWADY -- UNGH!... JUST NEED A LITTLE REST!
UM, ILLUSTRIOUS WIZARD... YOU'RE, UH... ARE YOU OKAY? WHAT'S THE MAT--?
WHOA! FINE -- I'M FINE! JUST A LITTLE TREMBLE. I'M --
AH...
OH MY! WHY IS YOUR STOMACH--?
...CHOOOOO!
DID YOUR STOMACH JUST SNEEZE?!
UM, UHH... WOULD YOU BELIEVE IT'S HAVING AN ALLERGIC REACTION? HEH...!
Too late! Sneezy's sneeze wakes every bat in the castle! The dwarfs scatter, but there's nowhere to run!...
WHAT TH--? GUARDS! GUARDS! INTRUDERS! IT'S THE DWARF GANG! SEIZE THEM! BRING THEM TO ME!

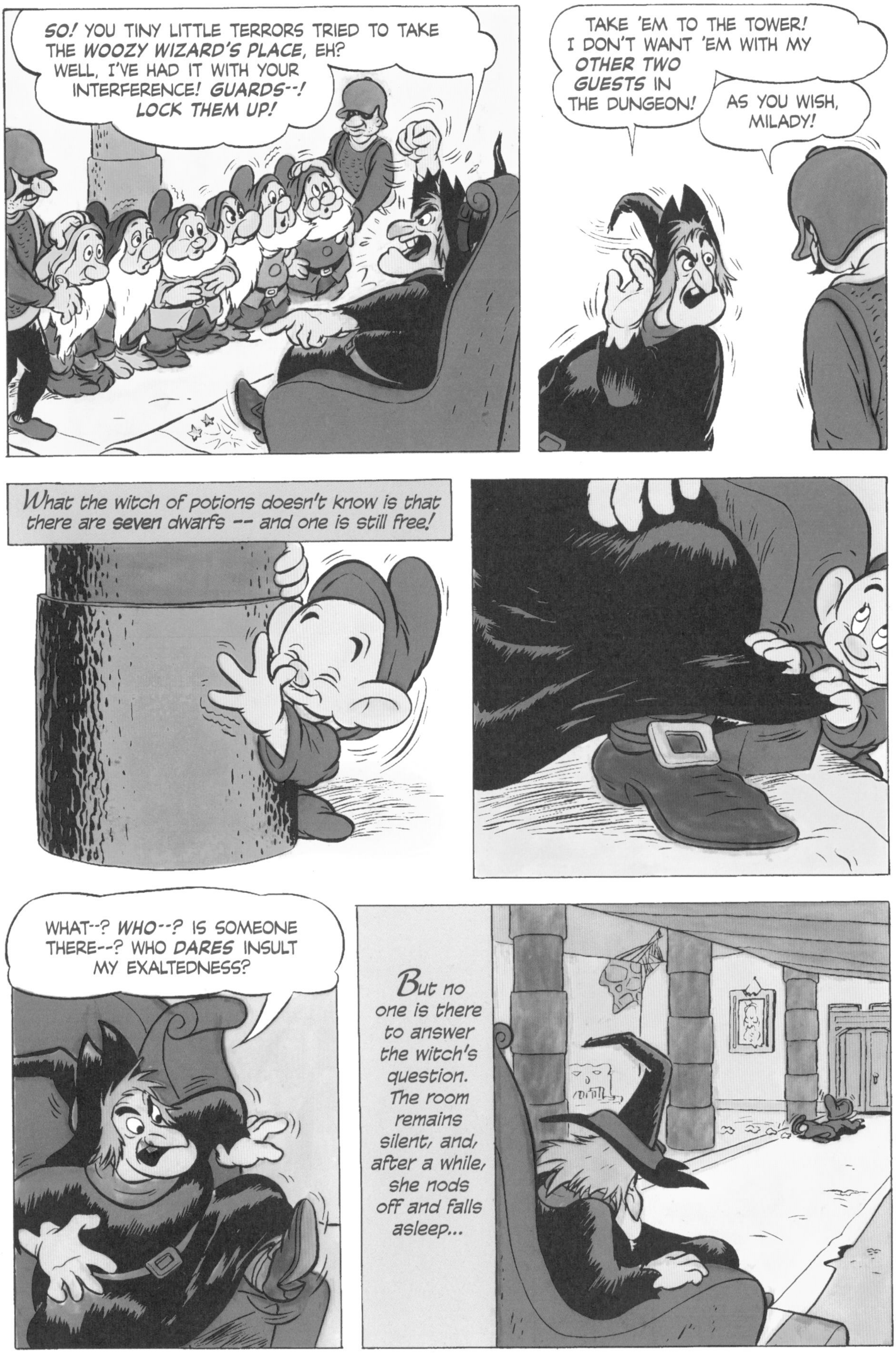
SO! YOU TINY LITTLE TERRORS TRIED TO TAKE THE WOOZY WIZARD'S PLACE, EH? WELL, I'VE HAD IT WITH YOUR INTERFERENCE! GUARDS--! LOCK THEM UP!
TAKE 'EM TO THE TOWER! I DON'T WANT 'EM WITH MY OTHER TWO GUESTS IN THE DUNGEON!
AS YOU WISH, MILADY!
What the witch of potions doesn't know is that there are seven dwarfs -- and one is still free!
WHAT--? WHO--? IS SOMEONE THERE--? WHO DARES INSULT MY EXALTEDNESS?
But no one is there to answer the witch's question. The room remains silent, and, after a while, she nods off and falls asleep...

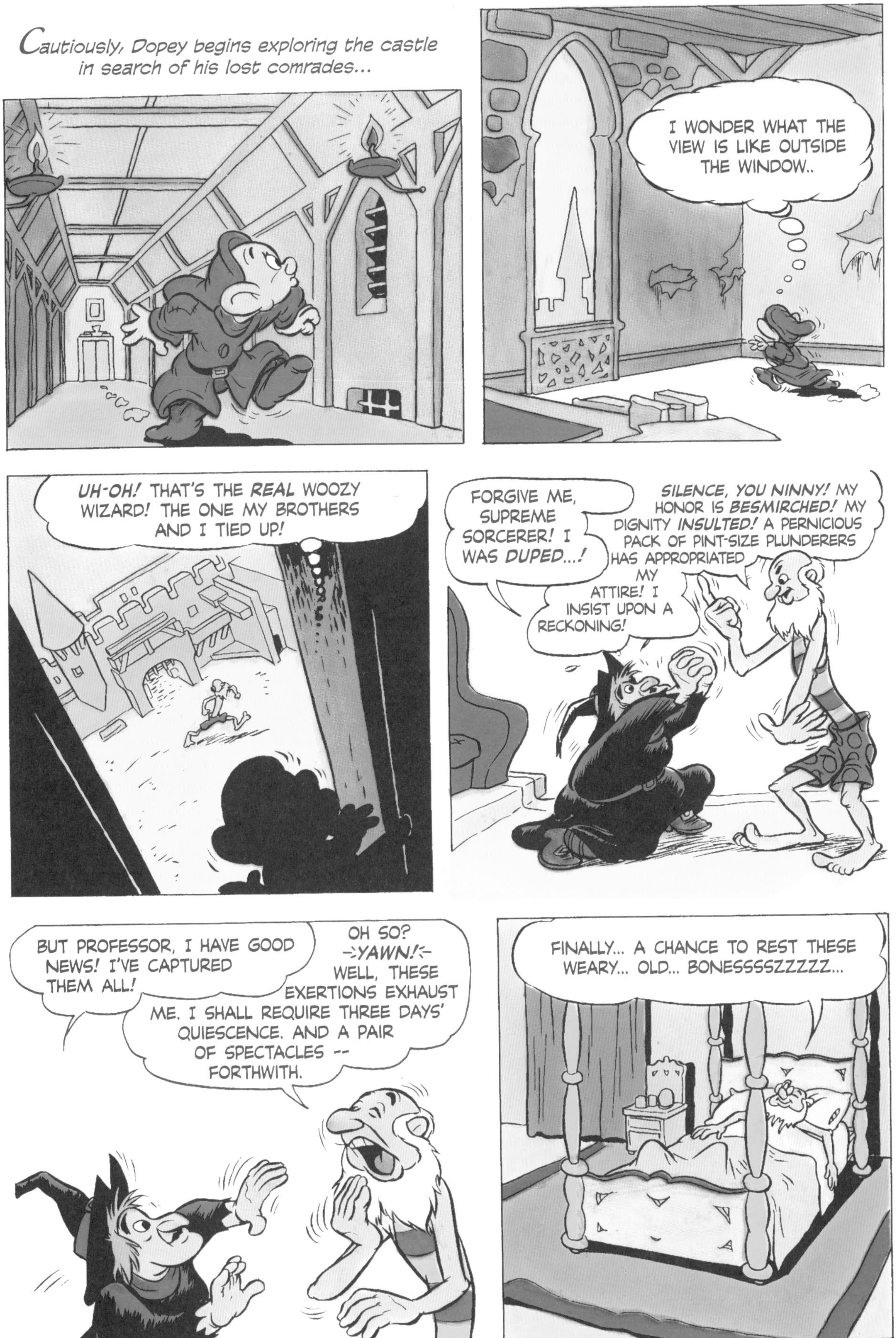
Cautiously, Dopey begins exploring the castle in search of his lost comrades...
I WONDER WHAT THE VIEW IS LIKE OUTSIDE THE WINDOW..
UH-OH! THAT'S THE REAL WOOZY WIZARD! THE ONE MY BROTHERS AND I TIED UP!
FORGIVE ME, SUPREME SORCERER! I WAS DUPED...!
SILENCE, YOU NINNY! MY HONOR IS BESMIRCHED! MY DIGNITY INSULTED! A PERNICIOUS PACK OF PINT-SIZE PLUNDERERS HAS APPROPRIATED MY ATTIRE! I INSIST UPON A RECKONING!
BUT PROFESSOR, I HAVE GOOD NEWS! I'VE CAPTURED THEM ALL!
OH SO? -YAWN!- WELL, THESE EXERTIONS EXHAUST ME. I SHALL REQUIRE THREE DAYS' QUIESCENCE. AND A PAIR OF SPECTACLES -- FORTHWITH.
FINALLY... A CHANCE TO REST THESE WEARY... OLD... BONESSSSZZZZZ...

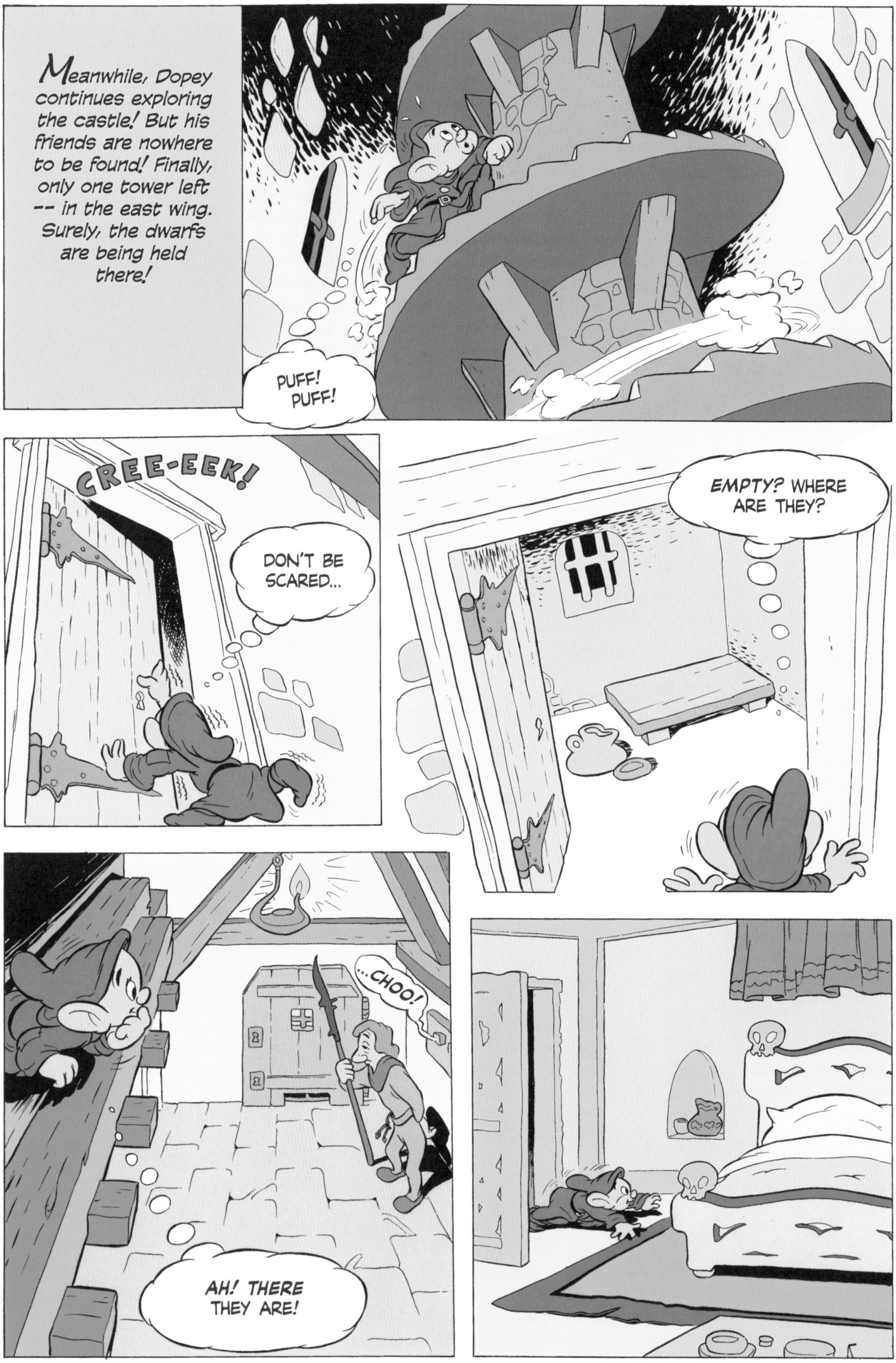

Meanwhile, Dopey continues exploring the castle! But his friends are nowhere to be found! Finally, only one tower left -- in the east wing. Surely, the dwarfs are being held there!
PUFF! PUFF!
CREE-EEK!
DON'T BE SCARED...
EMPTY? WHERE ARE THEY?
...CHOO!
AH! THERE THEY ARE!

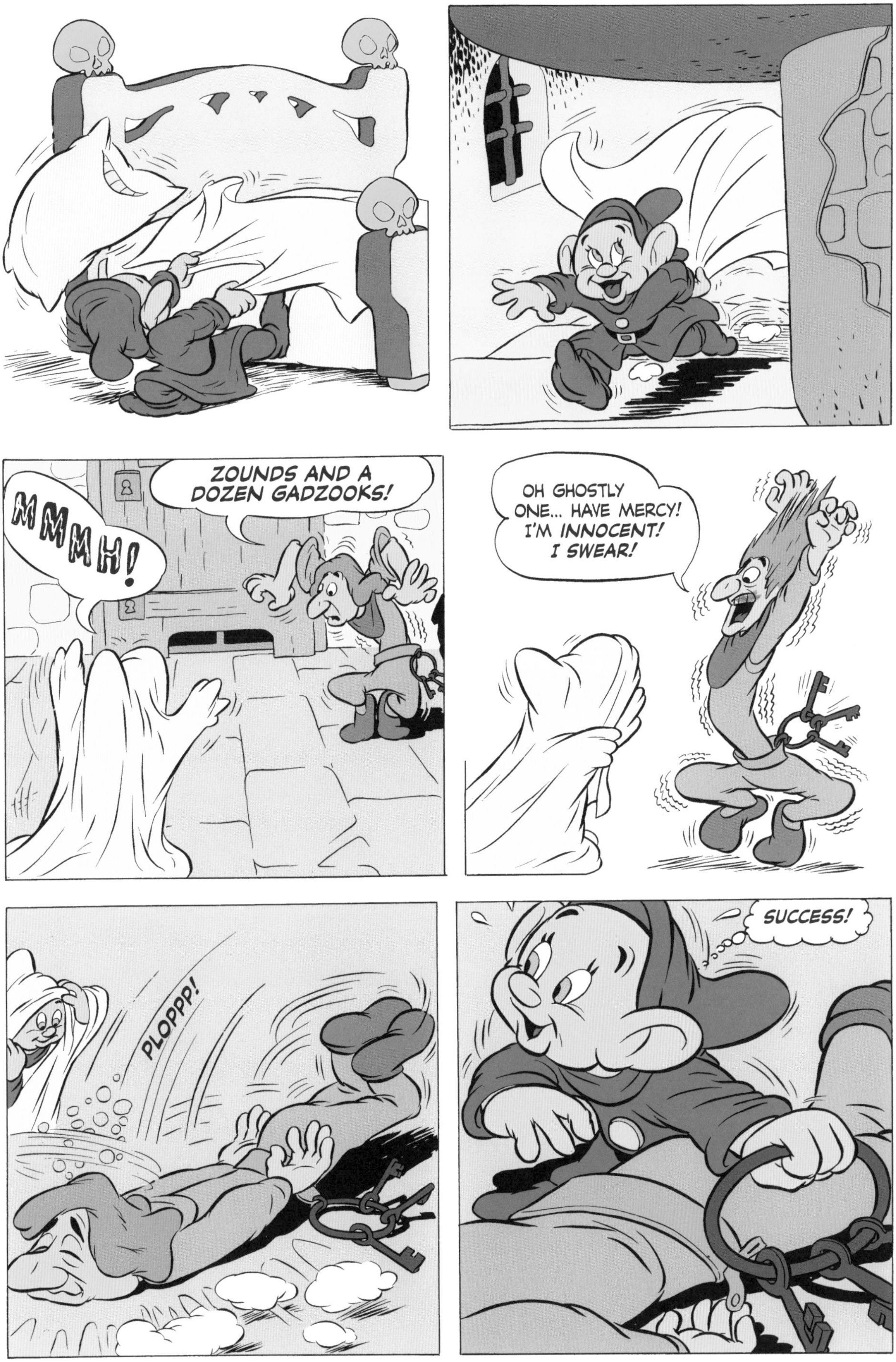
ZOUNDS AND A DOZEN GADZOOKS!
MMMH!
OH GHOSTLY ONE... HAVE MERCY! I'M INNOCENT! I SWEAR!
PLOPPP!
SUCCESS!

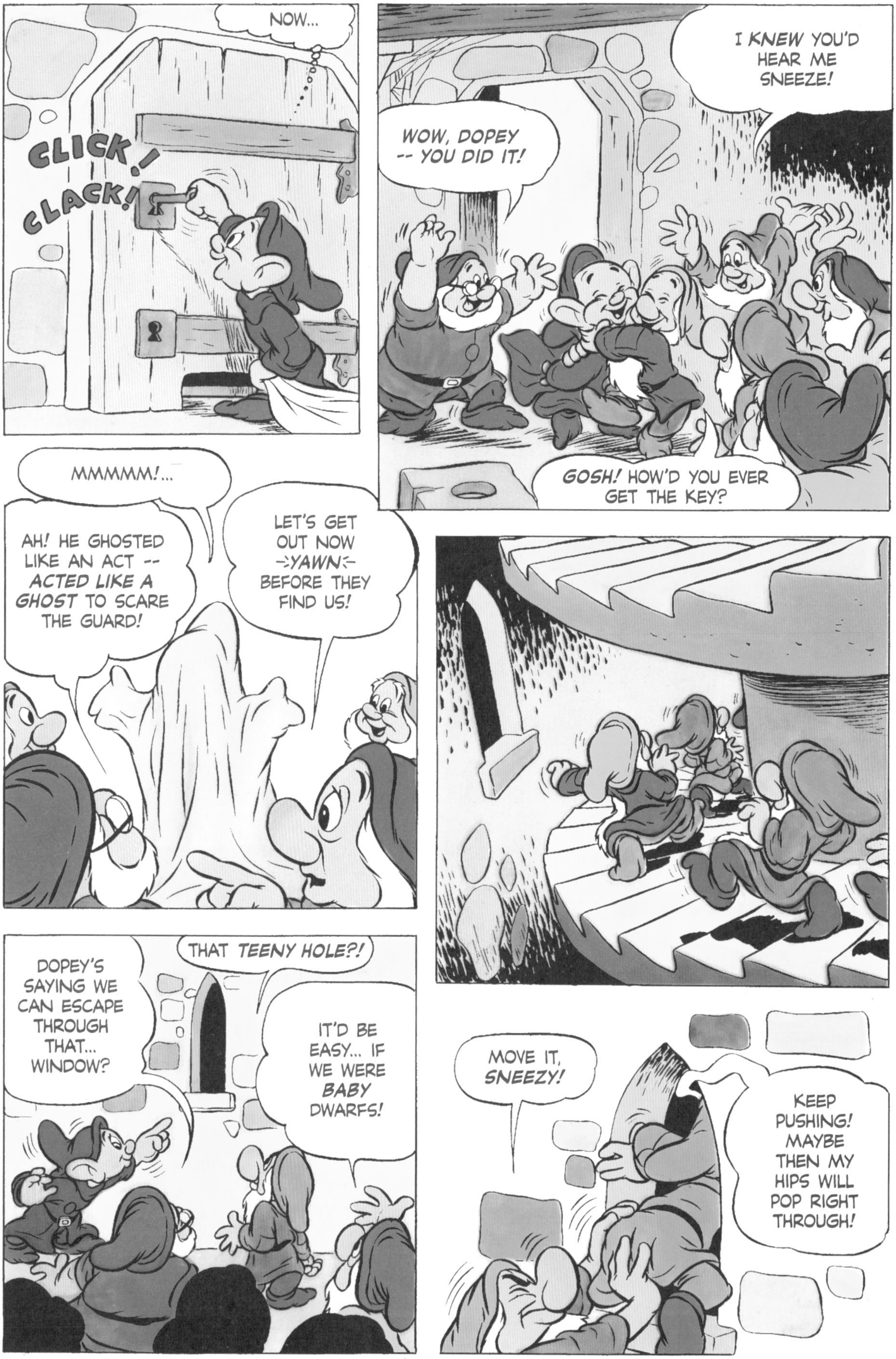
NOW...
CLICK! CLACK!
I KNEW YOU'D HEAR ME SNEEZE!
WOW, DOPEY -- YOU DID IT!
GOSH! HOW'D YOU EVER GET THE KEY?
MMMMM!...
AH! HE GHOSTED LIKE AN ACT -- ACTED LIKE A GHOST TO SCARE THE GUARD!
LET'S GET OUT NOW -YAWN- BEFORE THEY FIND US!
DOPEY'S SAYING WE CAN ESCAPE THROUGH THAT... WINDOW?
THAT TEENY HOLE?!
IT'D BE EASY... IF WE WERE BABY DWARFS!
MOVE IT, SNEEZY!
KEEP PUSHING! MAYBE THEN MY HIPS WILL POP RIGHT THROUGH!

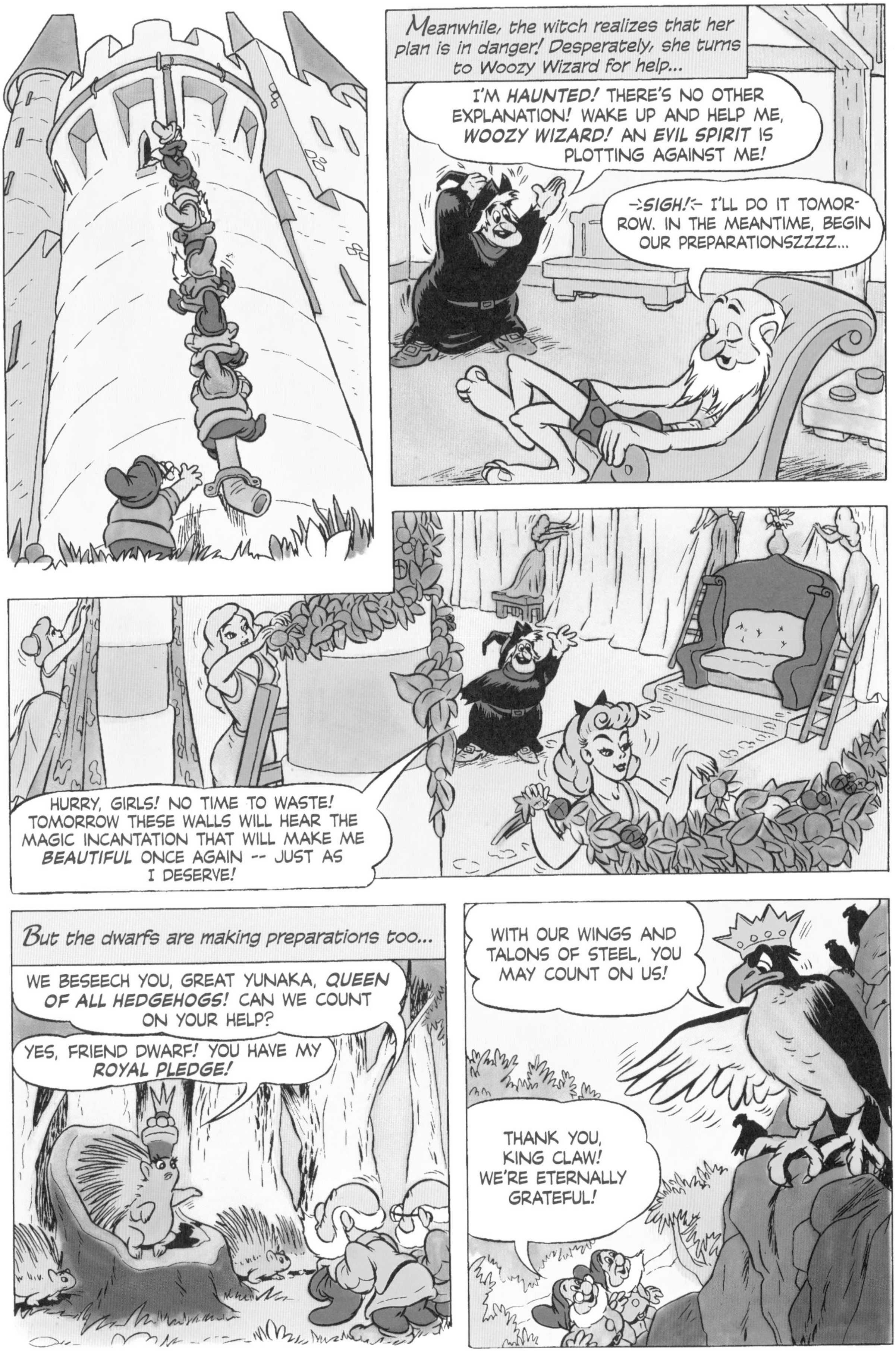
Meanwhile, the witch realizes that her plan is in danger! Desperately, she turns to Woozy Wizard for help...
I'M HAUNTED! THERE'S NO OTHER EXPLANATION! WAKE UP AND HELP ME, WOOZY WIZARD! AN EVIL SPIRIT IS PLOTTING AGAINST ME!
→SIGH!← I'LL DO IT TOMORROW. IN THE MEANTIME, BEGIN OUR PREPARATIONSZZZZ...
HURRY, GIRLS! NO TIME TO WASTE! TOMORROW THESE WALLS WILL HEAR THE MAGIC INCANTATION THAT WILL MAKE ME BEAUTIFUL ONCE AGAIN -- JUST AS I DESERVE!
But the dwarfs are making preparations too...
WE BESEECH YOU, GREAT YUNAKA, QUEEN OF ALL HEDGEHOGS! CAN WE COUNT ON YOUR HELP?
YES, FRIEND DWARF! YOU HAVE MY ROYAL PLEDGE!
WITH OUR WINGS AND TALONS OF STEEL, YOU MAY COUNT ON US!
THANK YOU, KING CLAW! WE'RE ETERNALLY GRATEFUL!

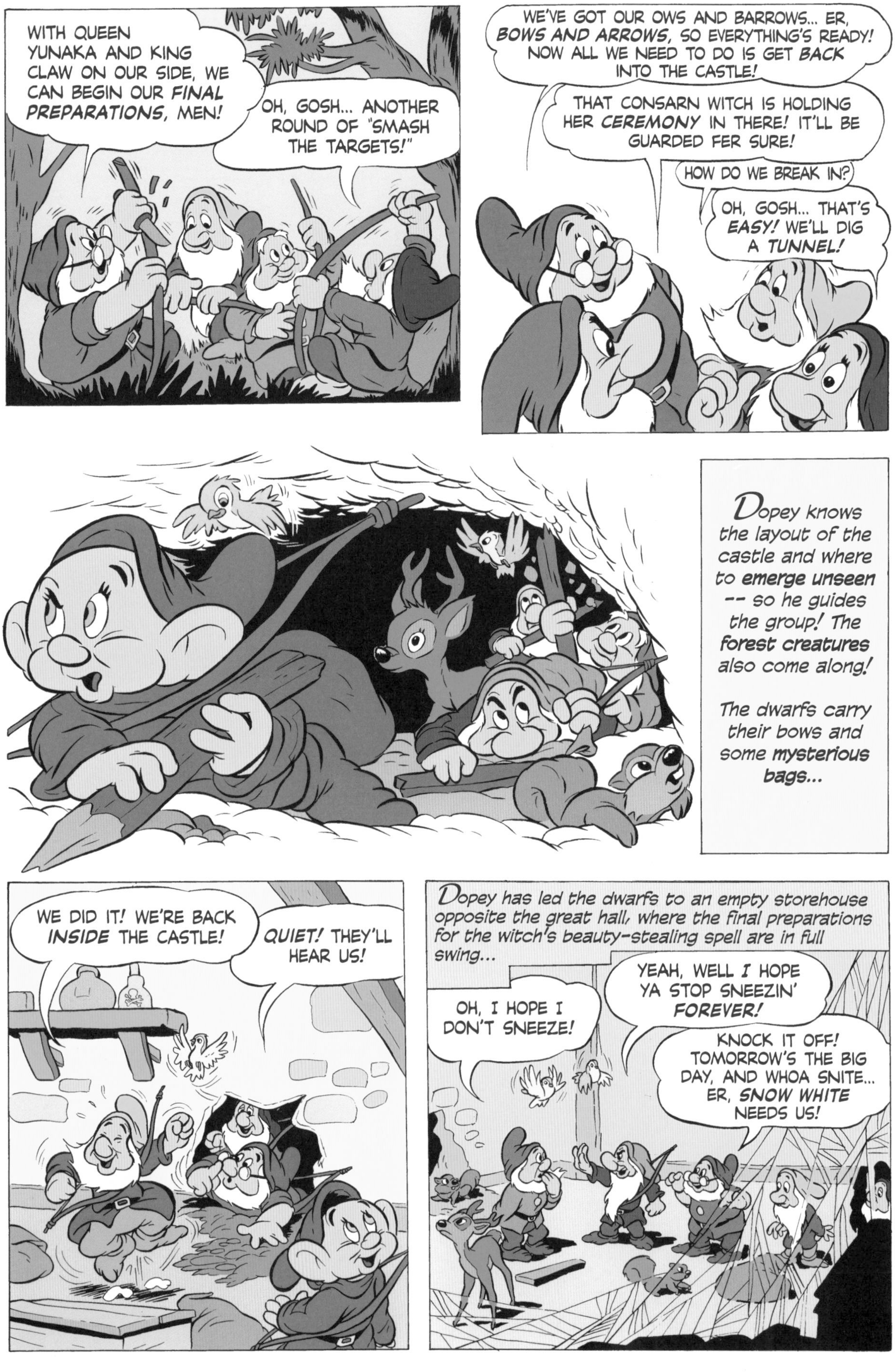
WITH QUEEN YUNAKA AND KING CLAW ON OUR SIDE, WE CAN BEGIN OUR *FINAL PREPARATIONS*, MEN!
OH, GOSH... ANOTHER ROUND OF "SMASH THE TARGETS!"
WE'VE GOT OUR OWS AND BARROWS... ER, *BOWS AND ARROWS*, SO EVERYTHING'S READY! NOW ALL WE NEED TO DO IS GET *BACK* INTO THE CASTLE!
THAT CONSARN WITCH IS HOLDING HER *CEREMONY* IN THERE! IT'LL BE GUARDED FER SURE!
HOW DO WE BREAK IN?
OH, GOSH... THAT'S *EASY!* WE'LL DIG A *TUNNEL!*
Dopey knows the layout of the castle and where to **emerge unseen** -- so he guides the group! The **forest creatures** also come along!
The dwarfs carry their bows and some **mysterious bags...**
WE DID IT! WE'RE BACK *INSIDE* THE CASTLE!
QUIET! THEY'LL HEAR US!
Dopey has led the dwarfs to an empty storehouse opposite the great hall, where the final preparations for the witch's beauty-stealing spell are in full swing...
OH, I HOPE I DON'T SNEEZE!
YEAH, WELL *I* HOPE YA STOP SNEEZIN' *FOREVER!*
KNOCK IT OFF! TOMORROW'S THE BIG DAY, AND WHOA SNITE... ER, *SNOW WHITE* NEEDS US!

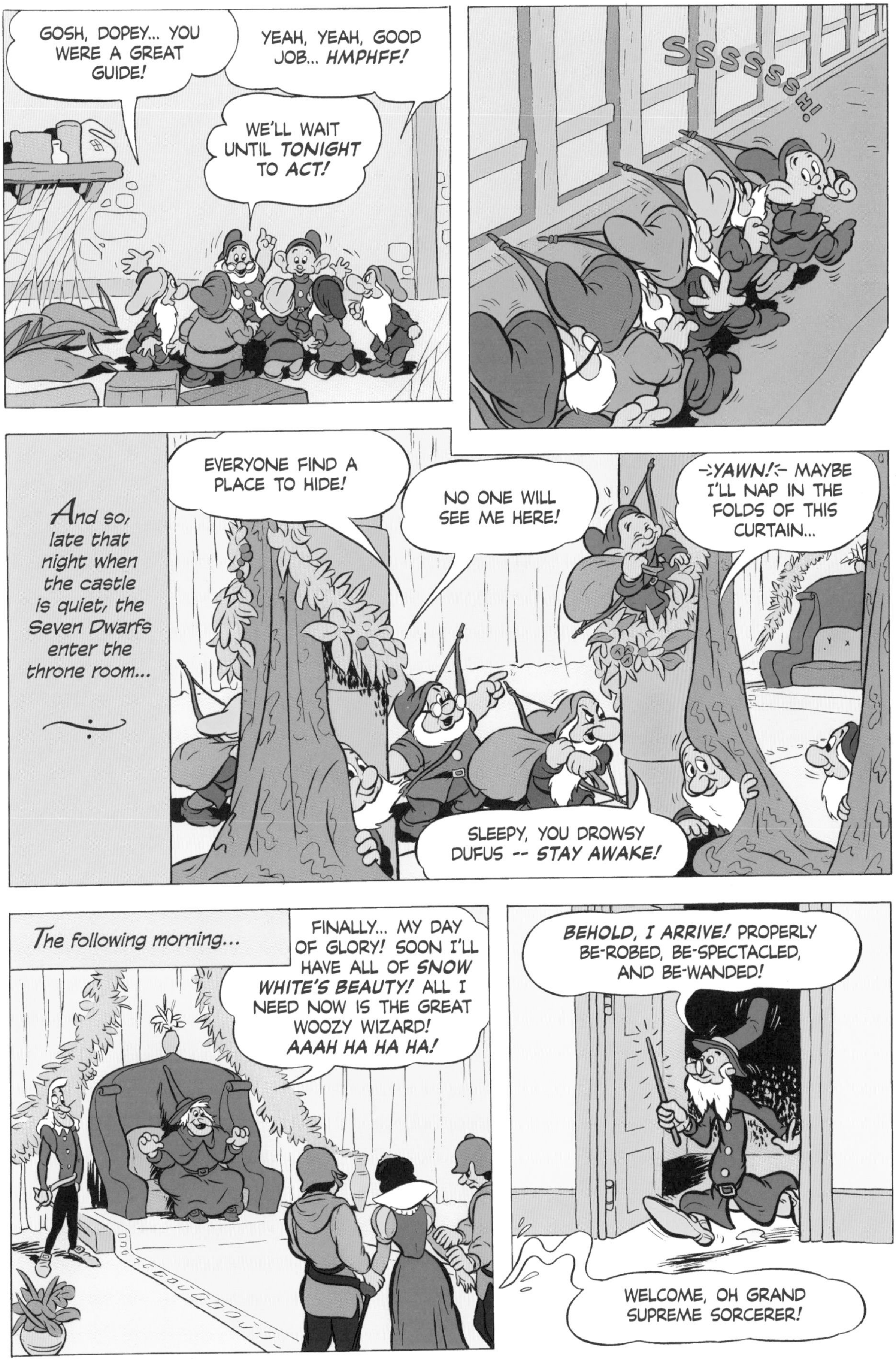

GOSH, DOPEY... YOU WERE A GREAT GUIDE!
YEAH, YEAH, GOOD JOB... HMPHFF!
WE'LL WAIT UNTIL TONIGHT TO ACT!
SSSSSSH!
And so, late that night when the castle is quiet, the Seven Dwarfs enter the throne room...
EVERYONE FIND A PLACE TO HIDE!
NO ONE WILL SEE ME HERE!
–YAWN!– MAYBE I'LL NAP IN THE FOLDS OF THIS CURTAIN...
SLEEPY, YOU DROWSY DUFUS -- STAY AWAKE!
The following morning...
FINALLY... MY DAY OF GLORY! SOON I'LL HAVE ALL OF SNOW WHITE'S BEAUTY! ALL I NEED NOW IS THE GREAT WOOZY WIZARD! AAAH HA HA HA!
BEHOLD, I ARRIVE! PROPERLY BE-ROBED, BE-SPECTACLED, AND BE-WANDED!
WELCOME, OH GRAND SUPREME SORCERER!

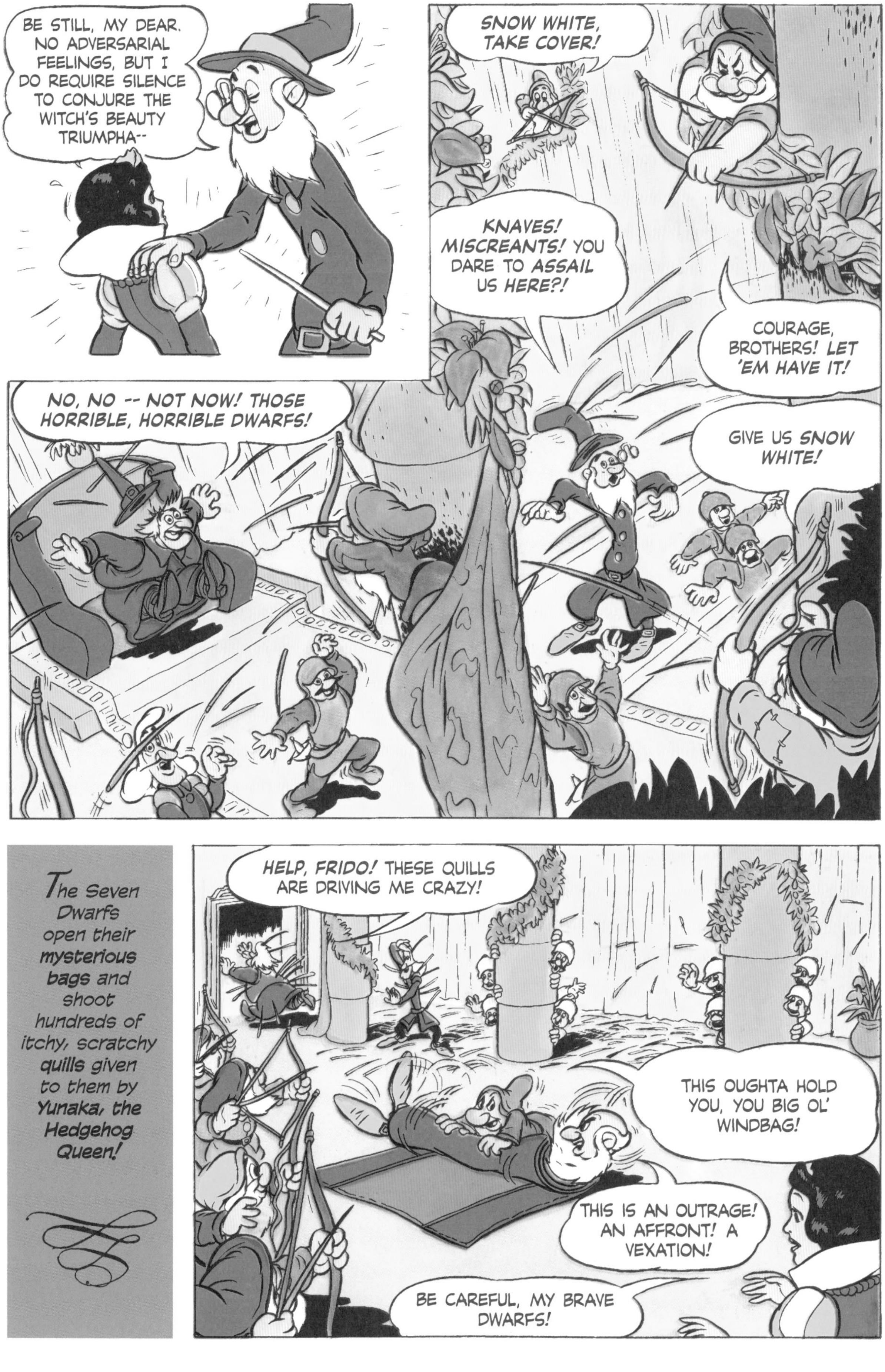
BE STILL, MY DEAR. NO ADVERSARIAL FEELINGS, BUT I DO REQUIRE SILENCE TO CONJURE THE WITCH'S BEAUTY TRIUMPHA--
SNOW WHITE, TAKE COVER!
KNAVES! MISCREANTS! YOU DARE TO ASSAIL US HERE?!
COURAGE, BROTHERS! LET 'EM HAVE IT!
NO, NO -- NOT NOW! THOSE HORRIBLE, HORRIBLE DWARFS!
GIVE US SNOW WHITE!
The Seven Dwarfs open their mysterious bags and shoot hundreds of itchy, scratchy quills given to them by Yunaka, the Hedgehog Queen!
HELP, FRIDO! THESE QUILLS ARE DRIVING ME CRAZY!
THIS OUGHTA HOLD YOU, YOU BIG OL' WINDBAG!
THIS IS AN OUTRAGE! AN AFFRONT! A VEXATION!
BE CAREFUL, MY BRAVE DWARFS!

EEEEK!

As the witch rushes from her castle, **King Claw** and his minions begin their role in the dwarfs' plan.

At a nod, they swoop in...

SPLASH!

And so, because witches immersed in water melt away forever, the reign of the Witch of Potions ends with a mighty splash.

With the witch gone, her spells are broken and her evil is undone. All of her subjects are freed from her power and revert to the side of good. All except one...

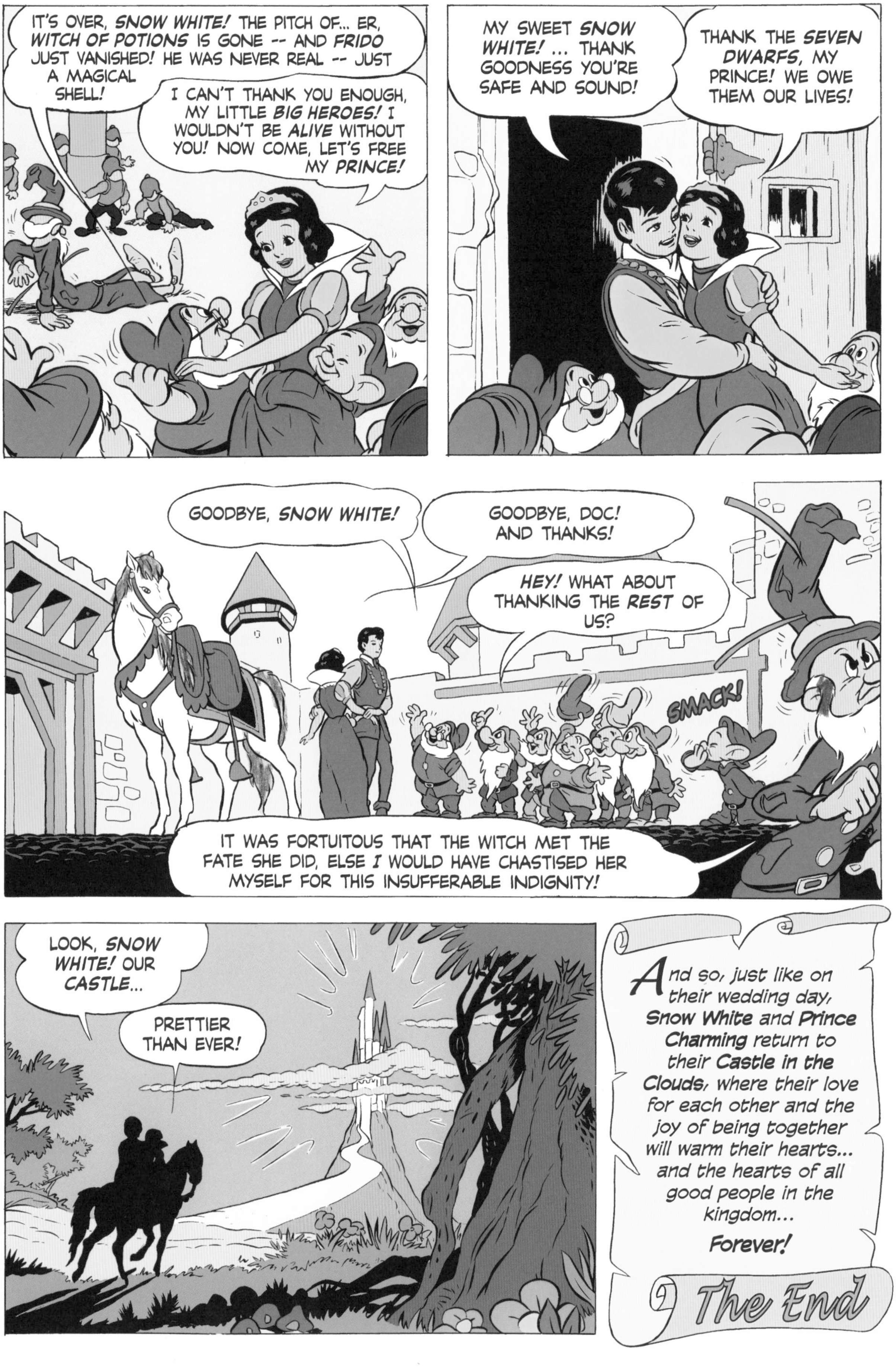
IT'S OVER, SNOW WHITE! THE PITCH OF... ER, WITCH OF POTIONS IS GONE -- AND FRIDO JUST VANISHED! HE WAS NEVER REAL -- JUST A MAGICAL SHELL!
I CAN'T THANK YOU ENOUGH, MY LITTLE BIG HEROES! I WOULDN'T BE ALIVE WITHOUT YOU! NOW COME, LET'S FREE MY PRINCE!
MY SWEET SNOW WHITE! ... THANK GOODNESS YOU'RE SAFE AND SOUND!
THANK THE SEVEN DWARFS, MY PRINCE! WE OWE THEM OUR LIVES!
GOODBYE, SNOW WHITE!
GOODBYE, DOC! AND THANKS!
HEY! WHAT ABOUT THANKING THE REST OF US?
SMACK!
IT WAS FORTUITOUS THAT THE WITCH MET THE FATE SHE DID, ELSE I WOULD HAVE CHASTISED HER MYSELF FOR THIS INSUFFERABLE INDIGNITY!
LOOK, SNOW WHITE! OUR CASTLE...
PRETTIER THAN EVER!
And so, just like on their wedding day, Snow White and Prince Charming return to their Castle in the Clouds, where their love for each other and the joy of being together will warm their hearts... and the hearts of all good people in the kingdom...
Forever!
The End

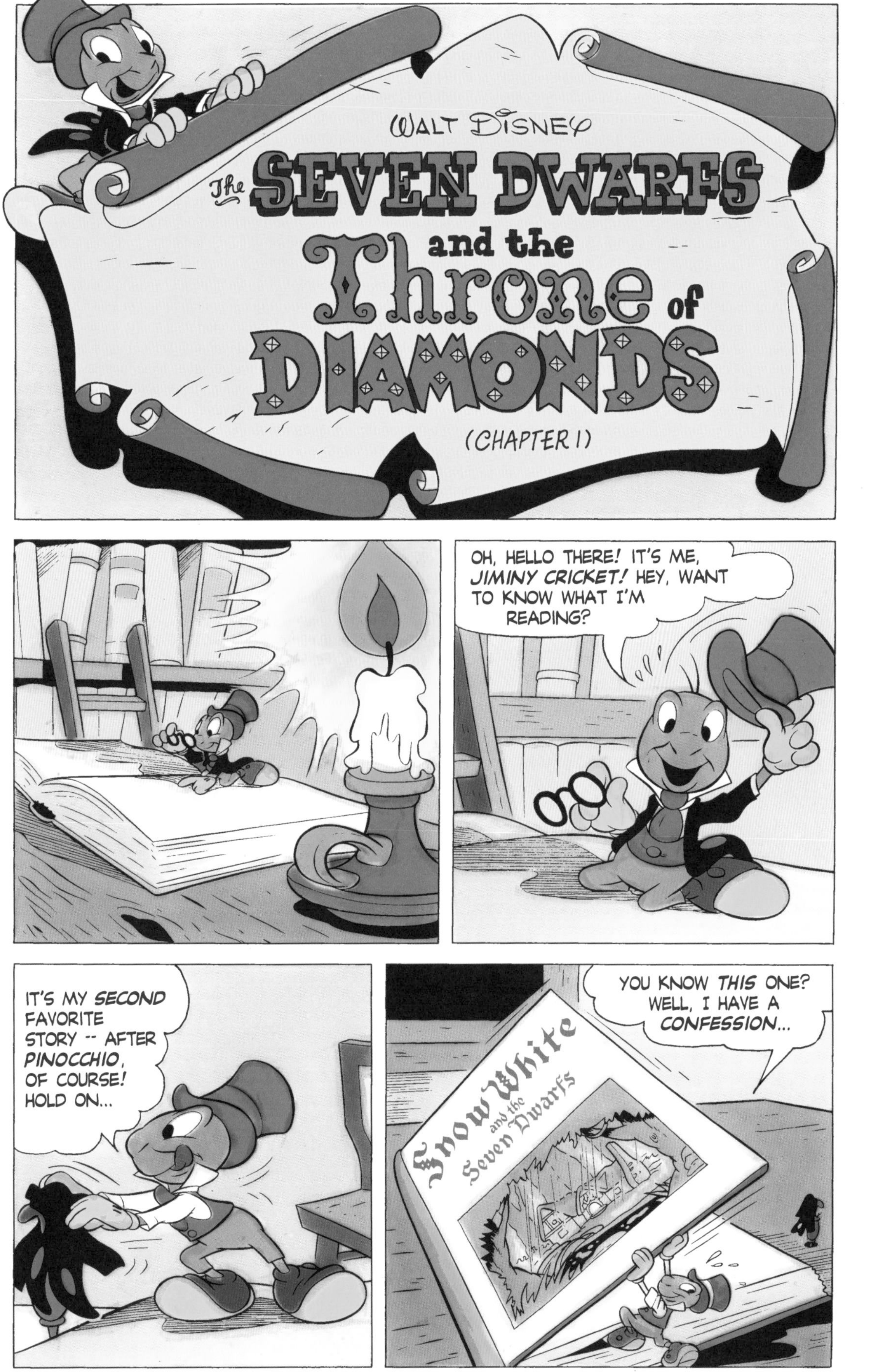
WALT DISNEY
The SEVEN DWARFS and the Throne of DIAMONDS
(CHAPTER 1)
OH, HELLO THERE! IT'S ME, JIMINY CRICKET! HEY, WANT TO KNOW WHAT I'M READING?
IT'S MY SECOND FAVORITE STORY -- AFTER PINOCCHIO, OF COURSE! HOLD ON...
YOU KNOW THIS ONE? WELL, I HAVE A CONFESSION...
Snow White and the Seven Dwarfs

STORY AND PENCILS: ROMANO SCARPA • INKS: LUCIANO GATTO
TRANSLATION: ALBERTO BECATTINI • DIALOG: JONATHAN H. GRAY WITH DAVID GERSTEIN
TITLE LETTERING: KEELI MCCARTHY • EDITING: J. MICHAEL CATRON

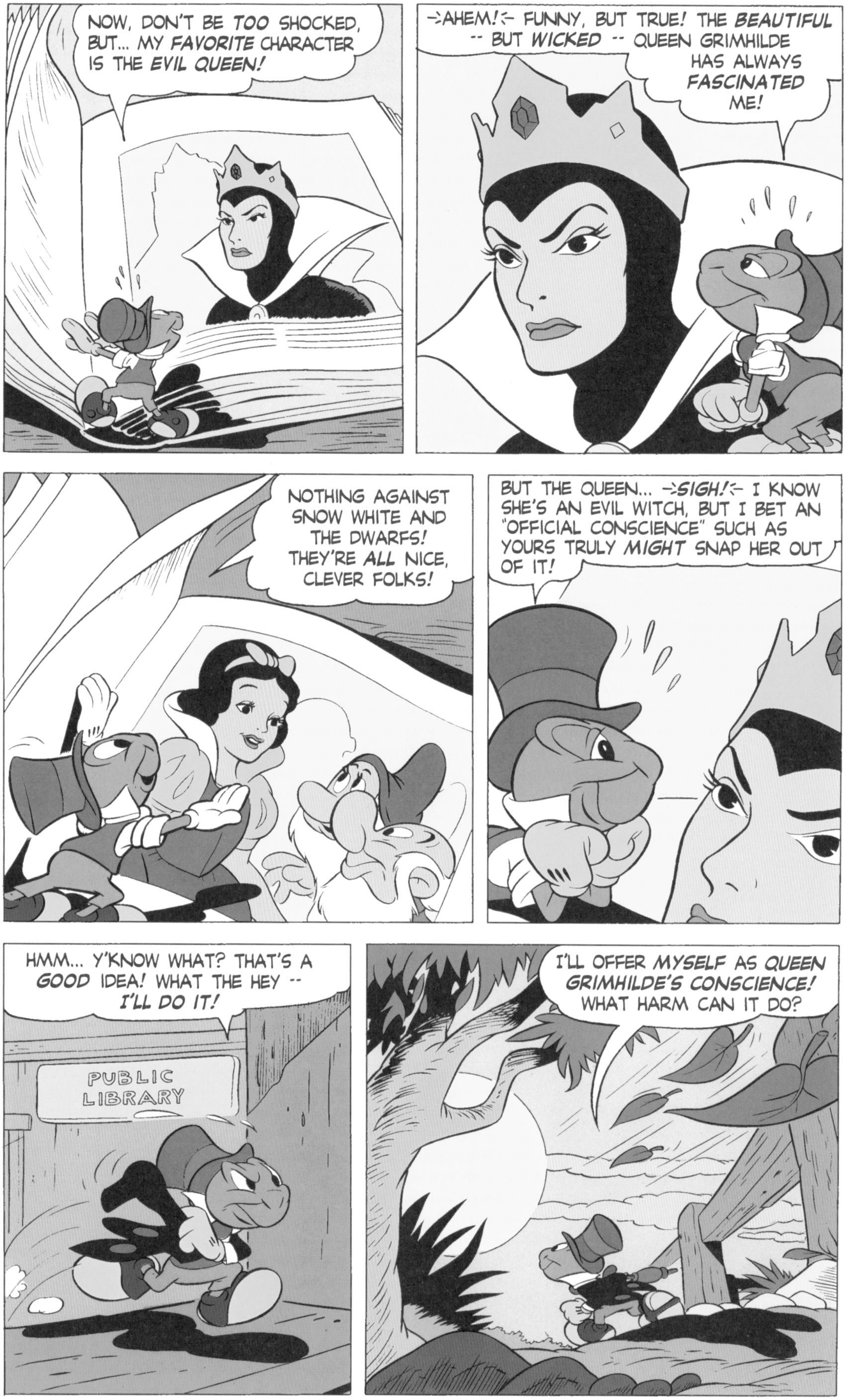
NOW, DON'T BE TOO SHOCKED, BUT... MY FAVORITE CHARACTER IS THE EVIL QUEEN!
–AHEM!– FUNNY, BUT TRUE! THE BEAUTIFUL -- BUT WICKED -- QUEEN GRIMHILDE HAS ALWAYS FASCINATED ME!
NOTHING AGAINST SNOW WHITE AND THE DWARFS! THEY'RE ALL NICE, CLEVER FOLKS!
BUT THE QUEEN... –SIGH!– I KNOW SHE'S AN EVIL WITCH, BUT I BET AN "OFFICIAL CONSCIENCE" SUCH AS YOURS TRULY MIGHT SNAP HER OUT OF IT!
HMM... Y'KNOW WHAT? THAT'S A GOOD IDEA! WHAT THE HEY -- I'LL DO IT!
PUBLIC LIBRARY
I'LL OFFER MYSELF AS QUEEN GRIMHILDE'S CONSCIENCE! WHAT HARM CAN IT DO?

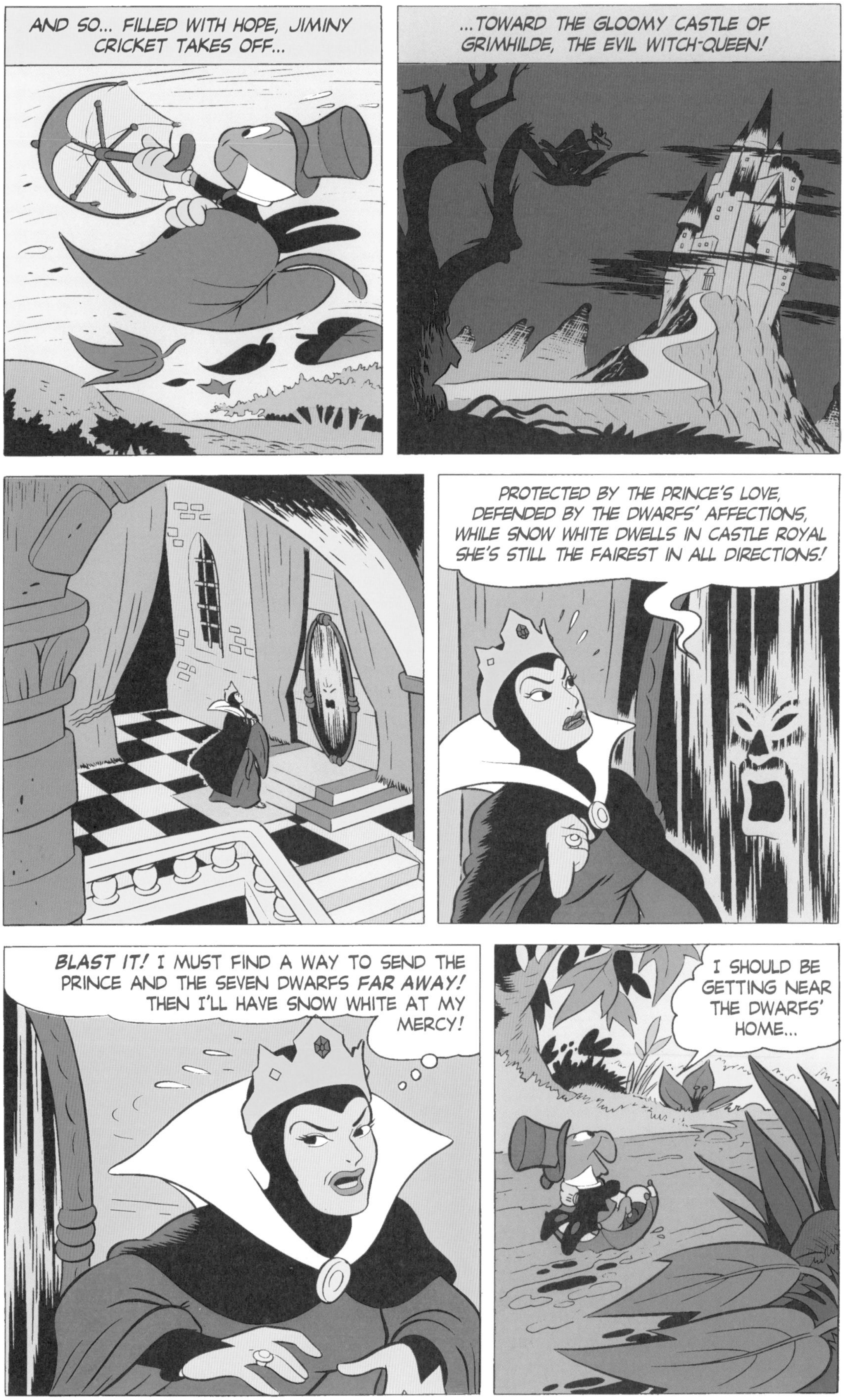
AND SO... FILLED WITH HOPE, JIMINY CRICKET TAKES OFF...
...TOWARD THE GLOOMY CASTLE OF GRIMHILDE, THE EVIL WITCH-QUEEN!
PROTECTED BY THE PRINCE'S LOVE, DEFENDED BY THE DWARFS' AFFECTIONS, WHILE SNOW WHITE DWELLS IN CASTLE ROYAL SHE'S STILL THE FAIREST IN ALL DIRECTIONS!
BLAST IT! I MUST FIND A WAY TO SEND THE PRINCE AND THE SEVEN DWARFS FAR AWAY! THEN I'LL HAVE SNOW WHITE AT MY MERCY!
I SHOULD BE GETTING NEAR THE DWARFS' HOME...

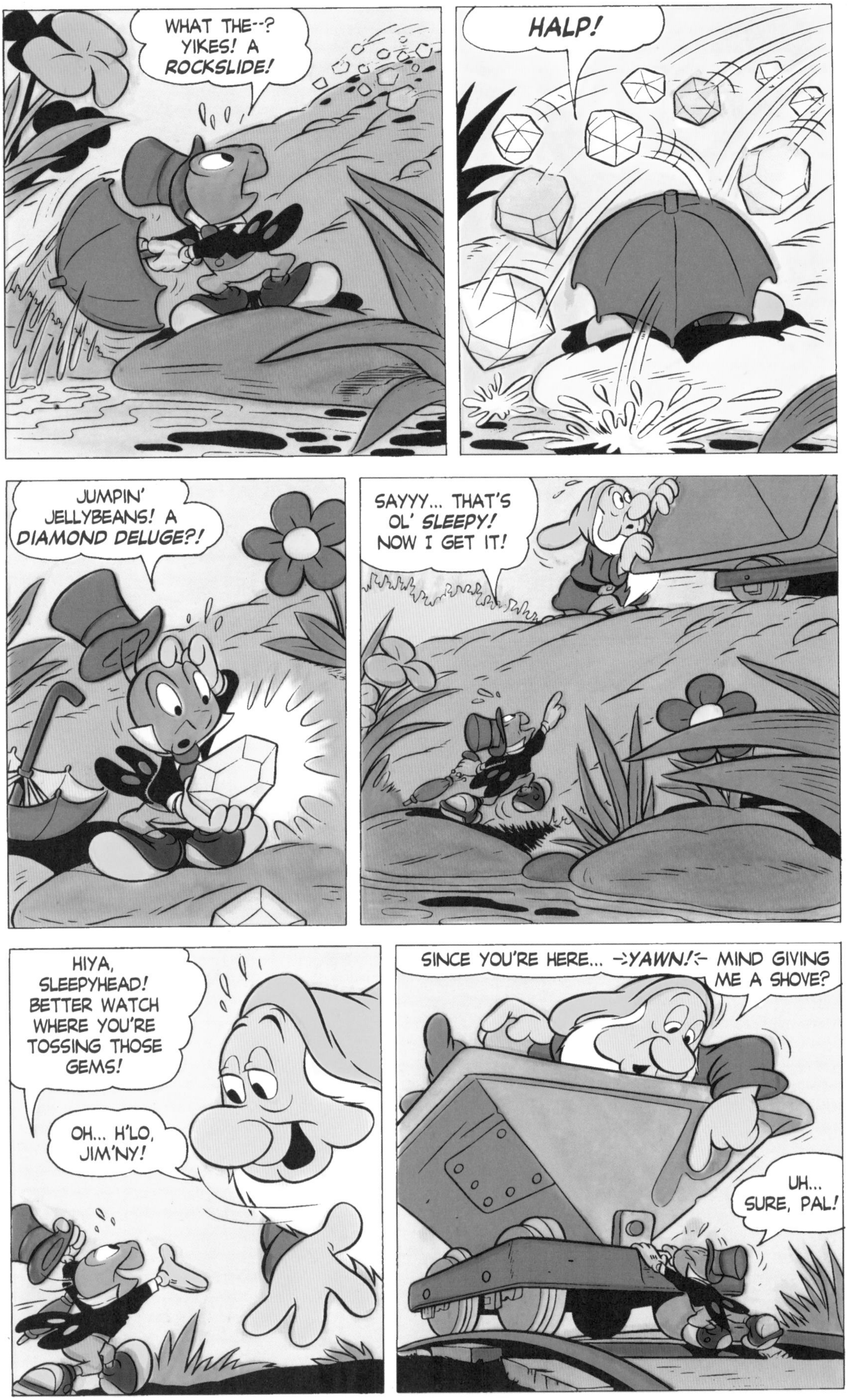
WHAT THE--? YIKES! A ROCKSLIDE!
HALP!
JUMPIN' JELLYBEANS! A DIAMOND DELUGE?!
SAYYY... THAT'S OL' SLEEPY! NOW I GET IT!
HIYA, SLEEPYHEAD! BETTER WATCH WHERE YOU'RE TOSSING THOSE GEMS!
OH... H'LO, JIM'NY!
SINCE YOU'RE HERE... -YAWN!- MIND GIVING ME A SHOVE?
UH... SURE, PAL!

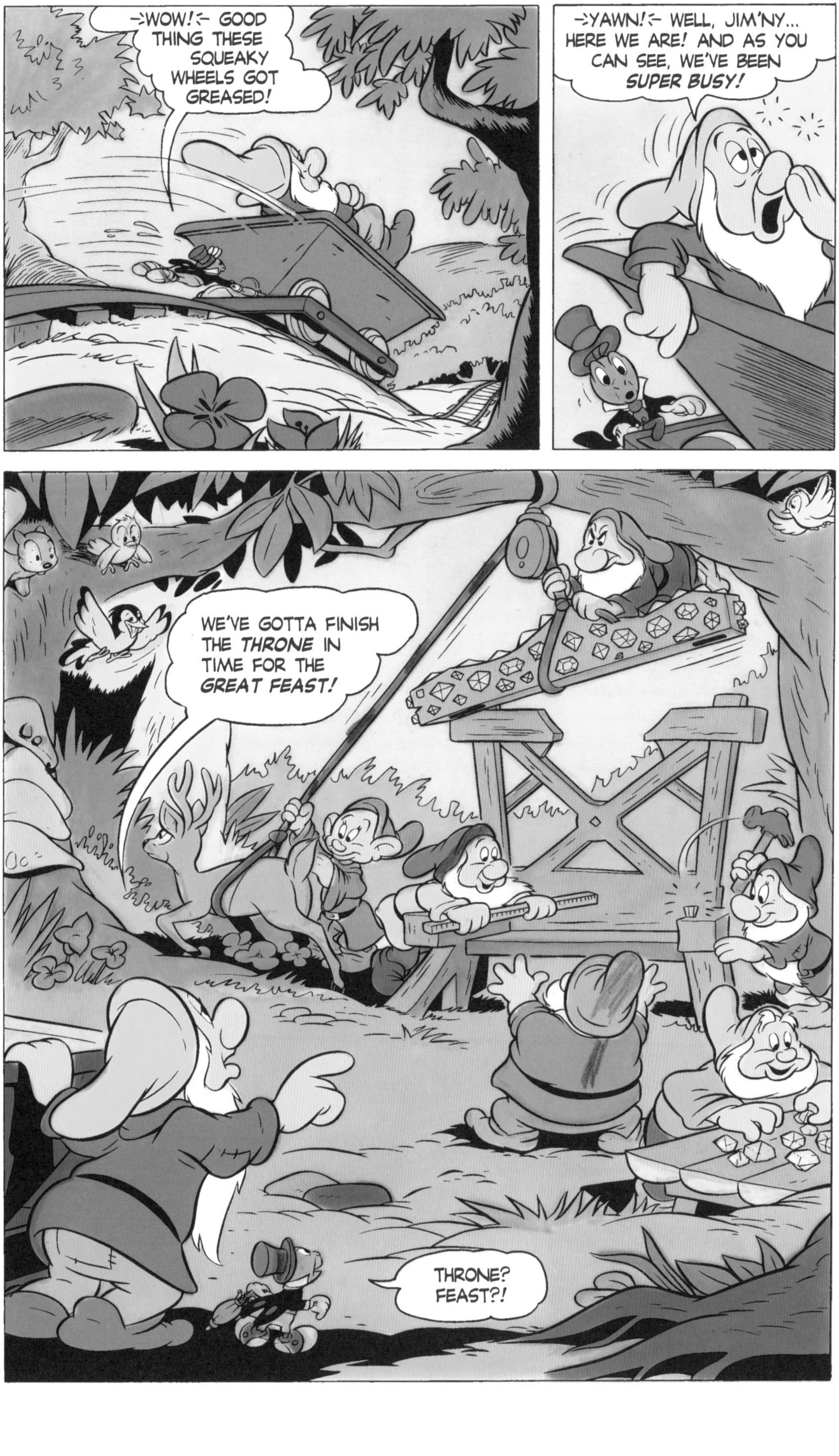
–>WOW!<– GOOD THING THESE SQUEAKY WHEELS GOT GREASED!
–>YAWN!<– WELL, JIM'NY... HERE WE ARE! AND AS YOU CAN SEE, WE'VE BEEN SUPER BUSY!
WE'VE GOTTA FINISH THE THRONE IN TIME FOR THE GREAT FEAST!
THRONE? FEAST?!

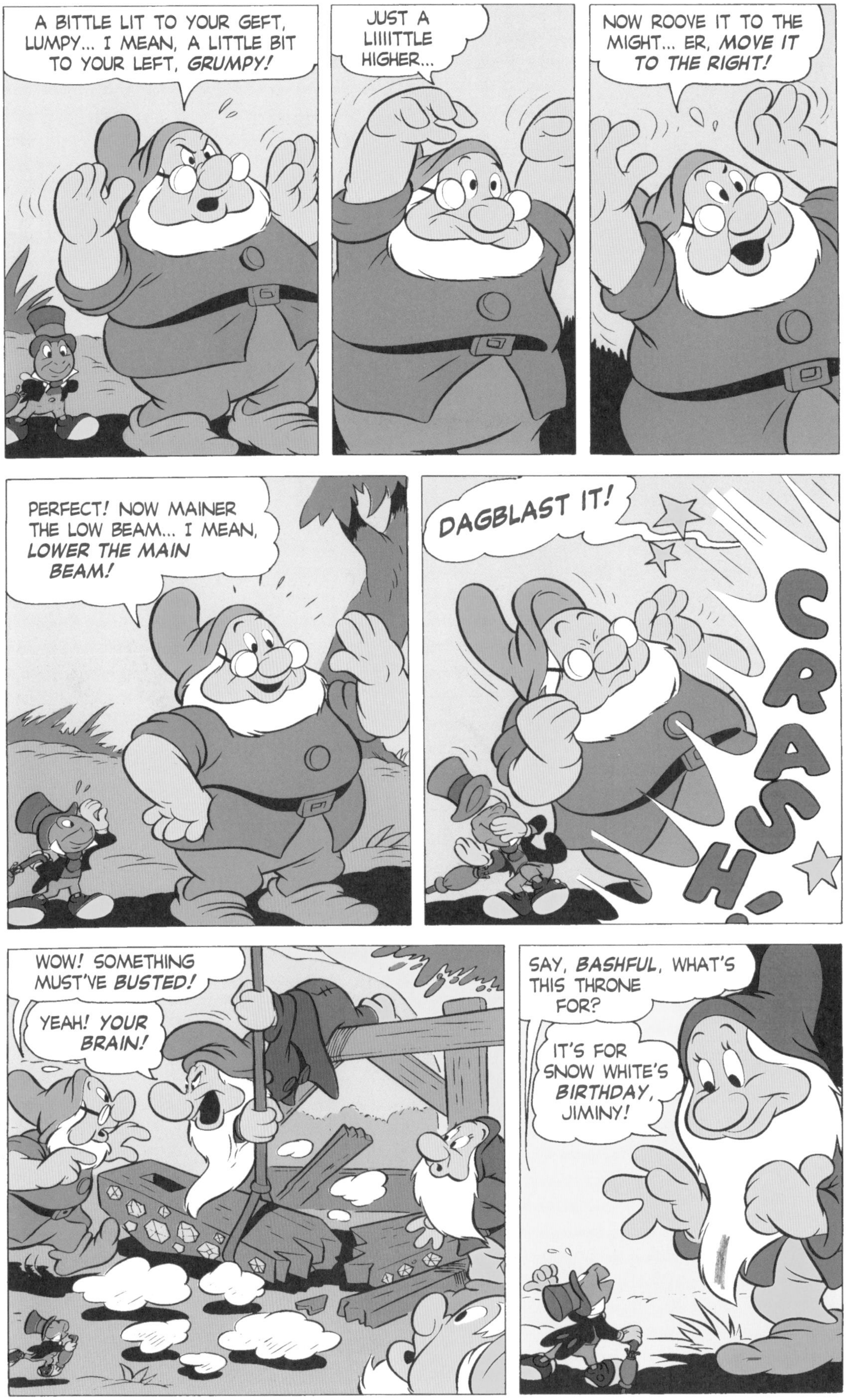
A BITTLE LIT TO YOUR GEFT, LUMPY... I MEAN, A LITTLE BIT TO YOUR LEFT, GRUMPY!
JUST A LIIIITTLE HIGHER...
NOW ROOVE IT TO THE MIGHT... ER, MOVE IT TO THE RIGHT!
PERFECT! NOW MAINER THE LOW BEAM... I MEAN, LOWER THE MAIN BEAM!
DAGBLAST IT!
CRASH!
WOW! SOMETHING MUST'VE BUSTED!
YEAH! YOUR BRAIN!
SAY, BASHFUL, WHAT'S THIS THRONE FOR?
IT'S FOR SNOW WHITE'S BIRTHDAY, JIMINY!

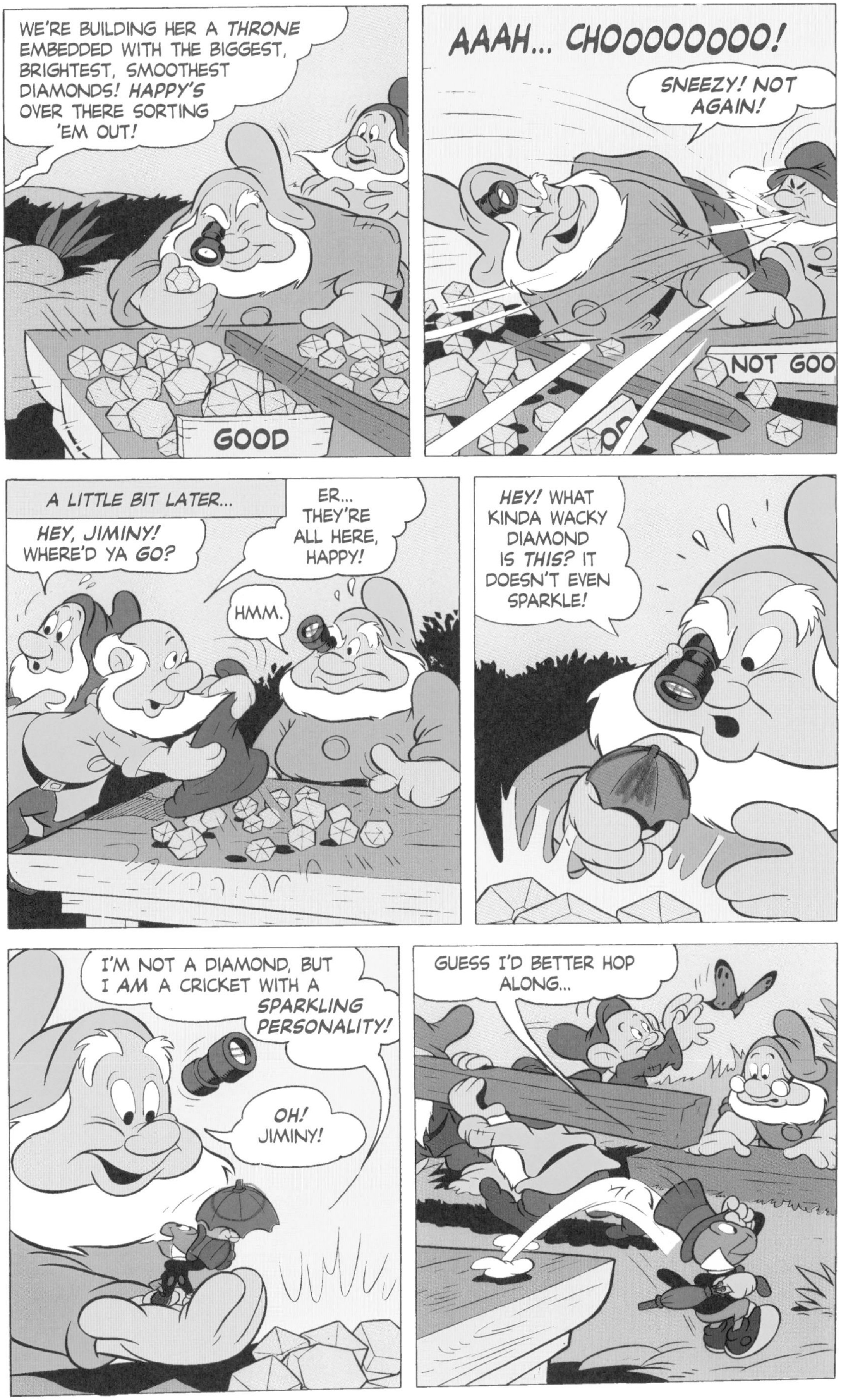
WE'RE BUILDING HER A THRONE EMBEDDED WITH THE BIGGEST, BRIGHTEST, SMOOTHEST DIAMONDS! HAPPY'S OVER THERE SORTING 'EM OUT!
GOOD
AAAH... CHOOOOOOOO!
SNEEZY! NOT AGAIN!
NOT GOO
A LITTLE BIT LATER...
HEY, JIMINY! WHERE'D YA GO?
ER... THEY'RE ALL HERE, HAPPY!
HMM.
HEY! WHAT KINDA WACKY DIAMOND IS THIS? IT DOESN'T EVEN SPARKLE!
I'M NOT A DIAMOND, BUT I AM A CRICKET WITH A SPARKLING PERSONALITY!
OH! JIMINY!
GUESS I'D BETTER HOP ALONG...

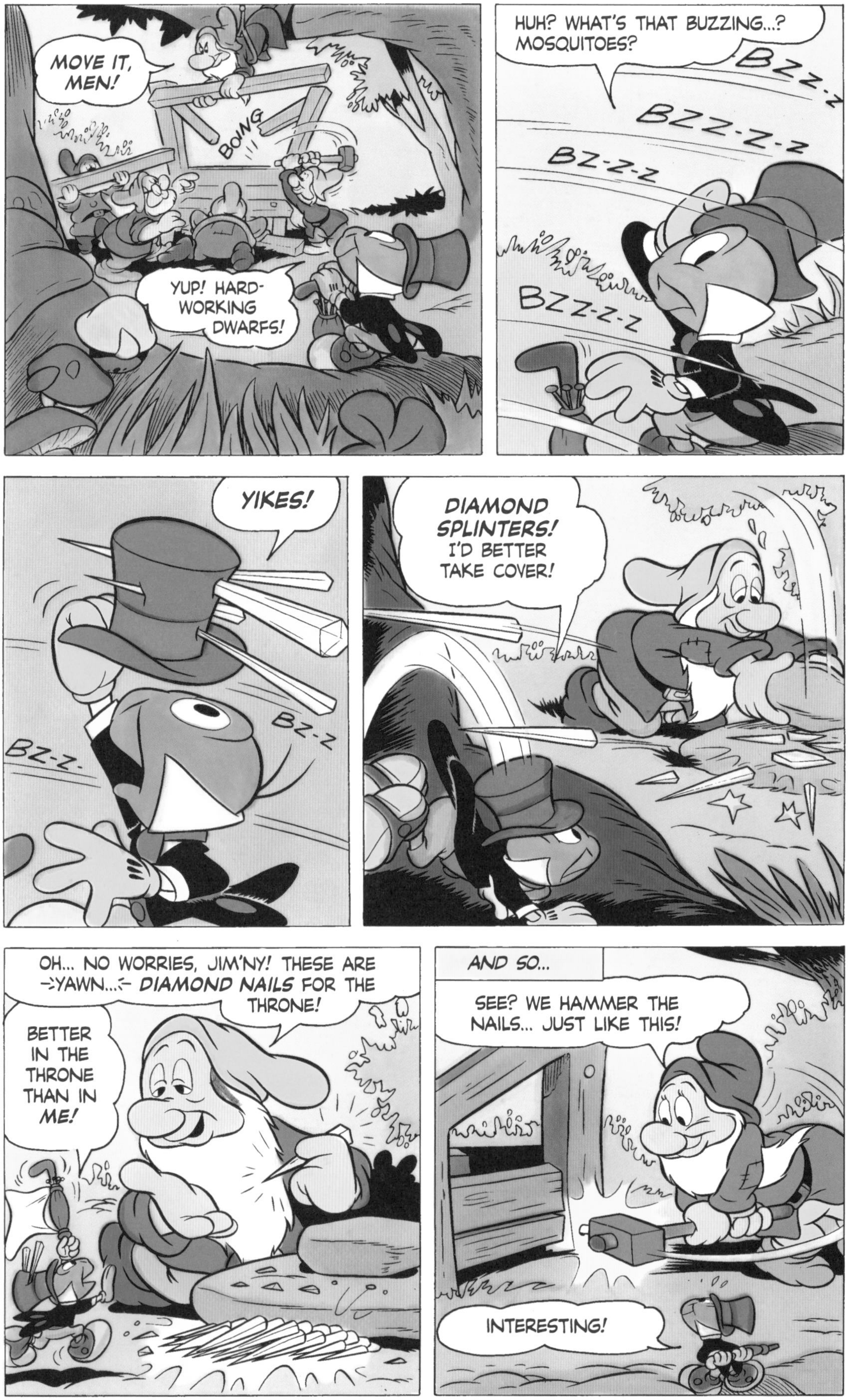
MOVE IT, MEN!
BOING
YUP! HARD-WORKING DWARFS!
HUH? WHAT'S THAT BUZZING...? MOSQUITOES?
BZZZ-Z
BZZ-Z-Z-Z
BZ-Z-Z
BZZ-Z-Z
YIKES!
BZ-Z
BZ-Z-
DIAMOND SPLINTERS! I'D BETTER TAKE COVER!
OH... NO WORRIES, JIM'NY! THESE ARE -YAWN...- DIAMOND NAILS FOR THE THRONE!
BETTER IN THE THRONE THAN IN ME!
AND SO...
SEE? WE HAMMER THE NAILS... JUST LIKE THIS!
INTERESTING!

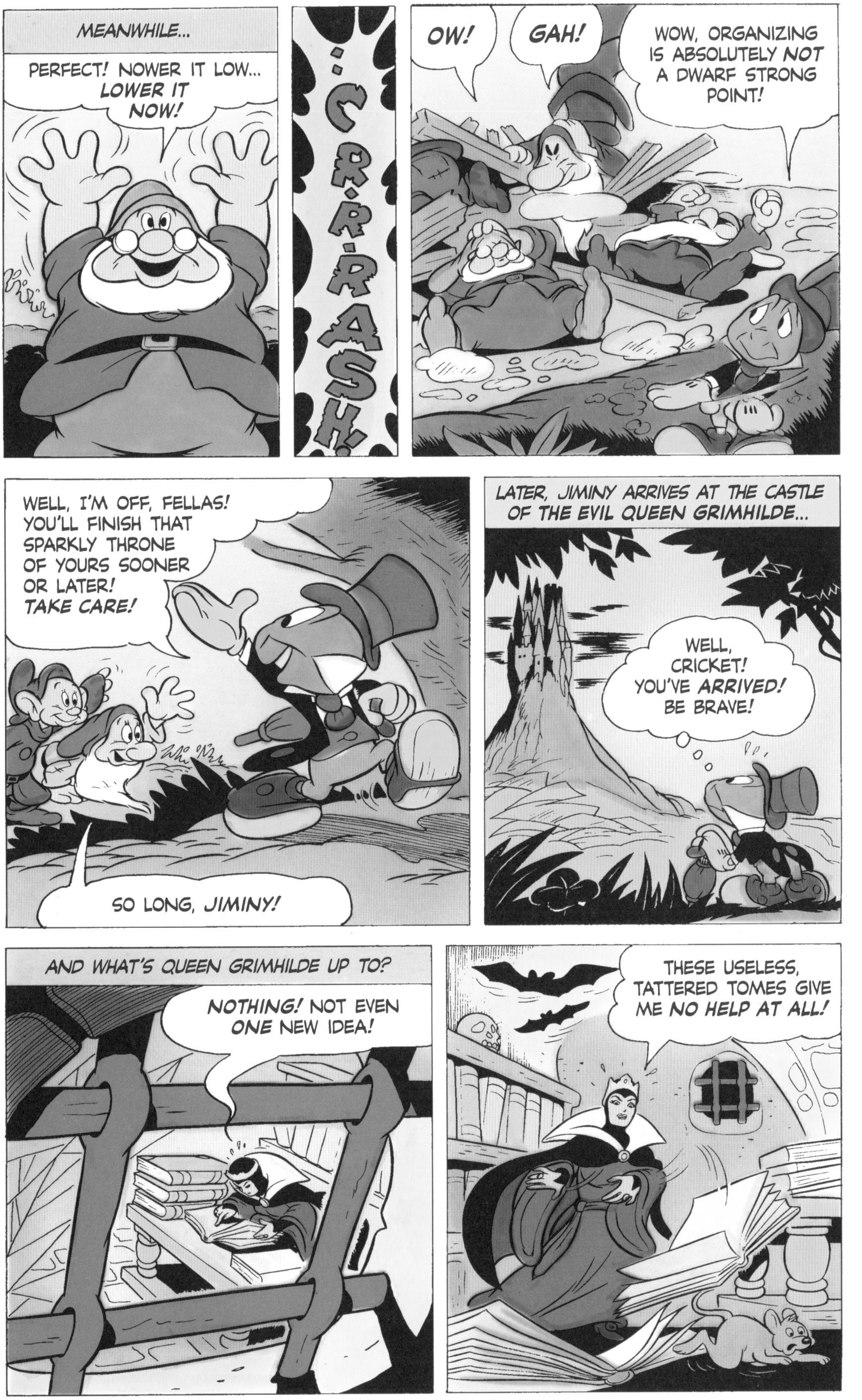
MEANWHILE...
PERFECT! NOWER IT LOW... LOWER IT NOW!
CR-R-RASH!
OW!
GAH!
WOW, ORGANIZING IS ABSOLUTELY NOT A DWARF STRONG POINT!
WELL, I'M OFF, FELLAS! YOU'LL FINISH THAT SPARKLY THRONE OF YOURS SOONER OR LATER! TAKE CARE!
SO LONG, JIMINY!
LATER, JIMINY ARRIVES AT THE CASTLE OF THE EVIL QUEEN GRIMHILDE...
WELL, CRICKET! YOU'VE ARRIVED! BE BRAVE!
AND WHAT'S QUEEN GRIMHILDE UP TO?
NOTHING! NOT EVEN ONE NEW IDEA!
THESE USELESS, TATTERED TOMES GIVE ME NO HELP AT ALL!

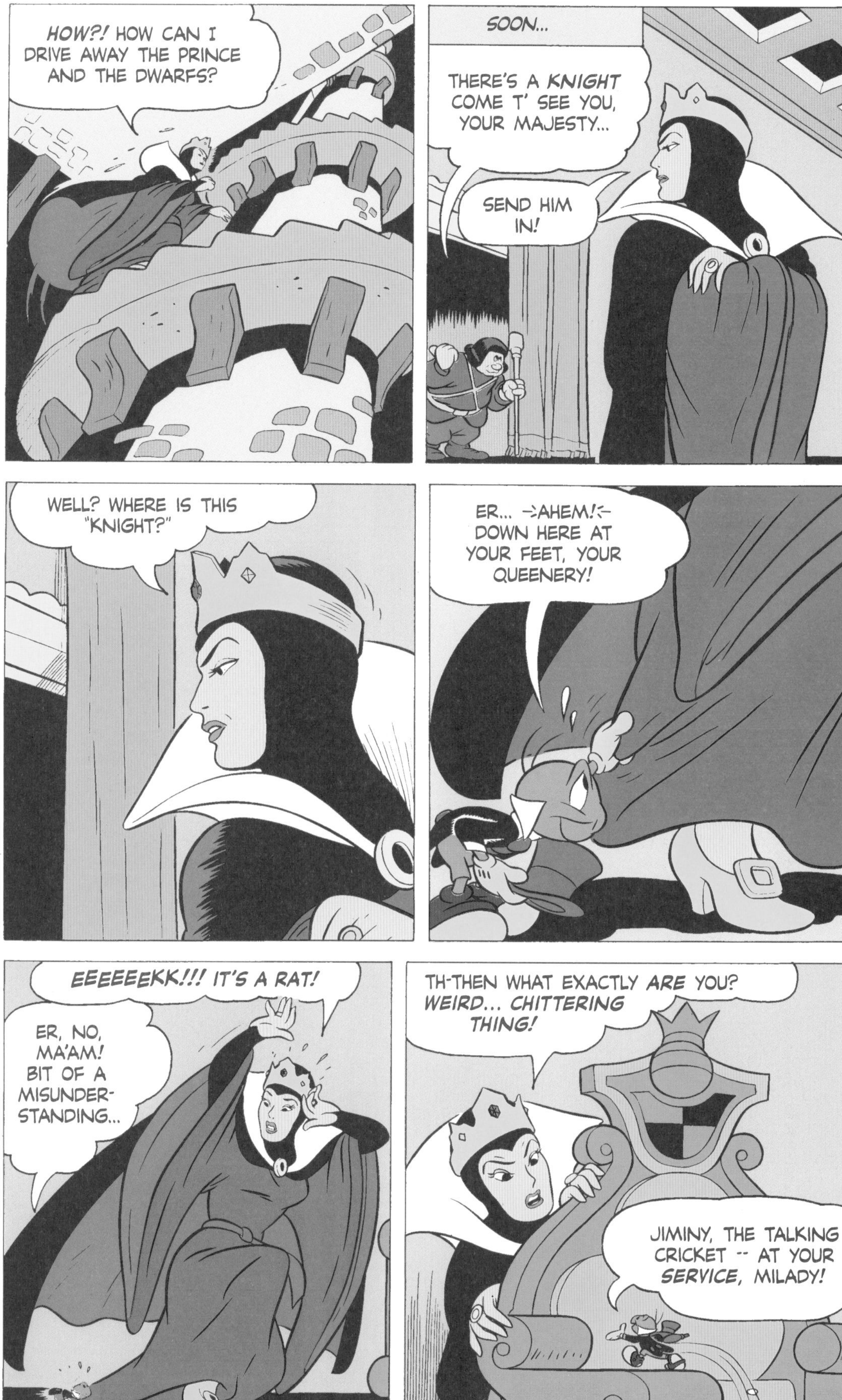
HOW?! HOW CAN I DRIVE AWAY THE PRINCE AND THE DWARFS?
SOON...
THERE'S A KNIGHT COME T' SEE YOU, YOUR MAJESTY...
SEND HIM IN!
WELL? WHERE IS THIS "KNIGHT?"
ER... AHEM! DOWN HERE AT YOUR FEET, YOUR QUEENERY!
EEEEEEKK!!! IT'S A RAT!
ER, NO, MA'AM! BIT OF A MISUNDER-STANDING...
TH-THEN WHAT EXACTLY ARE YOU? WEIRD... CHITTERING THING!
JIMINY, THE TALKING CRICKET -- AT YOUR SERVICE, MILADY!

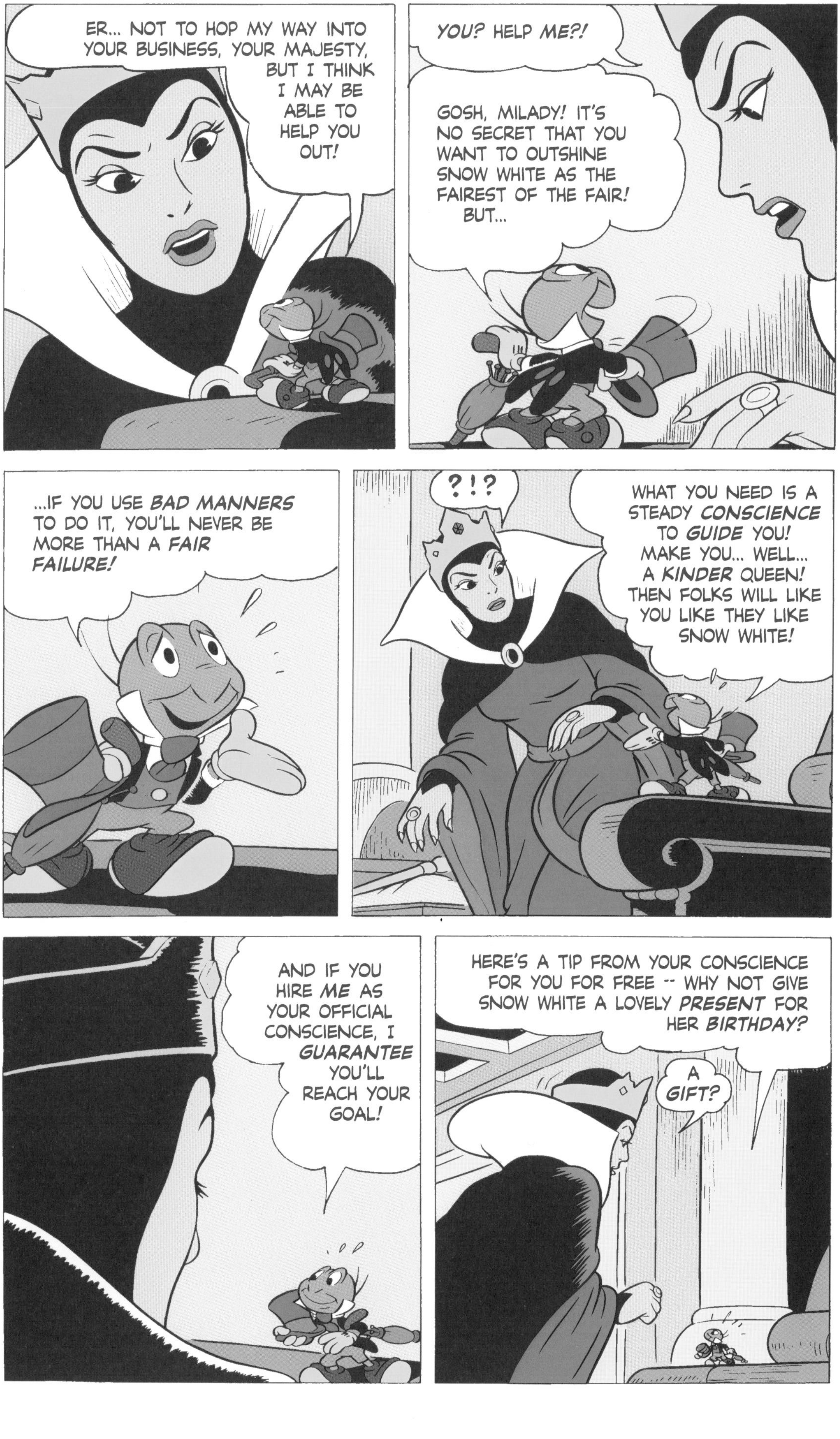
ER... NOT TO HOP MY WAY INTO YOUR BUSINESS, YOUR MAJESTY, BUT I THINK I MAY BE ABLE TO HELP YOU OUT!
YOU? HELP ME?!
GOSH, MILADY! IT'S NO SECRET THAT YOU WANT TO OUTSHINE SNOW WHITE AS THE FAIREST OF THE FAIR! BUT...
...IF YOU USE BAD MANNERS TO DO IT, YOU'LL NEVER BE MORE THAN A FAIR FAILURE!
?!?
WHAT YOU NEED IS A STEADY CONSCIENCE TO GUIDE YOU! MAKE YOU... WELL... A KINDER QUEEN! THEN FOLKS WILL LIKE YOU LIKE THEY LIKE SNOW WHITE!
AND IF YOU HIRE ME AS YOUR OFFICIAL CONSCIENCE, I GUARANTEE YOU'LL REACH YOUR GOAL!
HERE'S A TIP FROM YOUR CONSCIENCE FOR YOU FOR FREE -- WHY NOT GIVE SNOW WHITE A LOVELY PRESENT FOR HER BIRTHDAY?
A GIFT?

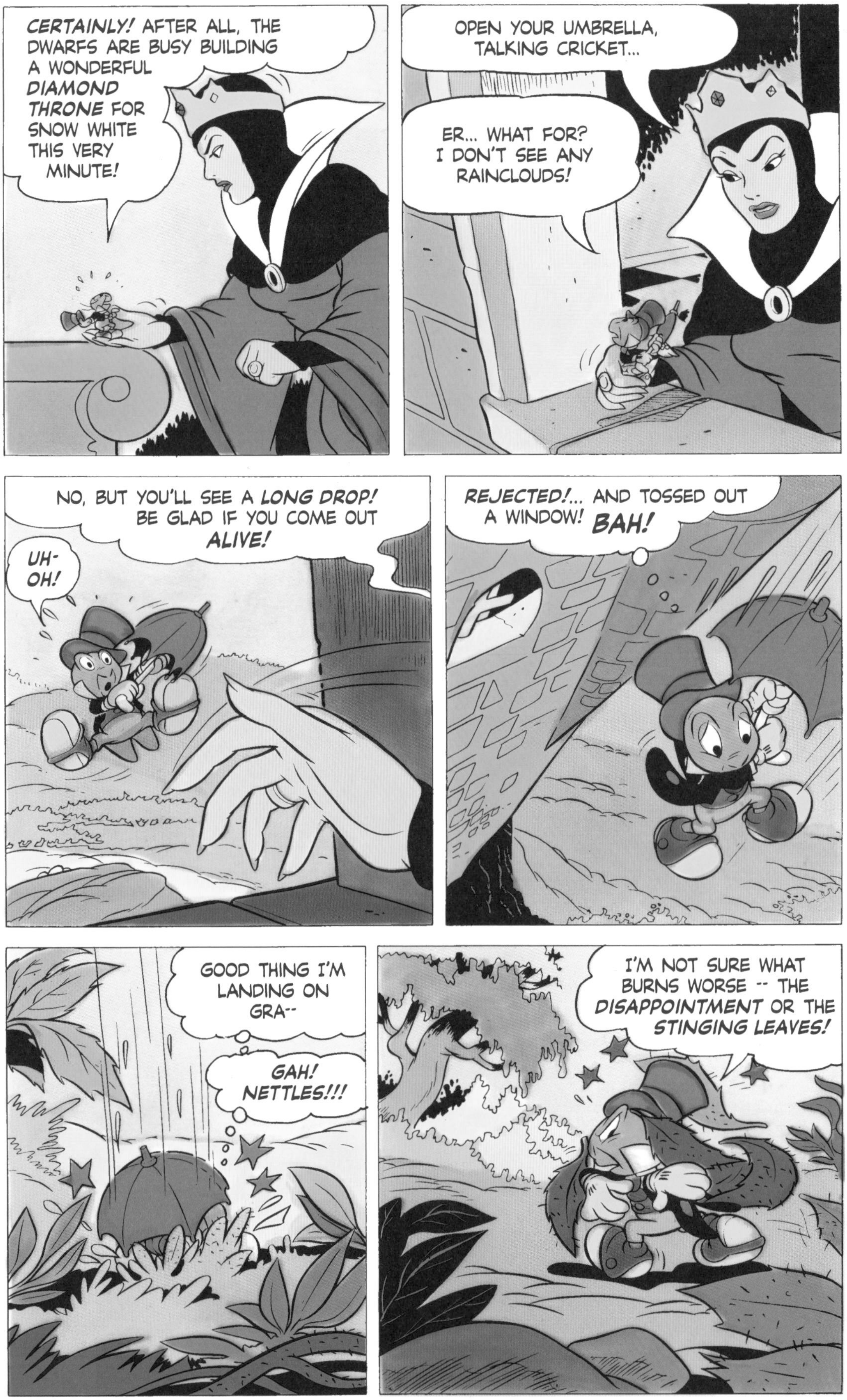
CERTAINLY! AFTER ALL, THE DWARFS ARE BUSY BUILDING A WONDERFUL DIAMOND THRONE FOR SNOW WHITE THIS VERY MINUTE!
OPEN YOUR UMBRELLA, TALKING CRICKET...
ER... WHAT FOR? I DON'T SEE ANY RAINCLOUDS!
NO, BUT YOU'LL SEE A LONG DROP! BE GLAD IF YOU COME OUT ALIVE!
UH-OH!
REJECTED!... AND TOSSED OUT A WINDOW! BAH!
GOOD THING I'M LANDING ON GRA--
GAH! NETTLES!!!
I'M NOT SURE WHAT BURNS WORSE -- THE DISAPPOINTMENT OR THE STINGING LEAVES!

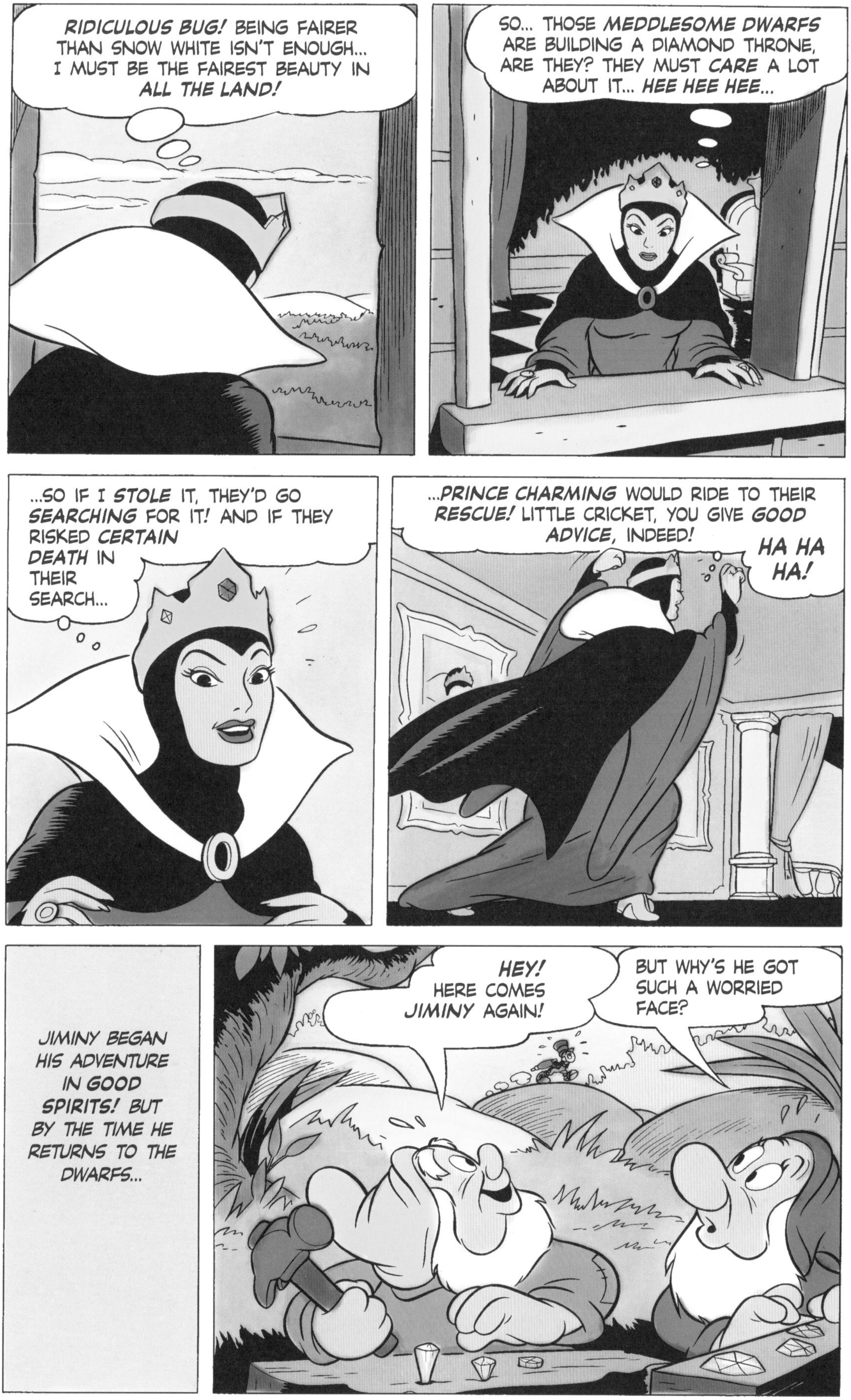
RIDICULOUS BUG! BEING FAIRER THAN SNOW WHITE ISN'T ENOUGH... I MUST BE THE FAIREST BEAUTY IN ALL THE LAND!
SO... THOSE MEDDLESOME DWARFS ARE BUILDING A DIAMOND THRONE, ARE THEY? THEY MUST CARE A LOT ABOUT IT... HEE HEE HEE...
...SO IF I STOLE IT, THEY'D GO SEARCHING FOR IT! AND IF THEY RISKED CERTAIN DEATH IN THEIR SEARCH...
...PRINCE CHARMING WOULD RIDE TO THEIR RESCUE! LITTLE CRICKET, YOU GIVE GOOD ADVICE, INDEED!
HA HA HA!
JIMINY BEGAN HIS ADVENTURE IN GOOD SPIRITS! BUT BY THE TIME HE RETURNS TO THE DWARFS...
HEY! HERE COMES JIMINY AGAIN!
BUT WHY'S HE GOT SUCH A WORRIED FACE?

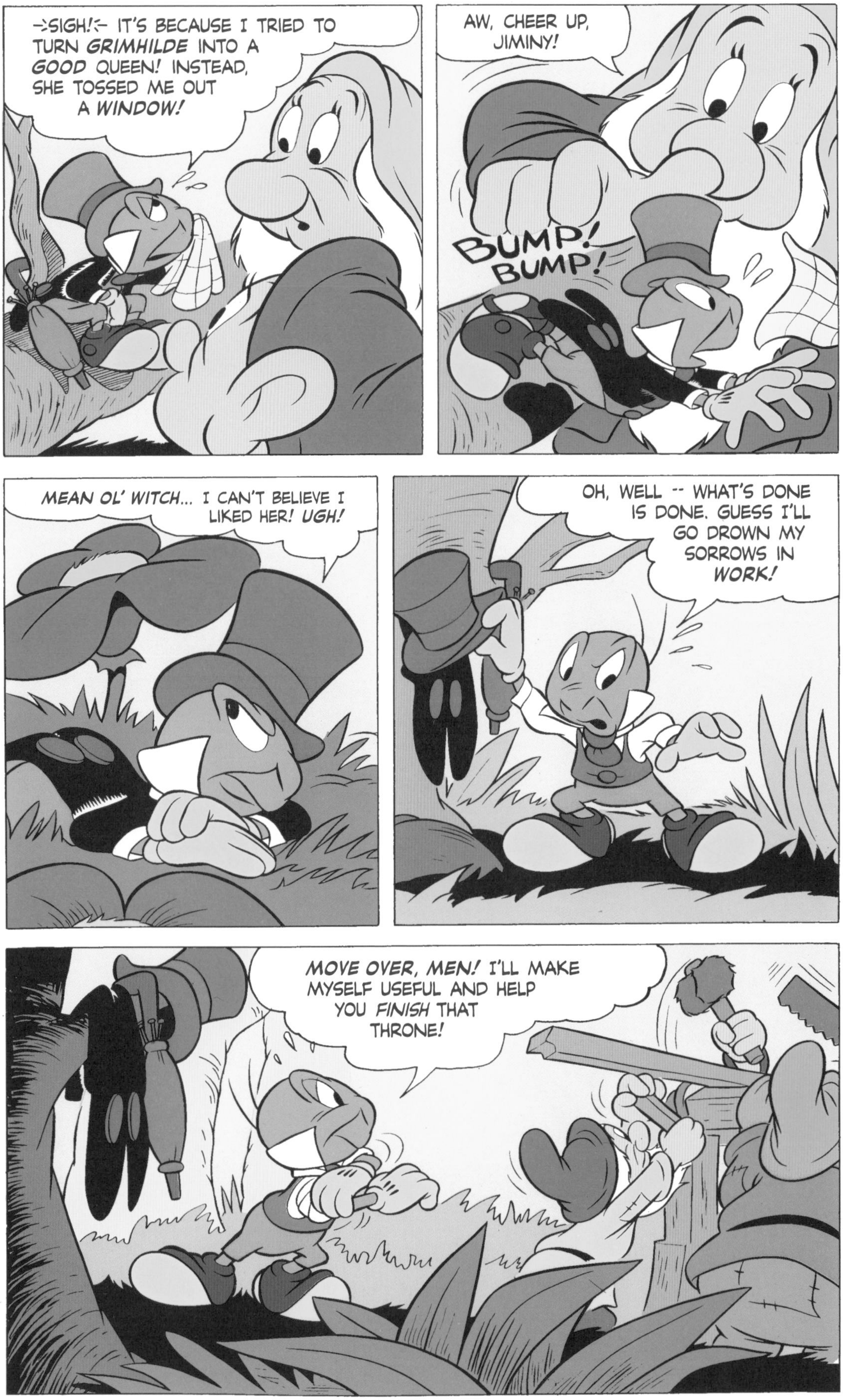
–SIGH!– IT'S BECAUSE I TRIED TO TURN GRIMHILDE INTO A GOOD QUEEN! INSTEAD, SHE TOSSED ME OUT A WINDOW!
AW, CHEER UP, JIMINY!
BUMP! BUMP!
MEAN OL' WITCH... I CAN'T BELIEVE I LIKED HER! UGH!
OH, WELL -- WHAT'S DONE IS DONE. GUESS I'LL GO DROWN MY SORROWS IN WORK!
MOVE OVER, MEN! I'LL MAKE MYSELF USEFUL AND HELP YOU FINISH THAT THRONE!

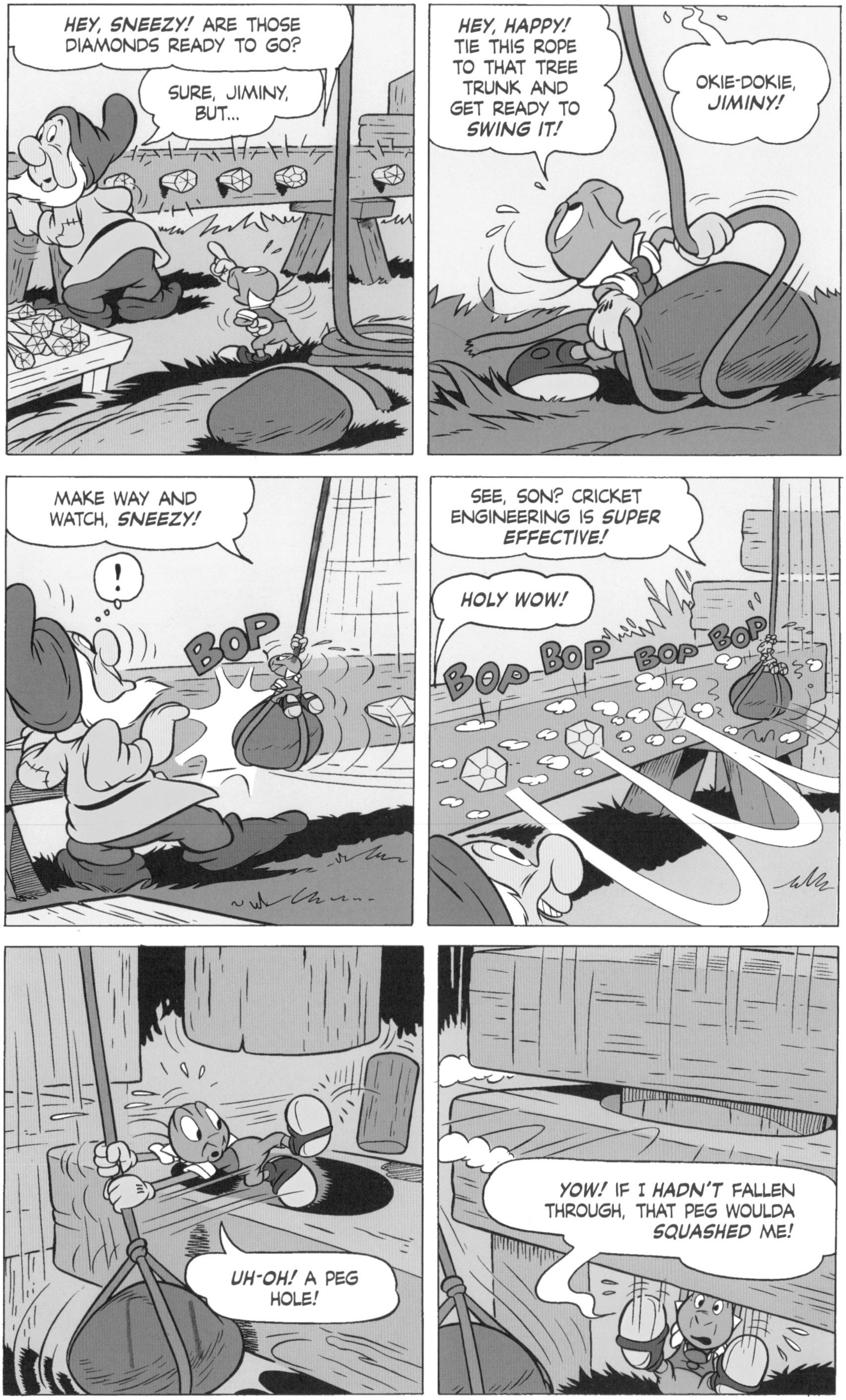
HEY, SNEEZY! ARE THOSE DIAMONDS READY TO GO?
SURE, JIMINY, BUT...
HEY, HAPPY! TIE THIS ROPE TO THAT TREE TRUNK AND GET READY TO SWING IT!
OKIE-DOKIE, JIMINY!
MAKE WAY AND WATCH, SNEEZY!
!
BOP
SEE, SON? CRICKET ENGINEERING IS SUPER EFFECTIVE!
HOLY WOW!
BOP BOP BOP BOP
UH-OH! A PEG HOLE!
YOW! IF I HADN'T FALLEN THROUGH, THAT PEG WOULDA SQUASHED ME!

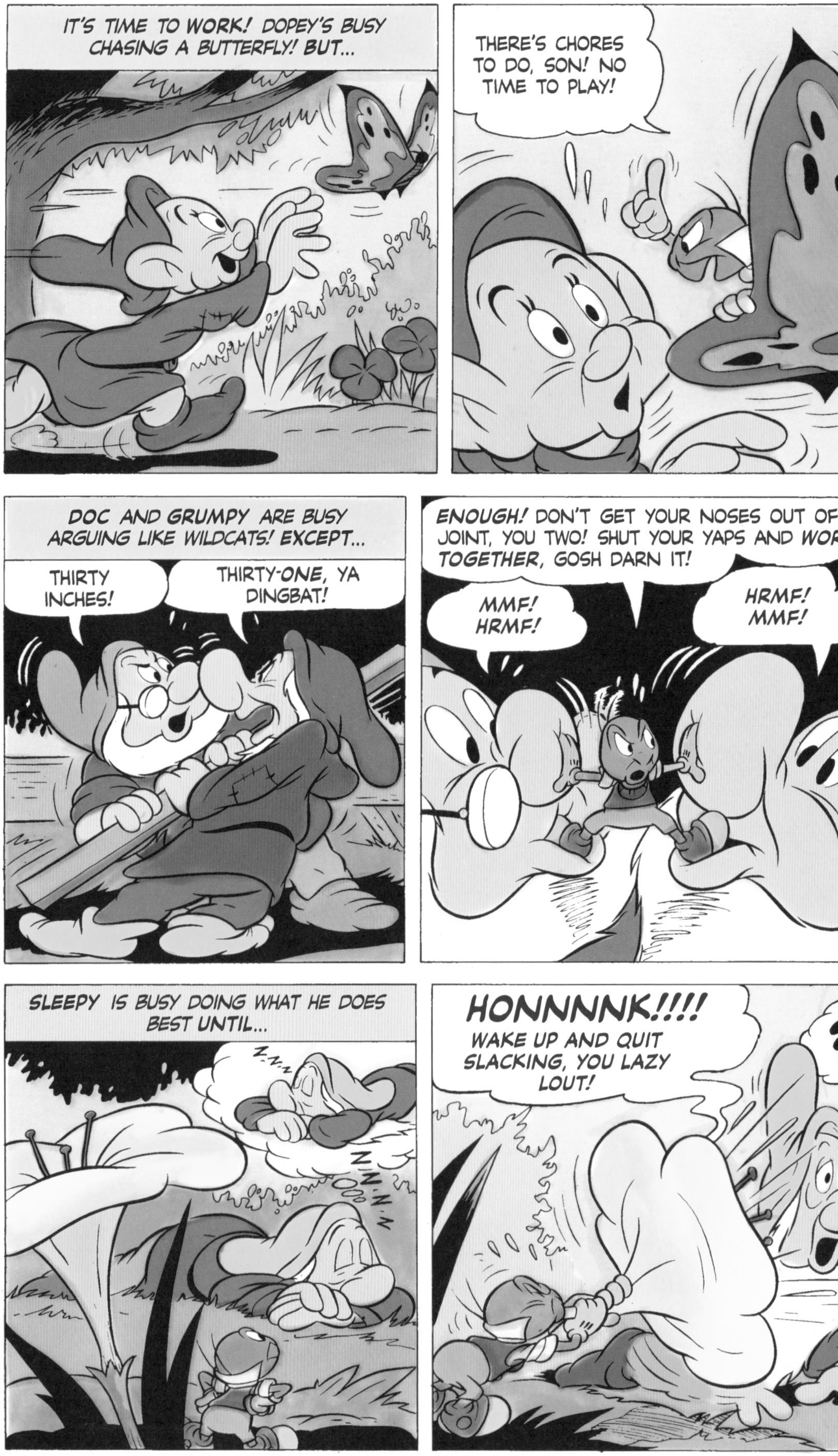
IT'S TIME TO WORK! DOPEY'S BUSY CHASING A BUTTERFLY! BUT...
THERE'S CHORES TO DO, SON! NO TIME TO PLAY!
DOC AND GRUMPY ARE BUSY ARGUING LIKE WILDCATS! EXCEPT...
THIRTY INCHES!
THIRTY-ONE, YA DINGBAT!
ENOUGH! DON'T GET YOUR NOSES OUT OF JOINT, YOU TWO! SHUT YOUR YAPS AND WORK TOGETHER, GOSH DARN IT!
MMF! HRMF!
HRMF! MMF!
SLEEPY IS BUSY DOING WHAT HE DOES BEST UNTIL...
Z-Z-Z
Z Z Z Z
HONNNNK!!!!
WAKE UP AND QUIT SLACKING, YOU LAZY LOUT!
?

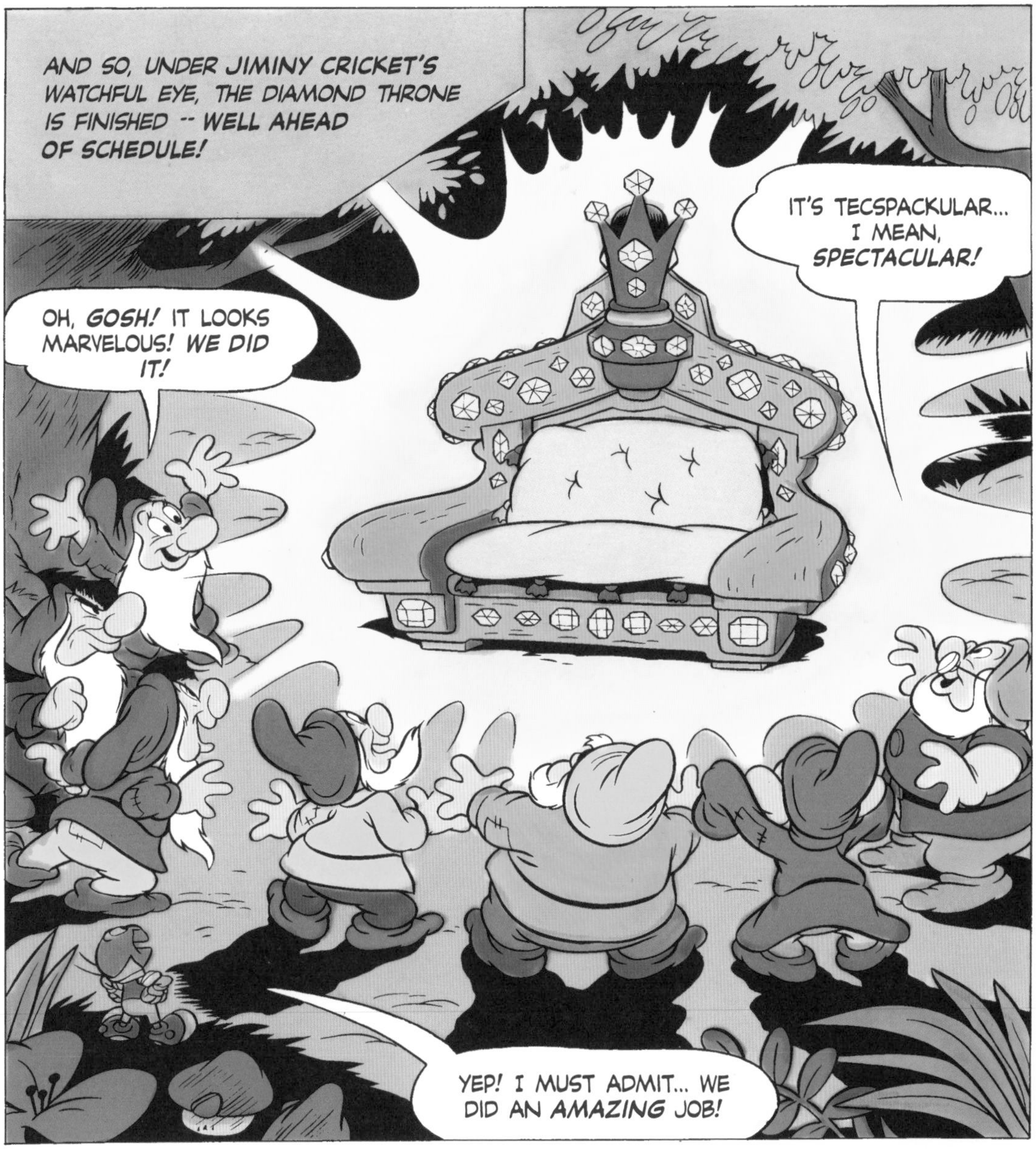
AND SO, UNDER JIMINY CRICKET'S WATCHFUL EYE, THE DIAMOND THRONE IS FINISHED -- WELL AHEAD OF SCHEDULE!
OH, GOSH! IT LOOKS MARVELOUS! WE DID IT!
IT'S TECSPACKULAR... I MEAN, SPECTACULAR!
YEP! I MUST ADMIT... WE DID AN AMAZING JOB!

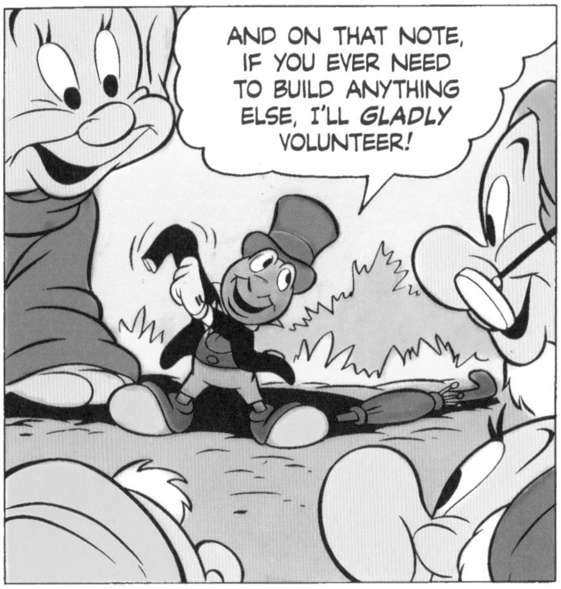
AND ON THAT NOTE, IF YOU EVER NEED TO BUILD ANYTHING ELSE, I'LL GLADLY VOLUNTEER!

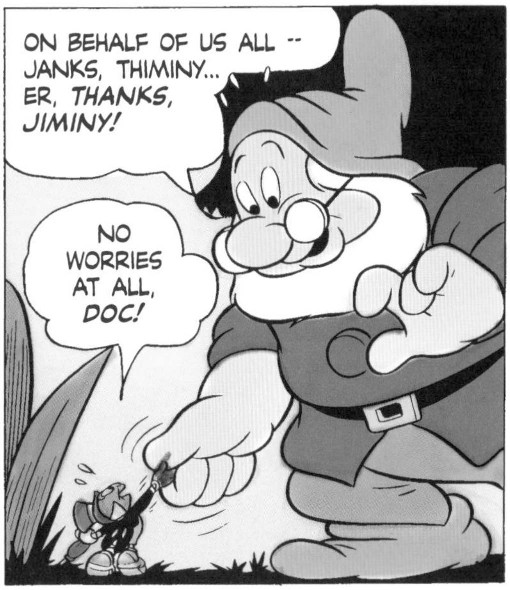
ON BEHALF OF US ALL -- JANKS, THIMINY... ER, THANKS, JIMINY!
NO WORRIES AT ALL, DOC!

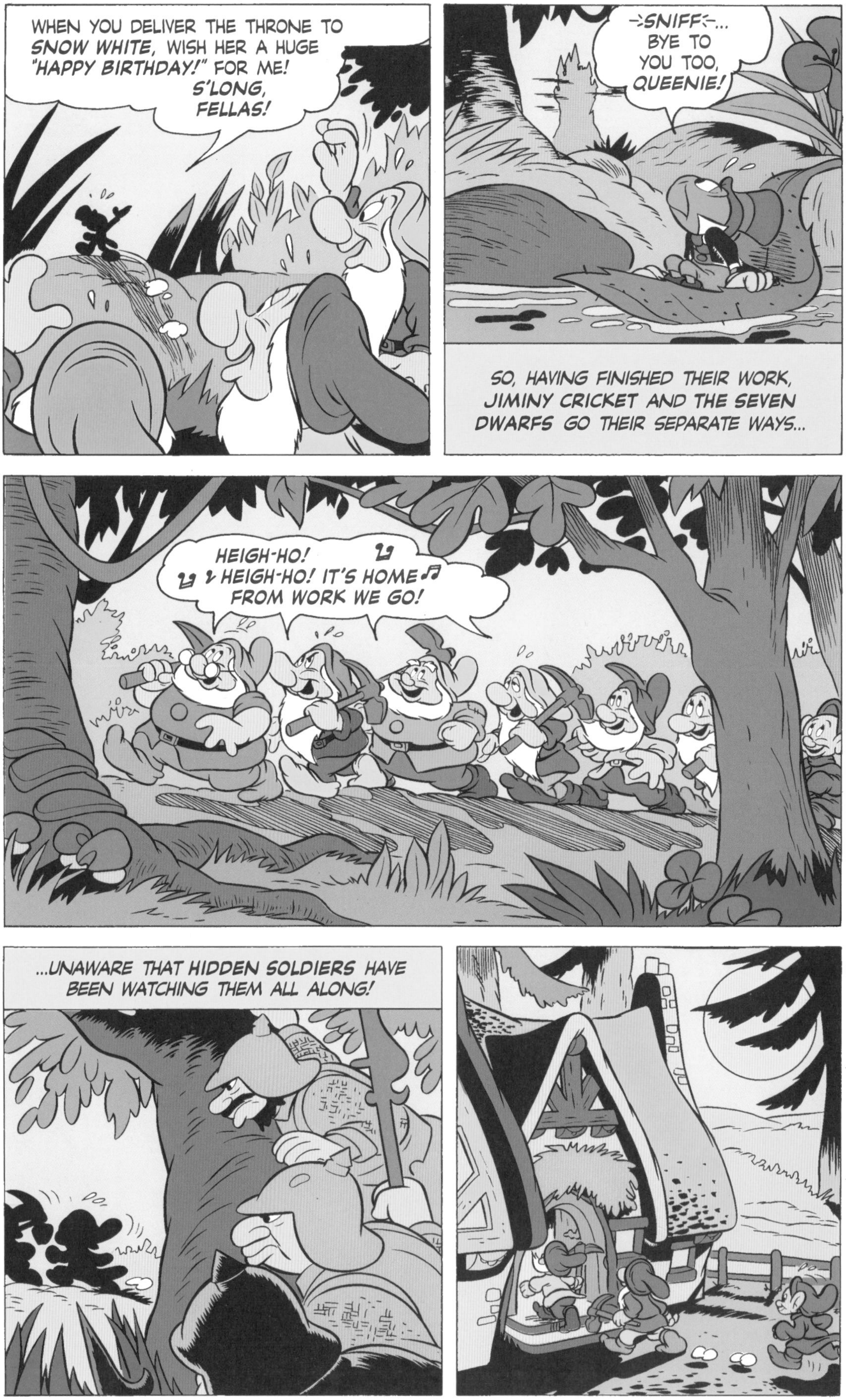
WHEN YOU DELIVER THE THRONE TO SNOW WHITE, WISH HER A HUGE "HAPPY BIRTHDAY!" FOR ME! S'LONG, FELLAS!
SNIFF... BYE TO YOU TOO, QUEENIE!
SO, HAVING FINISHED THEIR WORK, JIMINY CRICKET AND THE SEVEN DWARFS GO THEIR SEPARATE WAYS...
HEIGH-HO! HEIGH-HO! IT'S HOME FROM WORK WE GO!
...UNAWARE THAT HIDDEN SOLDIERS HAVE BEEN WATCHING THEM ALL ALONG!

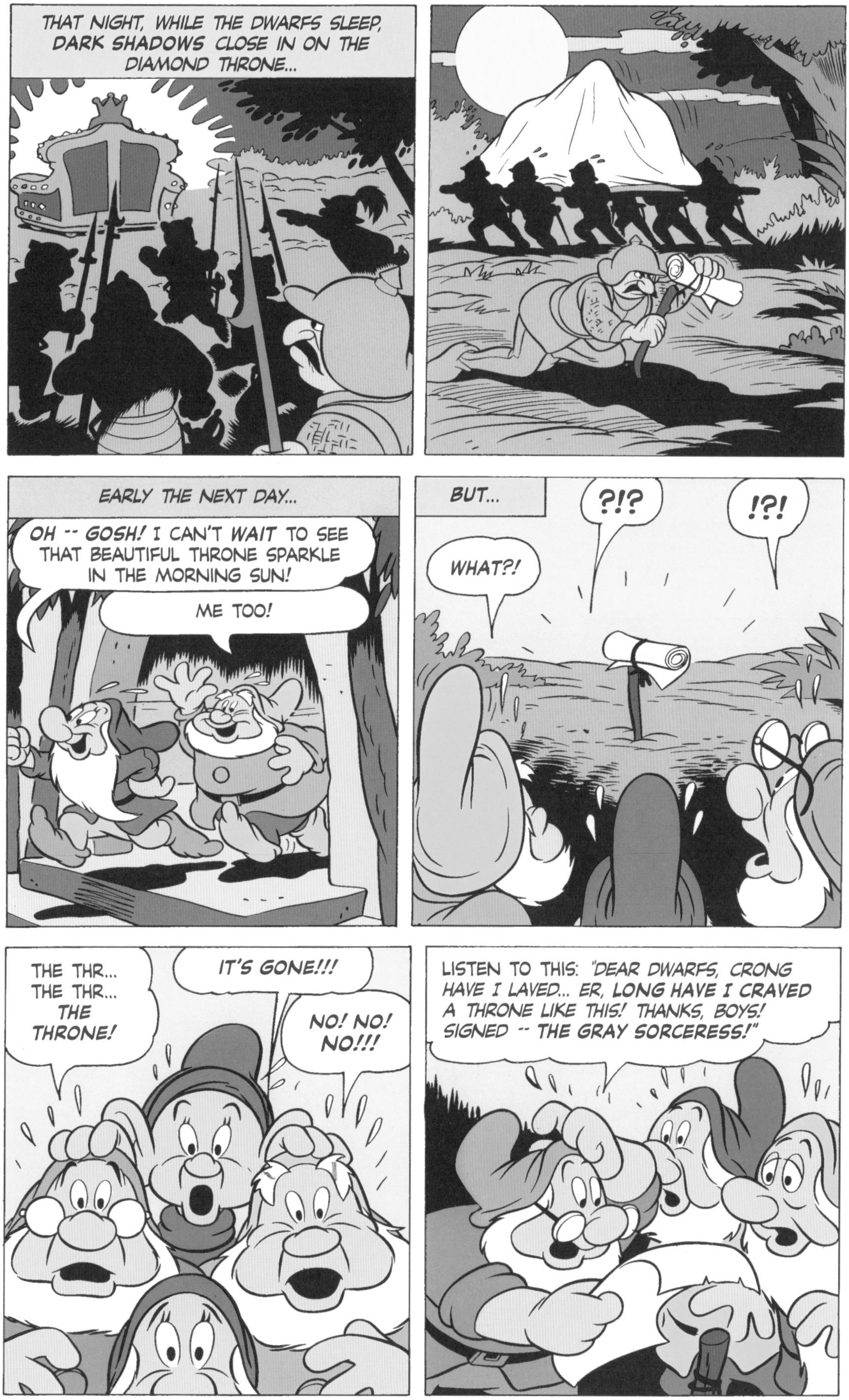
THAT NIGHT, WHILE THE DWARFS SLEEP, DARK SHADOWS CLOSE IN ON THE DIAMOND THRONE...
EARLY THE NEXT DAY...
OH -- GOSH! I CAN'T WAIT TO SEE THAT BEAUTIFUL THRONE SPARKLE IN THE MORNING SUN!
ME TOO!
BUT...
WHAT?!
?!?
!?!
THE THR... THE THR... THE THRONE!
IT'S GONE!!!
NO! NO! NO!!!
LISTEN TO THIS: "DEAR DWARFS, CRONG HAVE I LAVED... ER, LONG HAVE I CRAVED A THRONE LIKE THIS! THANKS, BOYS! SIGNED -- THE GRAY SORCERESS!"

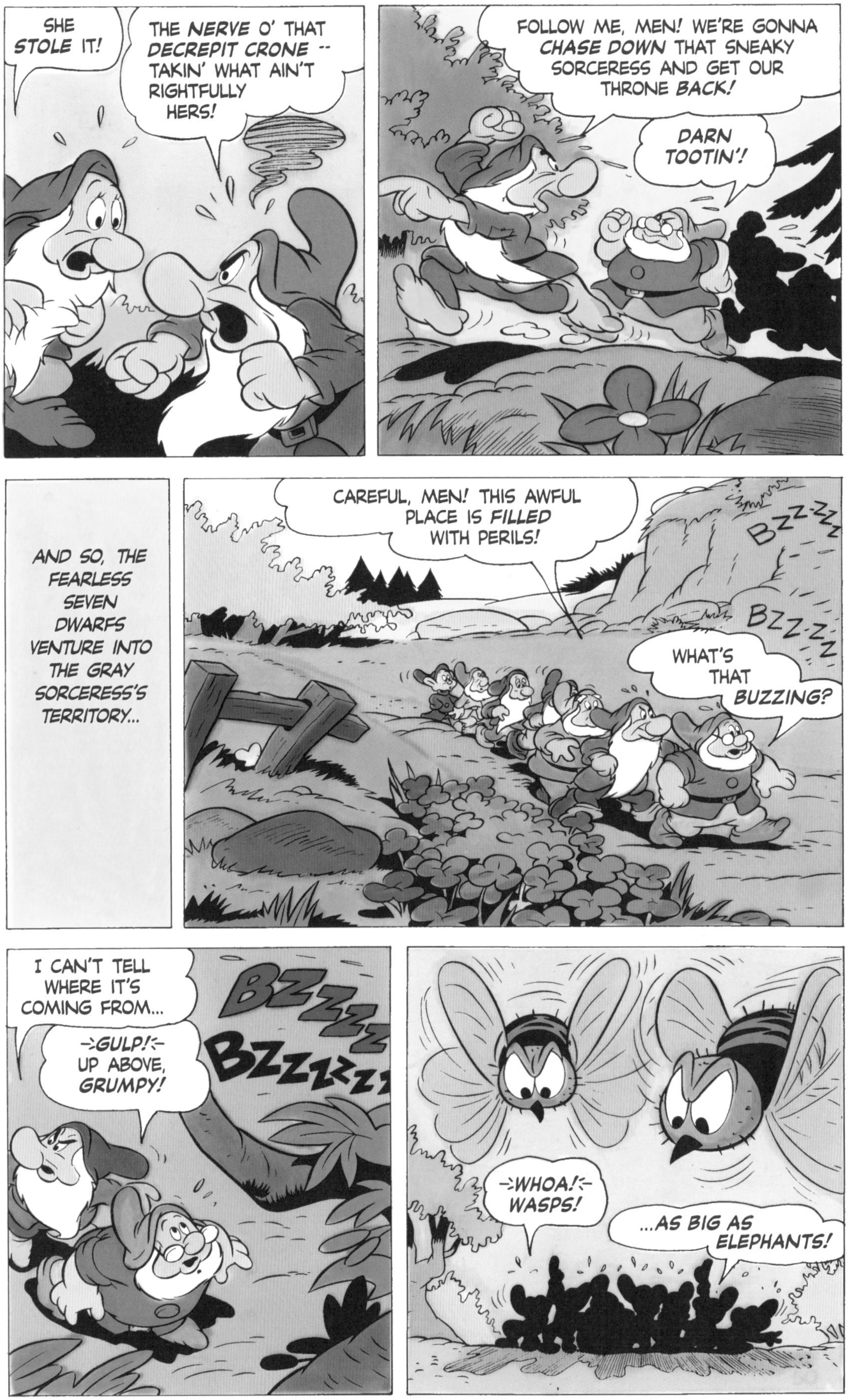
SHE STOLE IT!
THE NERVE O' THAT DECREPIT CRONE -- TAKIN' WHAT AIN'T RIGHTFULLY HERS!
FOLLOW ME, MEN! WE'RE GONNA CHASE DOWN THAT SNEAKY SORCERESS AND GET OUR THRONE BACK!
DARN TOOTIN'!
AND SO, THE FEARLESS SEVEN DWARFS VENTURE INTO THE GRAY SORCERESS'S TERRITORY...
CAREFUL, MEN! THIS AWFUL PLACE IS FILLED WITH PERILS!
BZZZZZ
BZZZZZ
WHAT'S THAT BUZZING?
I CAN'T TELL WHERE IT'S COMING FROM...
-GULP!- UP ABOVE, GRUMPY!
BZZZZ
BZZZZZZZ
-WHOA!- WASPS!
...AS BIG AS ELEPHANTS!

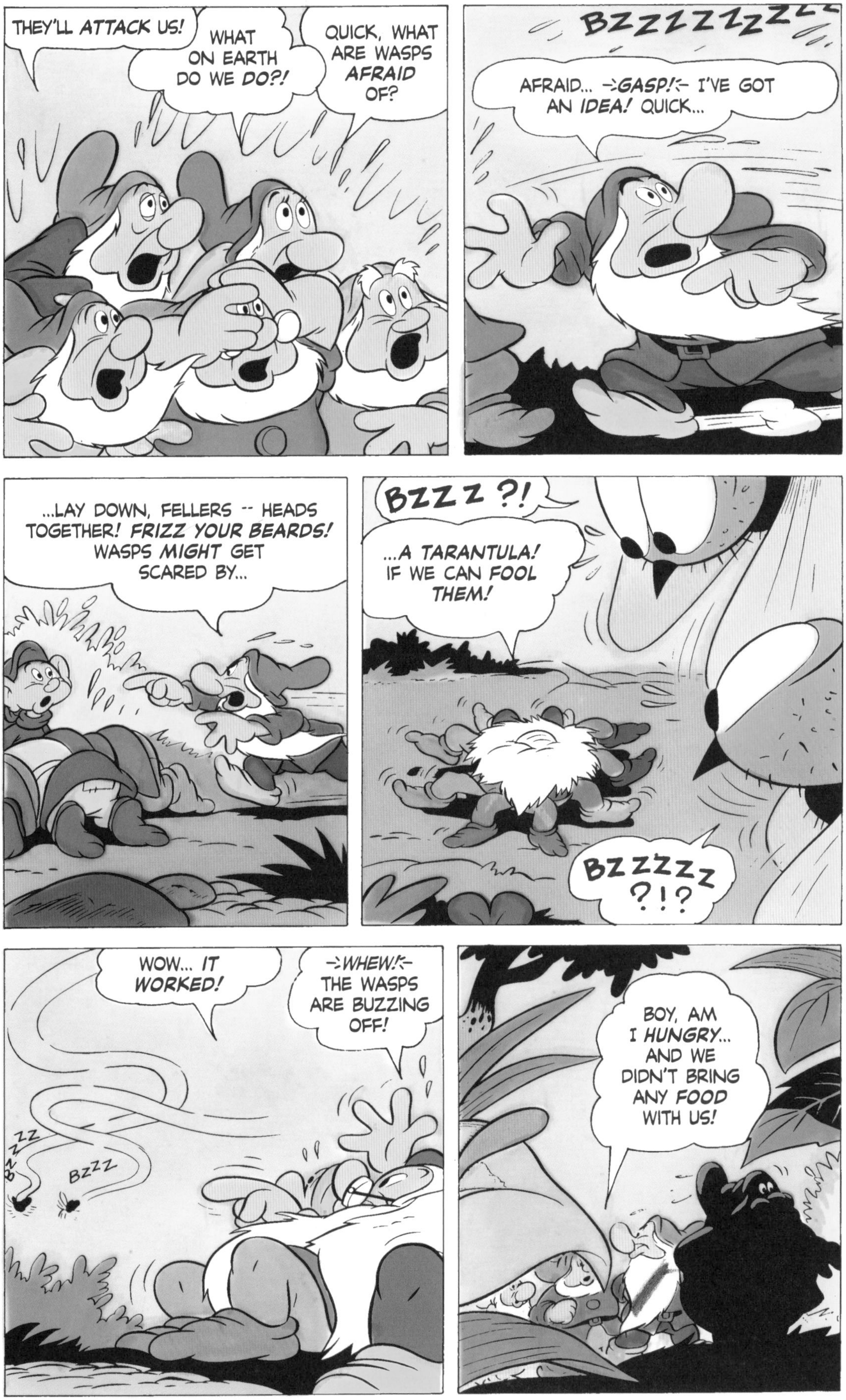
THEY'LL ATTACK US!
WHAT ON EARTH DO WE DO?!
QUICK, WHAT ARE WASPS AFRAID OF?
BZZZZZZZZ
AFRAID... GASP! I'VE GOT AN IDEA! QUICK...
...LAY DOWN, FELLERS -- HEADS TOGETHER! FRIZZ YOUR BEARDS! WASPS MIGHT GET SCARED BY...
BZZZ ?!
...A TARANTULA! IF WE CAN FOOL THEM!
BZZZZZ ?!?
WOW... IT WORKED!
WHEW! THE WASPS ARE BUZZING OFF!
BZZZ
BZZZ
BOY, AM I HUNGRY... AND WE DIDN'T BRING ANY FOOD WITH US!

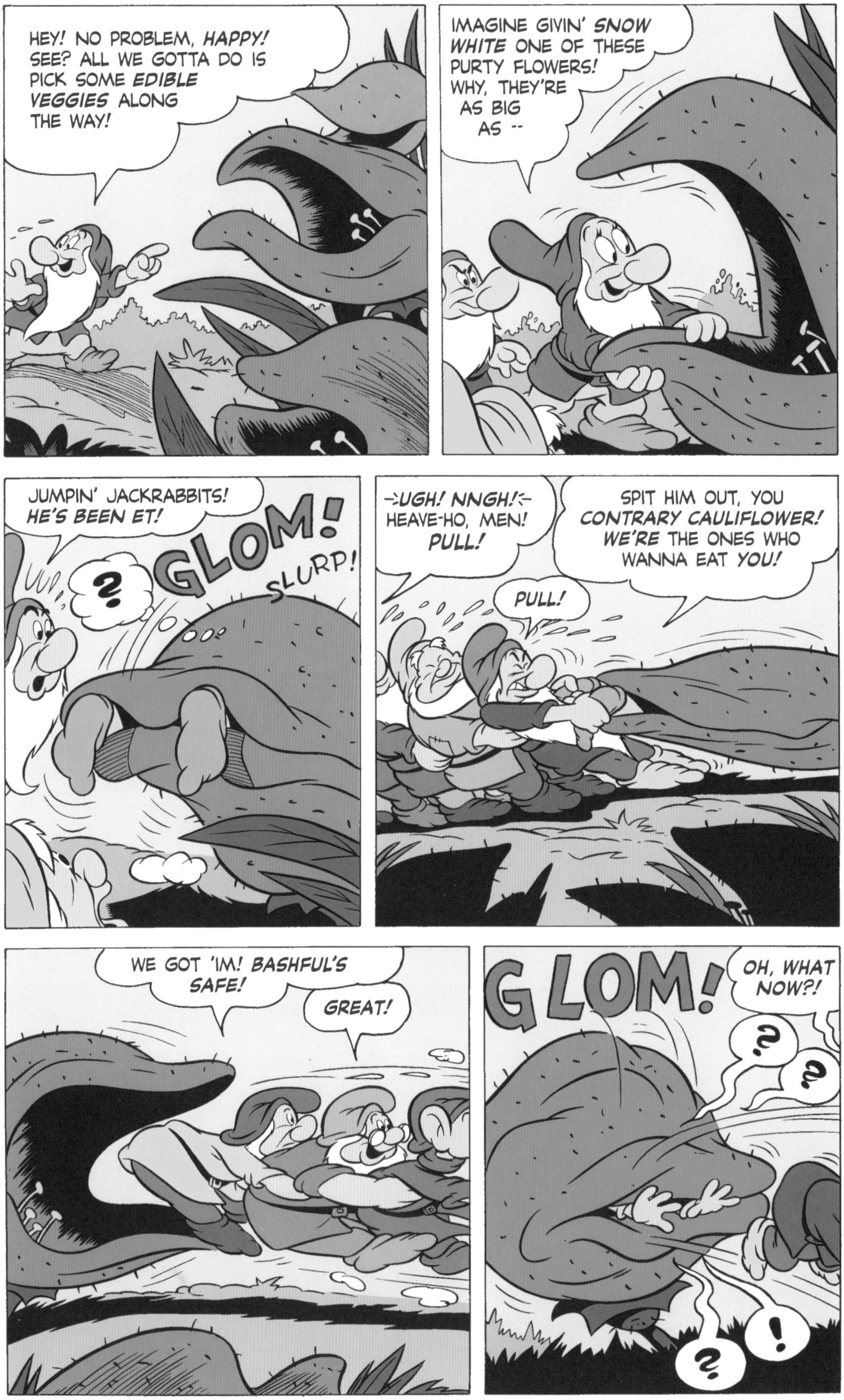
HEY! NO PROBLEM, HAPPY! SEE? ALL WE GOTTA DO IS PICK SOME EDIBLE VEGGIES ALONG THE WAY!
IMAGINE GIVIN' SNOW WHITE ONE OF THESE PURTY FLOWERS! WHY, THEY'RE AS BIG AS --
JUMPIN' JACKRABBITS! HE'S BEEN ET!
GLOM!
SLURP!
?
UGH! NNGH! HEAVE-HO, MEN! PULL!
SPIT HIM OUT, YOU CONTRARY CAULIFLOWER! WE'RE THE ONES WHO WANNA EAT YOU!
PULL!
WE GOT 'IM! BASHFUL'S SAFE!
GREAT!
GLOM!
OH, WHAT NOW?!
?
?
?
!

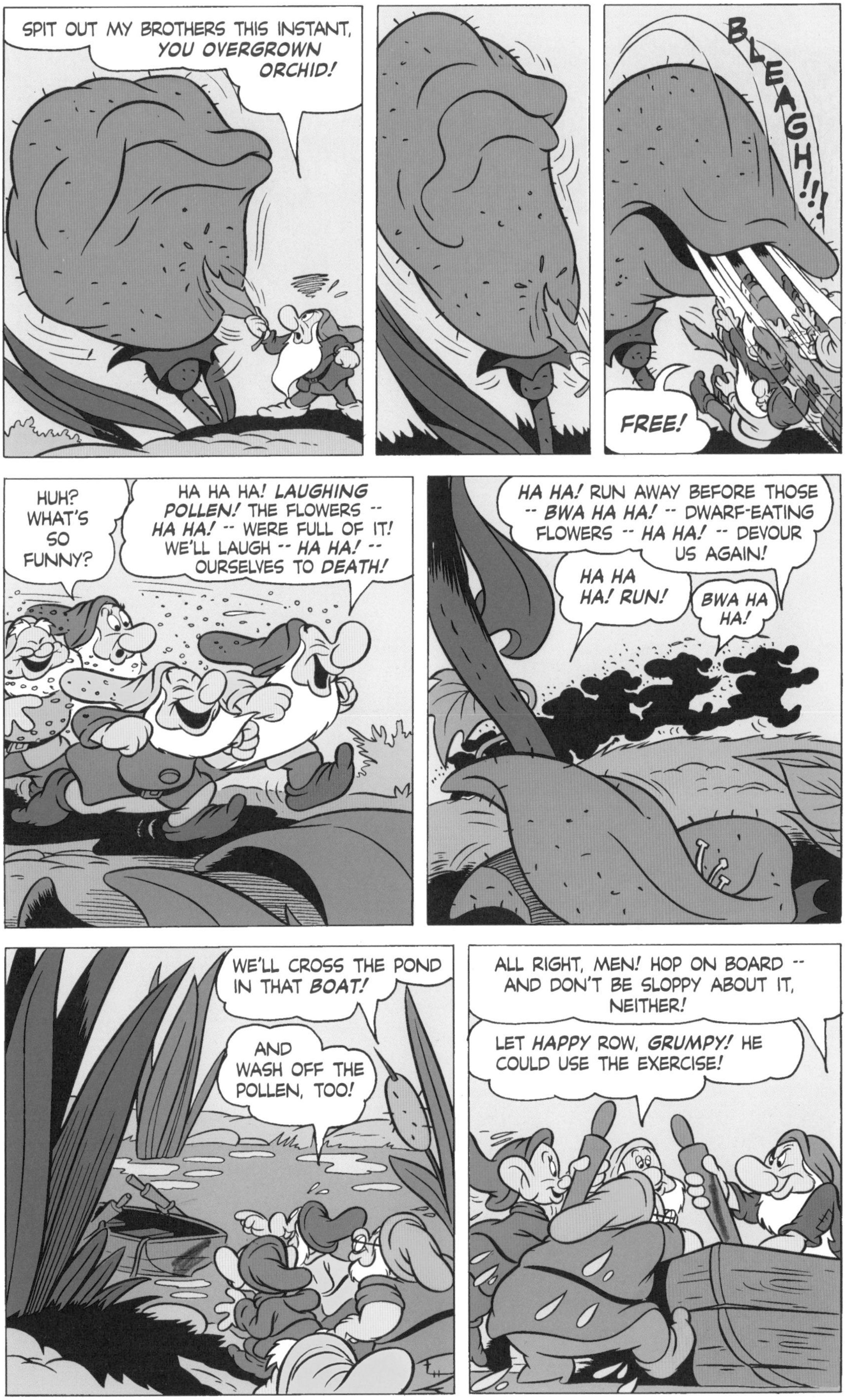

SPIT OUT MY BROTHERS THIS INSTANT, *YOU OVERGROWN ORCHID!*
BLEAGH!!!
FREE!
HUH? WHAT'S SO FUNNY?
HA HA HA! *LAUGHING POLLEN!* THE FLOWERS -- *HA HA!* -- WERE FULL OF IT! WE'LL LAUGH -- *HA HA!* -- OURSELVES TO *DEATH!*
HA HA! RUN AWAY BEFORE THOSE -- *BWA HA HA!* -- DWARF-EATING FLOWERS -- *HA HA!* -- DEVOUR US AGAIN!
HA HA HA! RUN!
BWA HA HA!
WE'LL CROSS THE POND IN THAT *BOAT!*
AND WASH OFF THE POLLEN, TOO!
ALL RIGHT, MEN! HOP ON BOARD -- AND DON'T BE SLOPPY ABOUT IT, NEITHER!
LET *HAPPY* ROW, *GRUMPY!* HE COULD USE THE EXERCISE!

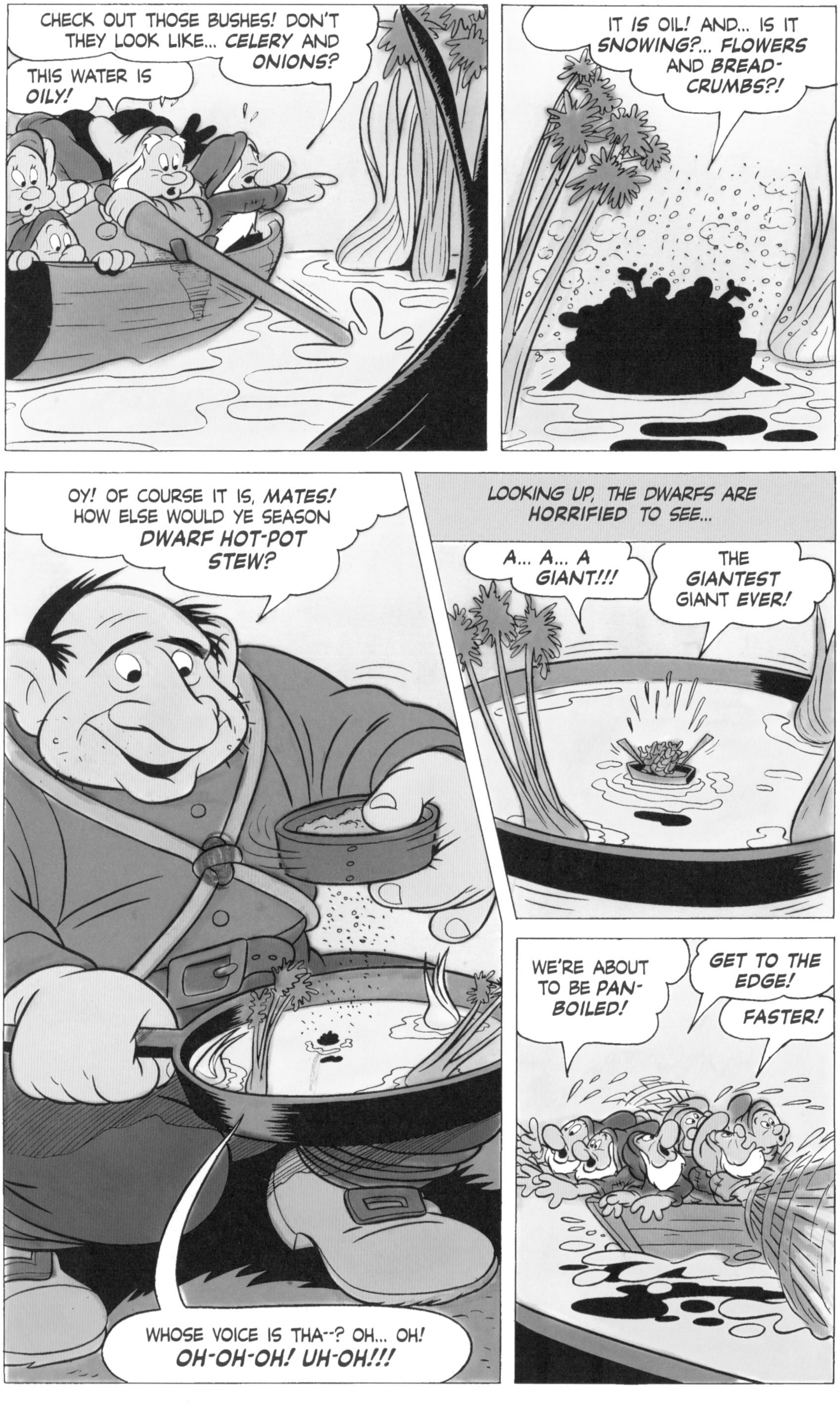
CHECK OUT THOSE BUSHES! DON'T THEY LOOK LIKE... CELERY AND ONIONS?
THIS WATER IS OILY!
IT IS OIL! AND... IS IT SNOWING?... FLOWERS AND BREAD-CRUMBS?!
OY! OF COURSE IT IS, MATES! HOW ELSE WOULD YE SEASON DWARF HOT-POT STEW?
WHOSE VOICE IS THA--? OH... OH! OH-OH-OH! UH-OH!!!
LOOKING UP, THE DWARFS ARE HORRIFIED TO SEE...
A... A... A GIANT!!!
THE GIANTEST GIANT EVER!
WE'RE ABOUT TO BE PAN-BOILED!
GET TO THE EDGE!
FASTER!

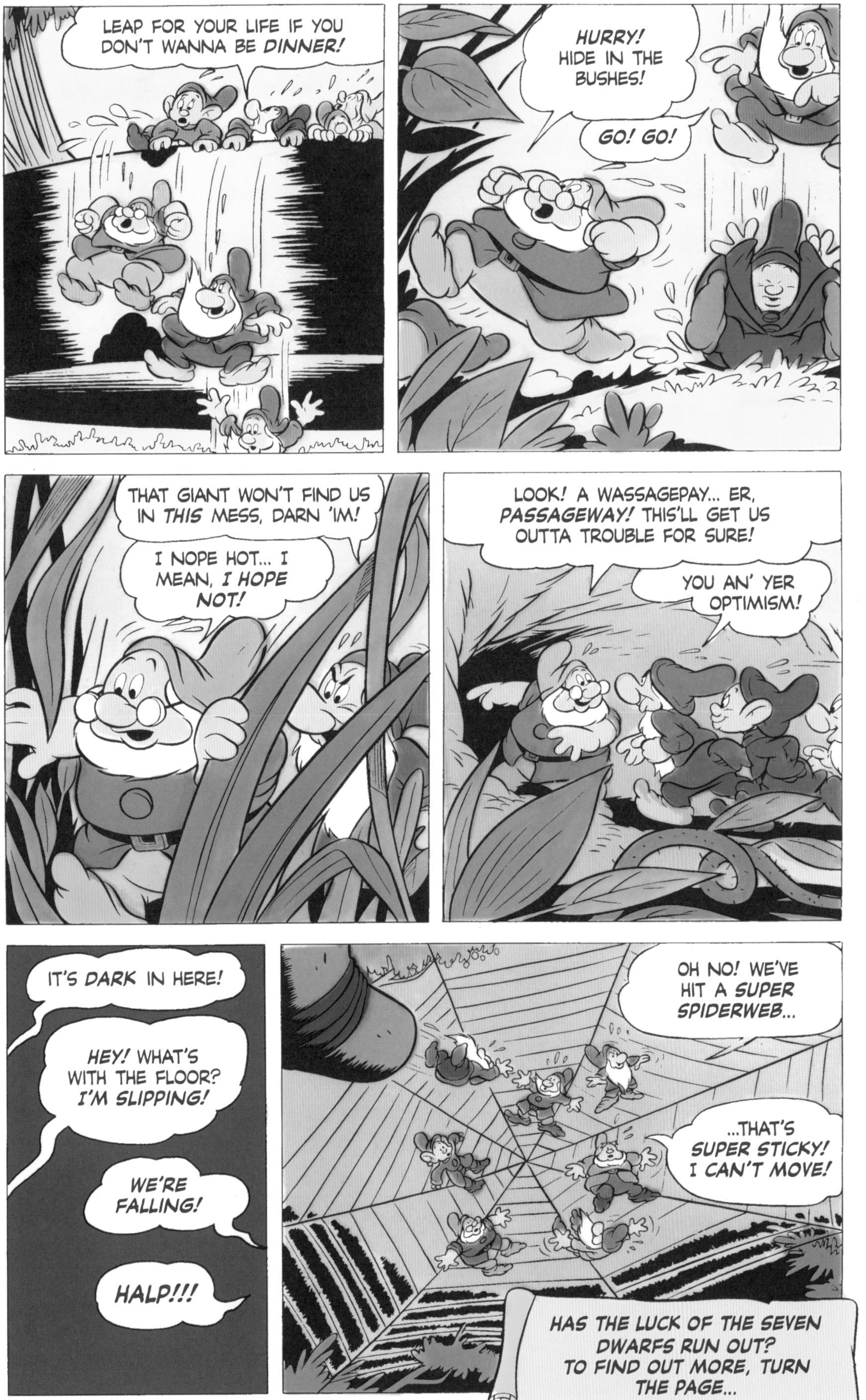
LEAP FOR YOUR LIFE IF YOU DON'T WANNA BE DINNER!
HURRY! HIDE IN THE BUSHES!
GO! GO!
THAT GIANT WON'T FIND US IN THIS MESS, DARN 'IM!
I NOPE HOT... I MEAN, I HOPE NOT!
LOOK! A WASSAGEPAY... ER, PASSAGEWAY! THIS'LL GET US OUTTA TROUBLE FOR SURE!
YOU AN' YER OPTIMISM!
IT'S DARK IN HERE!
HEY! WHAT'S WITH THE FLOOR? I'M SLIPPING!
WE'RE FALLING!
HALP!!!
OH NO! WE'VE HIT A SUPER SPIDERWEB...
...THAT'S SUPER STICKY! I CAN'T MOVE!
HAS THE LUCK OF THE SEVEN DWARFS RUN OUT? TO FIND OUT MORE, TURN THE PAGE...

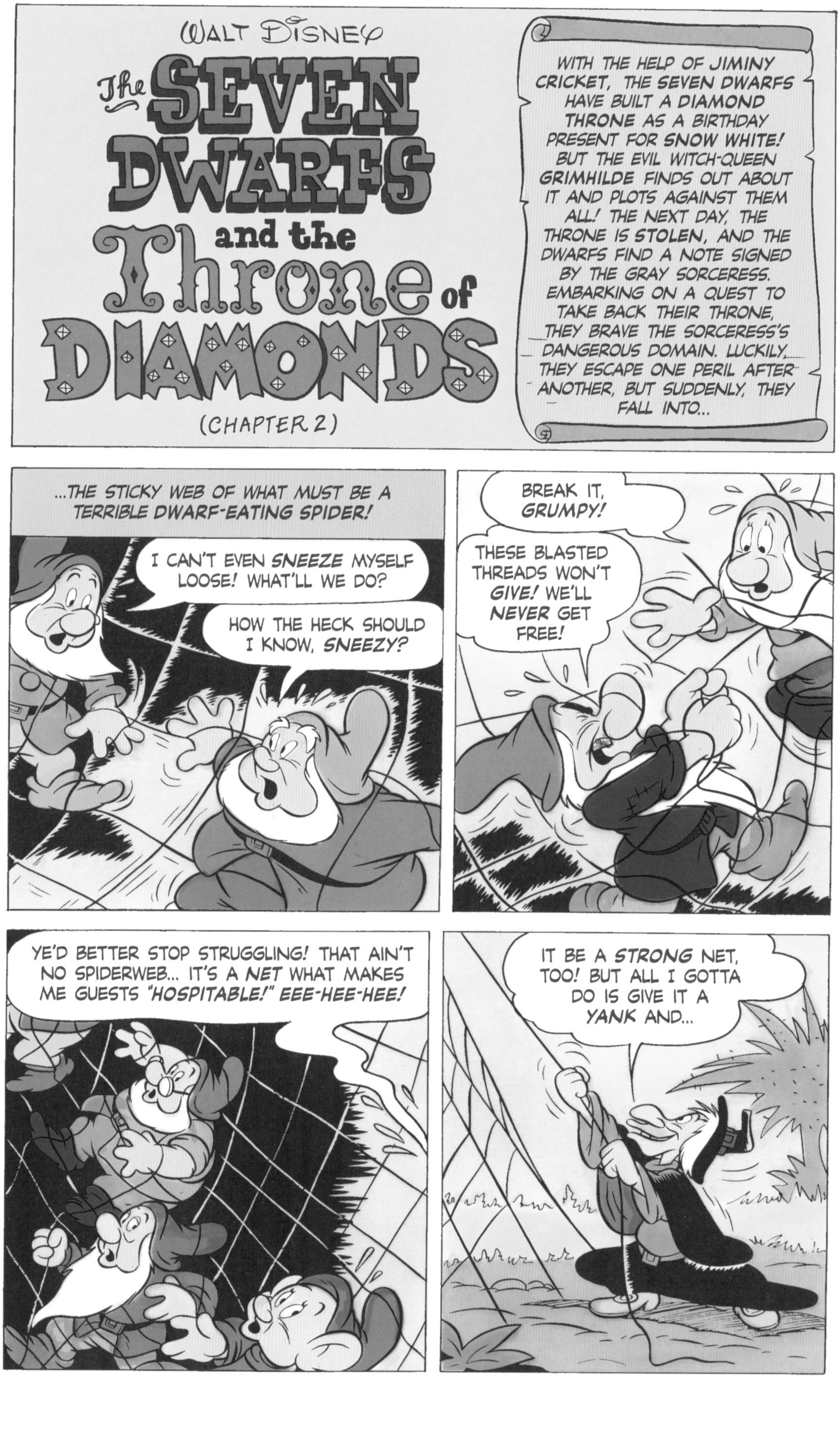
WALT DISNEY
The SEVEN DWARFS and the Throne of DIAMONDS
(CHAPTER 2)
WITH THE HELP OF JIMINY CRICKET, THE SEVEN DWARFS HAVE BUILT A DIAMOND THRONE AS A BIRTHDAY PRESENT FOR SNOW WHITE! BUT THE EVIL WITCH-QUEEN GRIMHILDE FINDS OUT ABOUT IT AND PLOTS AGAINST THEM ALL! THE NEXT DAY, THE THRONE IS STOLEN, AND THE DWARFS FIND A NOTE SIGNED BY THE GRAY SORCERESS. EMBARKING ON A QUEST TO TAKE BACK THEIR THRONE, THEY BRAVE THE SORCERESS'S DANGEROUS DOMAIN. LUCKILY, THEY ESCAPE ONE PERIL AFTER ANOTHER, BUT SUDDENLY, THEY FALL INTO...
...THE STICKY WEB OF WHAT MUST BE A TERRIBLE DWARF-EATING SPIDER!
I CAN'T EVEN SNEEZE MYSELF LOOSE! WHAT'LL WE DO?
HOW THE HECK SHOULD I KNOW, SNEEZY?
BREAK IT, GRUMPY!
THESE BLASTED THREADS WON'T GIVE! WE'LL NEVER GET FREE!
YE'D BETTER STOP STRUGGLING! THAT AIN'T NO SPIDERWEB... IT'S A NET WHAT MAKES ME GUESTS "HOSPITABLE!" EEE-HEE-HEE!
IT BE A STRONG NET, TOO! BUT ALL I GOTTA DO IS GIVE IT A YANK AND...

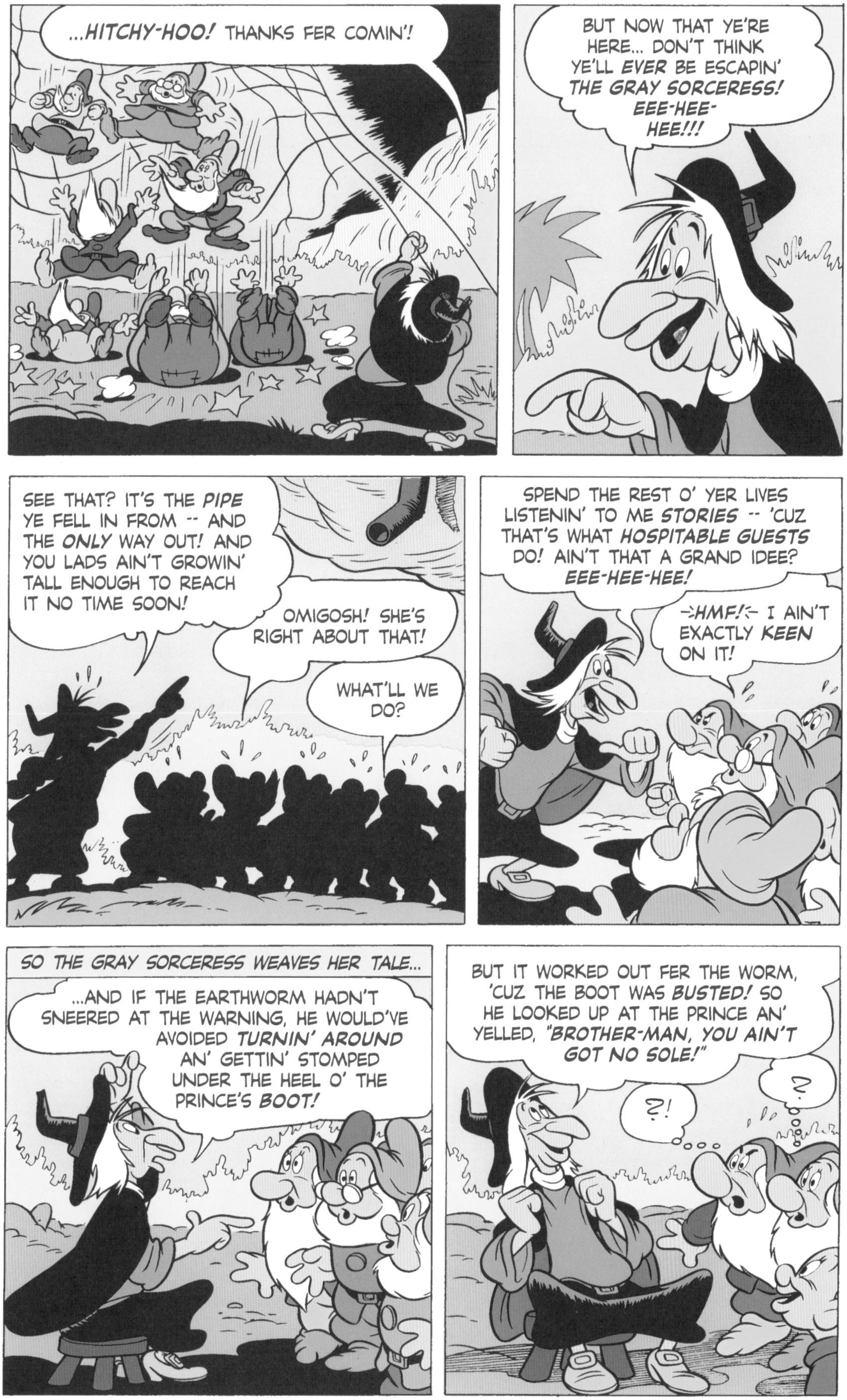
...HITCHY-HOO! THANKS FER COMIN'!
BUT NOW THAT YE'RE HERE... DON'T THINK YE'LL EVER BE ESCAPIN' THE GRAY SORCERESS! EEE-HEE-HEE!!!
SEE THAT? IT'S THE PIPE YE FELL IN FROM -- AND THE ONLY WAY OUT! AND YOU LADS AIN'T GROWIN' TALL ENOUGH TO REACH IT NO TIME SOON!
OMIGOSH! SHE'S RIGHT ABOUT THAT!
WHAT'LL WE DO?
SPEND THE REST O' YER LIVES LISTENIN' TO ME STORIES -- 'CUZ THAT'S WHAT HOSPITABLE GUESTS DO! AIN'T THAT A GRAND IDEE? EEE-HEE-HEE!
HMF! I AIN'T EXACTLY KEEN ON IT!
SO THE GRAY SORCERESS WEAVES HER TALE...
...AND IF THE EARTHWORM HADN'T SNEERED AT THE WARNING, HE WOULD'VE AVOIDED TURNIN' AROUND AN' GETTIN' STOMPED UNDER THE HEEL O' THE PRINCE'S BOOT!
BUT IT WORKED OUT FER THE WORM, 'CUZ THE BOOT WAS BUSTED! SO HE LOOKED UP AT THE PRINCE AN' YELLED, "BROTHER-MAN, YOU AIN'T GOT NO SOLE!"
?!
?

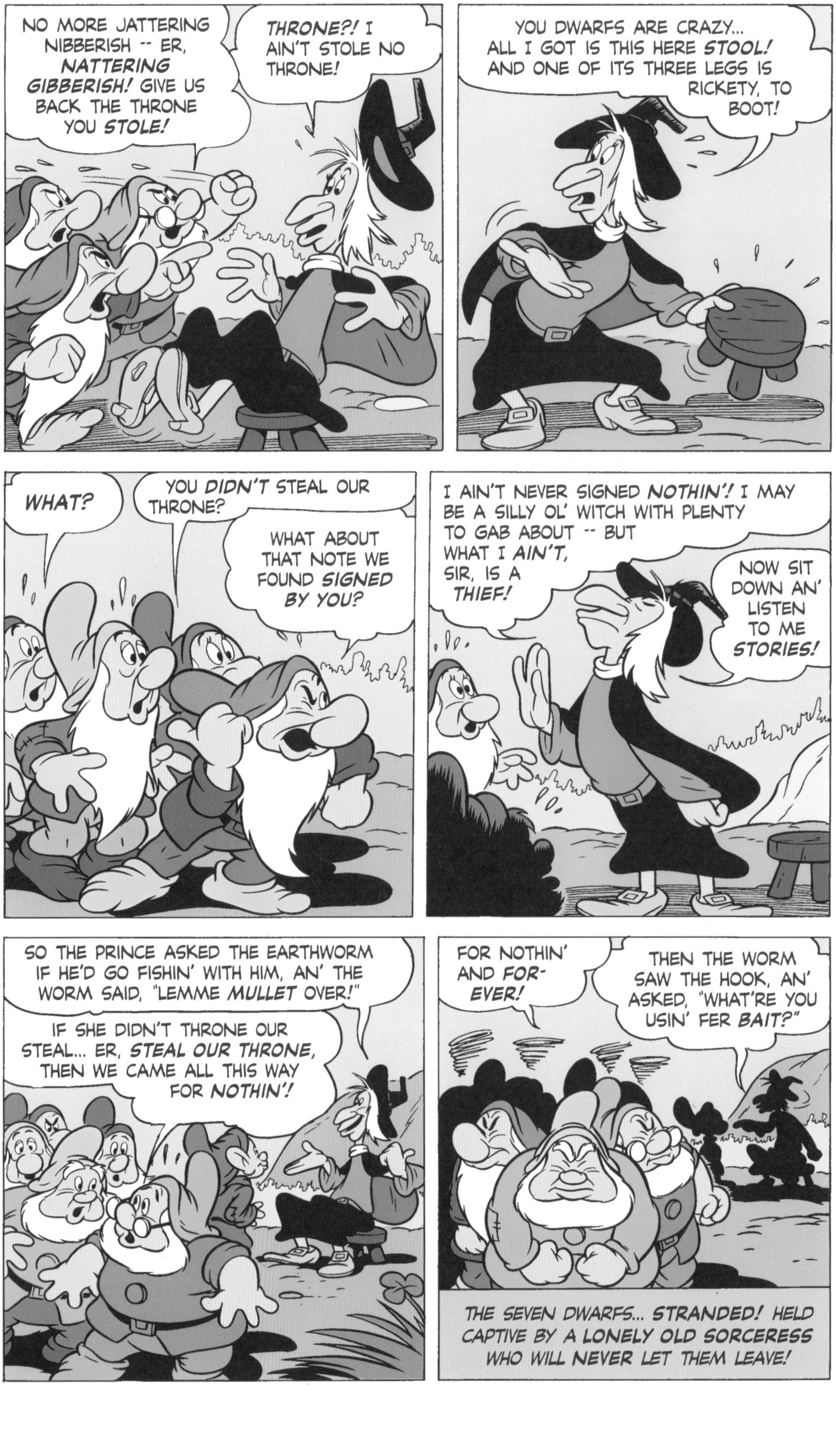

NO MORE JATTERING NIBBERISH -- ER, NATTERING GIBBERISH! GIVE US BACK THE THRONE YOU STOLE!
THRONE?! I AIN'T STOLE NO THRONE!
YOU DWARFS ARE CRAZY... ALL I GOT IS THIS HERE STOOL! AND ONE OF ITS THREE LEGS IS RICKETY, TO BOOT!
WHAT?
YOU DIDN'T STEAL OUR THRONE?
WHAT ABOUT THAT NOTE WE FOUND SIGNED BY YOU?
I AIN'T NEVER SIGNED NOTHIN'! I MAY BE A SILLY OL' WITCH WITH PLENTY TO GAB ABOUT -- BUT WHAT I AIN'T, SIR, IS A THIEF!
NOW SIT DOWN AN' LISTEN TO ME STORIES!
SO THE PRINCE ASKED THE EARTHWORM IF HE'D GO FISHIN' WITH HIM, AN' THE WORM SAID, "LEMME MULLET OVER!"
IF SHE DIDN'T THRONE OUR STEAL... ER, STEAL OUR THRONE, THEN WE CAME ALL THIS WAY FOR NOTHIN'!
FOR NOTHIN' AND FOR-EVER!
THEN THE WORM SAW THE HOOK, AN' ASKED, "WHAT'RE YOU USIN' FER BAIT?"
THE SEVEN DWARFS... STRANDED! HELD CAPTIVE BY A LONELY OLD SORCERESS WHO WILL NEVER LET THEM LEAVE!

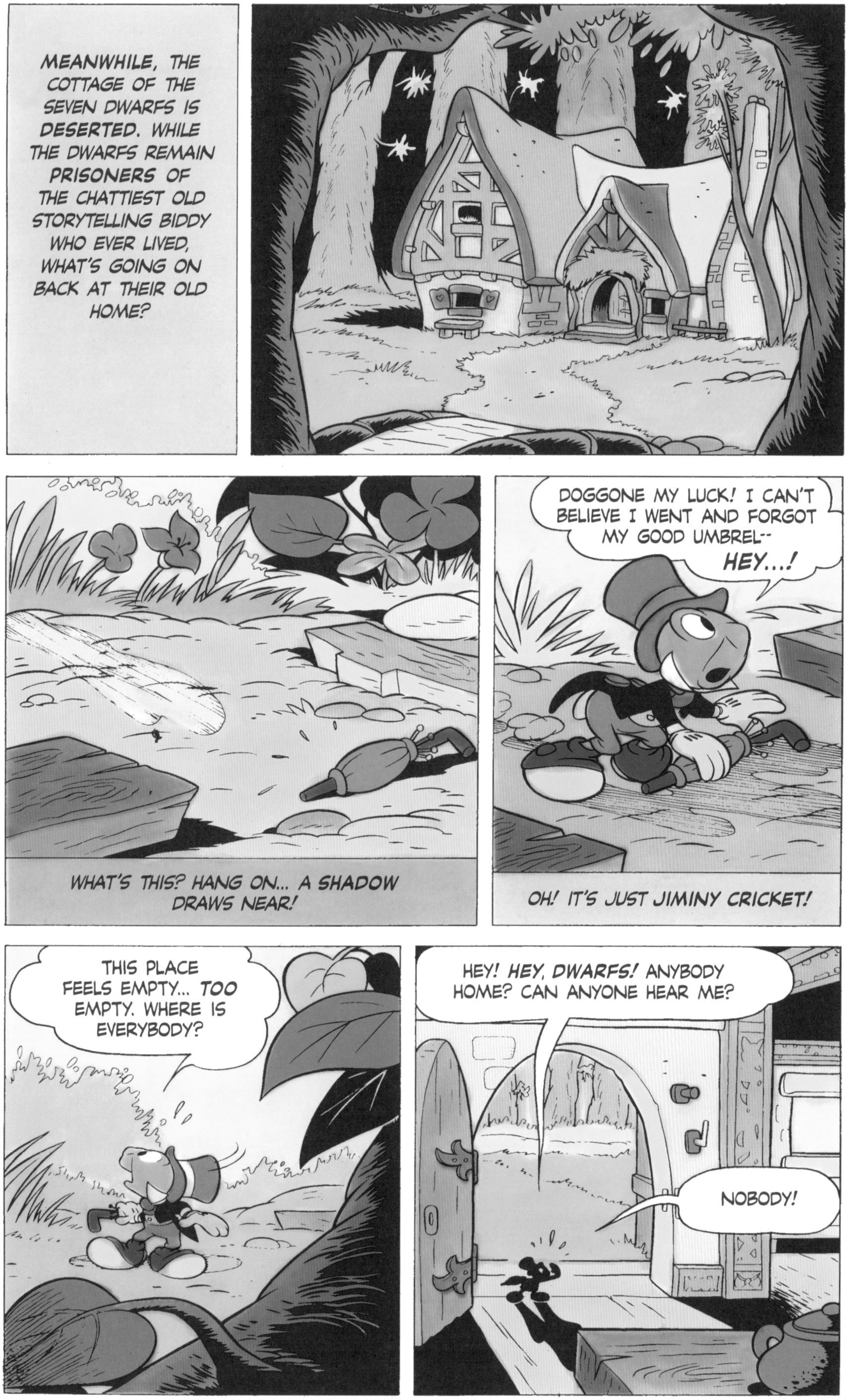
MEANWHILE, THE COTTAGE OF THE SEVEN DWARFS IS DESERTED. WHILE THE DWARFS REMAIN PRISONERS OF THE CHATTIEST OLD STORYTELLING BIDDY WHO EVER LIVED, WHAT'S GOING ON BACK AT THEIR OLD HOME?
WHAT'S THIS? HANG ON... A SHADOW DRAWS NEAR!
DOGGONE MY LUCK! I CAN'T BELIEVE I WENT AND FORGOT MY GOOD UMBREL-- HEY...!
OH! IT'S JUST JIMINY CRICKET!
THIS PLACE FEELS EMPTY... TOO EMPTY. WHERE IS EVERYBODY?
HEY! HEY, DWARFS! ANYBODY HOME? CAN ANYONE HEAR ME?
NOBODY!

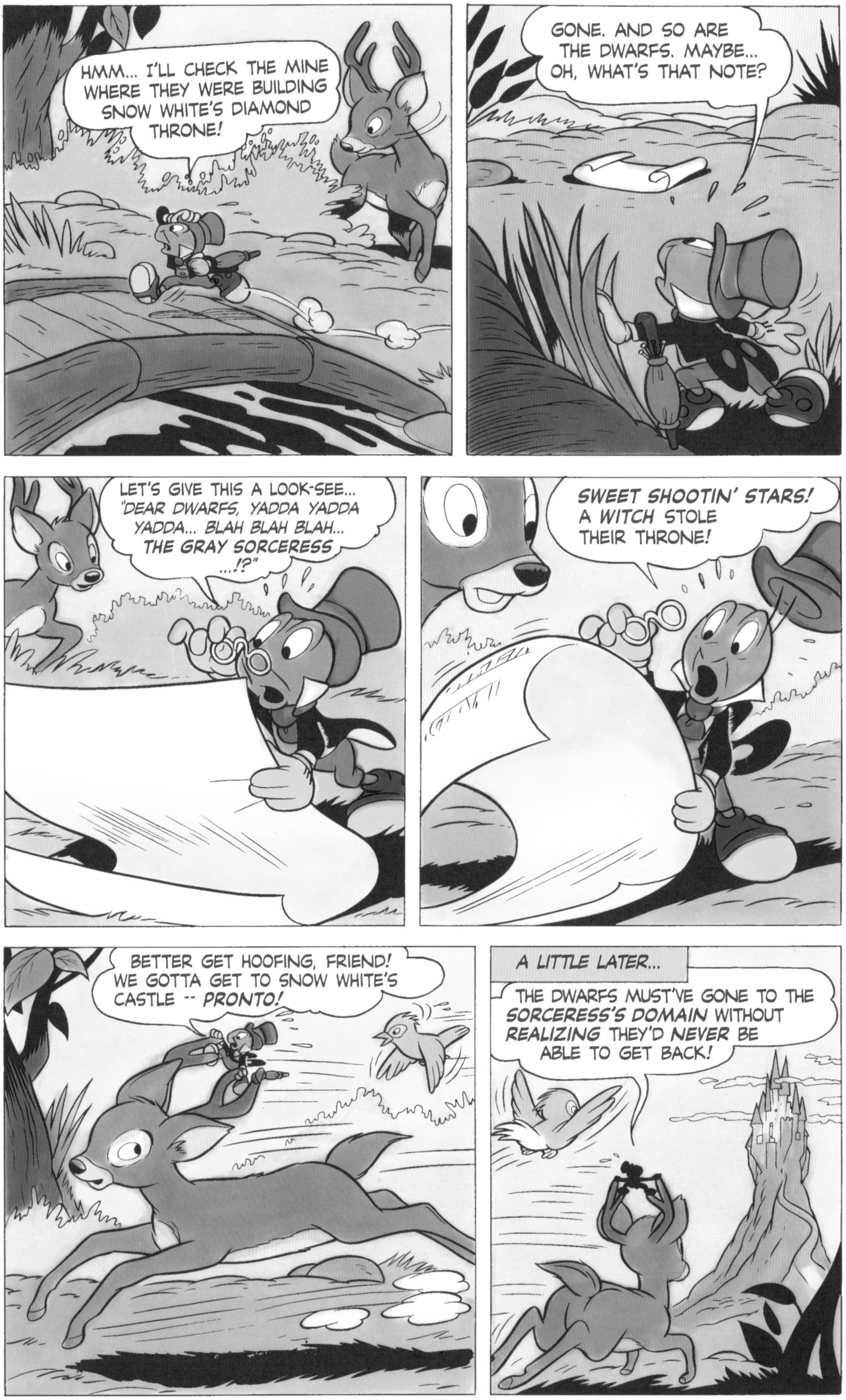
HMM... I'LL CHECK THE MINE WHERE THEY WERE BUILDING SNOW WHITE'S DIAMOND THRONE!
GONE. AND SO ARE THE DWARFS. MAYBE... OH, WHAT'S THAT NOTE?
LET'S GIVE THIS A LOOK-SEE... "DEAR DWARFS, YADDA YADDA YADDA... BLAH BLAH BLAH... THE GRAY SORCERESS ...!?"
SWEET SHOOTIN' STARS! A WITCH STOLE THEIR THRONE!
BETTER GET HOOFING, FRIEND! WE GOTTA GET TO SNOW WHITE'S CASTLE -- PRONTO!
A LITTLE LATER...
THE DWARFS MUST'VE GONE TO THE SORCERESS'S DOMAIN WITHOUT REALIZING THEY'D NEVER BE ABLE TO GET BACK!

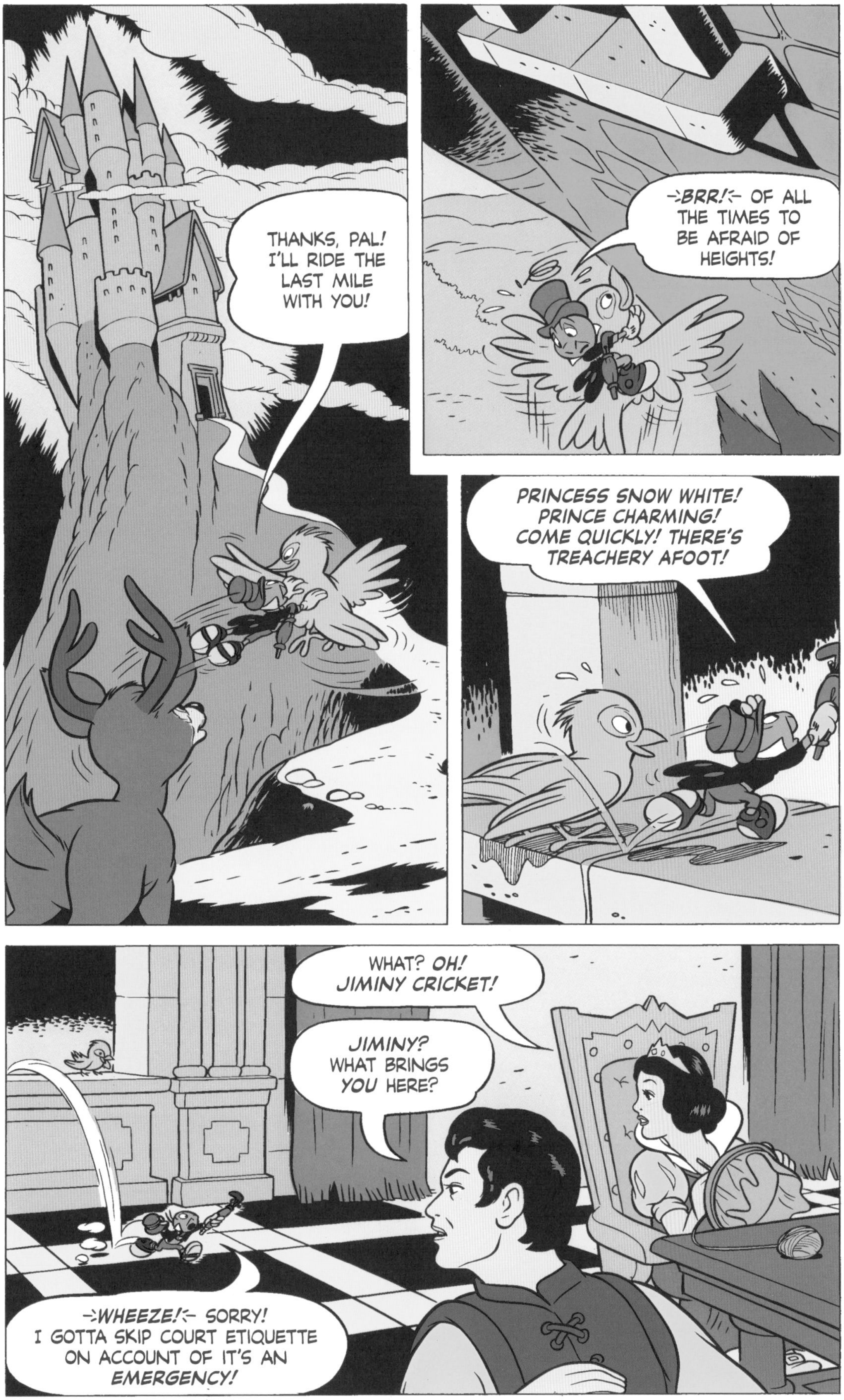
THANKS, PAL! I'LL RIDE THE LAST MILE WITH YOU!
-BRR!- OF ALL THE TIMES TO BE AFRAID OF HEIGHTS!
PRINCESS SNOW WHITE! PRINCE CHARMING! COME QUICKLY! THERE'S TREACHERY AFOOT!
WHAT? OH! JIMINY CRICKET!
JIMINY? WHAT BRINGS YOU HERE?
-WHEEZE!- SORRY! I GOTTA SKIP COURT ETIQUETTE ON ACCOUNT OF IT'S AN EMERGENCY!

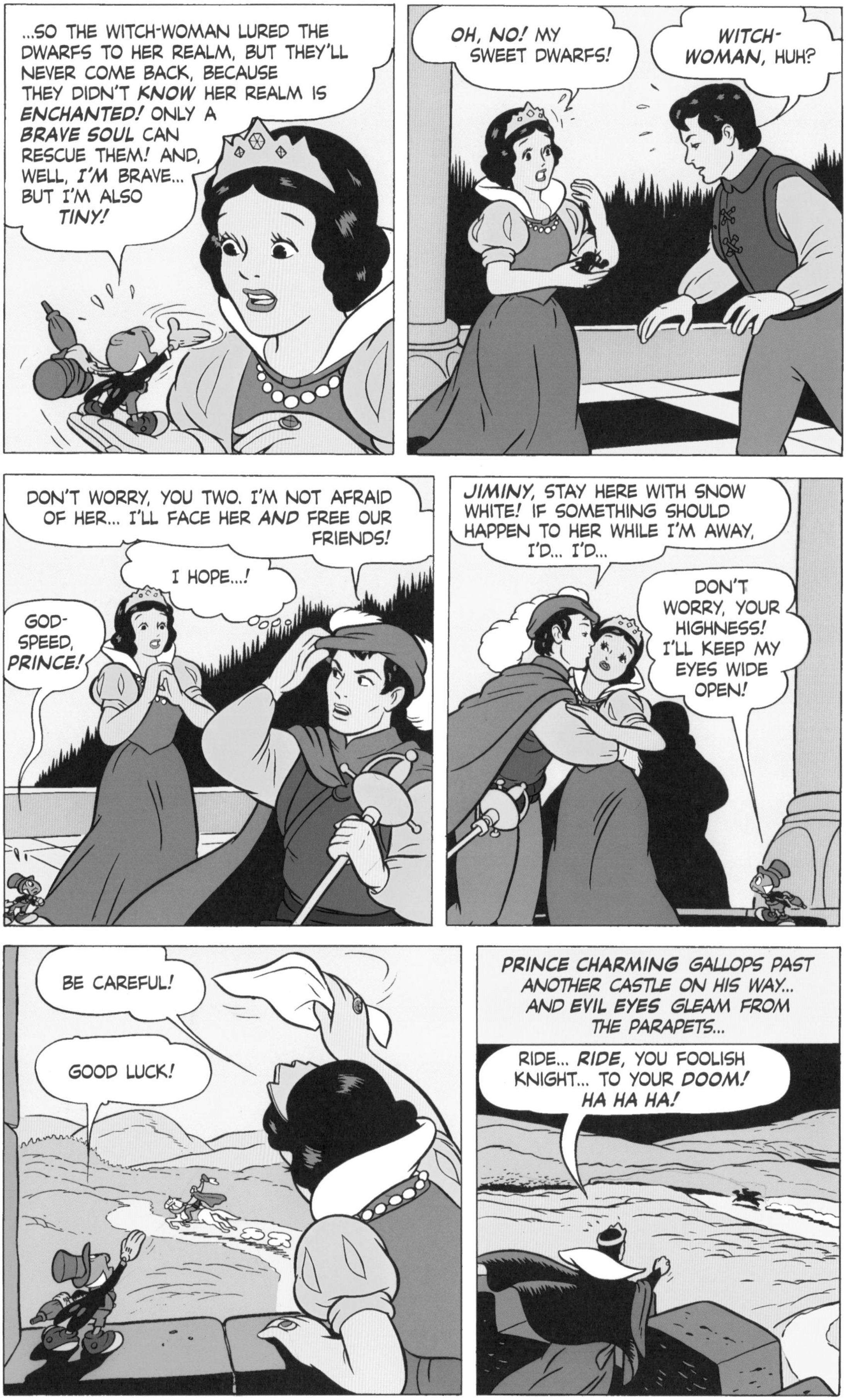
...SO THE WITCH-WOMAN LURED THE DWARFS TO HER REALM, BUT THEY'LL NEVER COME BACK, BECAUSE THEY DIDN'T KNOW HER REALM IS ENCHANTED! ONLY A BRAVE SOUL CAN RESCUE THEM! AND, WELL, I'M BRAVE... BUT I'M ALSO TINY!
OH, NO! MY SWEET DWARFS!
WITCH-WOMAN, HUH?
DON'T WORRY, YOU TWO. I'M NOT AFRAID OF HER... I'LL FACE HER AND FREE OUR FRIENDS!
I HOPE...!
GOD-SPEED, PRINCE!
JIMINY, STAY HERE WITH SNOW WHITE! IF SOMETHING SHOULD HAPPEN TO HER WHILE I'M AWAY, I'D... I'D...
DON'T WORRY, YOUR HIGHNESS! I'LL KEEP MY EYES WIDE OPEN!
BE CAREFUL!
GOOD LUCK!
PRINCE CHARMING GALLOPS PAST ANOTHER CASTLE ON HIS WAY... AND EVIL EYES GLEAM FROM THE PARAPETS...
RIDE... RIDE, YOU FOOLISH KNIGHT... TO YOUR DOOM! HA HA HA!

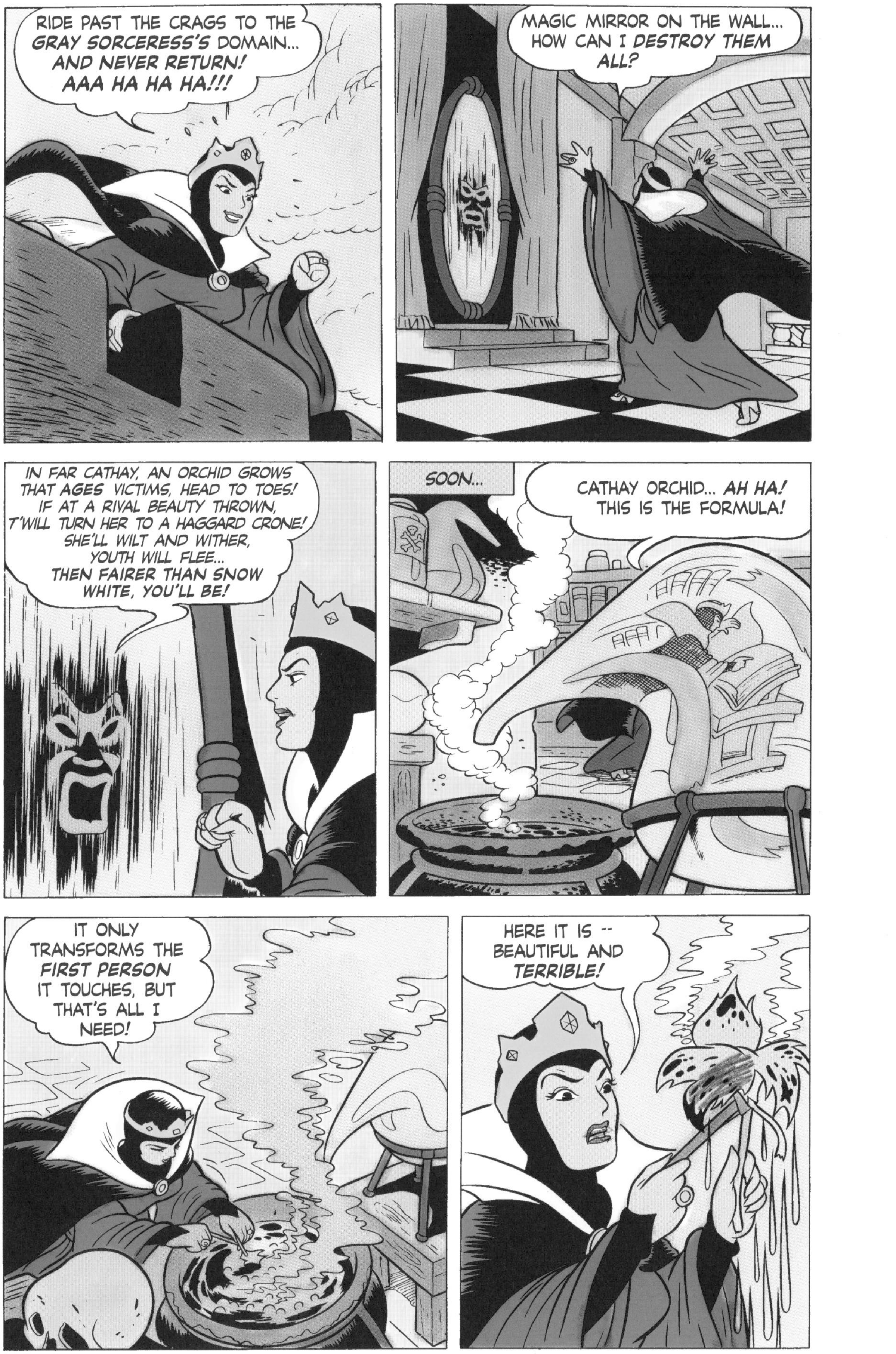
RIDE PAST THE CRAGS TO THE GRAY SORCERESS'S DOMAIN... AND NEVER RETURN! AAA HA HA HA!!!
MAGIC MIRROR ON THE WALL... HOW CAN I DESTROY THEM ALL?
IN FAR CATHAY, AN ORCHID GROWS THAT AGES VICTIMS, HEAD TO TOES! IF AT A RIVAL BEAUTY THROWN, T'WILL TURN HER TO A HAGGARD CRONE! SHE'LL WILT AND WITHER, YOUTH WILL FLEE... THEN FAIRER THAN SNOW WHITE, YOU'LL BE!
SOON...
CATHAY ORCHID... AH HA! THIS IS THE FORMULA!
IT ONLY TRANSFORMS THE FIRST PERSON IT TOUCHES, BUT THAT'S ALL I NEED!
HERE IT IS -- BEAUTIFUL AND TERRIBLE!

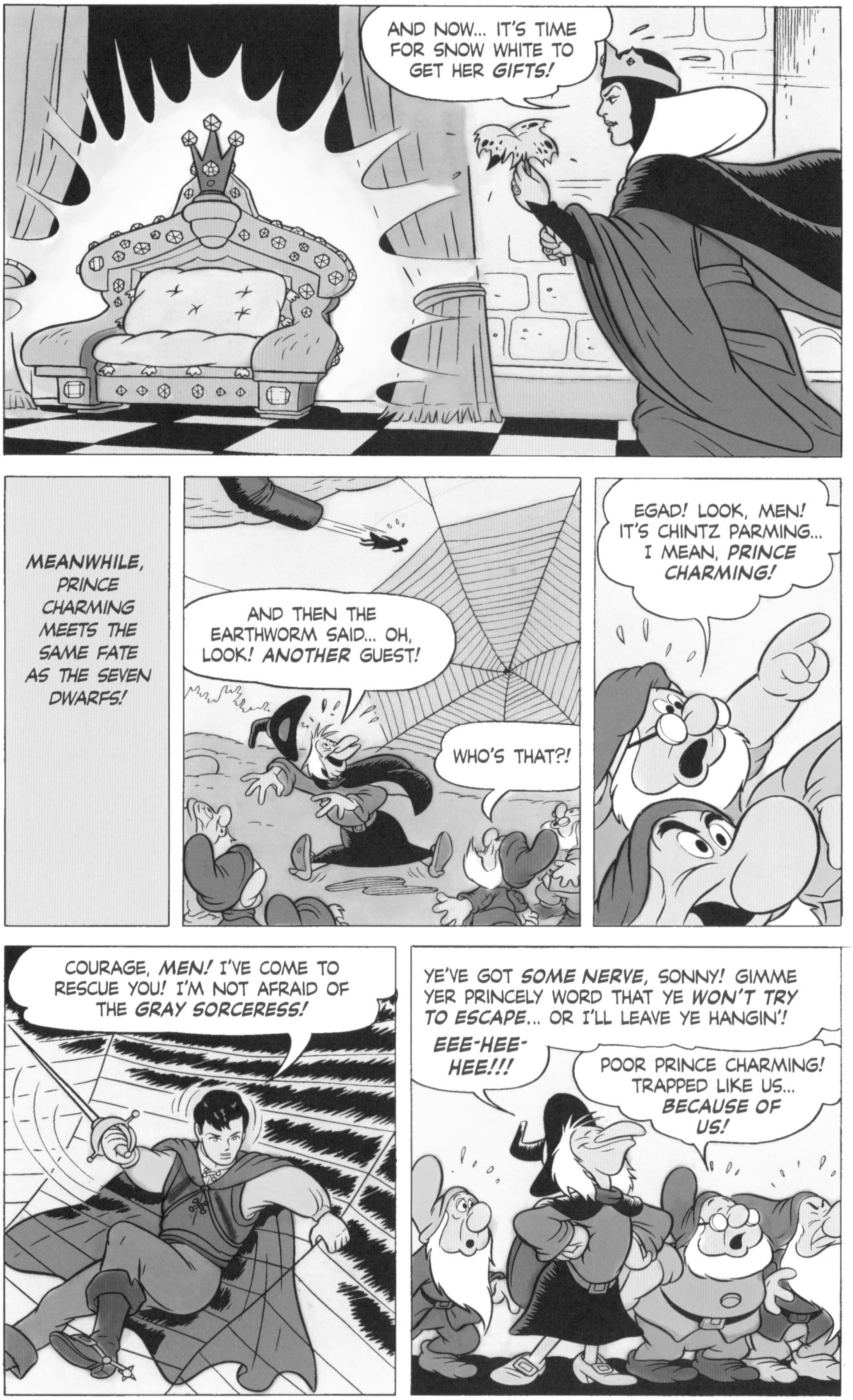
AND NOW... IT'S TIME FOR SNOW WHITE TO GET HER GIFTS!
MEANWHILE, PRINCE CHARMING MEETS THE SAME FATE AS THE SEVEN DWARFS!
AND THEN THE EARTHWORM SAID... OH, LOOK! ANOTHER GUEST!
WHO'S THAT?!
EGAD! LOOK, MEN! IT'S CHINTZ PARMING... I MEAN, PRINCE CHARMING!
COURAGE, MEN! I'VE COME TO RESCUE YOU! I'M NOT AFRAID OF THE GRAY SORCERESS!
YE'VE GOT SOME NERVE, SONNY! GIMME YER PRINCELY WORD THAT YE WON'T TRY TO ESCAPE... OR I'LL LEAVE YE HANGIN'!
EEE-HEE-HEE!!!
POOR PRINCE CHARMING! TRAPPED LIKE US... BECAUSE OF US!

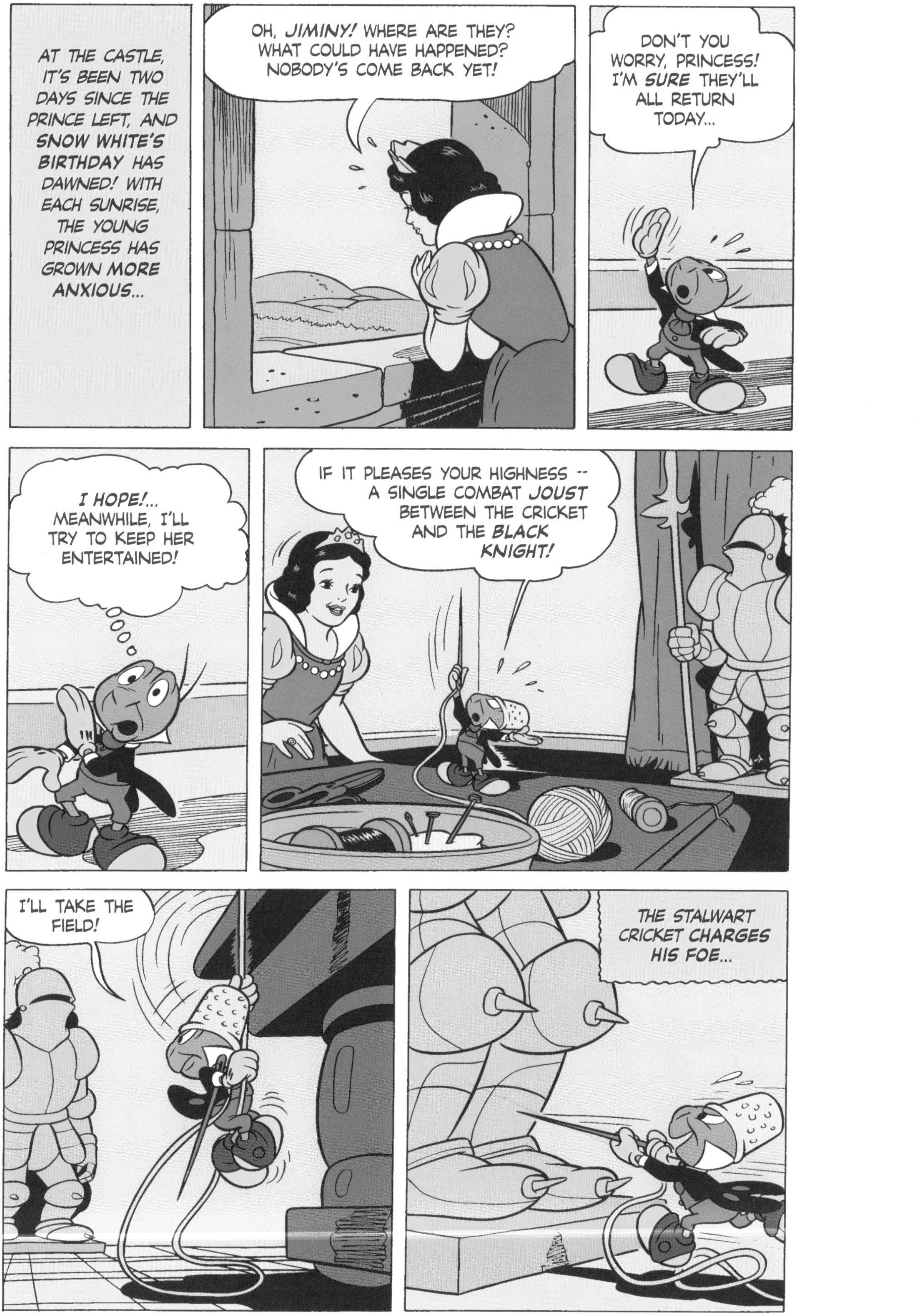
AT THE CASTLE, IT'S BEEN TWO DAYS SINCE THE PRINCE LEFT, AND SNOW WHITE'S BIRTHDAY HAS DAWNED! WITH EACH SUNRISE, THE YOUNG PRINCESS HAS GROWN MORE ANXIOUS...
OH, JIMINY! WHERE ARE THEY? WHAT COULD HAVE HAPPENED? NOBODY'S COME BACK YET!
DON'T YOU WORRY, PRINCESS! I'M SURE THEY'LL ALL RETURN TODAY...
I HOPE!... MEANWHILE, I'LL TRY TO KEEP HER ENTERTAINED!
IF IT PLEASES YOUR HIGHNESS -- A SINGLE COMBAT JOUST BETWEEN THE CRICKET AND THE BLACK KNIGHT!
I'LL TAKE THE FIELD!
THE STALWART CRICKET CHARGES HIS FOE...

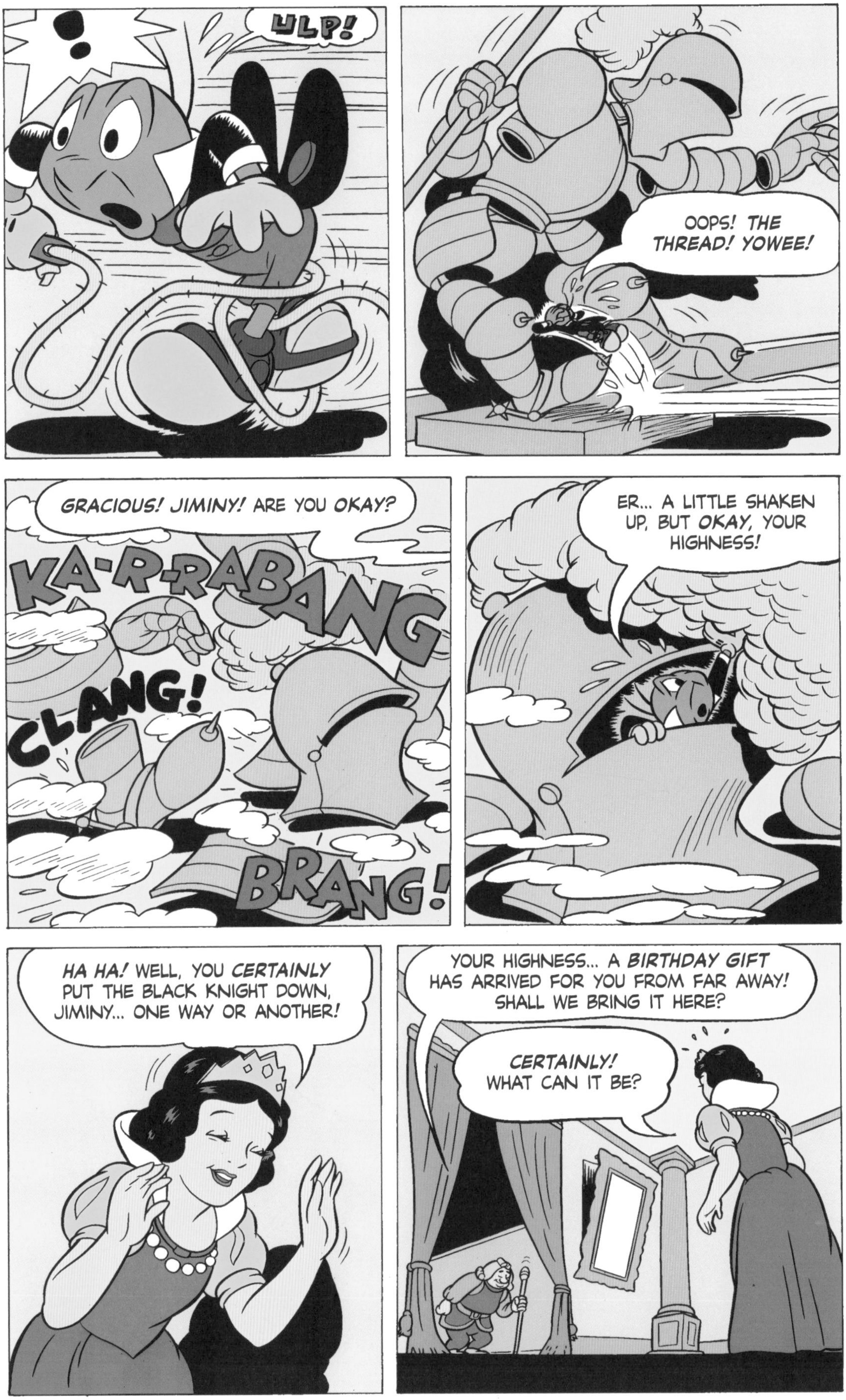
ULP!
OOPS! THE THREAD! YOWEE!
GRACIOUS! JIMINY! ARE YOU OKAY?
KA-R-RABANG
CLANG!
BRANG!
ER... A LITTLE SHAKEN UP, BUT OKAY, YOUR HIGHNESS!
HA HA! WELL, YOU CERTAINLY PUT THE BLACK KNIGHT DOWN, JIMINY... ONE WAY OR ANOTHER!
YOUR HIGHNESS... A BIRTHDAY GIFT HAS ARRIVED FOR YOU FROM FAR AWAY! SHALL WE BRING IT HERE?
CERTAINLY! WHAT CAN IT BE?

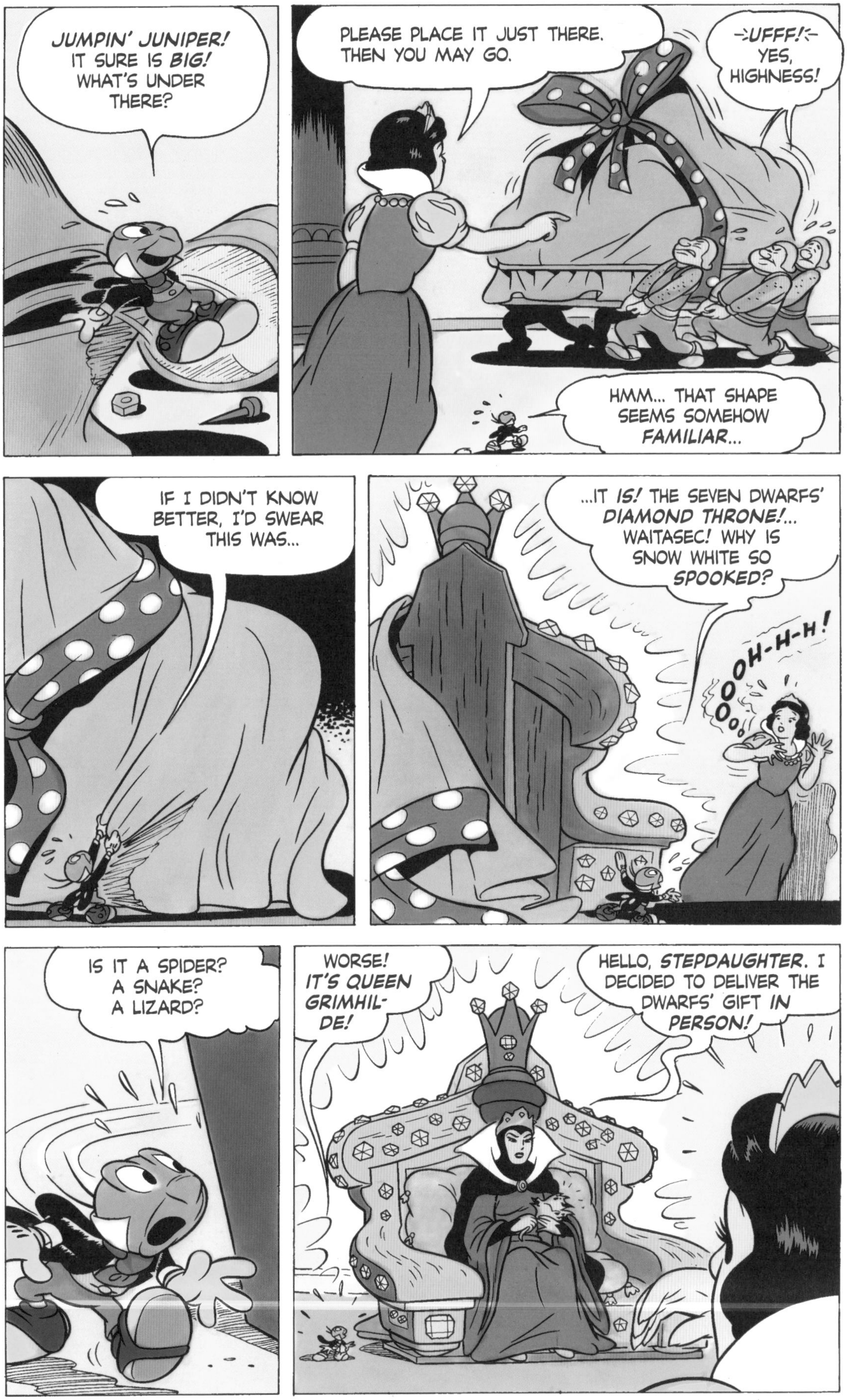
JUMPIN' JUNIPER! IT SURE IS BIG! WHAT'S UNDER THERE?
PLEASE PLACE IT JUST THERE. THEN YOU MAY GO.
UFFF! YES, HIGHNESS!
HMM... THAT SHAPE SEEMS SOMEHOW FAMILIAR...
IF I DIDN'T KNOW BETTER, I'D SWEAR THIS WAS...
...IT IS! THE SEVEN DWARFS' DIAMOND THRONE!... WAITASEC! WHY IS SNOW WHITE SO SPOOKED?
OOOOH-H-H!
IS IT A SPIDER? A SNAKE? A LIZARD?
WORSE! IT'S QUEEN GRIMHILDE!
HELLO, STEPDAUGHTER. I DECIDED TO DELIVER THE DWARFS' GIFT IN PERSON!

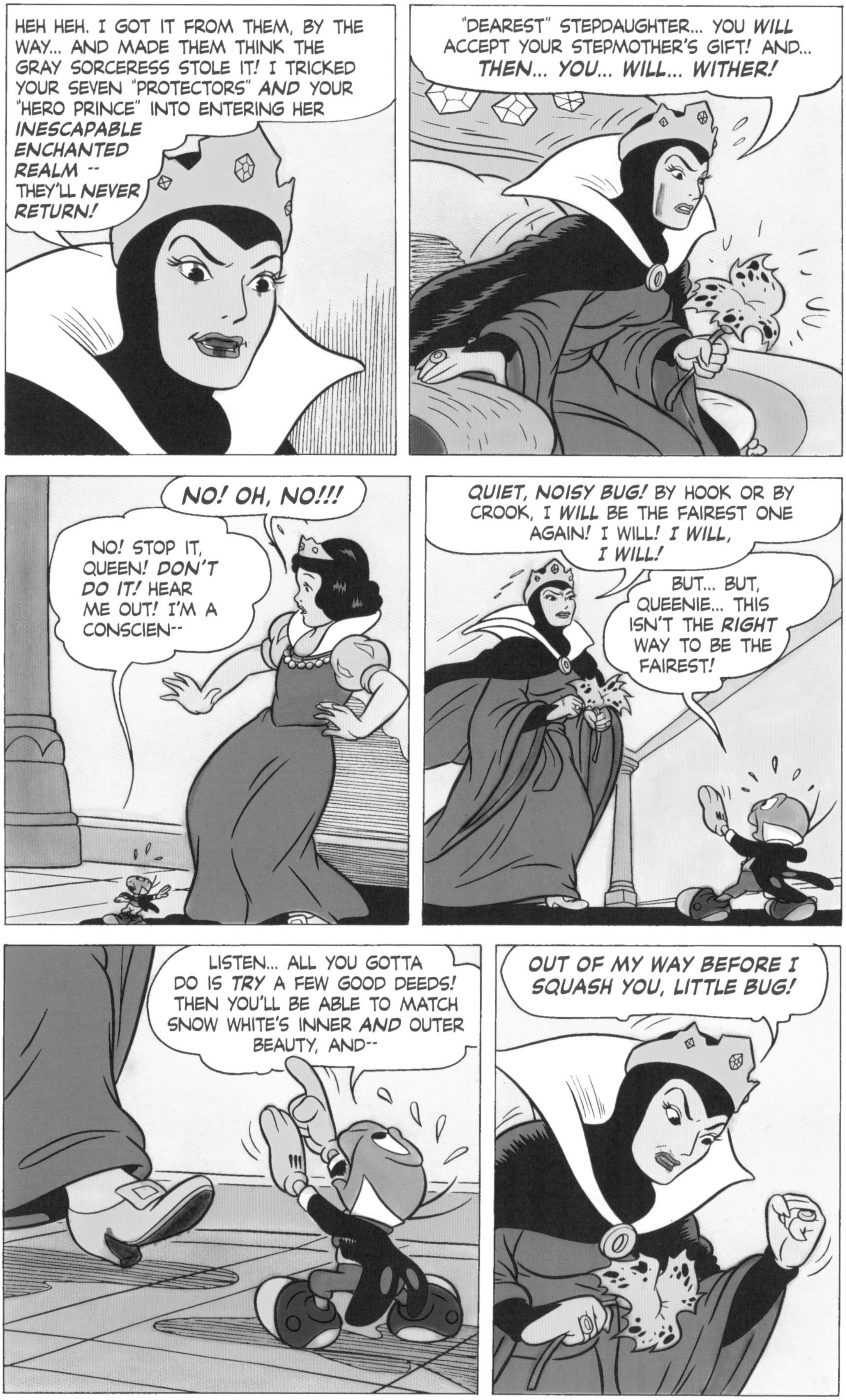
HEH HEH. I GOT IT FROM THEM, BY THE WAY... AND MADE THEM THINK THE GRAY SORCERESS STOLE IT! I TRICKED YOUR SEVEN "PROTECTORS" AND YOUR "HERO PRINCE" INTO ENTERING HER INESCAPABLE ENCHANTED REALM -- THEY'LL NEVER RETURN!
"DEAREST" STEPDAUGHTER... YOU WILL ACCEPT YOUR STEPMOTHER'S GIFT! AND... THEN... YOU... WILL... WITHER!
NO! OH, NO!!!
NO! STOP IT, QUEEN! DON'T DO IT! HEAR ME OUT! I'M A CONSCIEN--
QUIET, NOISY BUG! BY HOOK OR BY CROOK, I WILL BE THE FAIREST ONE AGAIN! I WILL! I WILL, I WILL!
BUT... BUT, QUEENIE... THIS ISN'T THE RIGHT WAY TO BE THE FAIREST!
LISTEN... ALL YOU GOTTA DO IS TRY A FEW GOOD DEEDS! THEN YOU'LL BE ABLE TO MATCH SNOW WHITE'S INNER AND OUTER BEAUTY, AND--
OUT OF MY WAY BEFORE I SQUASH YOU, LITTLE BUG!

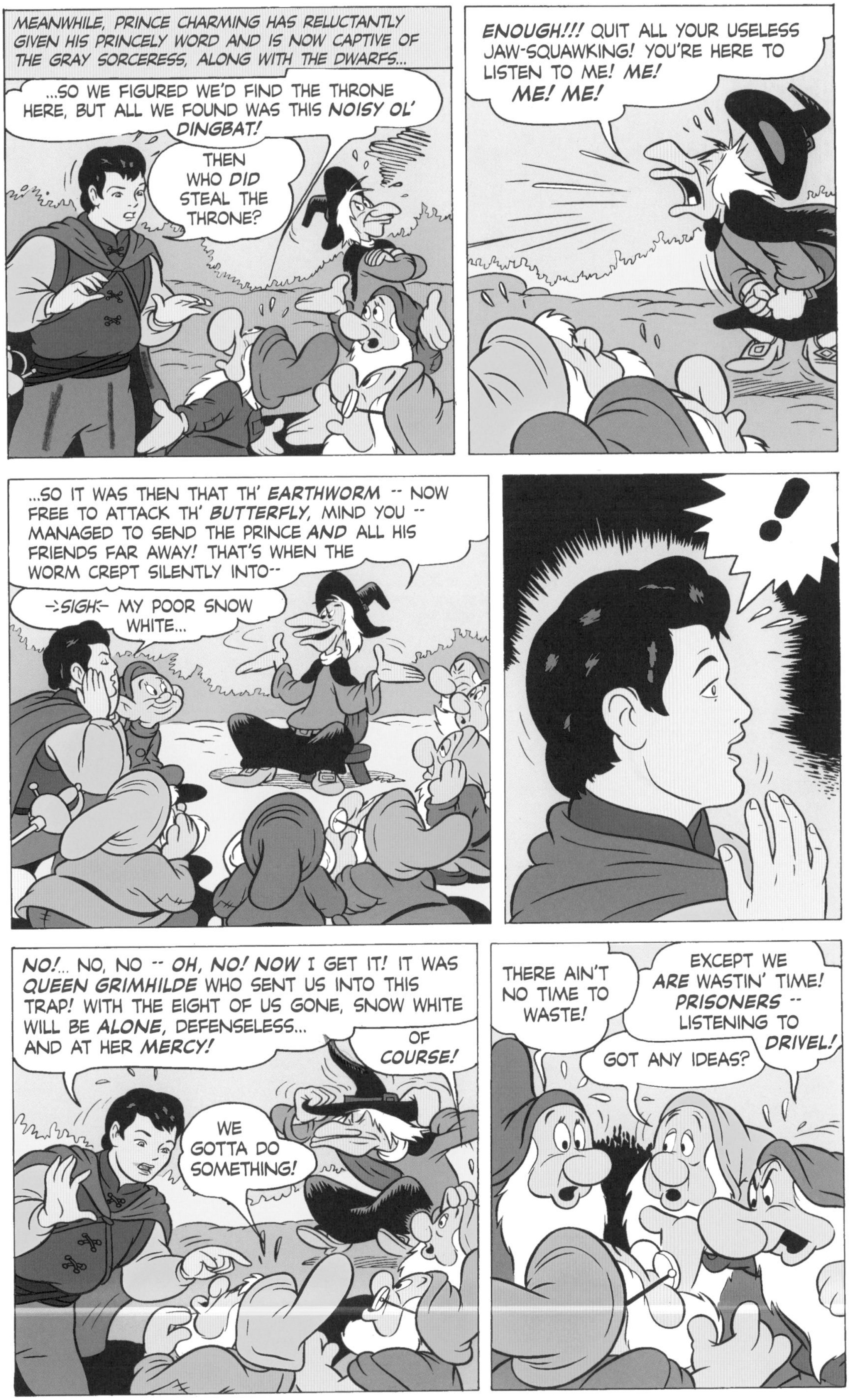

MEANWHILE, PRINCE CHARMING HAS RELUCTANTLY GIVEN HIS PRINCELY WORD AND IS NOW CAPTIVE OF THE GRAY SORCERESS, ALONG WITH THE DWARFS...
...SO WE FIGURED WE'D FIND THE THRONE HERE, BUT ALL WE FOUND WAS THIS NOISY OL' DINGBAT!
THEN WHO DID STEAL THE THRONE?
ENOUGH!!! QUIT ALL YOUR USELESS JAW-SQUAWKING! YOU'RE HERE TO LISTEN TO ME! ME! ME! ME!
...SO IT WAS THEN THAT TH' EARTHWORM -- NOW FREE TO ATTACK TH' BUTTERFLY, MIND YOU -- MANAGED TO SEND THE PRINCE AND ALL HIS FRIENDS FAR AWAY! THAT'S WHEN THE WORM CREPT SILENTLY INTO--
-SIGH- MY POOR SNOW WHITE...
!
NO!... NO, NO -- OH, NO! NOW I GET IT! IT WAS QUEEN GRIMHILDE WHO SENT US INTO THIS TRAP! WITH THE EIGHT OF US GONE, SNOW WHITE WILL BE ALONE, DEFENSELESS... AND AT HER MERCY!
OF COURSE!
WE GOTTA DO SOMETHING!
THERE AIN'T NO TIME TO WASTE!
EXCEPT WE ARE WASTIN' TIME! PRISONERS -- LISTENING TO DRIVEL!
GOT ANY IDEAS?

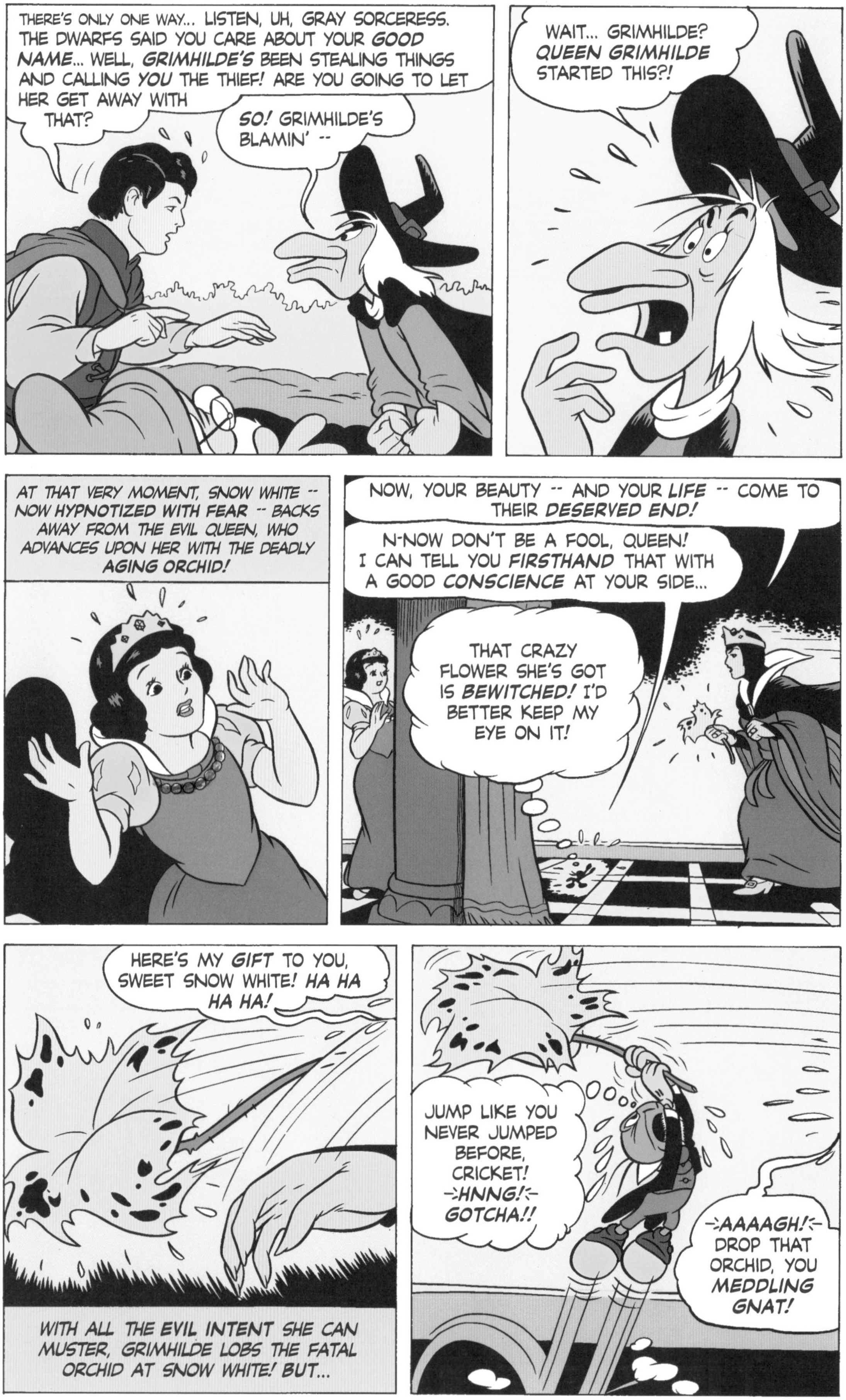
THERE'S ONLY ONE WAY... LISTEN, UH, GRAY SORCERESS. THE DWARFS SAID YOU CARE ABOUT YOUR GOOD NAME... WELL, GRIMHILDE'S BEEN STEALING THINGS AND CALLING YOU THE THIEF! ARE YOU GOING TO LET HER GET AWAY WITH THAT?
SO! GRIMHILDE'S BLAMIN' --
WAIT... GRIMHILDE? QUEEN GRIMHILDE STARTED THIS?!
AT THAT VERY MOMENT, SNOW WHITE -- NOW HYPNOTIZED WITH FEAR -- BACKS AWAY FROM THE EVIL QUEEN, WHO ADVANCES UPON HER WITH THE DEADLY AGING ORCHID!
NOW, YOUR BEAUTY -- AND YOUR LIFE -- COME TO THEIR DESERVED END!
N-NOW DON'T BE A FOOL, QUEEN! I CAN TELL YOU FIRSTHAND THAT WITH A GOOD CONSCIENCE AT YOUR SIDE...
THAT CRAZY FLOWER SHE'S GOT IS BEWITCHED! I'D BETTER KEEP MY EYE ON IT!
HERE'S MY GIFT TO YOU, SWEET SNOW WHITE! HA HA HA HA!
WITH ALL THE EVIL INTENT SHE CAN MUSTER, GRIMHILDE LOBS THE FATAL ORCHID AT SNOW WHITE! BUT...
JUMP LIKE YOU NEVER JUMPED BEFORE, CRICKET! -HNNG!- GOTCHA!!
-AAAAGH!- DROP THAT ORCHID, YOU MEDDLING GNAT!

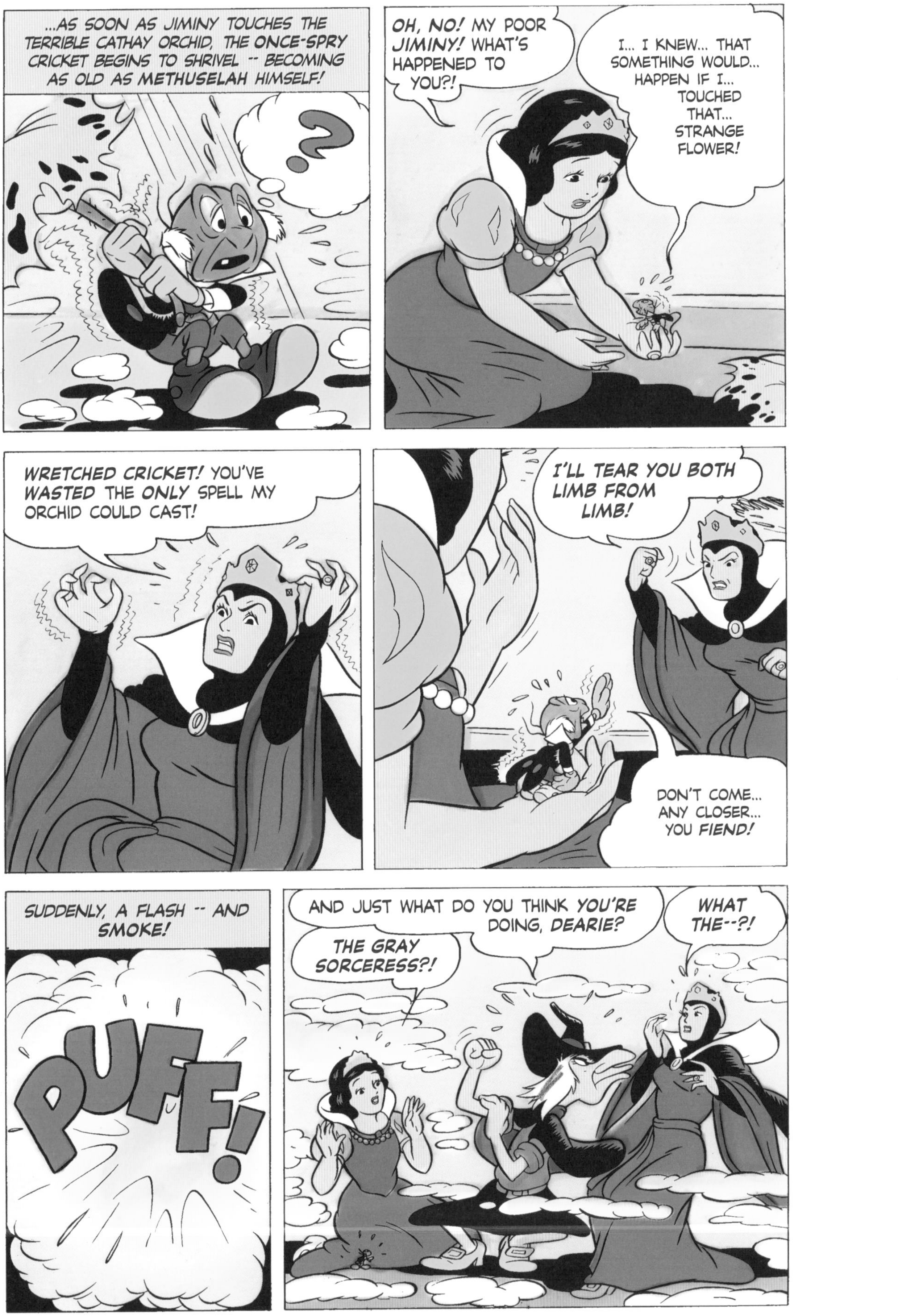
...AS SOON AS JIMINY TOUCHES THE TERRIBLE CATHAY ORCHID, THE ONCE-SPRY CRICKET BEGINS TO SHRIVEL -- BECOMING AS OLD AS METHUSELAH HIMSELF!
?
OH, NO! MY POOR JIMINY! WHAT'S HAPPENED TO YOU?!
I... I KNEW... THAT SOMETHING WOULD... HAPPEN IF I... TOUCHED THAT... STRANGE FLOWER!
WRETCHED CRICKET! YOU'VE WASTED THE ONLY SPELL MY ORCHID COULD CAST!
I'LL TEAR YOU BOTH LIMB FROM LIMB!
DON'T COME... ANY CLOSER... YOU FIEND!
SUDDENLY, A FLASH -- AND SMOKE!
PUFF!
AND JUST WHAT DO YOU THINK YOU'RE DOING, DEARIE?
THE GRAY SORCERESS?!
WHAT THE--?!

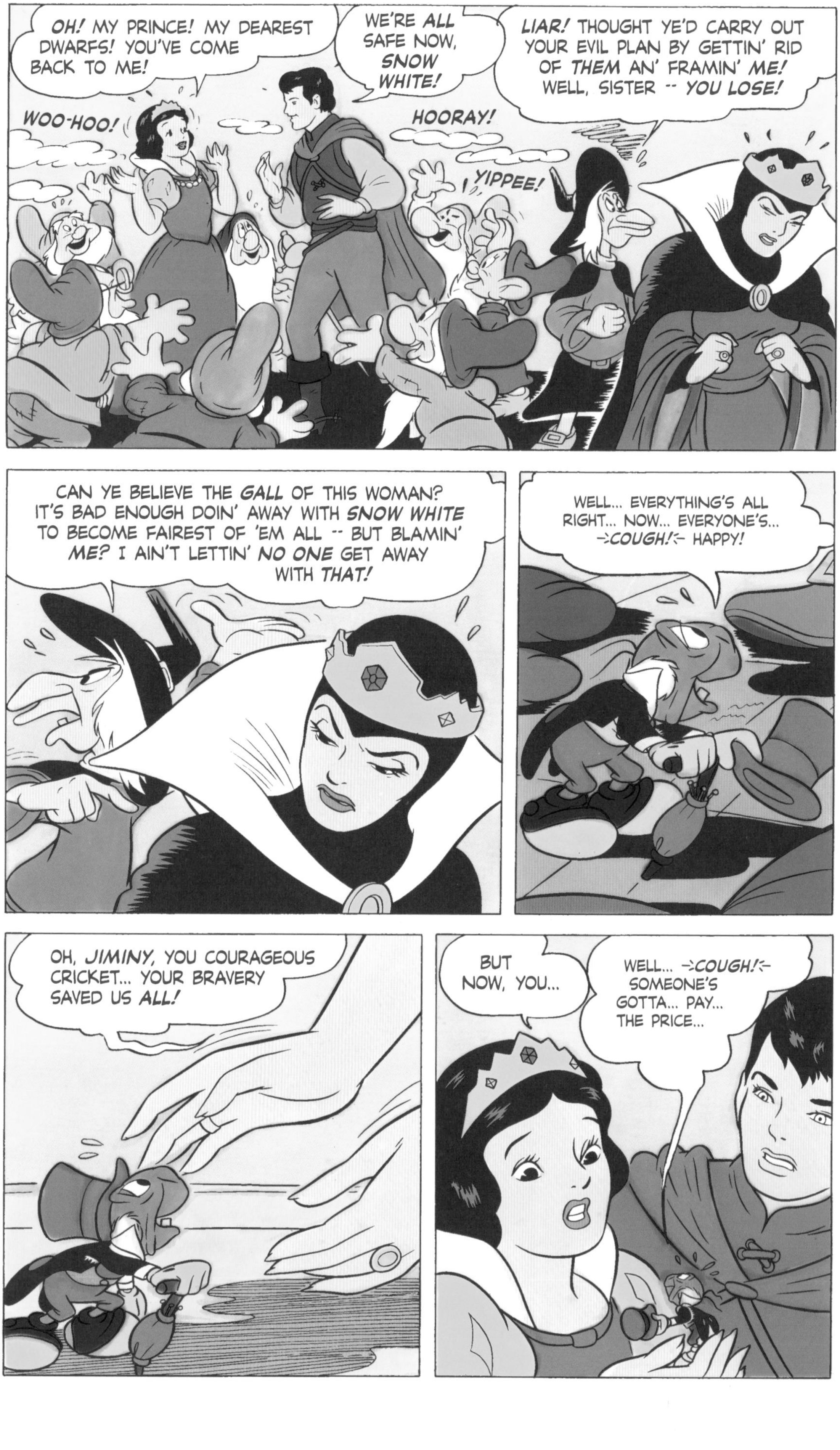
OH! MY PRINCE! MY DEAREST DWARFS! YOU'VE COME BACK TO ME!
WE'RE ALL SAFE NOW, SNOW WHITE!
LIAR! THOUGHT YE'D CARRY OUT YOUR EVIL PLAN BY GETTIN' RID OF THEM AN' FRAMIN' ME! WELL, SISTER -- YOU LOSE!
WOO-HOO!
HOORAY!
YIPPEE!
CAN YE BELIEVE THE GALL OF THIS WOMAN? IT'S BAD ENOUGH DOIN' AWAY WITH SNOW WHITE TO BECOME FAIREST OF 'EM ALL -- BUT BLAMIN' ME? I AIN'T LETTIN' NO ONE GET AWAY WITH THAT!
WELL... EVERYTHING'S ALL RIGHT... NOW... EVERYONE'S... -COUGH!- HAPPY!
OH, JIMINY, YOU COURAGEOUS CRICKET... YOUR BRAVERY SAVED US ALL!
BUT NOW, YOU...
WELL... -COUGH!- SOMEONE'S GOTTA... PAY... THE PRICE...

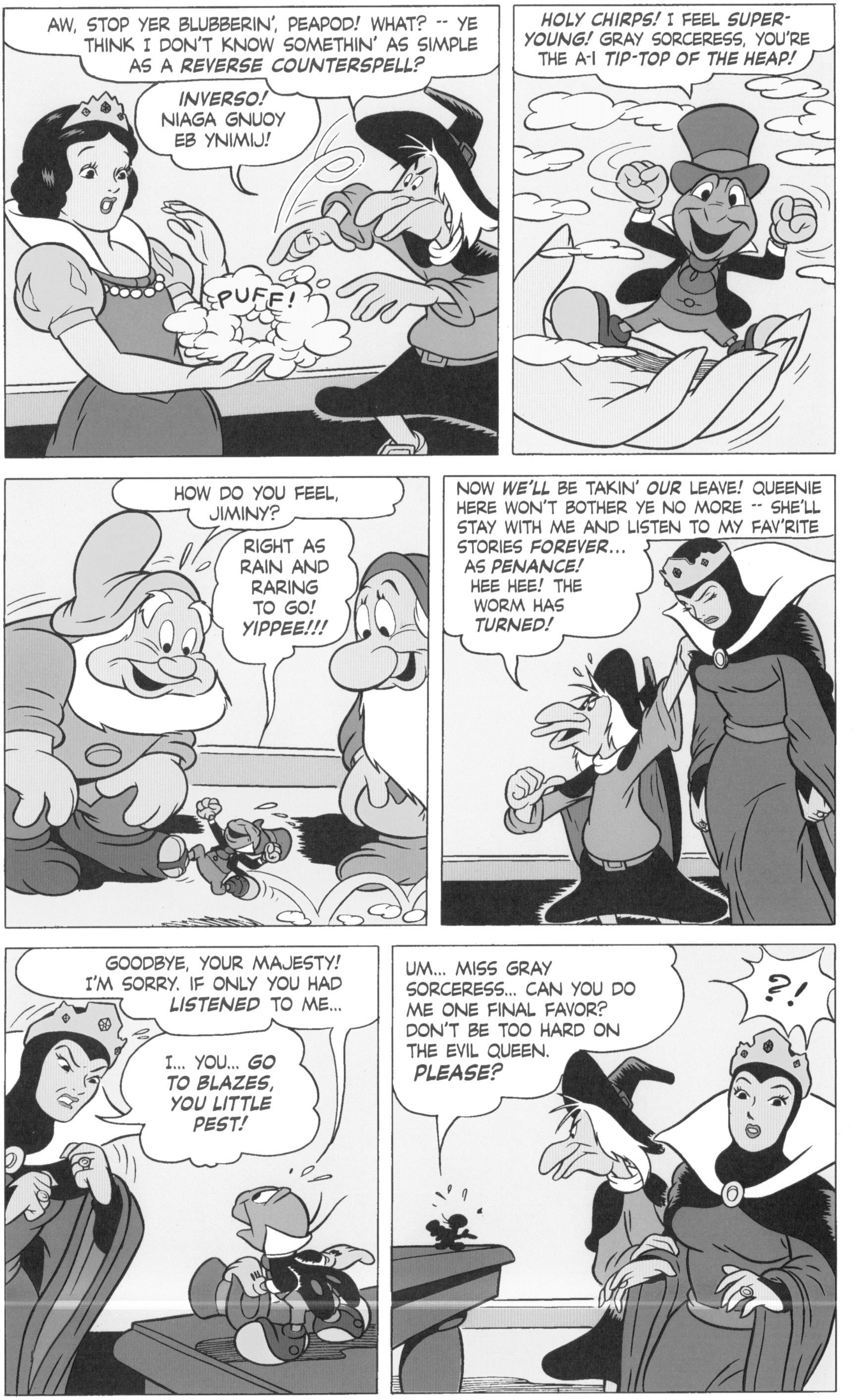
AW, STOP YER BLUBBERIN', PEAPOD! WHAT? -- YE THINK I DON'T KNOW SOMETHIN' AS SIMPLE AS A REVERSE COUNTERSPELL?
INVERSO! NIAGA GNUOY EB YNIMIJ!
PUFF!
HOLY CHIRPS! I FEEL SUPER-YOUNG! GRAY SORCERESS, YOU'RE THE A-1 TIP-TOP OF THE HEAP!
HOW DO YOU FEEL, JIMINY?
RIGHT AS RAIN AND RARING TO GO! YIPPEE!!!
NOW WE'LL BE TAKIN' OUR LEAVE! QUEENIE HERE WON'T BOTHER YE NO MORE -- SHE'LL STAY WITH ME AND LISTEN TO MY FAV'RITE STORIES FOREVER... AS PENANCE! HEE HEE! THE WORM HAS TURNED!
GOODBYE, YOUR MAJESTY! I'M SORRY. IF ONLY YOU HAD LISTENED TO ME...
I... YOU... GO TO BLAZES, YOU LITTLE PEST!
UM... MISS GRAY SORCERESS... CAN YOU DO ME ONE FINAL FAVOR? DON'T BE TOO HARD ON THE EVIL QUEEN. PLEASE?
?!

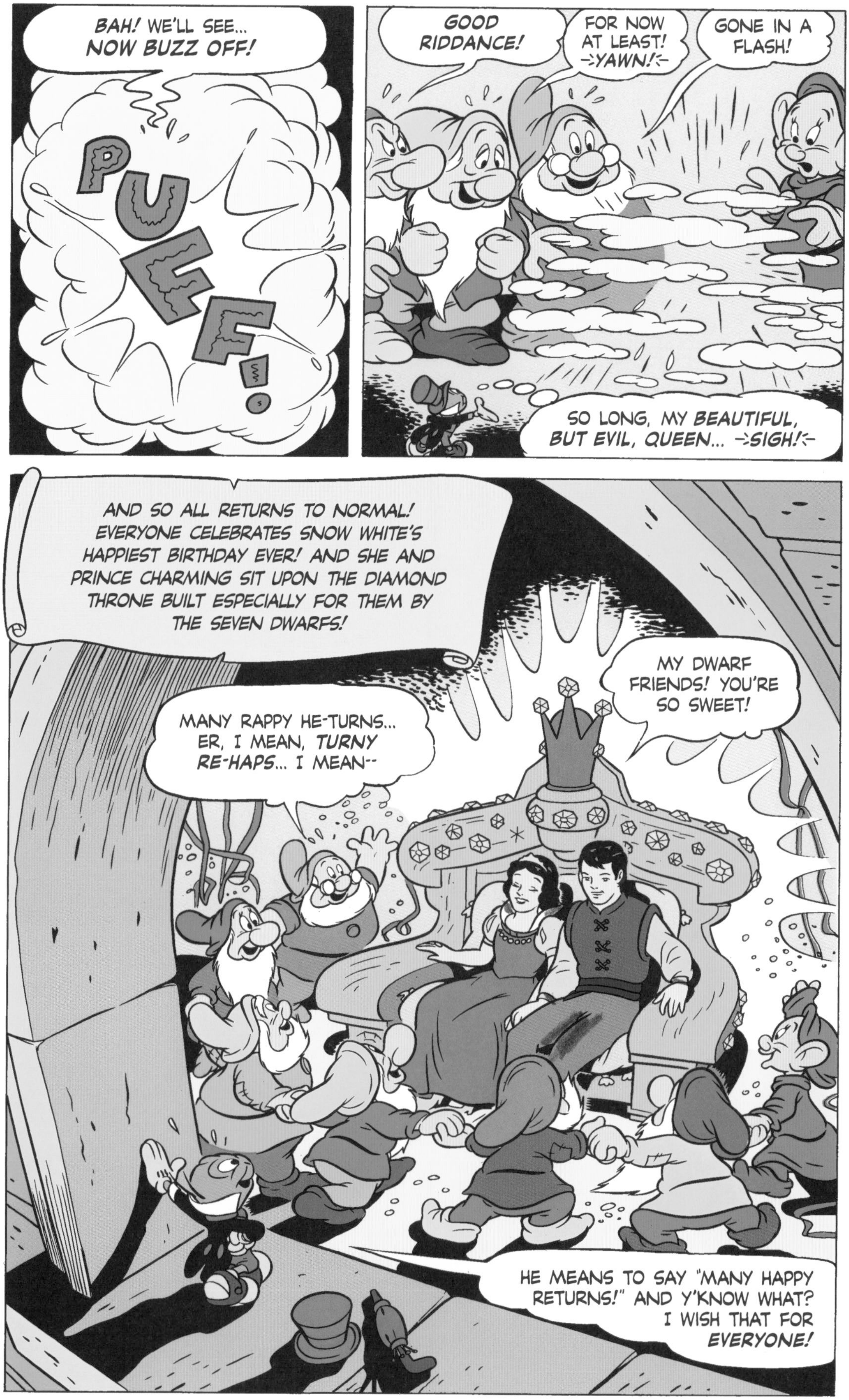
BAH! WE'LL SEE... NOW BUZZ OFF!
PUFF!
GOOD RIDDANCE!
FOR NOW AT LEAST! -YAWN!-
GONE IN A FLASH!
SO LONG, MY BEAUTIFUL, BUT EVIL, QUEEN... -SIGH!-
AND SO ALL RETURNS TO NORMAL! EVERYONE CELEBRATES SNOW WHITE'S HAPPIEST BIRTHDAY EVER! AND SHE AND PRINCE CHARMING SIT UPON THE DIAMOND THRONE BUILT ESPECIALLY FOR THEM BY THE SEVEN DWARFS!
MANY RAPPY HE-TURNS... ER, I MEAN, TURNY RE-HAPS... I MEAN--
MY DWARF FRIENDS! YOU'RE SO SWEET!
HE MEANS TO SAY "MANY HAPPY RETURNS!" AND Y'KNOW WHAT? I WISH THAT FOR EVERYONE!

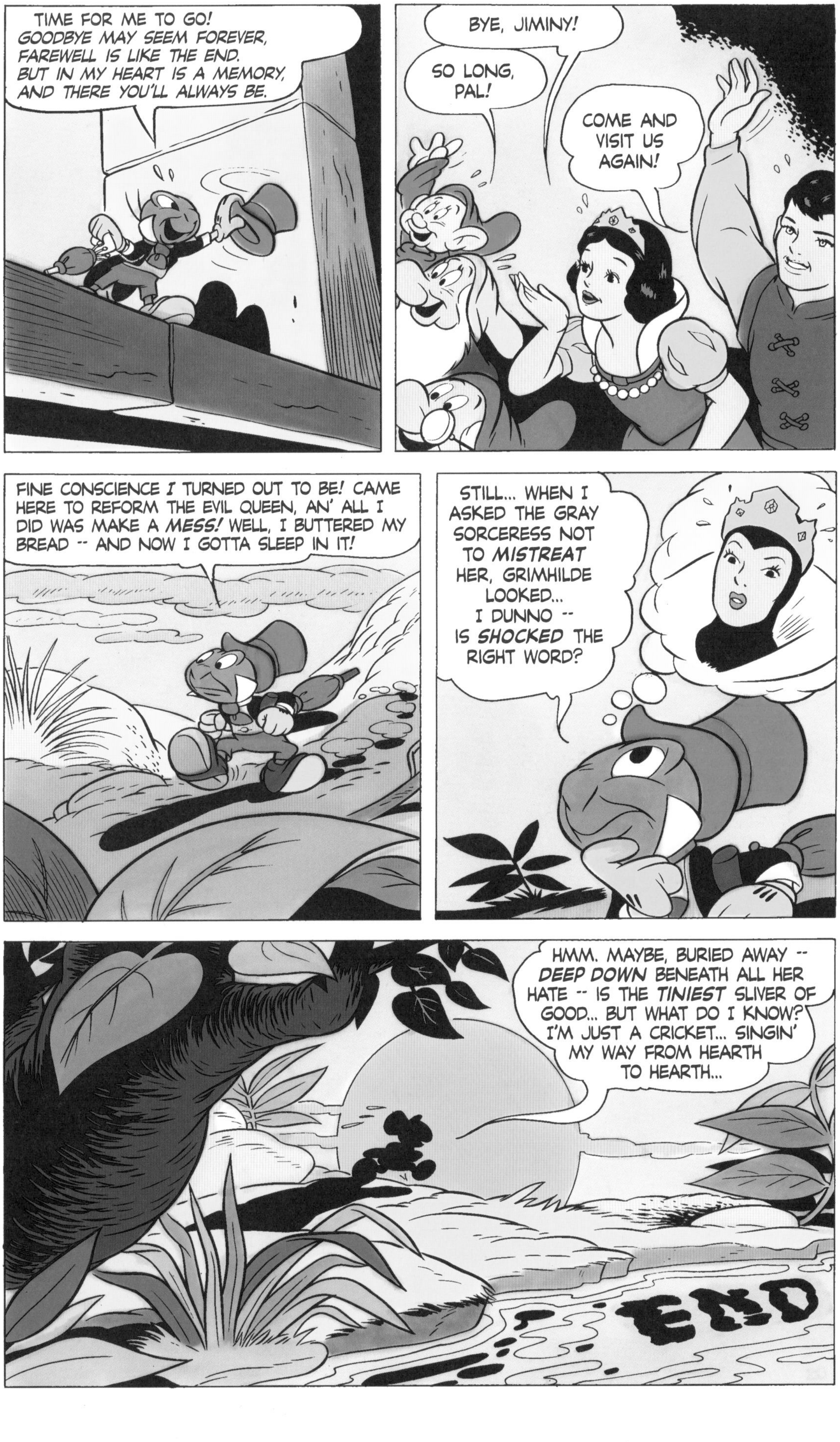
TIME FOR ME TO GO! GOODBYE MAY SEEM FOREVER, FAREWELL IS LIKE THE END. BUT IN MY HEART IS A MEMORY, AND THERE YOU'LL ALWAYS BE.
BYE, JIMINY!
SO LONG, PAL!
COME AND VISIT US AGAIN!
FINE CONSCIENCE I TURNED OUT TO BE! CAME HERE TO REFORM THE EVIL QUEEN, AN' ALL I DID WAS MAKE A MESS! WELL, I BUTTERED MY BREAD -- AND NOW I GOTTA SLEEP IN IT!
STILL... WHEN I ASKED THE GRAY SORCERESS NOT TO MISTREAT HER, GRIMHILDE LOOKED... I DUNNO -- IS SHOCKED THE RIGHT WORD?
HMM. MAYBE, BURIED AWAY -- DEEP DOWN BENEATH ALL HER HATE -- IS THE TINIEST SLIVER OF GOOD... BUT WHAT DO I KNOW? I'M JUST A CRICKET... SINGIN' MY WAY FROM HEARTH TO HEARTH...
END

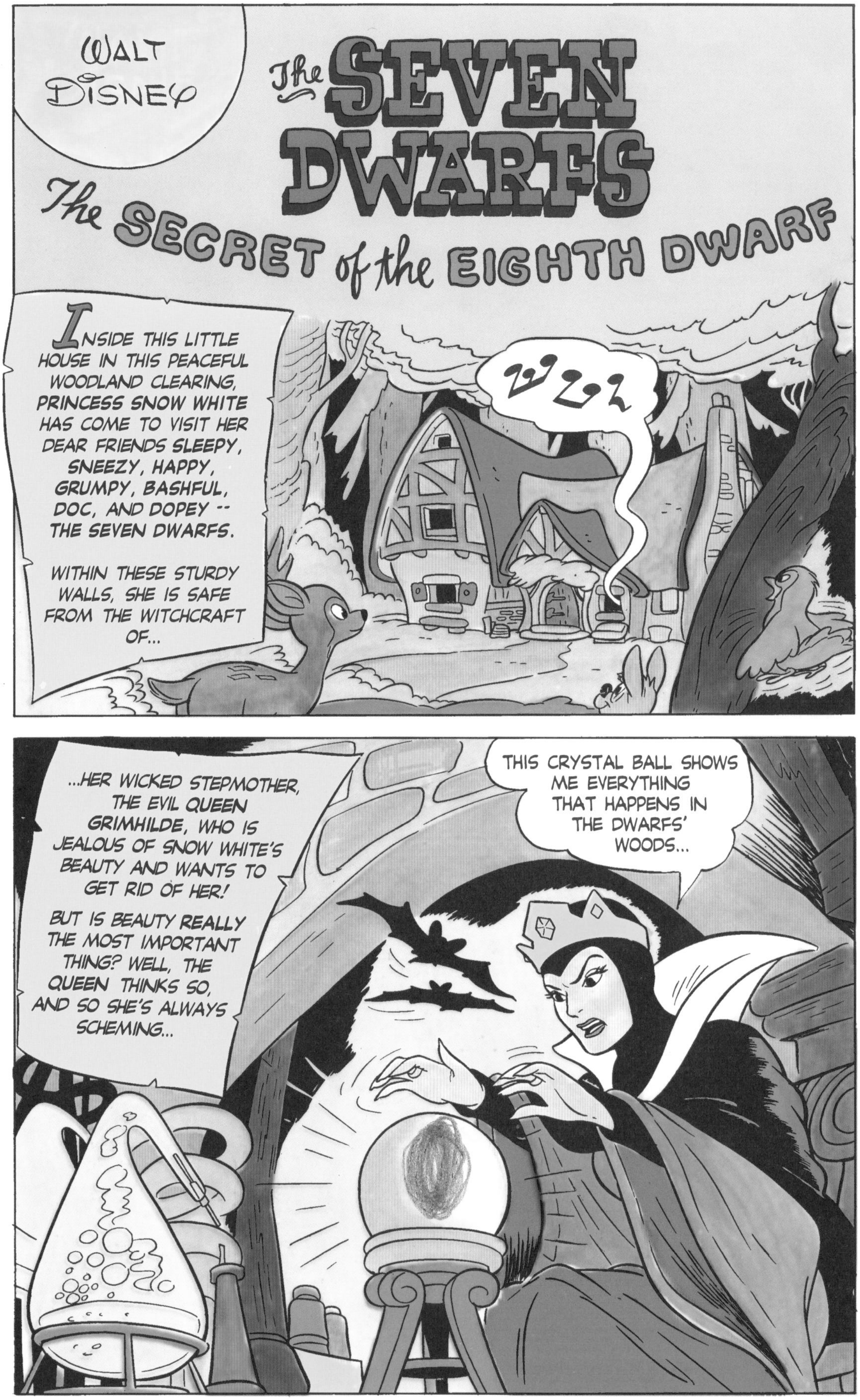
Walt Disney
The Seven Dwarfs
The Secret of the Eighth Dwarf
Inside this little house in this peaceful woodland clearing, Princess Snow White has come to visit her dear friends Sleepy, Sneezy, Happy, Grumpy, Bashful, Doc, and Dopey -- the Seven Dwarfs.
Within these sturdy walls, she is safe from the witchcraft of...
zzzz
...her wicked stepmother, the evil Queen Grimhilde, who is jealous of Snow White's beauty and wants to get rid of her!
But is beauty really the most important thing? Well, the Queen thinks so, and so she's always scheming...
This crystal ball shows me everything that happens in the Dwarfs' woods...

STORY AND PENCILS: ROMANO SCARPA • INKS: RODOLFO CIMINO
TRANSLATION: SIMONE CASTALDI • DIALOG CONTINUITY: JONATHAN H. GRAY WITH DAVID GERSTEIN
TITLE LETTERING: KEELI MCCARTHY • EDITING: J. MICHAEL CATRON

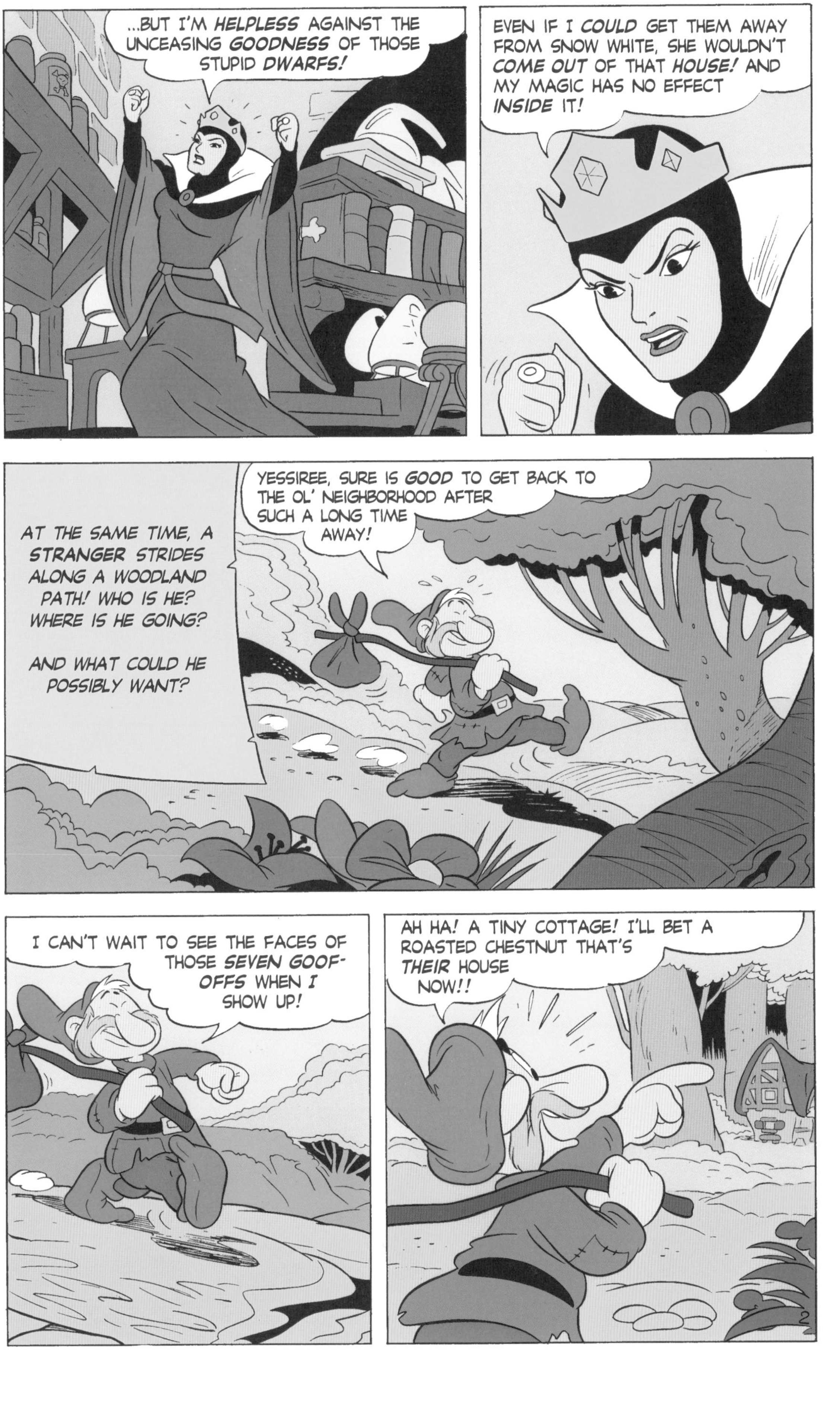
...BUT I'M HELPLESS AGAINST THE UNCEASING GOODNESS OF THOSE STUPID DWARFS!
EVEN IF I COULD GET THEM AWAY FROM SNOW WHITE, SHE WOULDN'T COME OUT OF THAT HOUSE! AND MY MAGIC HAS NO EFFECT INSIDE IT!
AT THE SAME TIME, A STRANGER STRIDES ALONG A WOODLAND PATH! WHO IS HE? WHERE IS HE GOING?
AND WHAT COULD HE POSSIBLY WANT?
YESSIREE, SURE IS GOOD TO GET BACK TO THE OL' NEIGHBORHOOD AFTER SUCH A LONG TIME AWAY!
I CAN'T WAIT TO SEE THE FACES OF THOSE SEVEN GOOF-OFFS WHEN I SHOW UP!
AH HA! A TINY COTTAGE! I'LL BET A ROASTED CHESTNUT THAT'S THEIR HOUSE NOW!!
2

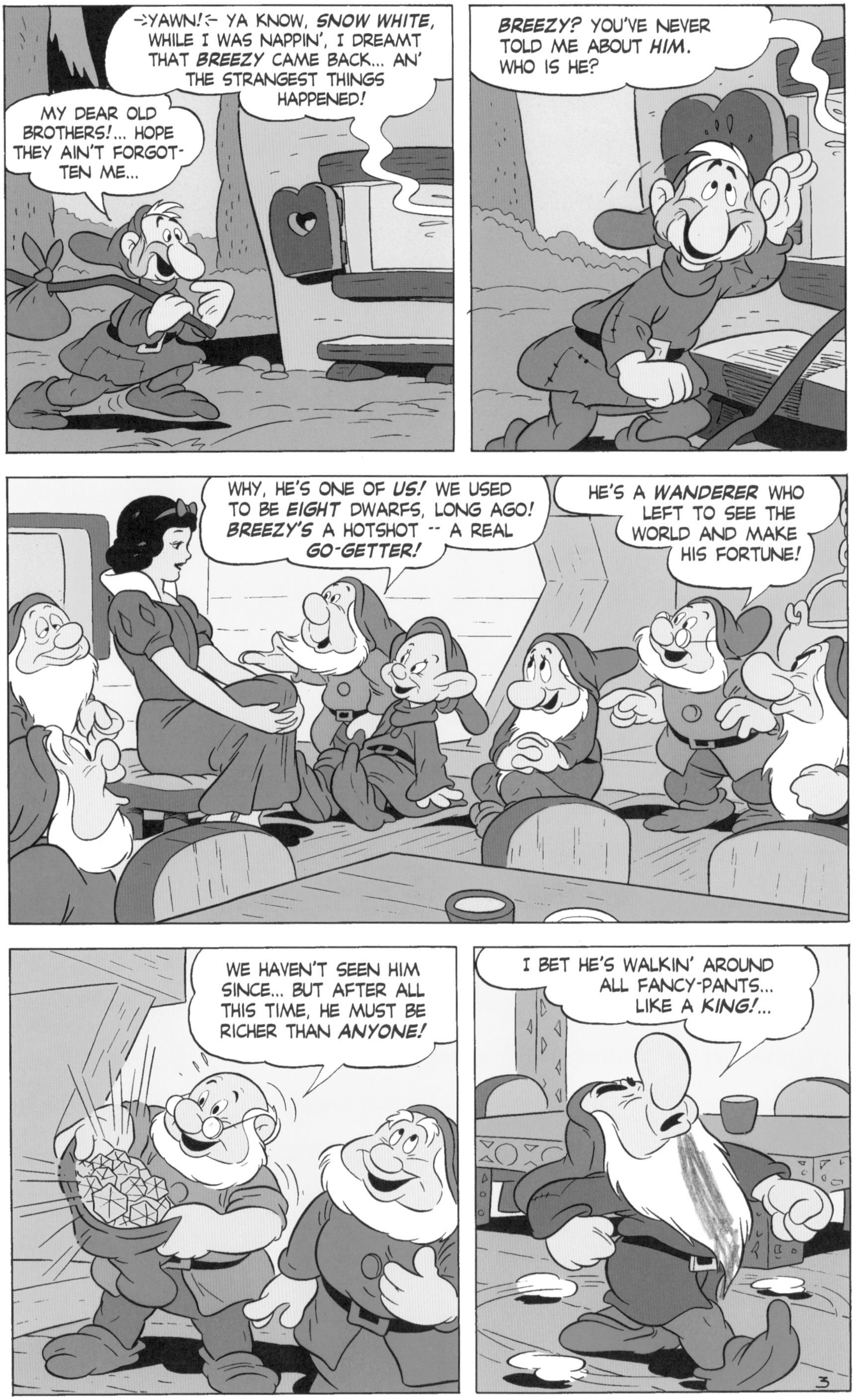

MY DEAR OLD BROTHERS!... HOPE THEY AIN'T FORGOT-TEN ME...
-YAWN!- YA KNOW, SNOW WHITE, WHILE I WAS NAPPIN', I DREAMT THAT BREEZY CAME BACK... AN' THE STRANGEST THINGS HAPPENED!
BREEZY? YOU'VE NEVER TOLD ME ABOUT HIM. WHO IS HE?
WHY, HE'S ONE OF US! WE USED TO BE EIGHT DWARFS, LONG AGO! BREEZY'S A HOTSHOT -- A REAL GO-GETTER!
HE'S A WANDERER WHO LEFT TO SEE THE WORLD AND MAKE HIS FORTUNE!
WE HAVEN'T SEEN HIM SINCE... BUT AFTER ALL THIS TIME, HE MUST BE RICHER THAN ANYONE!
I BET HE'S WALKIN' AROUND ALL FANCY-PANTS... LIKE A KING!...
3

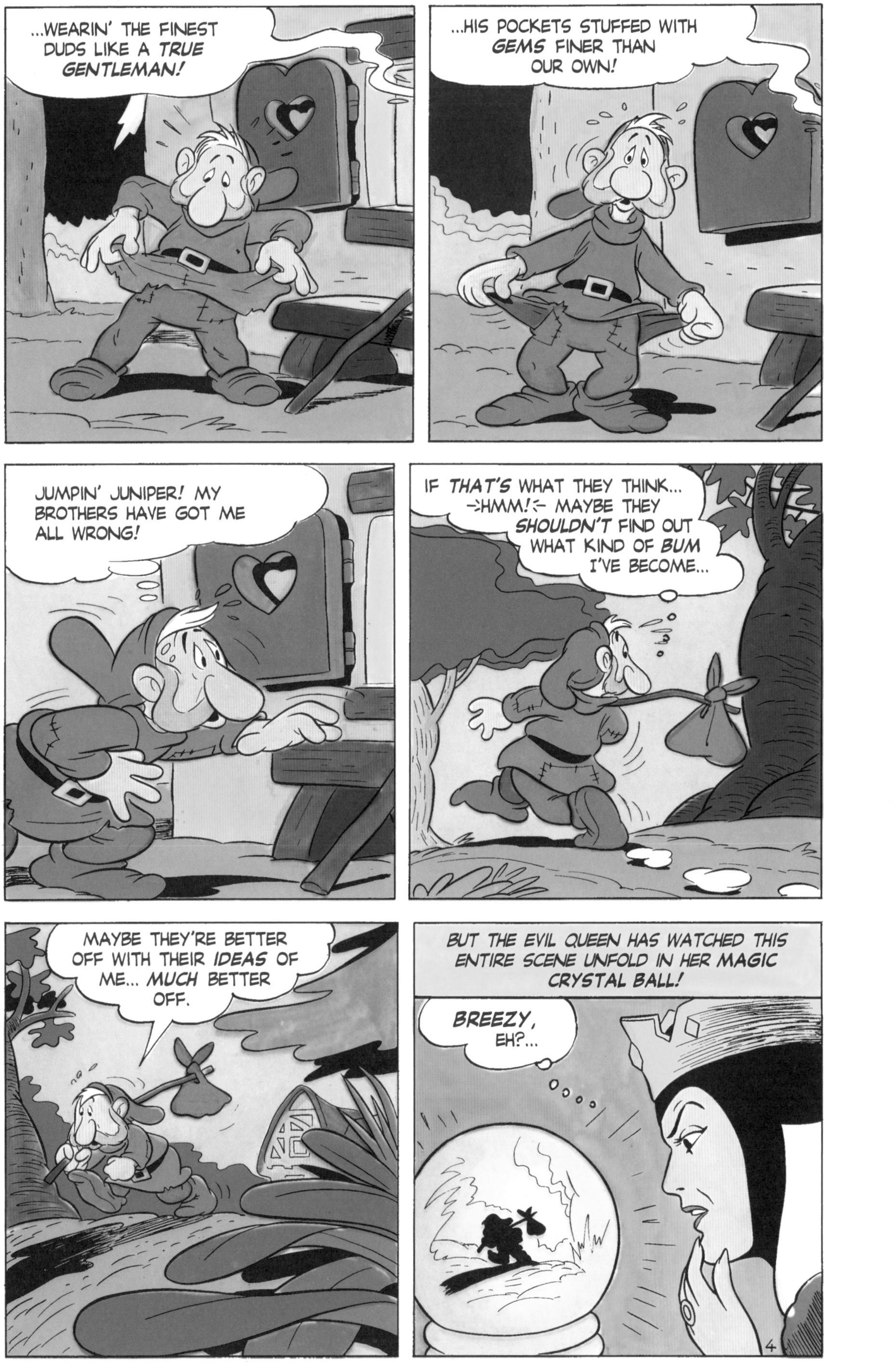
...WEARIN' THE FINEST DUDS LIKE A TRUE GENTLEMAN!
...HIS POCKETS STUFFED WITH GEMS FINER THAN OUR OWN!
JUMPIN' JUNIPER! MY BROTHERS HAVE GOT ME ALL WRONG!
IF THAT'S WHAT THEY THINK... -HMM!- MAYBE THEY SHOULDN'T FIND OUT WHAT KIND OF BUM I'VE BECOME...
MAYBE THEY'RE BETTER OFF WITH THEIR IDEAS OF ME... MUCH BETTER OFF.
BUT THE EVIL QUEEN HAS WATCHED THIS ENTIRE SCENE UNFOLD IN HER MAGIC CRYSTAL BALL!
BREEZY, EH?...
4

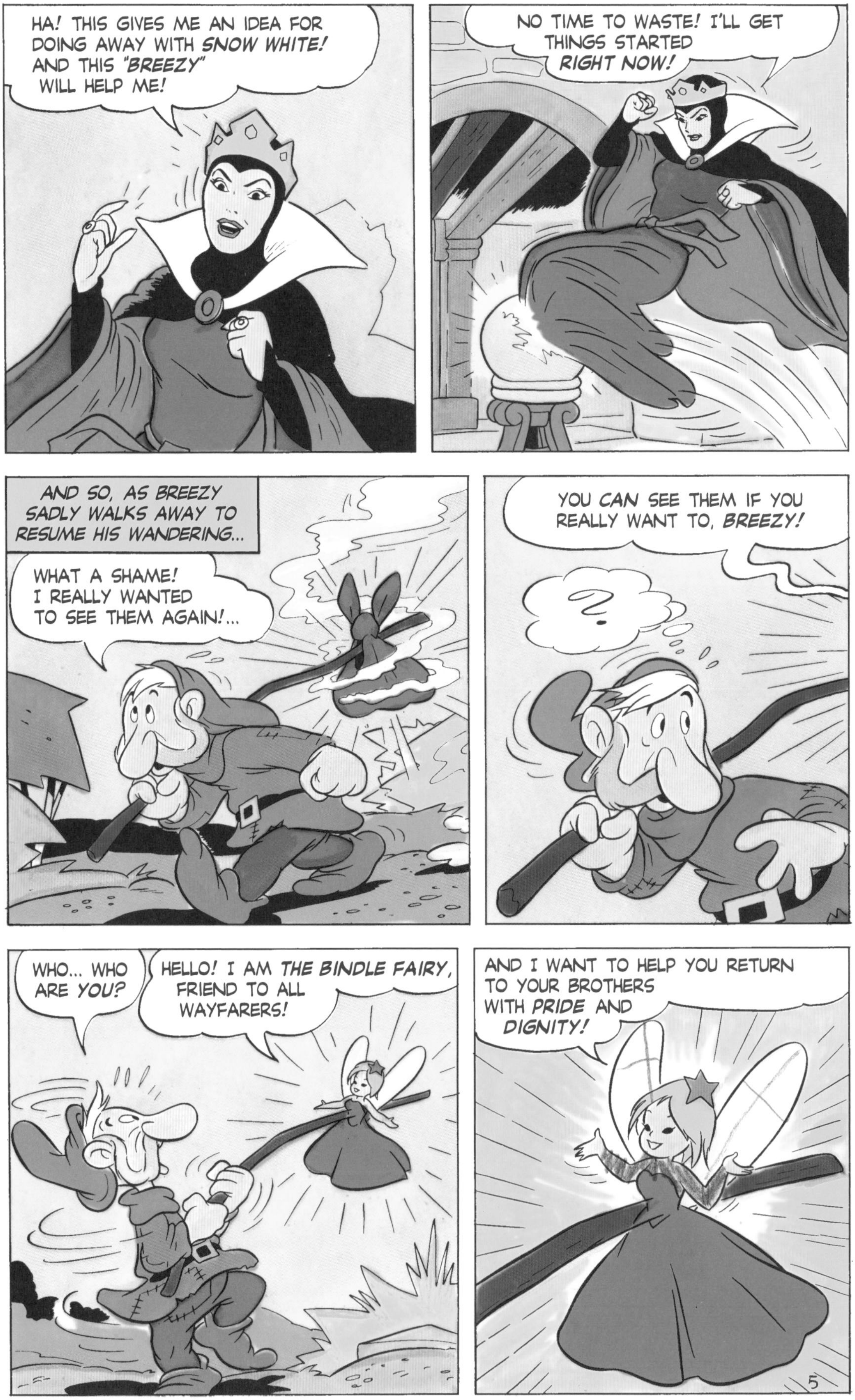
HA! THIS GIVES ME AN IDEA FOR DOING AWAY WITH SNOW WHITE! AND THIS "BREEZY" WILL HELP ME!
NO TIME TO WASTE! I'LL GET THINGS STARTED RIGHT NOW!
AND SO, AS BREEZY SADLY WALKS AWAY TO RESUME HIS WANDERING...
WHAT A SHAME! I REALLY WANTED TO SEE THEM AGAIN!...
YOU CAN SEE THEM IF YOU REALLY WANT TO, BREEZY!
?
WHO... WHO ARE YOU?
HELLO! I AM THE BINDLE FAIRY, FRIEND TO ALL WAYFARERS!
AND I WANT TO HELP YOU RETURN TO YOUR BROTHERS WITH PRIDE AND DIGNITY!
5

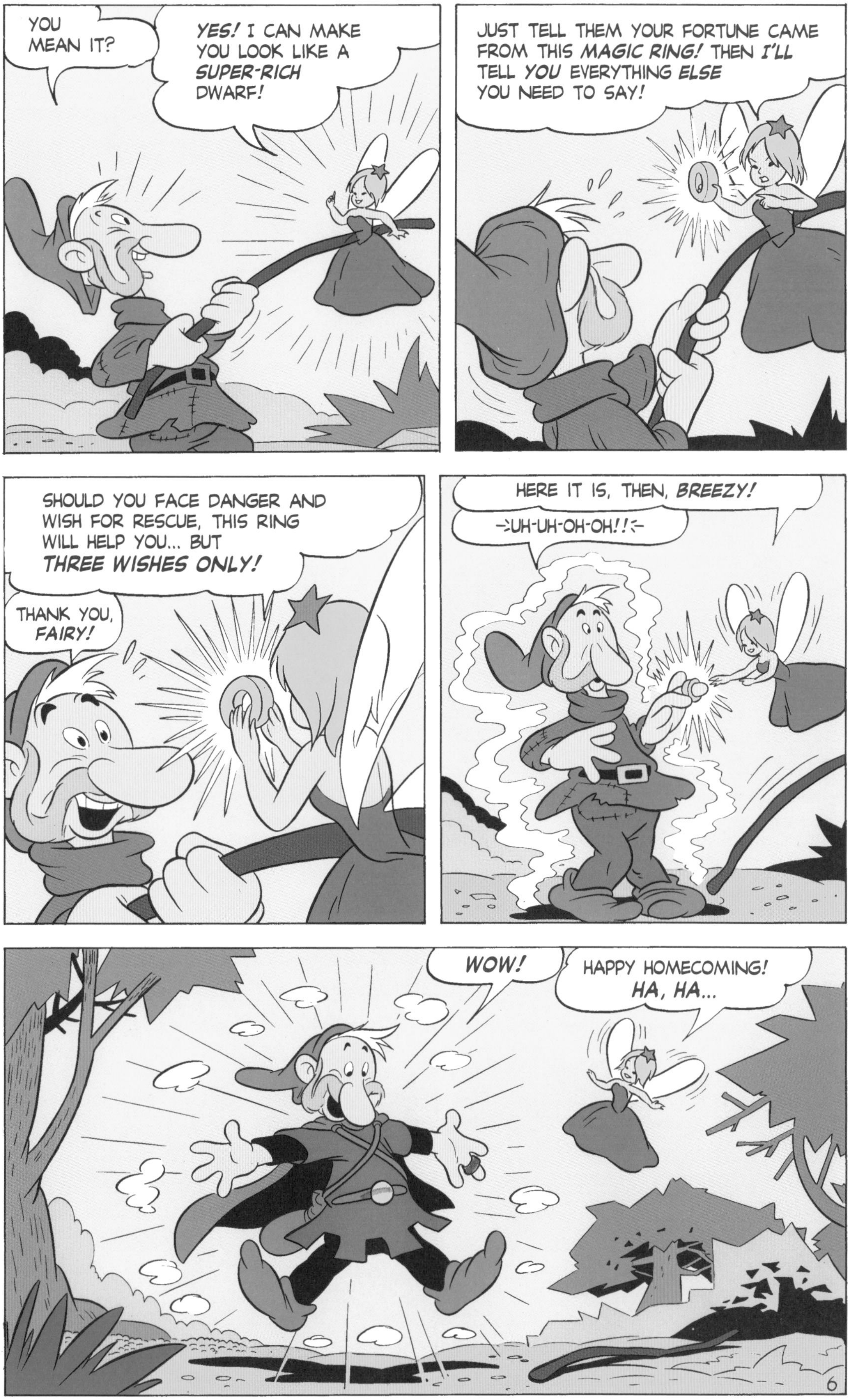
YOU MEAN IT?
YES! I CAN MAKE YOU LOOK LIKE A SUPER-RICH DWARF!
JUST TELL THEM YOUR FORTUNE CAME FROM THIS MAGIC RING! THEN I'LL TELL YOU EVERYTHING ELSE YOU NEED TO SAY!
SHOULD YOU FACE DANGER AND WISH FOR RESCUE, THIS RING WILL HELP YOU... BUT THREE WISHES ONLY!
THANK YOU, FAIRY!
HERE IT IS, THEN, BREEZY!
UH-UH-OH-OH!!
WOW!
HAPPY HOMECOMING! HA, HA...
6

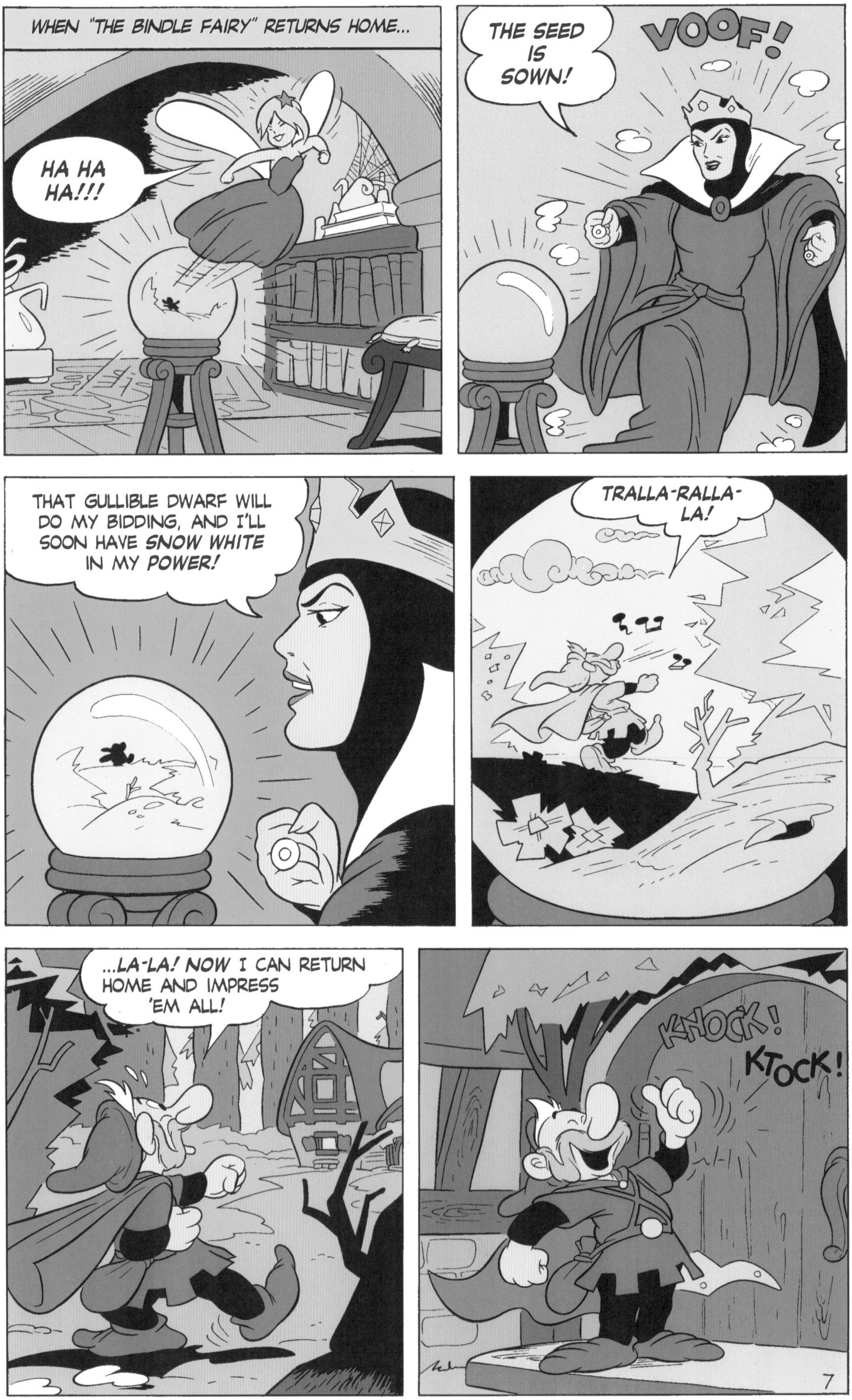
WHEN "THE BINDLE FAIRY" RETURNS HOME...
HA HA HA!!!
THE SEED IS SOWN!
VOOF!
THAT GULLIBLE DWARF WILL DO MY BIDDING, AND I'LL SOON HAVE SNOW WHITE IN MY POWER!
TRALLA-RALLA-LA!
...LA-LA! NOW I CAN RETURN HOME AND IMPRESS 'EM ALL!
KNOCK!
KTOCK!
7

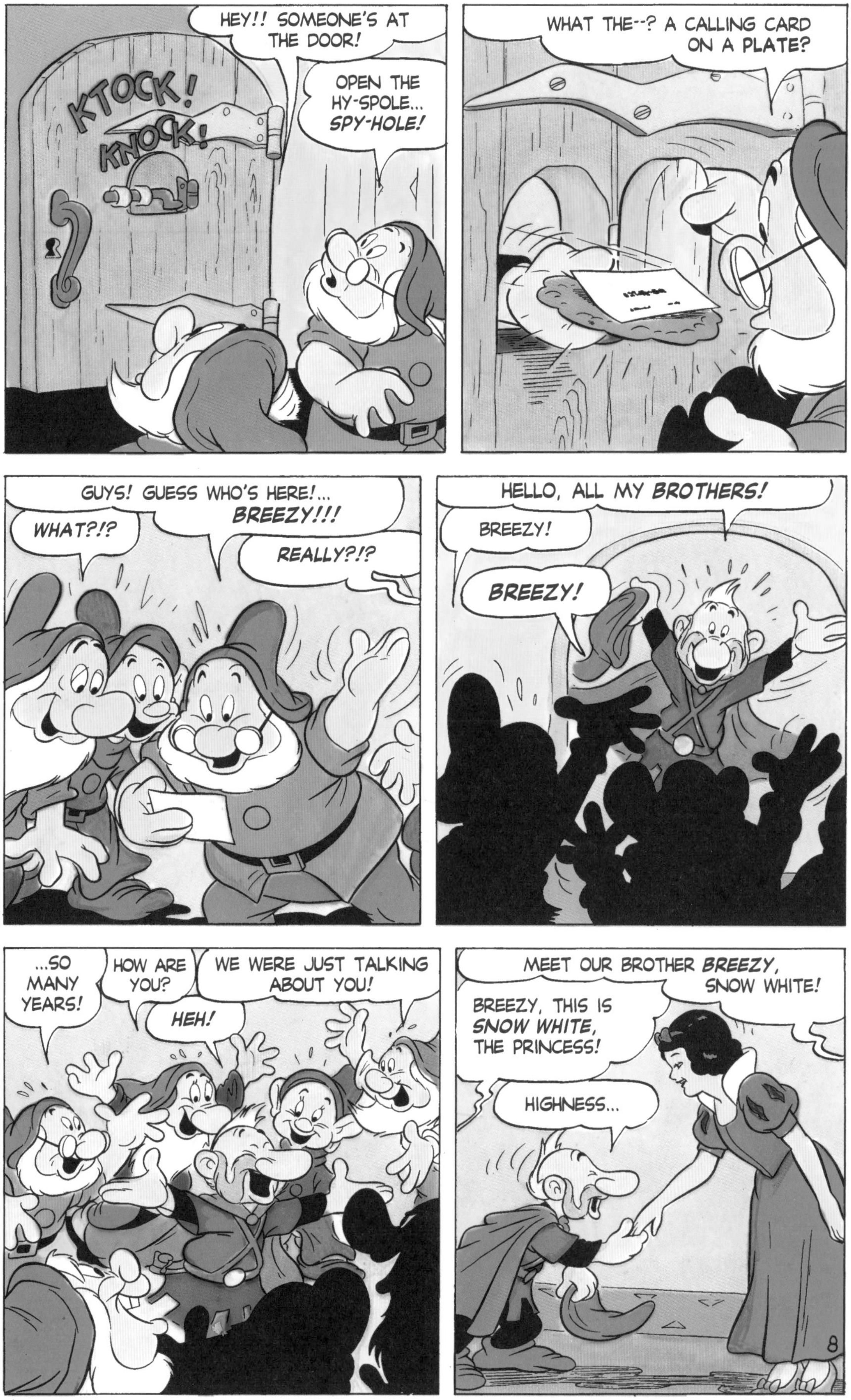
KTOCK! KNOCK!
HEY!! SOMEONE'S AT THE DOOR!
OPEN THE HY-SPOLE... SPY-HOLE!
WHAT THE--? A CALLING CARD ON A PLATE?
GUYS! GUESS WHO'S HERE!... BREEZY!!!
WHAT?!?
REALLY?!?
HELLO, ALL MY BROTHERS!
BREEZY!
BREEZY!
...SO MANY YEARS!
HOW ARE YOU?
WE WERE JUST TALKING ABOUT YOU!
HEH!
MEET OUR BROTHER BREEZY, SNOW WHITE!
BREEZY, THIS IS SNOW WHITE, THE PRINCESS!
HIGHNESS...
8

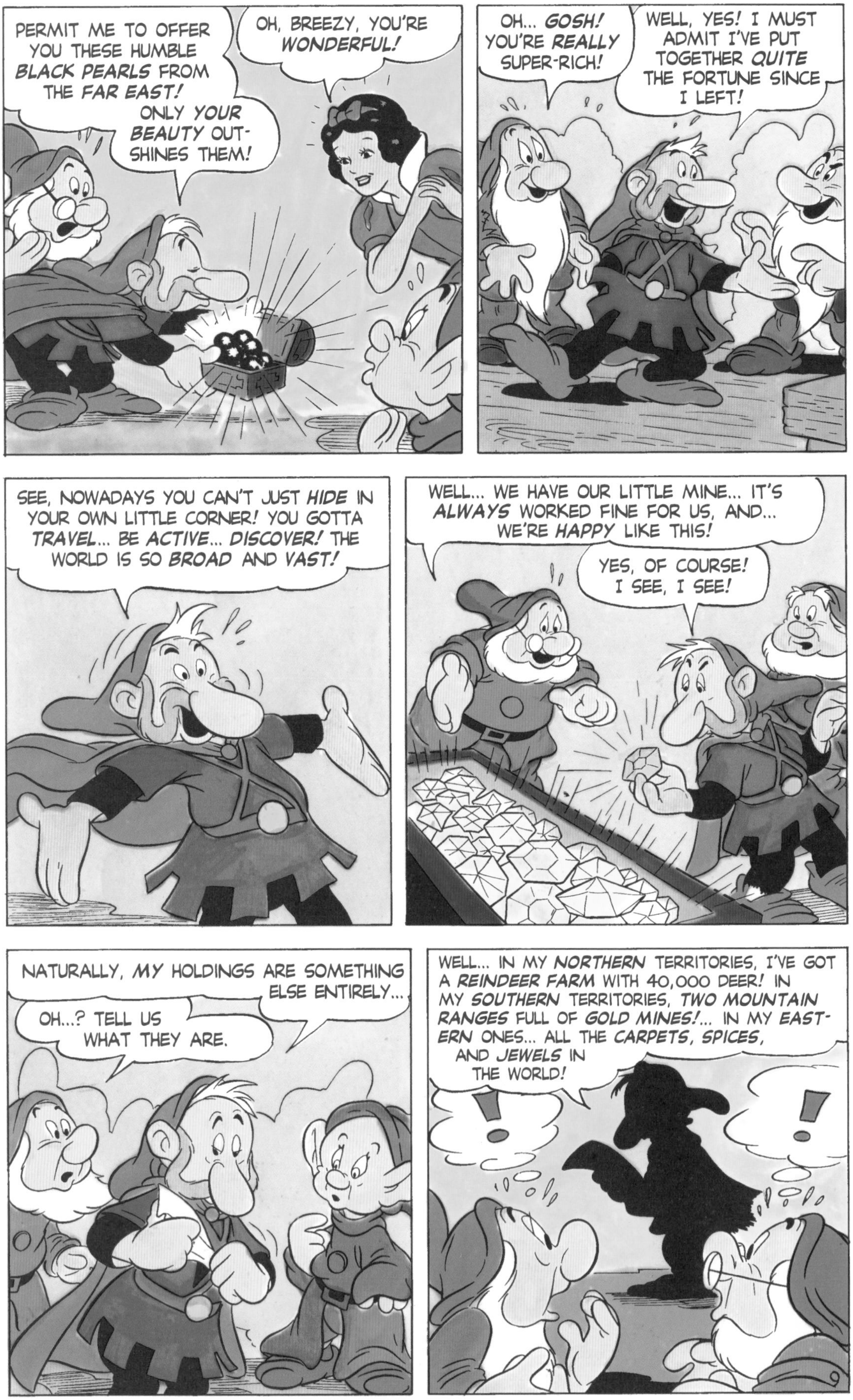

PERMIT ME TO OFFER YOU THESE HUMBLE BLACK PEARLS FROM THE FAR EAST!
ONLY YOUR BEAUTY OUT-SHINES THEM!
OH, BREEZY, YOU'RE WONDERFUL!
OH... GOSH! YOU'RE REALLY SUPER-RICH!
WELL, YES! I MUST ADMIT I'VE PUT TOGETHER QUITE THE FORTUNE SINCE I LEFT!
SEE, NOWADAYS YOU CAN'T JUST HIDE IN YOUR OWN LITTLE CORNER! YOU GOTTA TRAVEL... BE ACTIVE... DISCOVER! THE WORLD IS SO BROAD AND VAST!
WELL... WE HAVE OUR LITTLE MINE... IT'S ALWAYS WORKED FINE FOR US, AND... WE'RE HAPPY LIKE THIS!
YES, OF COURSE! I SEE, I SEE!
NATURALLY, MY HOLDINGS ARE SOMETHING ELSE ENTIRELY...
OH...? TELL US WHAT THEY ARE.
WELL... IN MY NORTHERN TERRITORIES, I'VE GOT A REINDEER FARM WITH 40,000 DEER! IN MY SOUTHERN TERRITORIES, TWO MOUNTAIN RANGES FULL OF GOLD MINES!... IN MY EAST-ERN ONES... ALL THE CARPETS, SPICES, AND JEWELS IN THE WORLD!
!
!
9

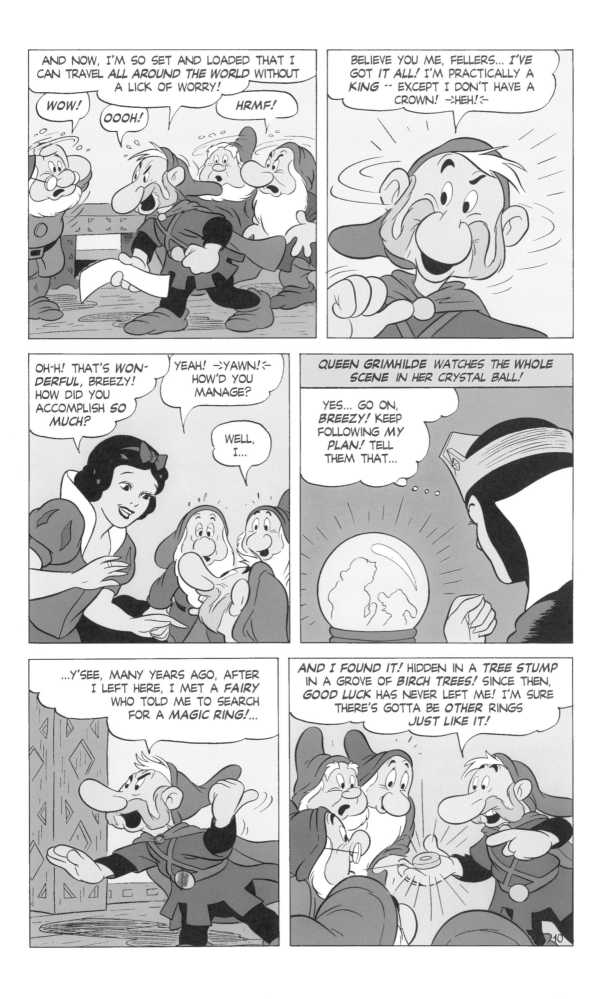

AND NOW, I'M SO SET AND LOADED THAT I CAN TRAVEL *ALL AROUND THE WORLD* WITHOUT A LICK OF WORRY!

WOW!

OOOH!

HRMF!

BELIEVE YOU ME, FELLERS... *I'VE GOT IT ALL!* I'M PRACTICALLY A *KING* -- EXCEPT I DON'T HAVE A CROWN! →HEH!←

OH-H! THAT'S *WONDERFUL*, BREEZY! HOW DID YOU ACCOMPLISH *SO MUCH?*

YEAH! →YAWN!← HOW'D YOU MANAGE?

WELL, I...

QUEEN GRIMHILDE WATCHES THE WHOLE SCENE IN HER CRYSTAL BALL!

YES... GO ON, *BREEZY!* KEEP FOLLOWING *MY PLAN!* TELL THEM THAT...

...Y'SEE, MANY YEARS AGO, AFTER I LEFT HERE, I MET A *FAIRY* WHO TOLD ME TO SEARCH FOR A *MAGIC RING!*...

AND I FOUND IT! HIDDEN IN A *TREE STUMP* IN A GROVE OF *BIRCH TREES!* SINCE THEN, *GOOD LUCK* HAS NEVER LEFT ME! I'M SURE THERE'S GOTTA BE *OTHER* RINGS *JUST LIKE IT!*

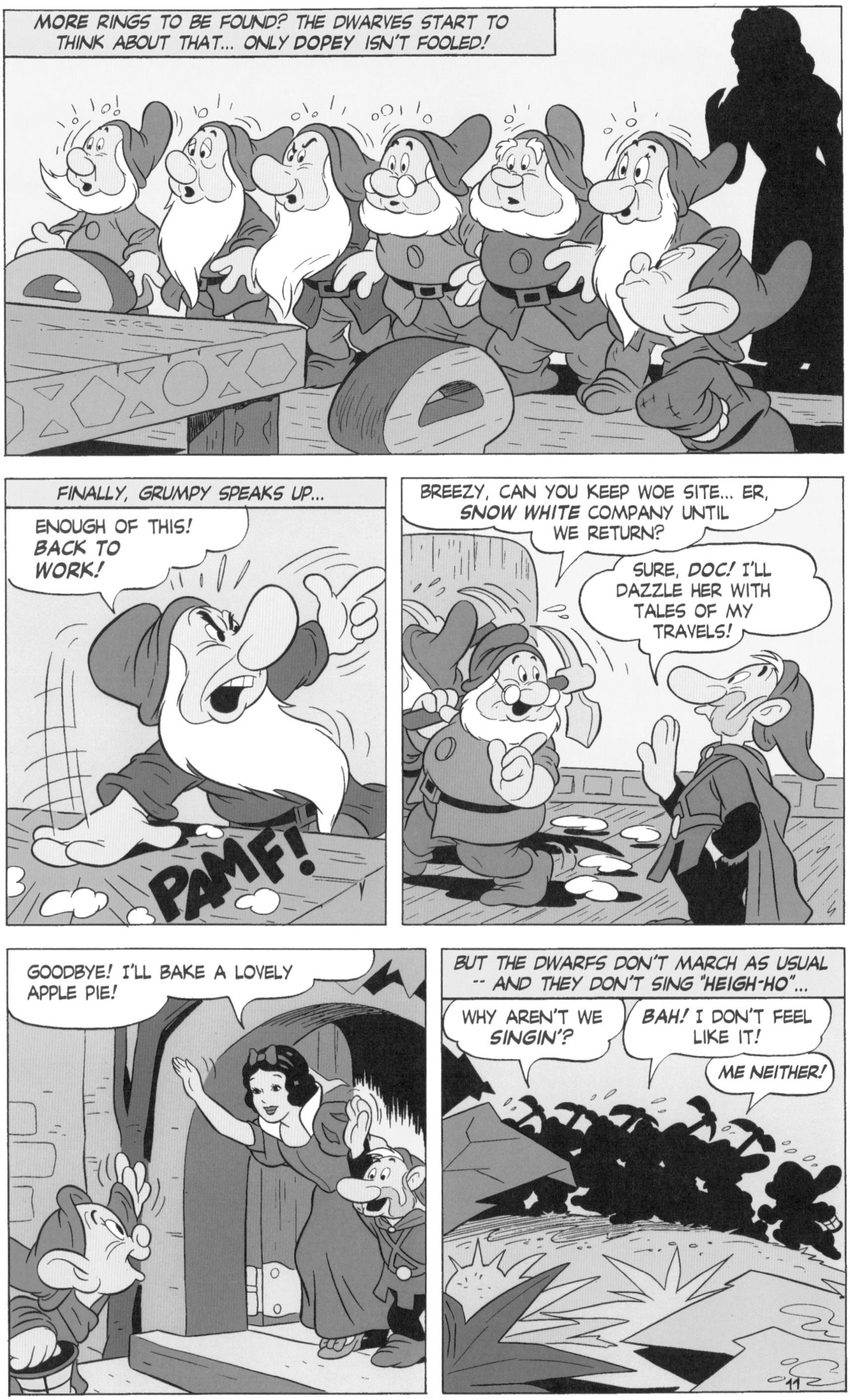
MORE RINGS TO BE FOUND? THE DWARVES START TO THINK ABOUT THAT... ONLY DOPEY ISN'T FOOLED!
FINALLY, GRUMPY SPEAKS UP...
ENOUGH OF THIS! BACK TO WORK!
PAMF!
BREEZY, CAN YOU KEEP WOE SITE... ER, SNOW WHITE COMPANY UNTIL WE RETURN?
SURE, DOC! I'LL DAZZLE HER WITH TALES OF MY TRAVELS!
GOODBYE! I'LL BAKE A LOVELY APPLE PIE!
BUT THE DWARFS DON'T MARCH AS USUAL -- AND THEY DON'T SING "HEIGH-HO"...
WHY AREN'T WE SINGIN'?
BAH! I DON'T FEEL LIKE IT!
ME NEITHER!

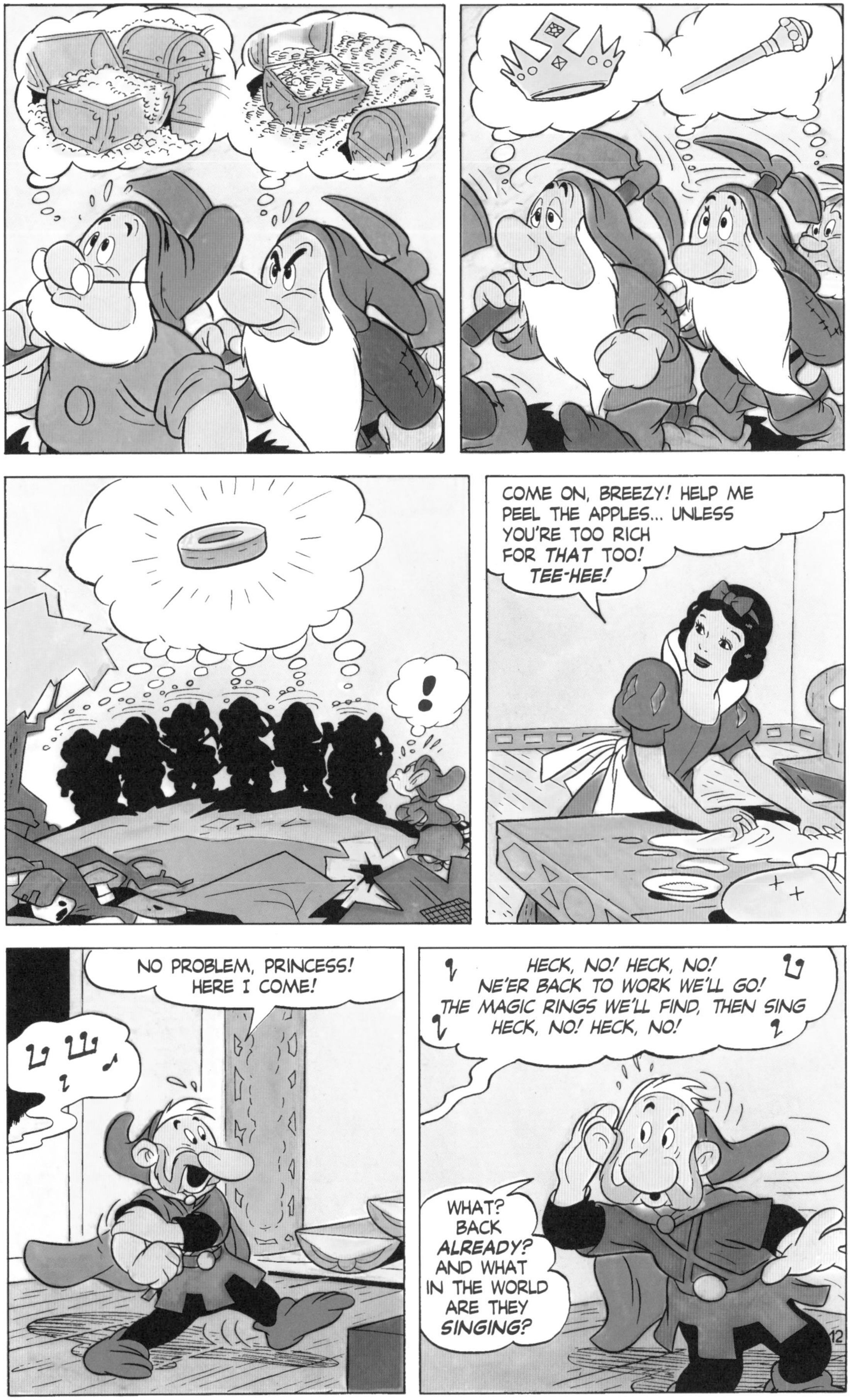

COME ON, BREEZY! HELP ME PEEL THE APPLES... UNLESS YOU'RE TOO RICH FOR THAT TOO! TEE-HEE!
NO PROBLEM, PRINCESS! HERE I COME!
HECK, NO! HECK, NO! NE'ER BACK TO WORK WE'LL GO! THE MAGIC RINGS WE'LL FIND, THEN SING HECK, NO! HECK, NO!
WHAT? BACK ALREADY? AND WHAT IN THE WORLD ARE THEY SINGING?
12

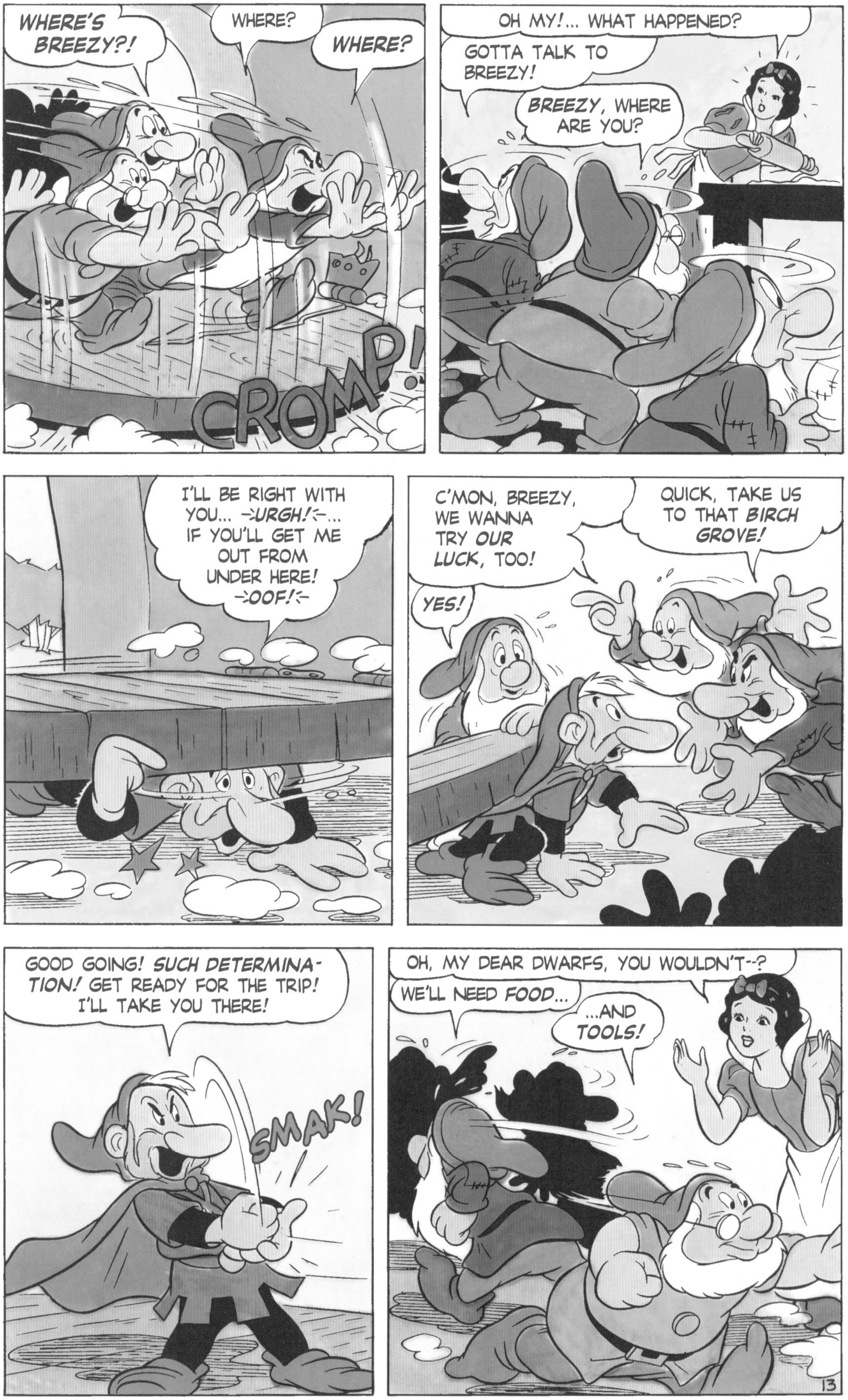
WHERE'S BREEZY?!
WHERE?
WHERE?
CROMP!
OH MY!... WHAT HAPPENED?
GOTTA TALK TO BREEZY!
BREEZY, WHERE ARE YOU?
I'LL BE RIGHT WITH YOU... URGH!... IF YOU'LL GET ME OUT FROM UNDER HERE! OOF!
C'MON, BREEZY, WE WANNA TRY OUR LUCK, TOO!
QUICK, TAKE US TO THAT BIRCH GROVE!
YES!
GOOD GOING! SUCH DETERMINATION! GET READY FOR THE TRIP! I'LL TAKE YOU THERE!
SMAK!
OH, MY DEAR DWARFS, YOU WOULDN'T--?
WE'LL NEED FOOD...
...AND TOOLS!
13

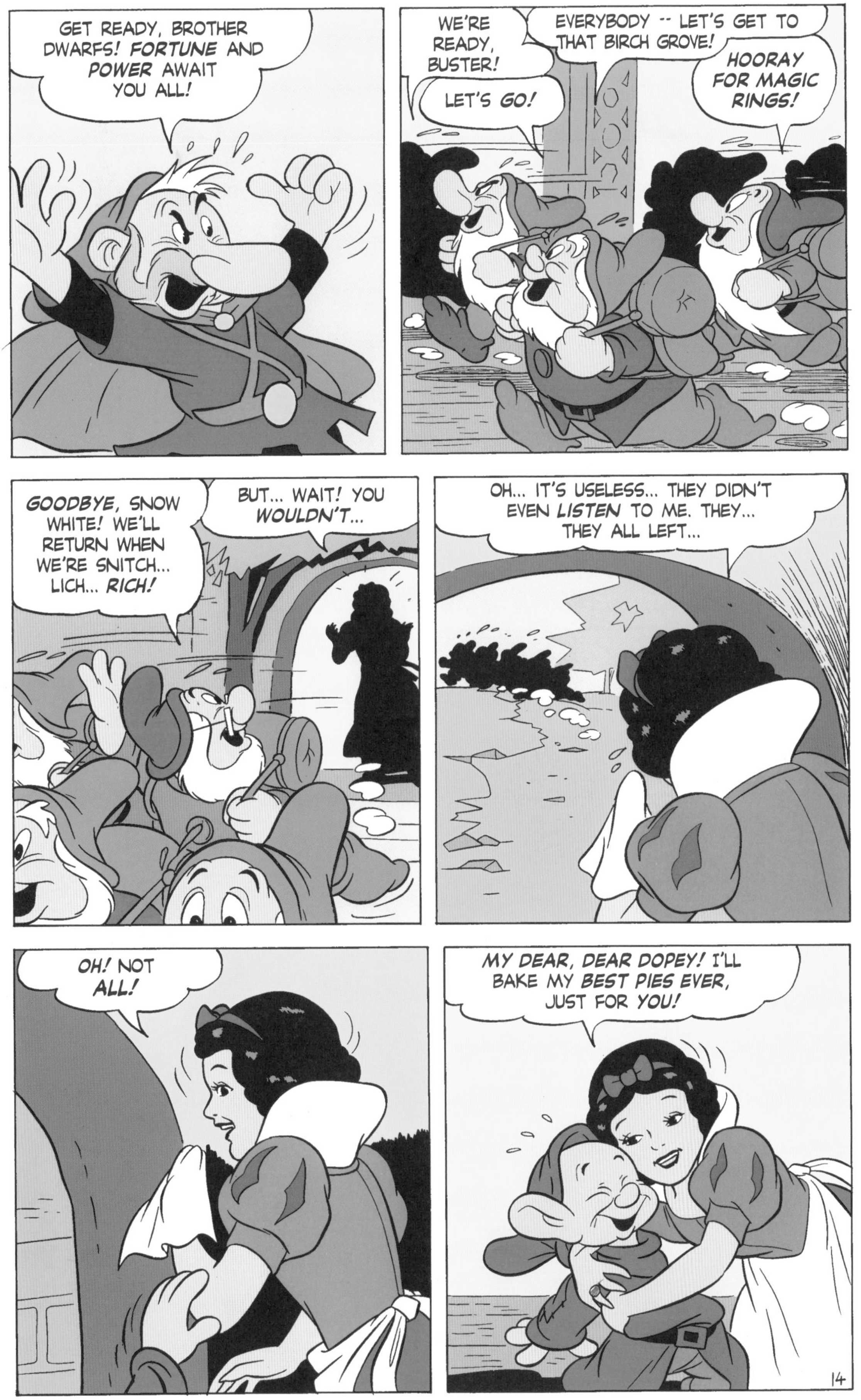
GET READY, BROTHER DWARFS! FORTUNE AND POWER AWAIT YOU ALL!
WE'RE READY, BUSTER!
EVERYBODY -- LET'S GET TO THAT BIRCH GROVE!
LET'S GO!
HOORAY FOR MAGIC RINGS!
GOODBYE, SNOW WHITE! WE'LL RETURN WHEN WE'RE SNITCH... LICH... RICH!
BUT... WAIT! YOU WOULDN'T...
OH... IT'S USELESS... THEY DIDN'T EVEN LISTEN TO ME. THEY... THEY ALL LEFT...
OH! NOT ALL!
MY DEAR, DEAR DOPEY! I'LL BAKE MY BEST PIES EVER, JUST FOR YOU!
14

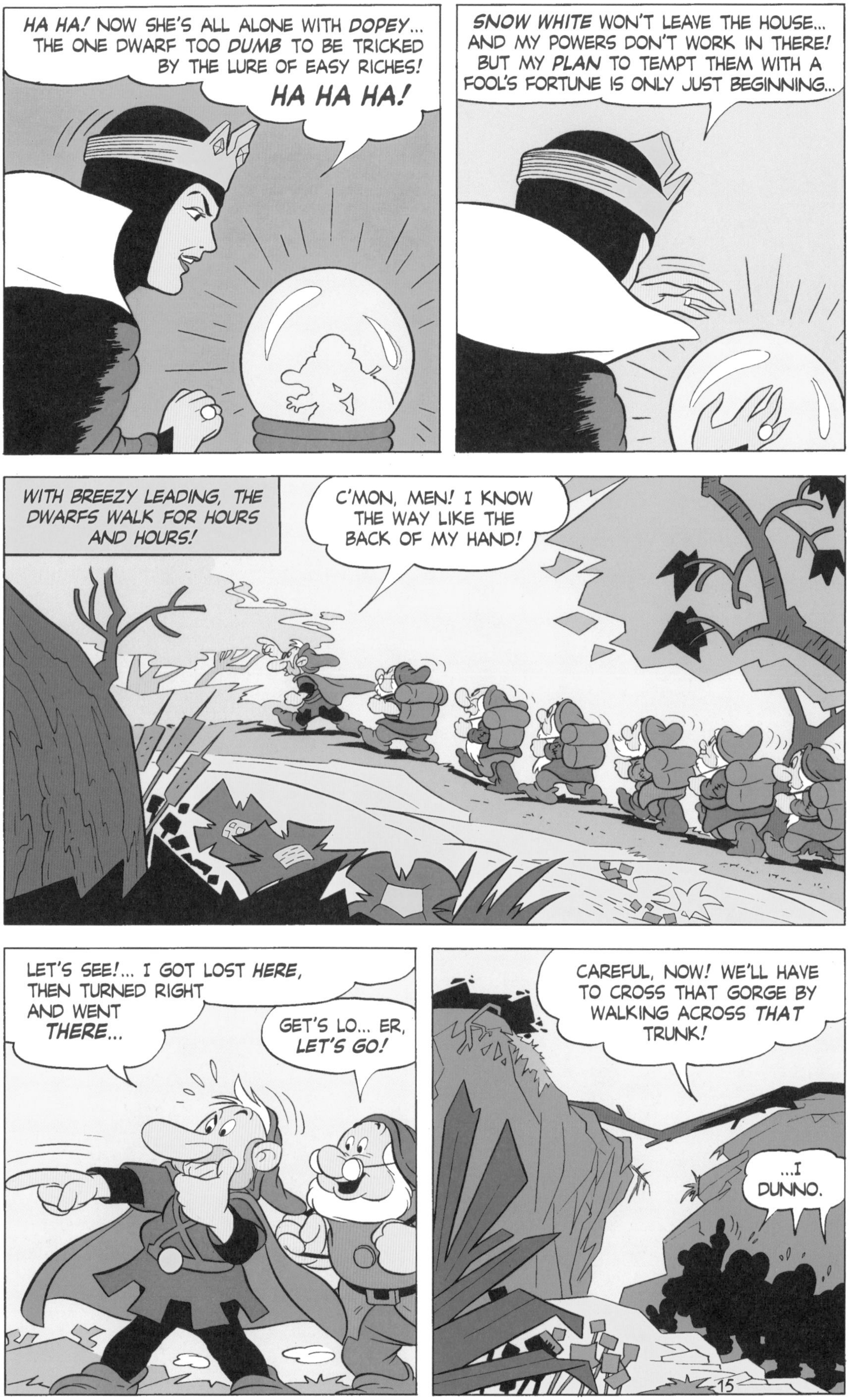
HA HA! NOW SHE'S ALL ALONE WITH DOPEY... THE ONE DWARF TOO DUMB TO BE TRICKED BY THE LURE OF EASY RICHES!
HA HA HA!
SNOW WHITE WON'T LEAVE THE HOUSE... AND MY POWERS DON'T WORK IN THERE! BUT MY PLAN TO TEMPT THEM WITH A FOOL'S FORTUNE IS ONLY JUST BEGINNING...
WITH BREEZY LEADING, THE DWARFS WALK FOR HOURS AND HOURS!
C'MON, MEN! I KNOW THE WAY LIKE THE BACK OF MY HAND!
LET'S SEE!... I GOT LOST HERE, THEN TURNED RIGHT AND WENT THERE...
GET'S LO... ER, LET'S GO!
CAREFUL, NOW! WE'LL HAVE TO CROSS THAT GORGE BY WALKING ACROSS THAT TRUNK!
...I DUNNO.

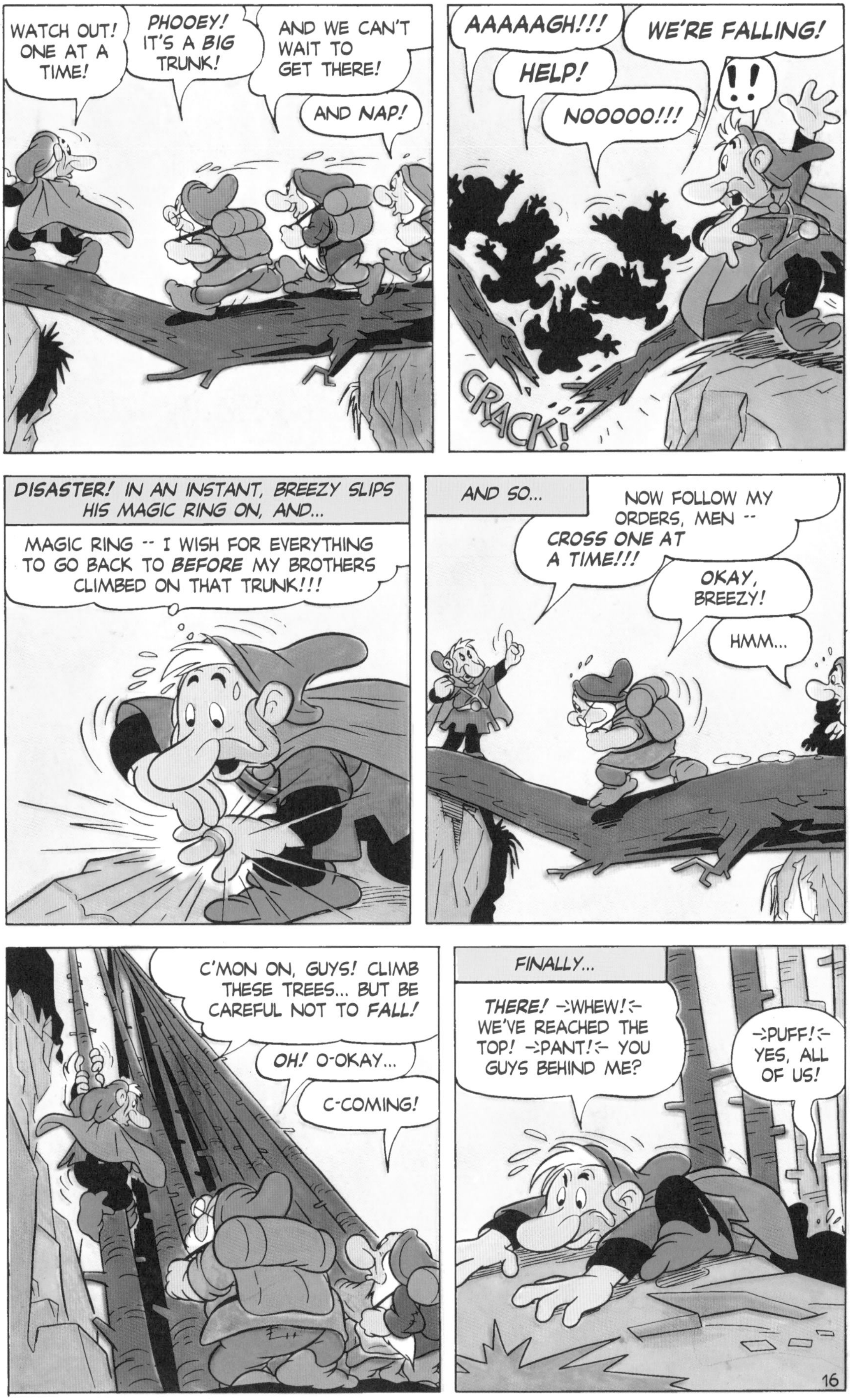
WATCH OUT! ONE AT A TIME!
PHOOEY! IT'S A BIG TRUNK!
AND WE CAN'T WAIT TO GET THERE!
AND NAP!
AAAAAGH!!!
HELP!
WE'RE FALLING!
NOOOOO!!!
!!
CRACK!
DISASTER! IN AN INSTANT, BREEZY SLIPS HIS MAGIC RING ON, AND...
MAGIC RING -- I WISH FOR EVERYTHING TO GO BACK TO BEFORE MY BROTHERS CLIMBED ON THAT TRUNK!!!
AND SO...
NOW FOLLOW MY ORDERS, MEN -- CROSS ONE AT A TIME!!!
OKAY, BREEZY!
HMM...
C'MON ON, GUYS! CLIMB THESE TREES... BUT BE CAREFUL NOT TO FALL!
OH! O-OKAY...
C-COMING!
FINALLY...
THERE! -WHEW!- WE'VE REACHED THE TOP! -PANT!- YOU GUYS BEHIND ME?
-PUFF!- YES, ALL OF US!
16

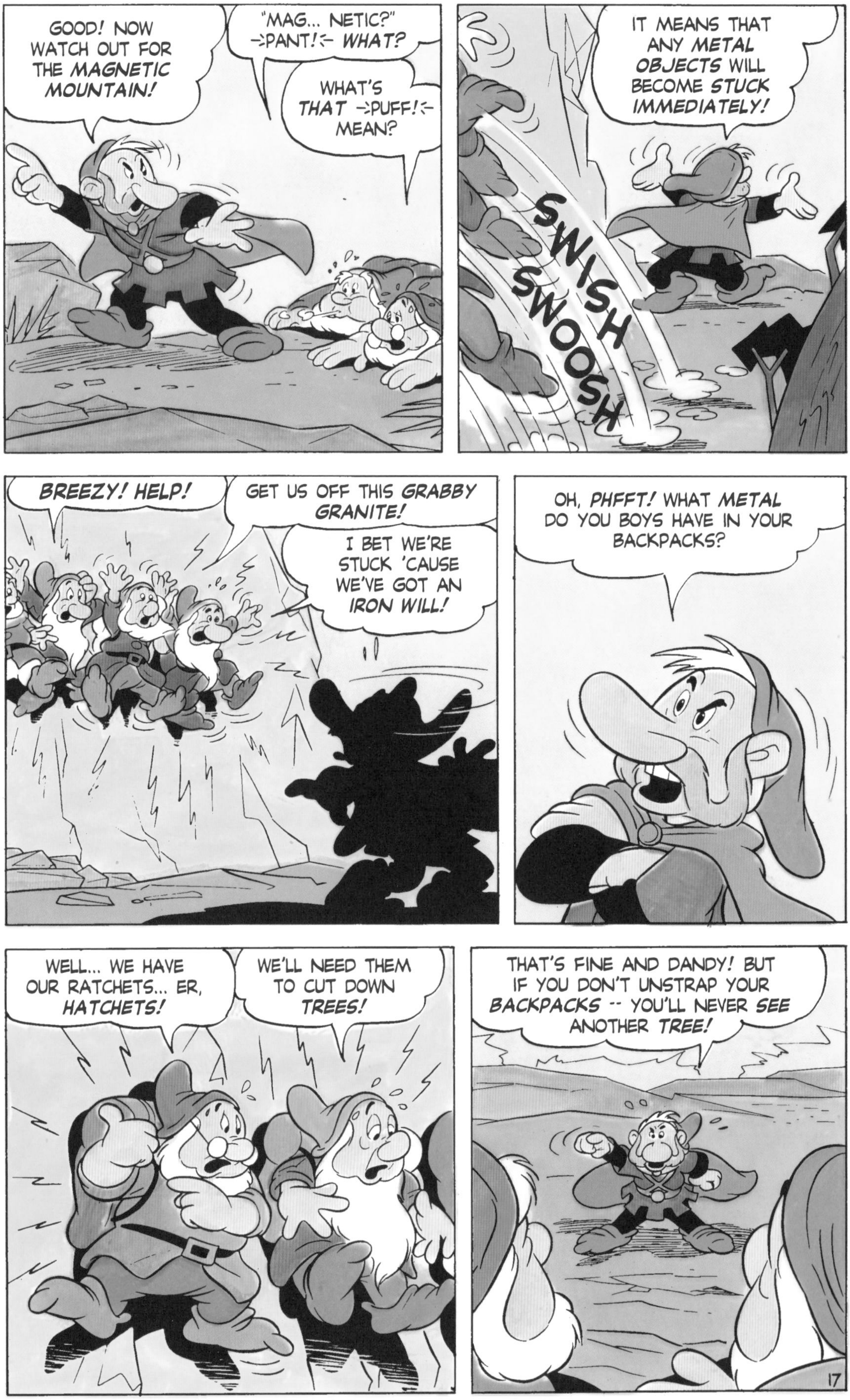
GOOD! NOW WATCH OUT FOR THE MAGNETIC MOUNTAIN!
"MAG... NETIC?" ~PANT!~ WHAT?
WHAT'S THAT ~PUFF!~ MEAN?
IT MEANS THAT ANY METAL OBJECTS WILL BECOME STUCK IMMEDIATELY!
SWISH
SWOOSH
BREEZY! HELP!
GET US OFF THIS GRABBY GRANITE!
I BET WE'RE STUCK 'CAUSE WE'VE GOT AN IRON WILL!
OH, PHFFT! WHAT METAL DO YOU BOYS HAVE IN YOUR BACKPACKS?
WELL... WE HAVE OUR RATCHETS... ER, HATCHETS!
WE'LL NEED THEM TO CUT DOWN TREES!
THAT'S FINE AND DANDY! BUT IF YOU DON'T UNSTRAP YOUR BACKPACKS -- YOU'LL NEVER SEE ANOTHER TREE!
17

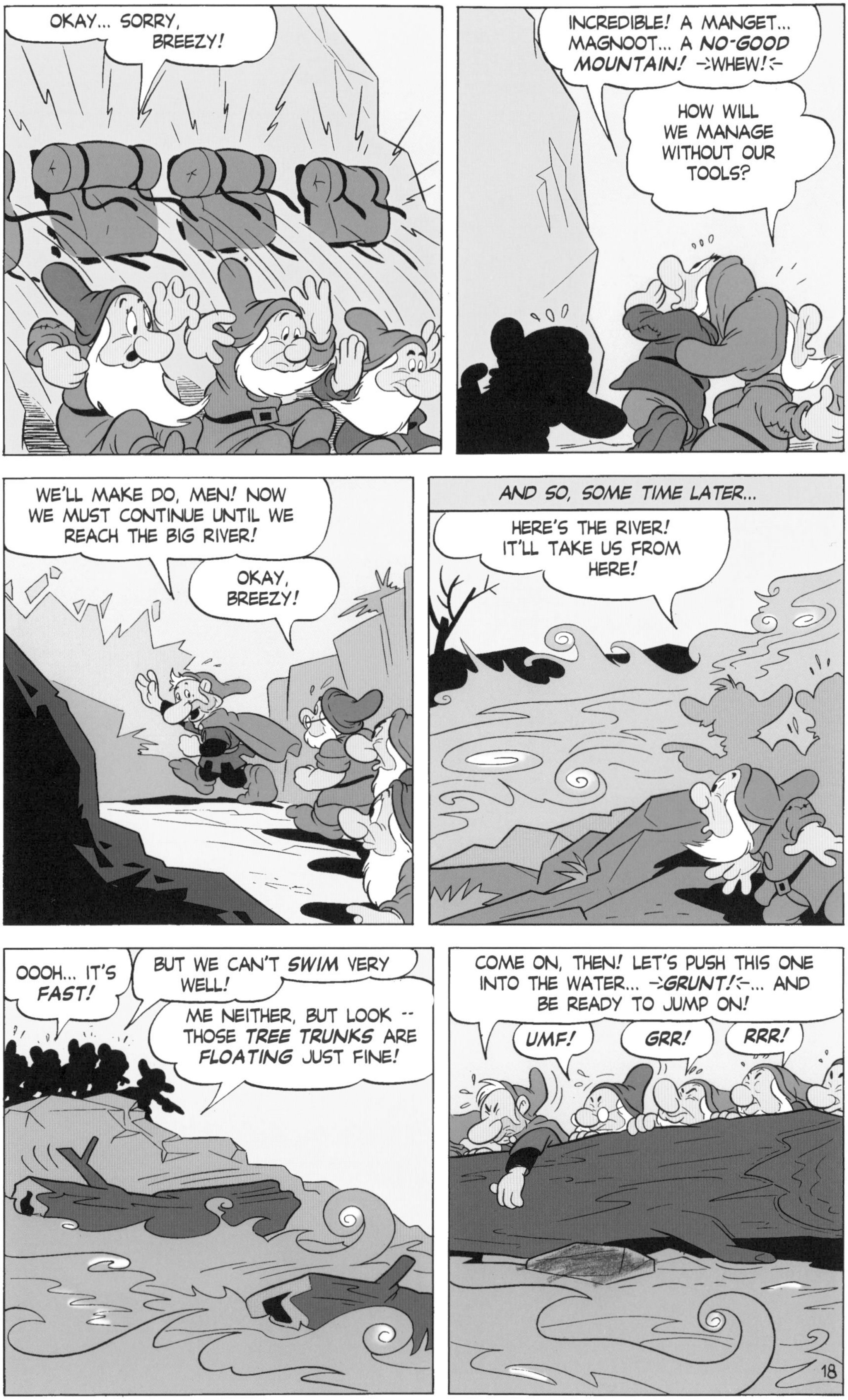
OKAY... SORRY, BREEZY!
INCREDIBLE! A MANGET... MAGNOOT... A NO-GOOD MOUNTAIN! ->WHEW!<-
HOW WILL WE MANAGE WITHOUT OUR TOOLS?
WE'LL MAKE DO, MEN! NOW WE MUST CONTINUE UNTIL WE REACH THE BIG RIVER!
OKAY, BREEZY!
AND SO, SOME TIME LATER...
HERE'S THE RIVER! IT'LL TAKE US FROM HERE!
OOOH... IT'S FAST!
BUT WE CAN'T SWIM VERY WELL!
ME NEITHER, BUT LOOK -- THOSE TREE TRUNKS ARE FLOATING JUST FINE!
COME ON, THEN! LET'S PUSH THIS ONE INTO THE WATER... ->GRUNT!<-... AND BE READY TO JUMP ON!
UMF!
GRR!
RRR!
18

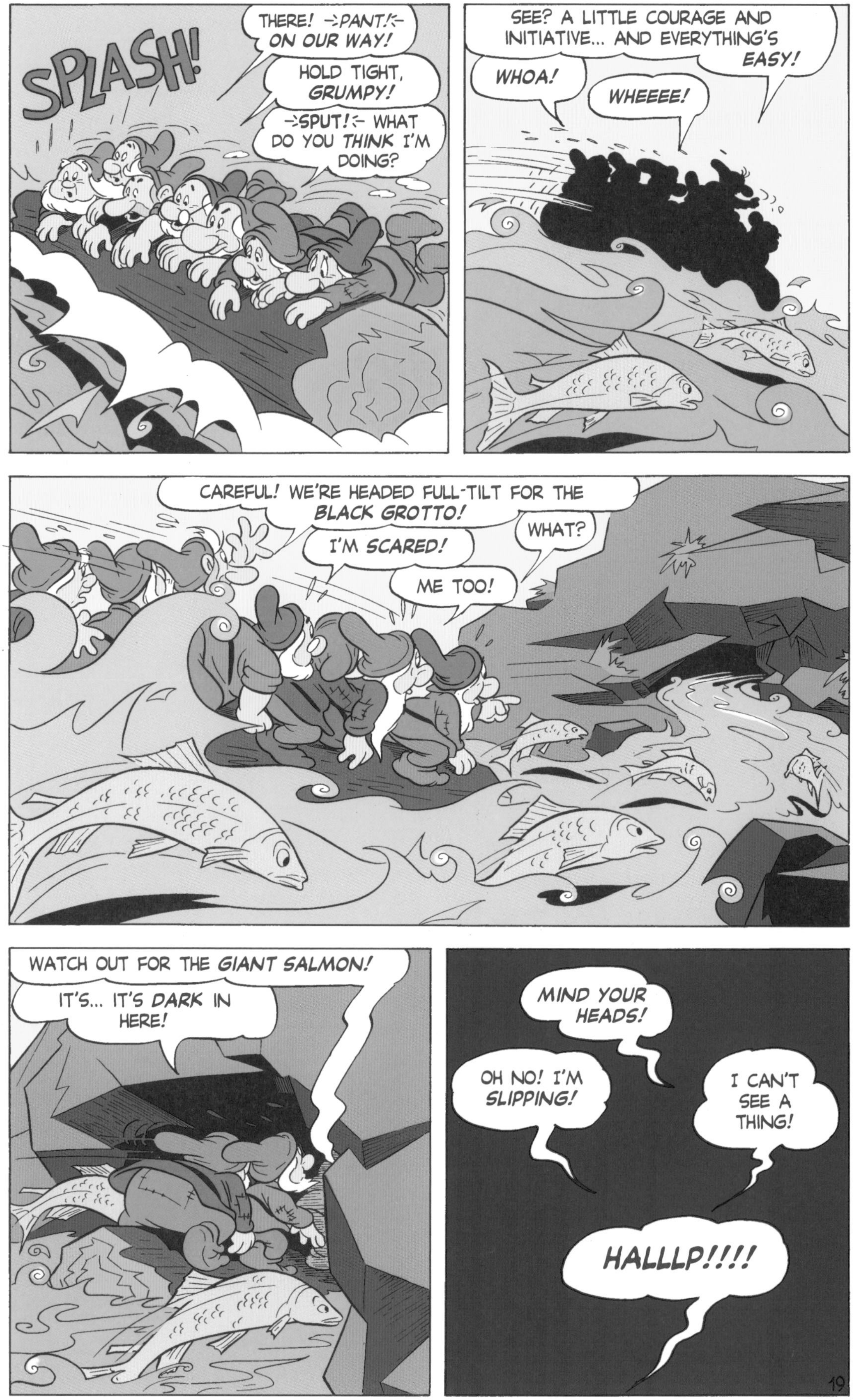
SPLASH!
THERE! -PANT!- ON OUR WAY!
HOLD TIGHT, GRUMPY!
-SPUT!- WHAT DO YOU THINK I'M DOING?
SEE? A LITTLE COURAGE AND INITIATIVE... AND EVERYTHING'S EASY!
WHOA!
WHEEEE!
CAREFUL! WE'RE HEADED FULL-TILT FOR THE BLACK GROTTO!
I'M SCARED!
WHAT?
ME TOO!
WATCH OUT FOR THE GIANT SALMON!
IT'S... IT'S DARK IN HERE!
MIND YOUR HEADS!
OH NO! I'M SLIPPING!
I CAN'T SEE A THING!
HALLLP!!!!
19

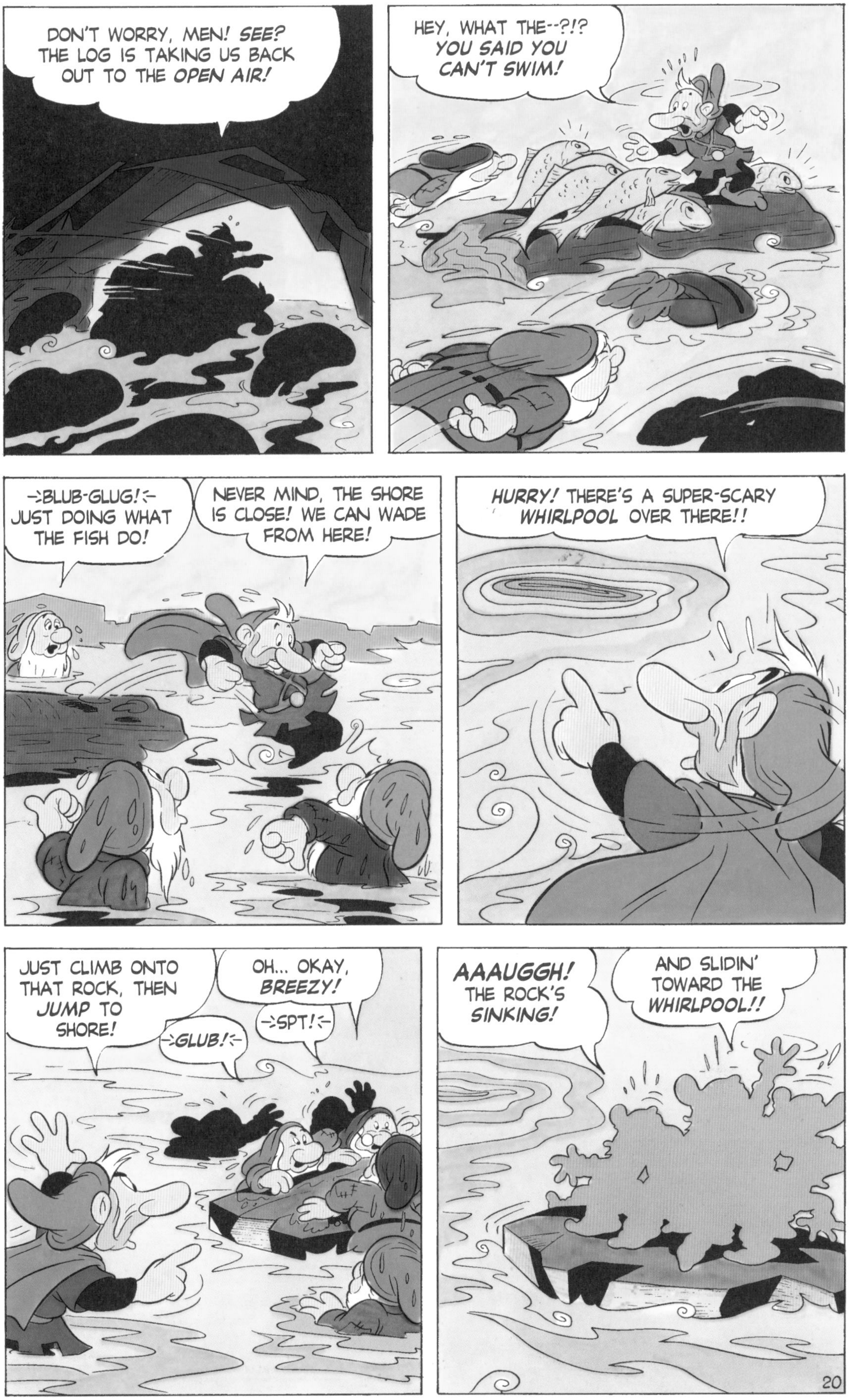
DON'T WORRY, MEN! SEE? THE LOG IS TAKING US BACK OUT TO THE OPEN AIR!
HEY, WHAT THE--?!? YOU SAID YOU CAN'T SWIM!
-BLUB-GLUG!- JUST DOING WHAT THE FISH DO!
NEVER MIND, THE SHORE IS CLOSE! WE CAN WADE FROM HERE!
HURRY! THERE'S A SUPER-SCARY WHIRLPOOL OVER THERE!!
JUST CLIMB ONTO THAT ROCK, THEN JUMP TO SHORE!
-GLUB!-
OH... OKAY, BREEZY!
-SPT!-
AAAUGGH! THE ROCK'S SINKING!
AND SLIDIN' TOWARD THE WHIRLPOOL!!
20

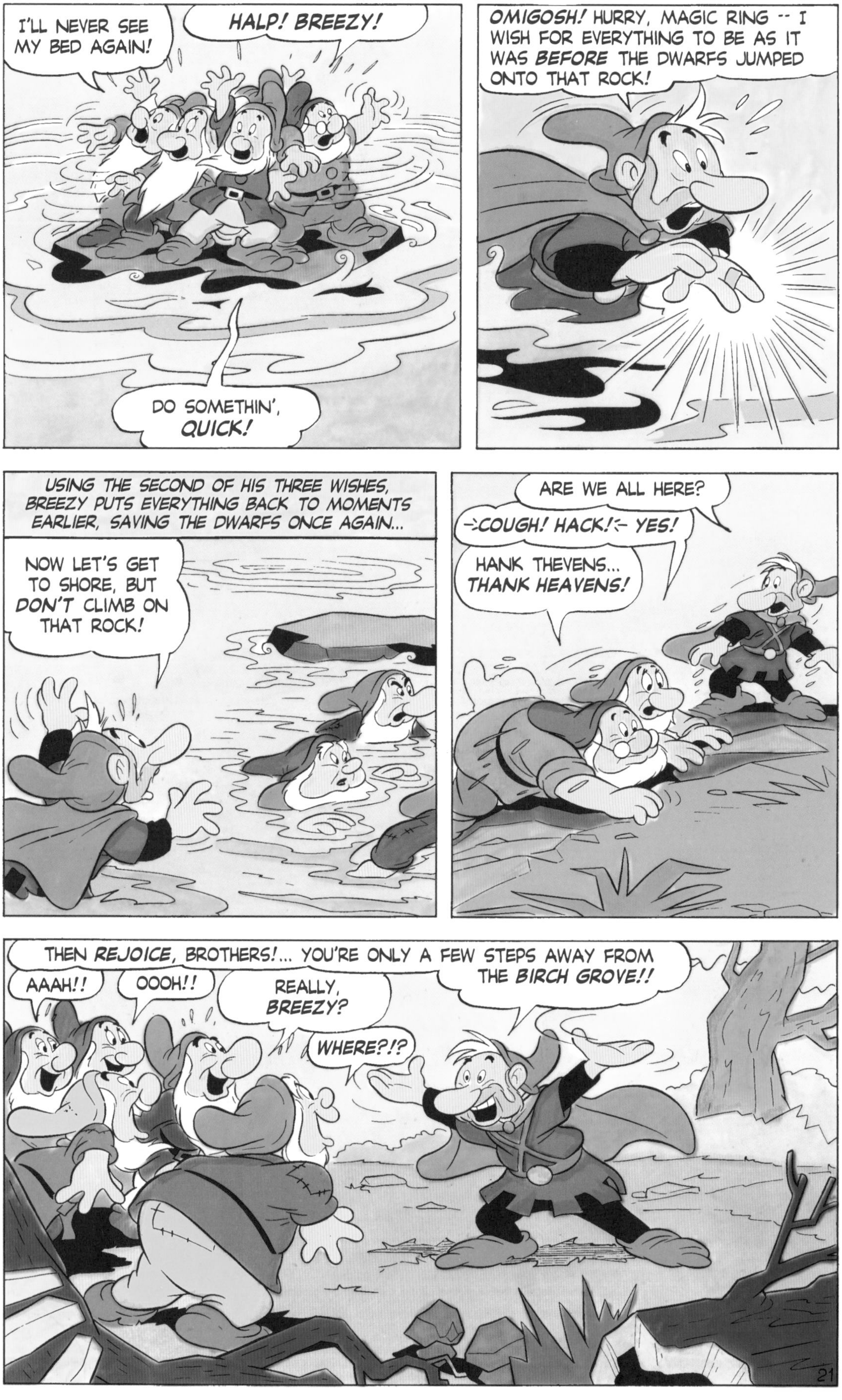
I'LL NEVER SEE MY BED AGAIN!
HALP! BREEZY!
DO SOMETHIN', QUICK!
OMIGOSH! HURRY, MAGIC RING -- I WISH FOR EVERYTHING TO BE AS IT WAS BEFORE THE DWARFS JUMPED ONTO THAT ROCK!
USING THE SECOND OF HIS THREE WISHES, BREEZY PUTS EVERYTHING BACK TO MOMENTS EARLIER, SAVING THE DWARFS ONCE AGAIN...
NOW LET'S GET TO SHORE, BUT DON'T CLIMB ON THAT ROCK!
ARE WE ALL HERE?
-COUGH! HACK!- YES!
HANK THEVENS... THANK HEAVENS!
THEN REJOICE, BROTHERS!... YOU'RE ONLY A FEW STEPS AWAY FROM THE BIRCH GROVE!!
AAAH!!
OOOH!!
REALLY, BREEZY?
WHERE?!?
21

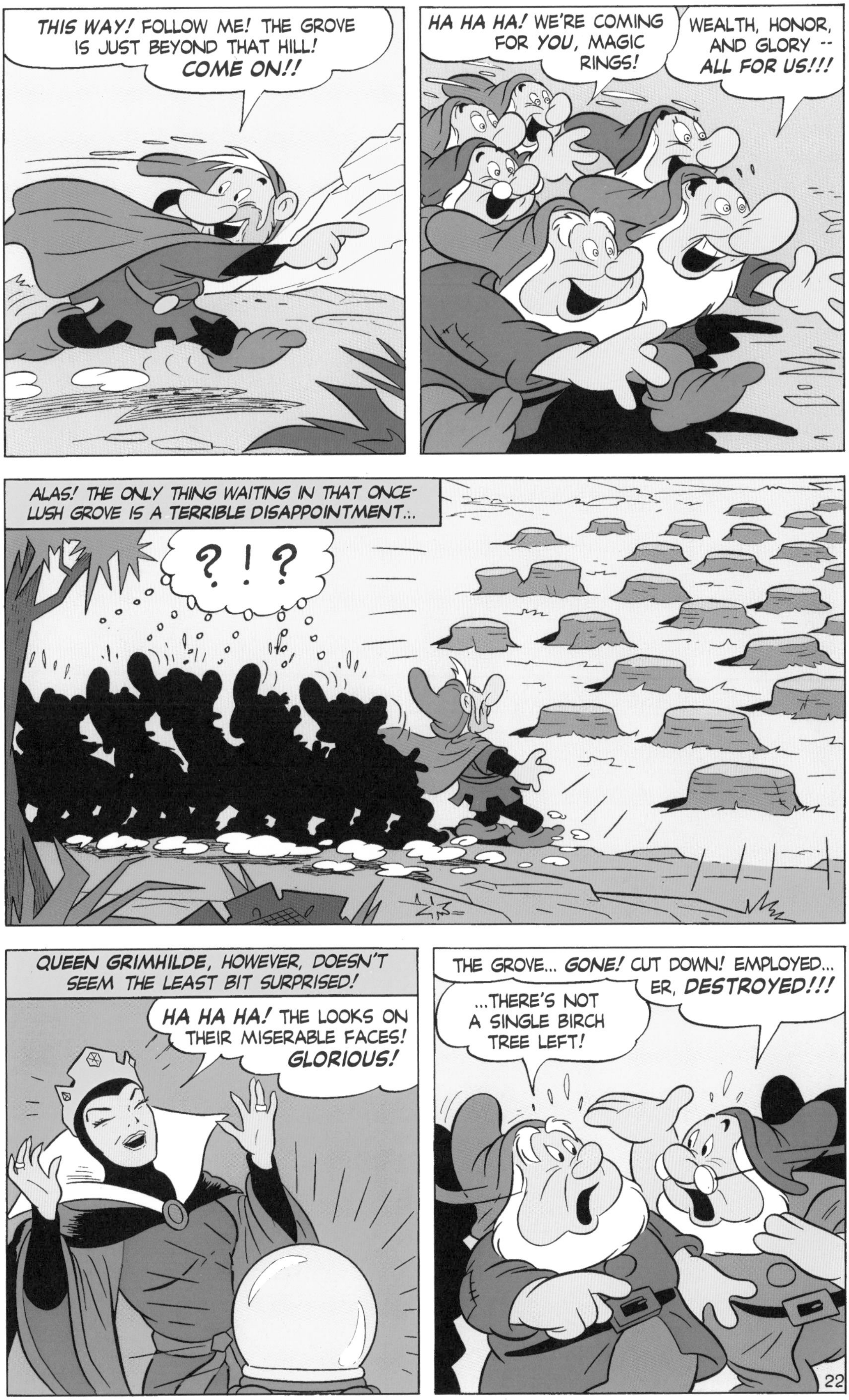
THIS WAY! FOLLOW ME! THE GROVE IS JUST BEYOND THAT HILL! COME ON!!
HA HA HA! WE'RE COMING FOR YOU, MAGIC RINGS!
WEALTH, HONOR, AND GLORY -- ALL FOR US!!!
ALAS! THE ONLY THING WAITING IN THAT ONCE-LUSH GROVE IS A TERRIBLE DISAPPOINTMENT...
?!?
QUEEN GRIMHILDE, HOWEVER, DOESN'T SEEM THE LEAST BIT SURPRISED!
HA HA HA! THE LOOKS ON THEIR MISERABLE FACES! GLORIOUS!
THE GROVE... GONE! CUT DOWN! EMPLOYED... ER, DESTROYED!!!
...THERE'S NOT A SINGLE BIRCH TREE LEFT!
22

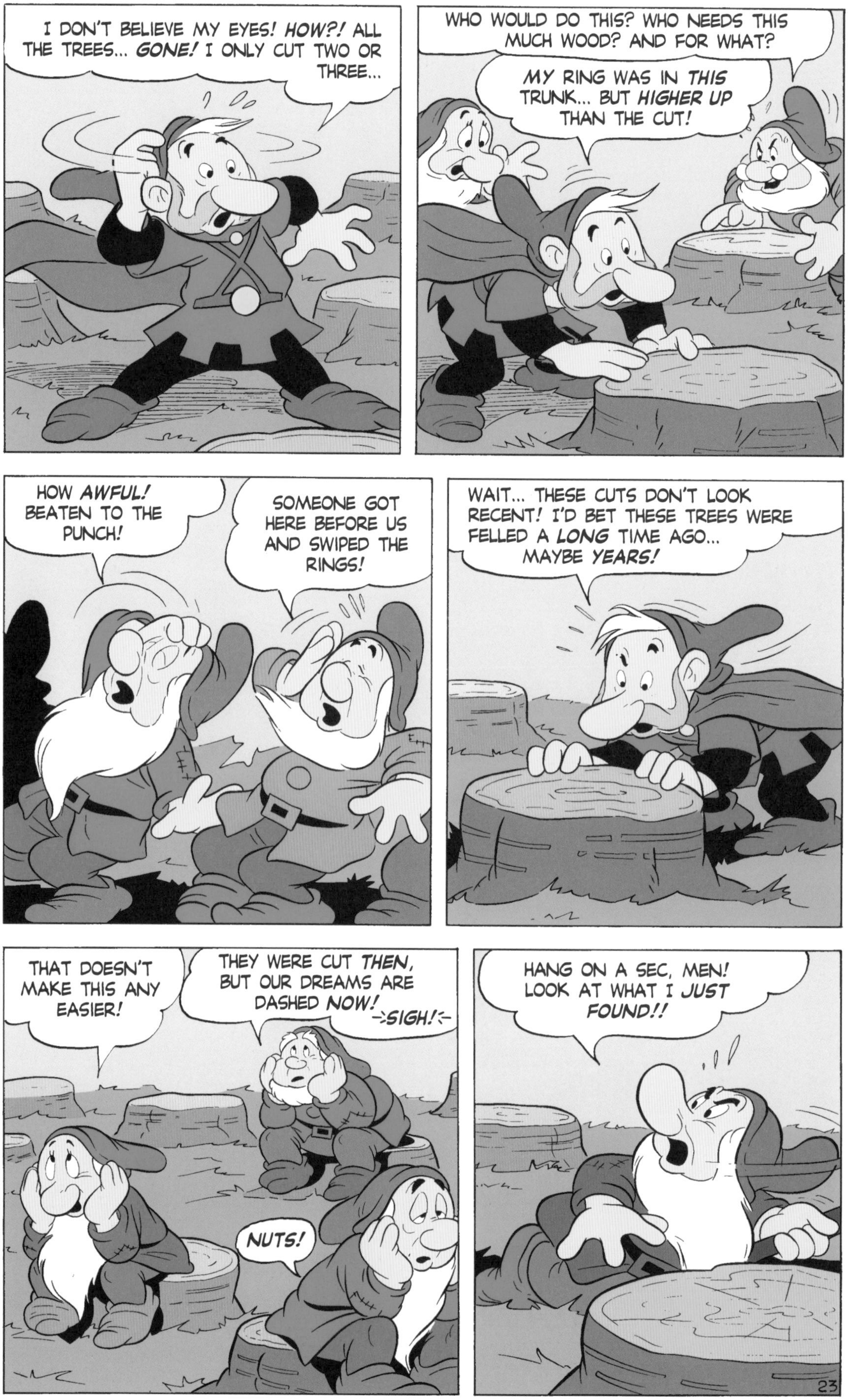
I DON'T BELIEVE MY EYES! HOW?! ALL THE TREES... GONE! I ONLY CUT TWO OR THREE...
WHO WOULD DO THIS? WHO NEEDS THIS MUCH WOOD? AND FOR WHAT?
MY RING WAS IN THIS TRUNK... BUT HIGHER UP THAN THE CUT!
HOW AWFUL! BEATEN TO THE PUNCH!
SOMEONE GOT HERE BEFORE US AND SWIPED THE RINGS!
WAIT... THESE CUTS DON'T LOOK RECENT! I'D BET THESE TREES WERE FELLED A LONG TIME AGO... MAYBE YEARS!
THAT DOESN'T MAKE THIS ANY EASIER!
THEY WERE CUT THEN, BUT OUR DREAMS ARE DASHED NOW!
-SIGH!-
NUTS!
HANG ON A SEC, MEN! LOOK AT WHAT I JUST FOUND!!
23

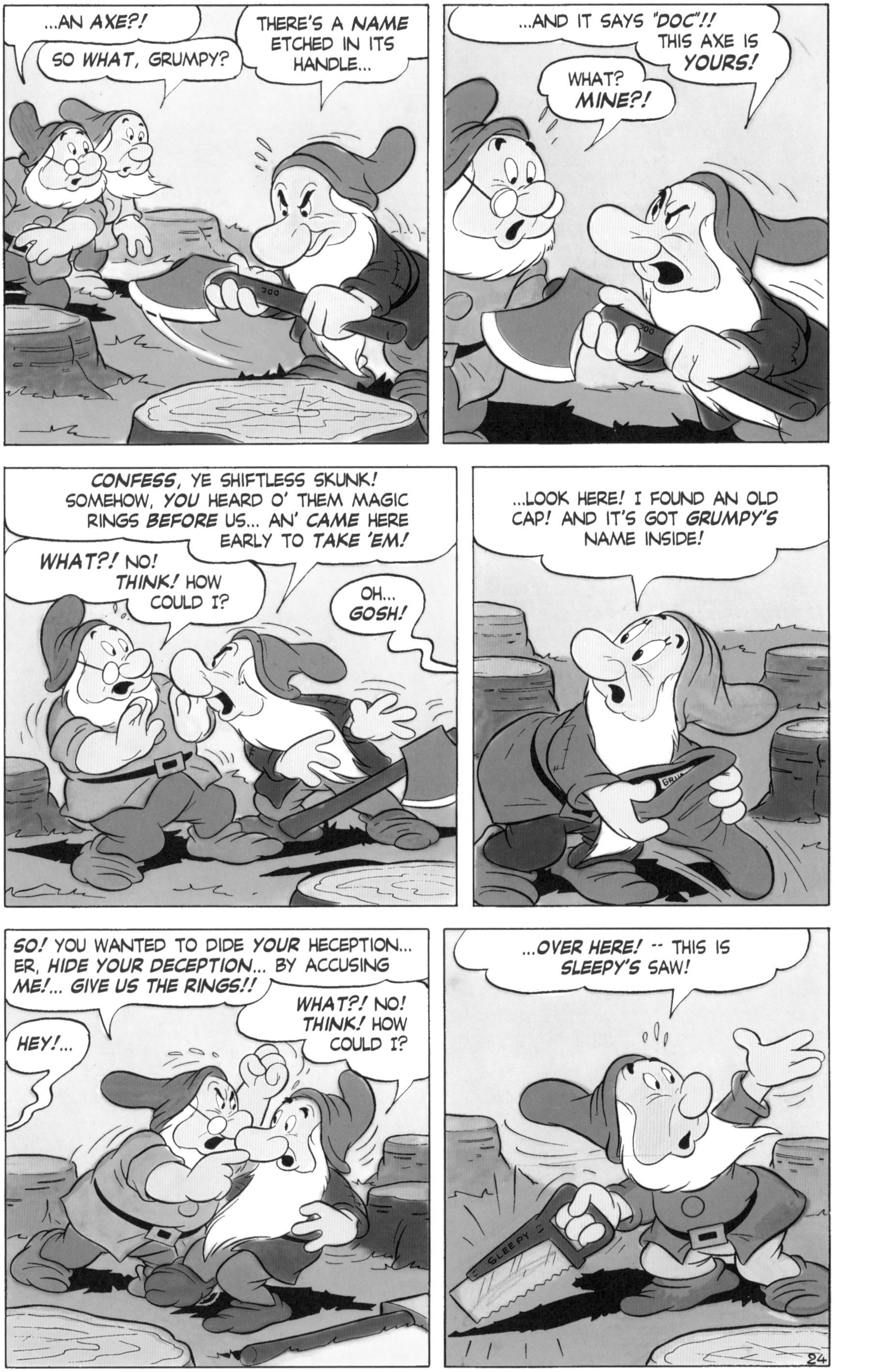
...AN AXE?!
SO WHAT, GRUMPY?
THERE'S A NAME ETCHED IN ITS HANDLE...
DOC
...AND IT SAYS "DOC"!! THIS AXE IS YOURS!
WHAT? MINE?!
DOC
CONFESS, YE SHIFTLESS SKUNK! SOMEHOW, YOU HEARD O' THEM MAGIC RINGS BEFORE US... AN' CAME HERE EARLY TO TAKE 'EM!
WHAT?! NO! THINK! HOW COULD I?
OH... GOSH!
...LOOK HERE! I FOUND AN OLD CAP! AND IT'S GOT GRUMPY'S NAME INSIDE!
SO! YOU WANTED TO DIDE YOUR HECEPTION... ER, HIDE YOUR DECEPTION... BY ACCUSING ME!... GIVE US THE RINGS!!
WHAT?! NO! THINK! HOW COULD I?
HEY!...
...OVER HERE! -- THIS IS SLEEPY'S SAW!
SLEEPY
24

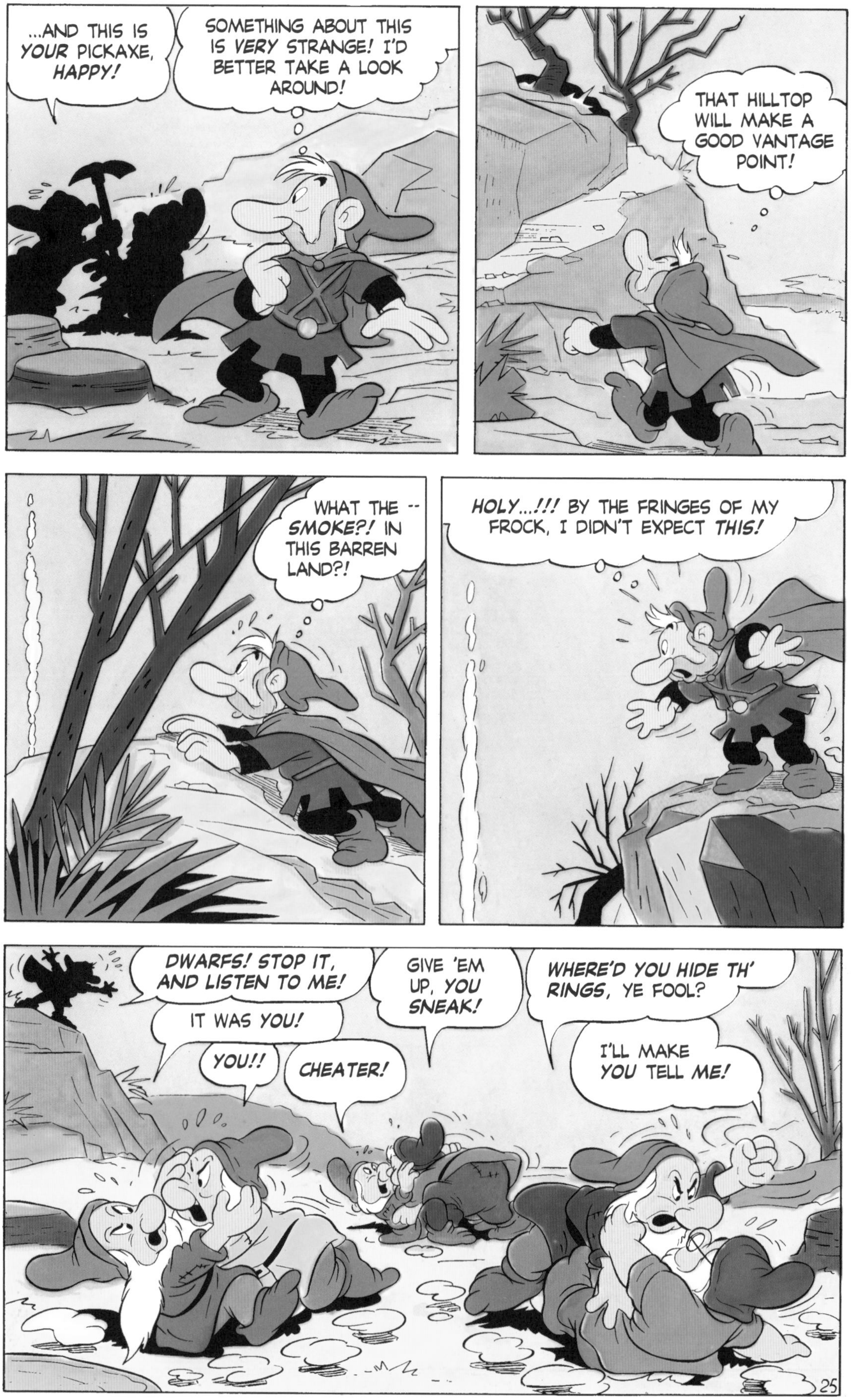
...AND THIS IS YOUR PICKAXE, HAPPY!
SOMETHING ABOUT THIS IS VERY STRANGE! I'D BETTER TAKE A LOOK AROUND!
THAT HILLTOP WILL MAKE A GOOD VANTAGE POINT!
WHAT THE -- SMOKE?! IN THIS BARREN LAND?!
HOLY...!!! BY THE FRINGES OF MY FROCK, I DIDN'T EXPECT THIS!
DWARFS! STOP IT, AND LISTEN TO ME!
IT WAS YOU!
YOU!!
CHEATER!
GIVE 'EM UP, YOU SNEAK!
WHERE'D YOU HIDE TH' RINGS, YE FOOL?
I'LL MAKE YOU TELL ME!
25

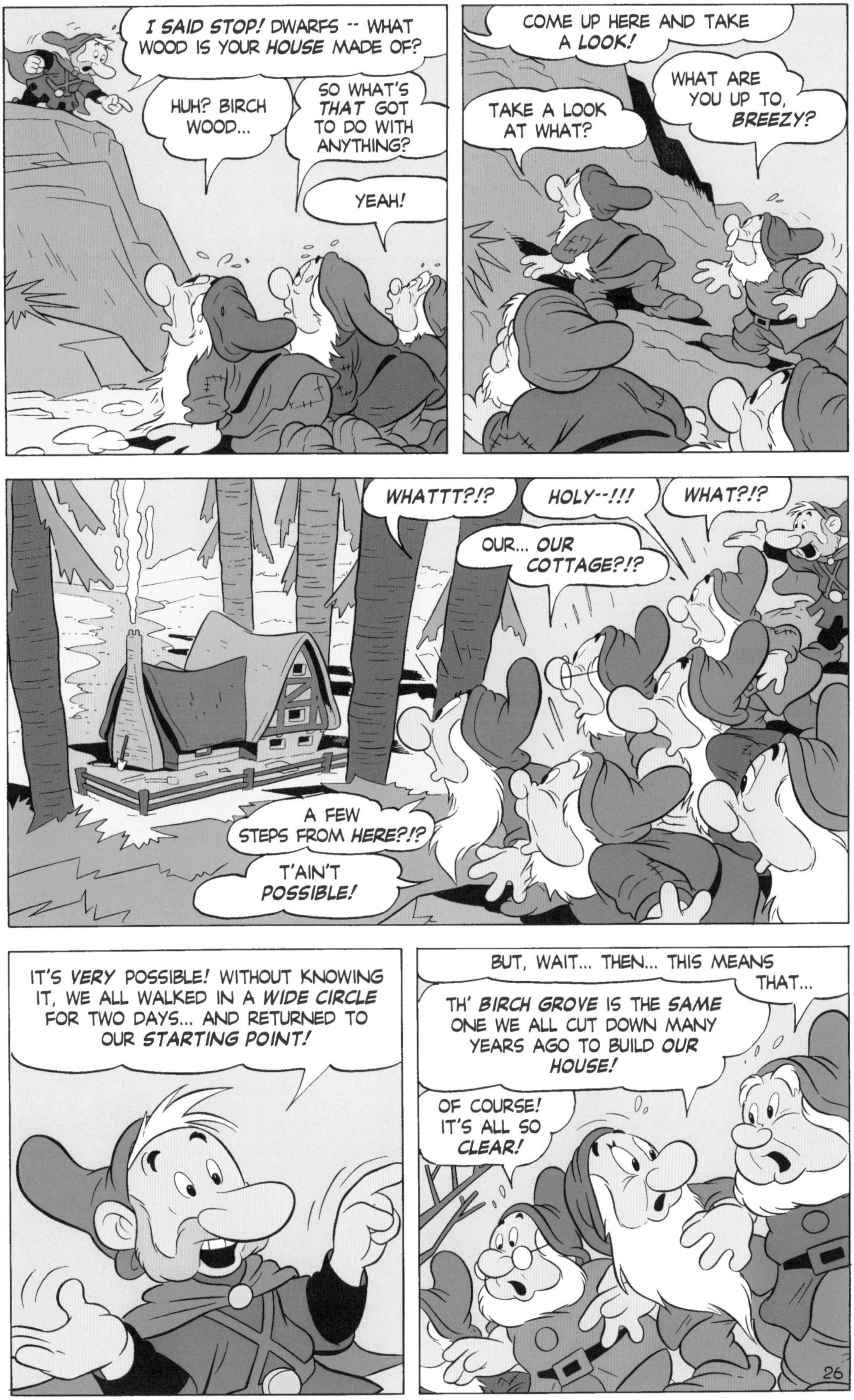
I SAID STOP! DWARFS -- WHAT WOOD IS YOUR HOUSE MADE OF?
HUH? BIRCH WOOD...
SO WHAT'S THAT GOT TO DO WITH ANYTHING?
YEAH!
COME UP HERE AND TAKE A LOOK!
TAKE A LOOK AT WHAT?
WHAT ARE YOU UP TO, BREEZY?
WHATTT?!?
HOLY--!!!
WHAT?!?
OUR... OUR COTTAGE?!?
A FEW STEPS FROM HERE?!?
T'AIN'T POSSIBLE!
IT'S VERY POSSIBLE! WITHOUT KNOWING IT, WE ALL WALKED IN A WIDE CIRCLE FOR TWO DAYS... AND RETURNED TO OUR STARTING POINT!
BUT, WAIT... THEN... THIS MEANS THAT...
TH' BIRCH GROVE IS THE SAME ONE WE ALL CUT DOWN MANY YEARS AGO TO BUILD OUR HOUSE!
OF COURSE! IT'S ALL SO CLEAR!
26

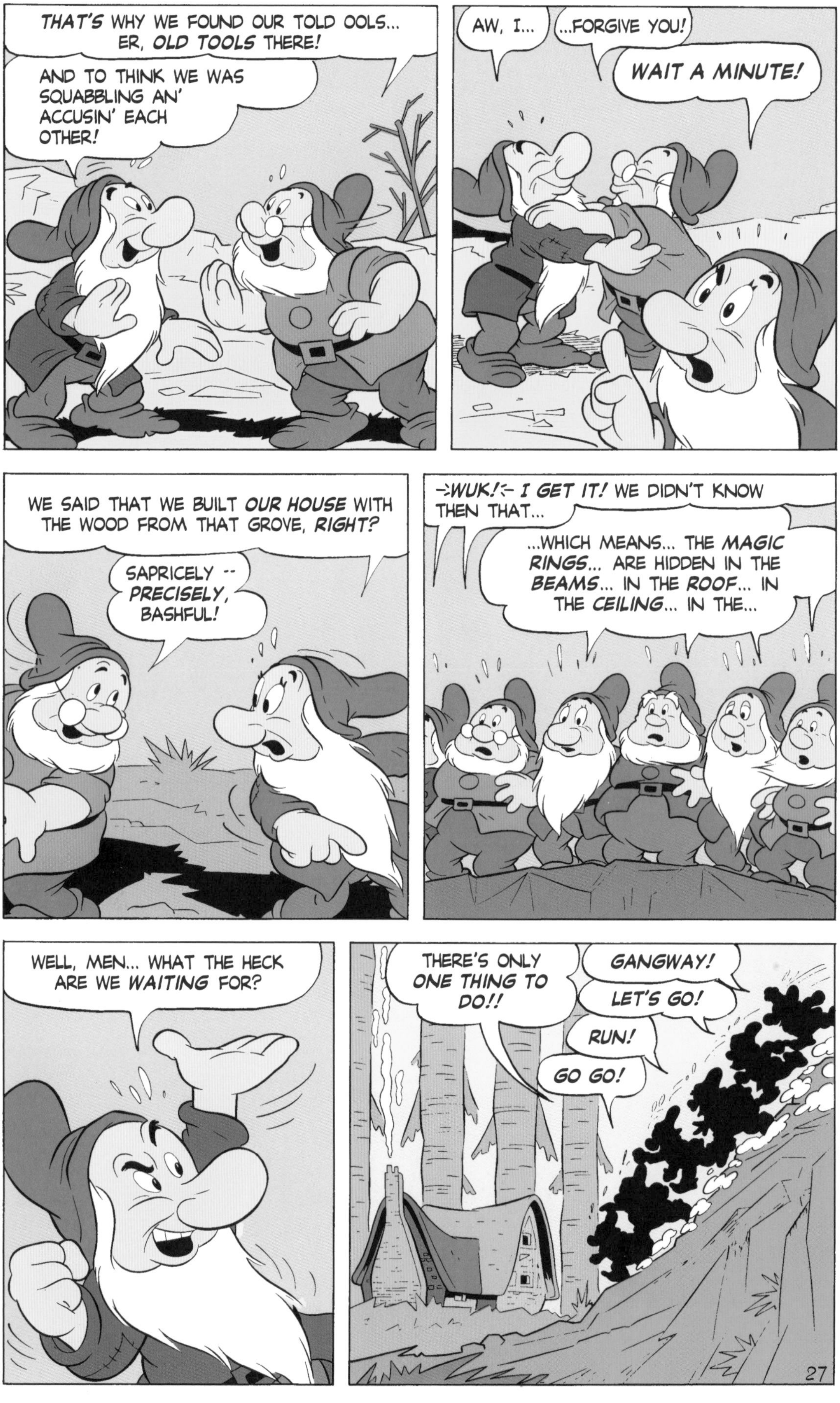

THAT'S WHY WE FOUND OUR TOLD OOLS... ER, OLD TOOLS THERE!
AND TO THINK WE WAS SQUABBLING AN' ACCUSIN' EACH OTHER!
AW, I...
...FORGIVE YOU!
WAIT A MINUTE!
WE SAID THAT WE BUILT OUR HOUSE WITH THE WOOD FROM THAT GROVE, RIGHT?
SAPRICELY -- PRECISELY, BASHFUL!
-WUK!- I GET IT! WE DIDN'T KNOW THEN THAT...
...WHICH MEANS... THE MAGIC RINGS... ARE HIDDEN IN THE BEAMS... IN THE ROOF... IN THE CEILING... IN THE...
WELL, MEN... WHAT THE HECK ARE WE WAITING FOR?
THERE'S ONLY ONE THING TO DO!!
GANGWAY!
LET'S GO!
RUN!
GO GO!
27

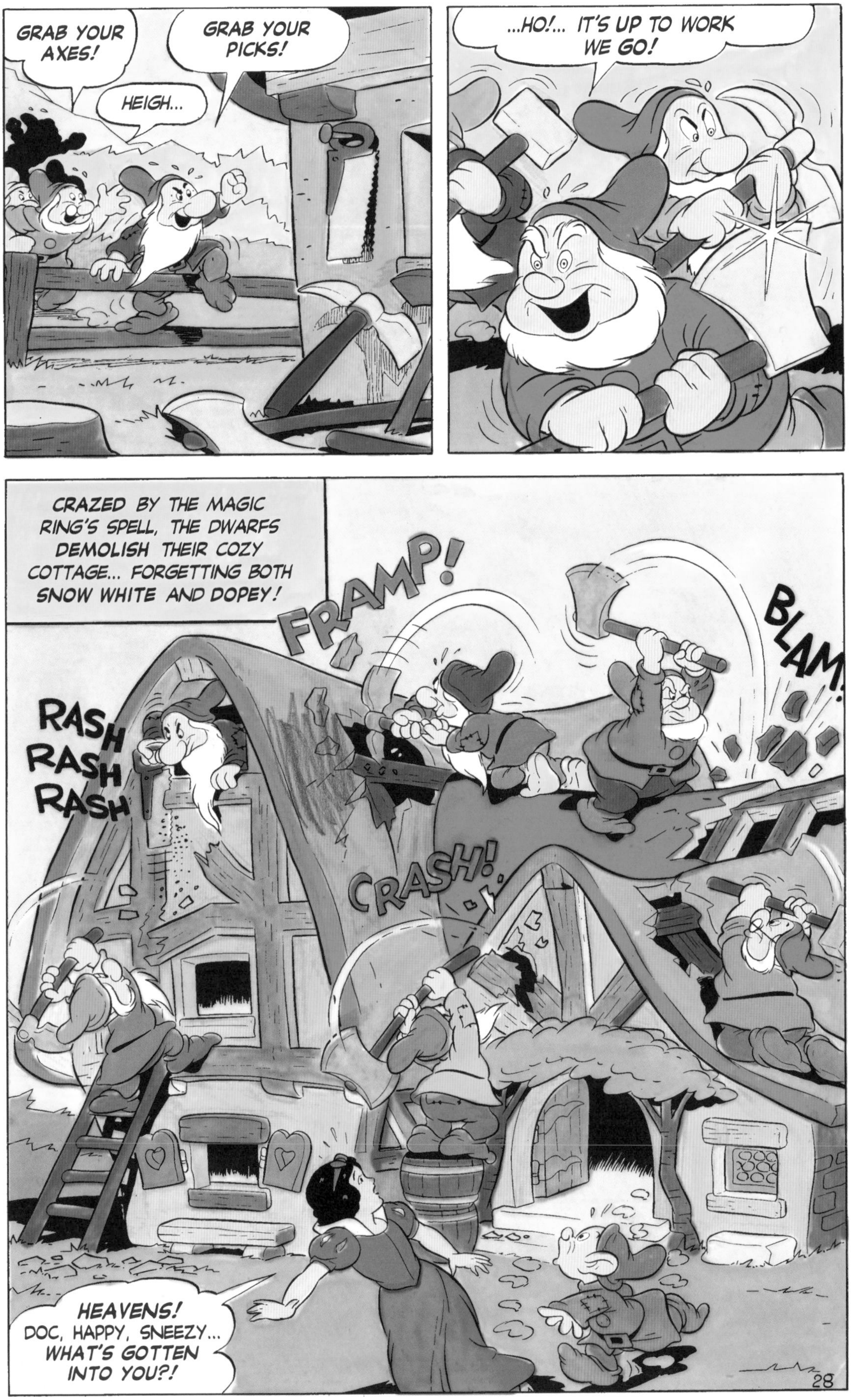
GRAB YOUR AXES!
GRAB YOUR PICKS!
HEIGH...
...HO!... IT'S UP TO WORK WE GO!
CRAZED BY THE MAGIC RING'S SPELL, THE DWARFS DEMOLISH THEIR COZY COTTAGE... FORGETTING BOTH SNOW WHITE AND DOPEY!
FRAMP!
BLAM!
RASH RASH RASH
CRASH!
HEAVENS! DOC, HAPPY, SNEEZY... WHAT'S GOTTEN INTO YOU?!
28

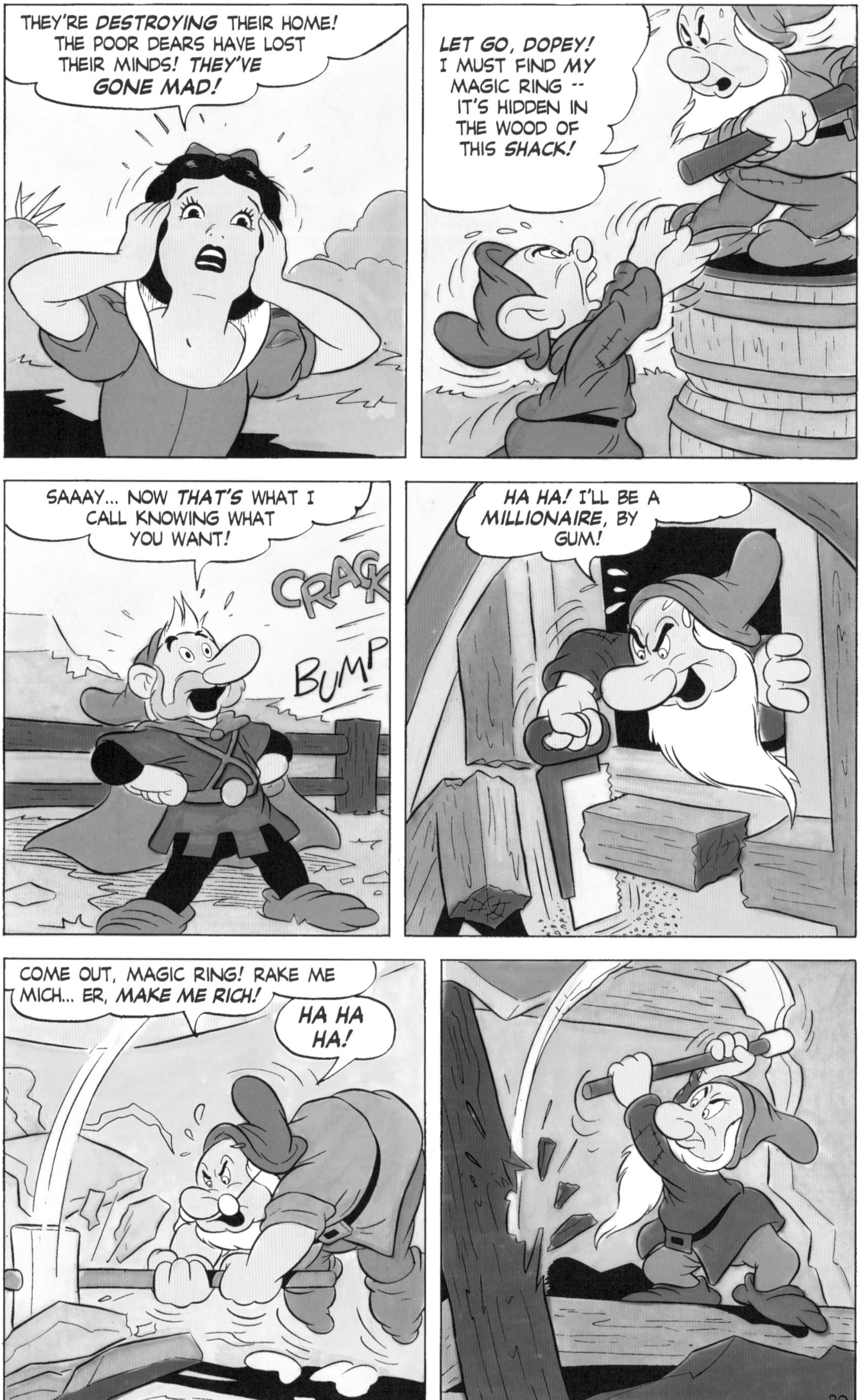
THEY'RE DESTROYING THEIR HOME! THE POOR DEARS HAVE LOST THEIR MINDS! THEY'VE GONE MAD!
LET GO, DOPEY! I MUST FIND MY MAGIC RING -- IT'S HIDDEN IN THE WOOD OF THIS SHACK!
SAAAY... NOW THAT'S WHAT I CALL KNOWING WHAT YOU WANT!
CRACK
BUMP
HA HA! I'LL BE A MILLIONAIRE, BY GUM!
COME OUT, MAGIC RING! RAKE ME MICH... ER, MAKE ME RICH!
HA HA HA!
29

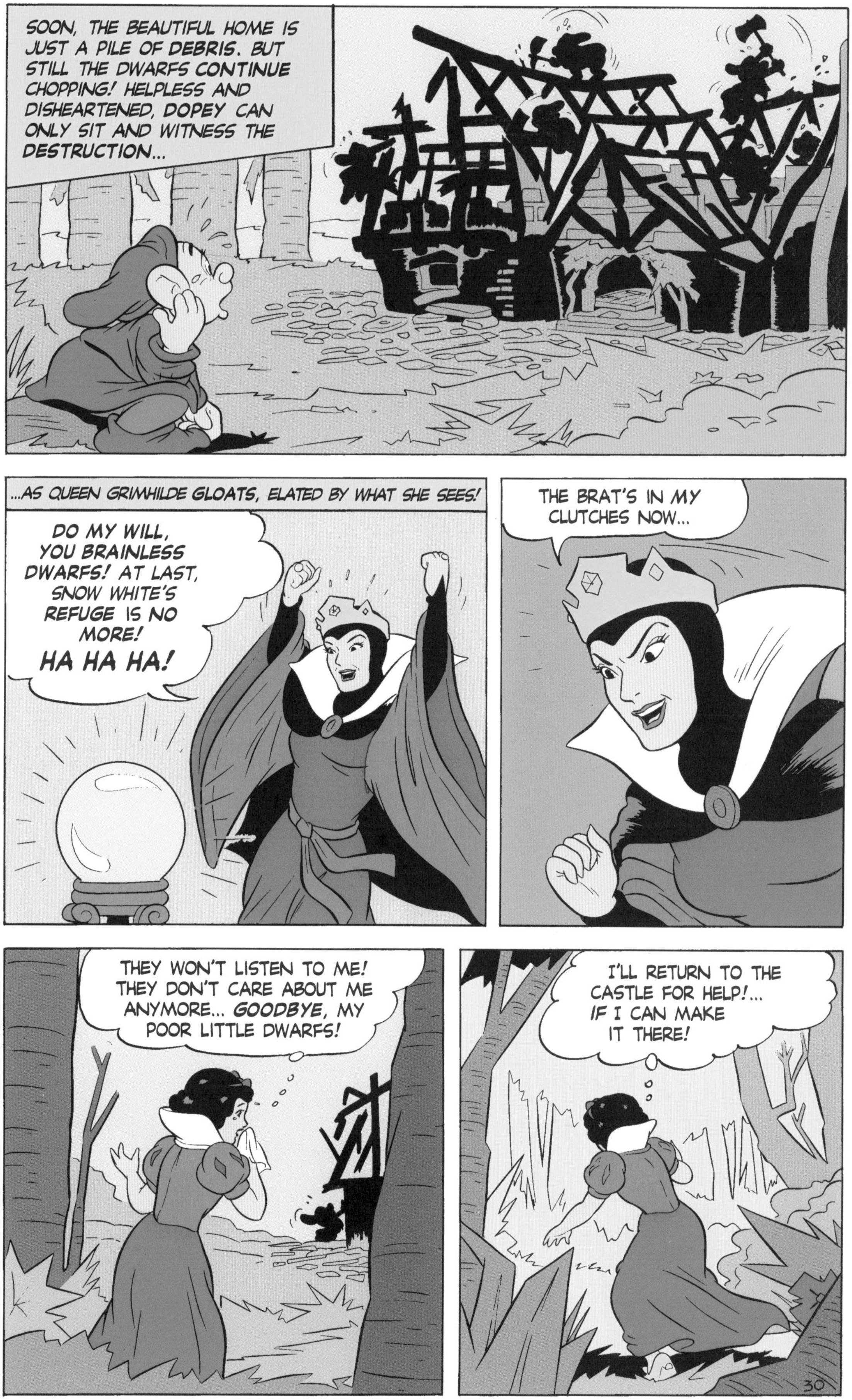
SOON, THE BEAUTIFUL HOME IS JUST A PILE OF DEBRIS. BUT STILL THE DWARFS CONTINUE CHOPPING! HELPLESS AND DISHEARTENED, DOPEY CAN ONLY SIT AND WITNESS THE DESTRUCTION...
...AS QUEEN GRIMHILDE GLOATS, ELATED BY WHAT SHE SEES!
DO MY WILL, YOU BRAINLESS DWARFS! AT LAST, SNOW WHITE'S REFUGE IS NO MORE! HA HA HA!
THE BRAT'S IN MY CLUTCHES NOW...
THEY WON'T LISTEN TO ME! THEY DON'T CARE ABOUT ME ANYMORE... GOODBYE, MY POOR LITTLE DWARFS!
I'LL RETURN TO THE CASTLE FOR HELP!... IF I CAN MAKE IT THERE!
30

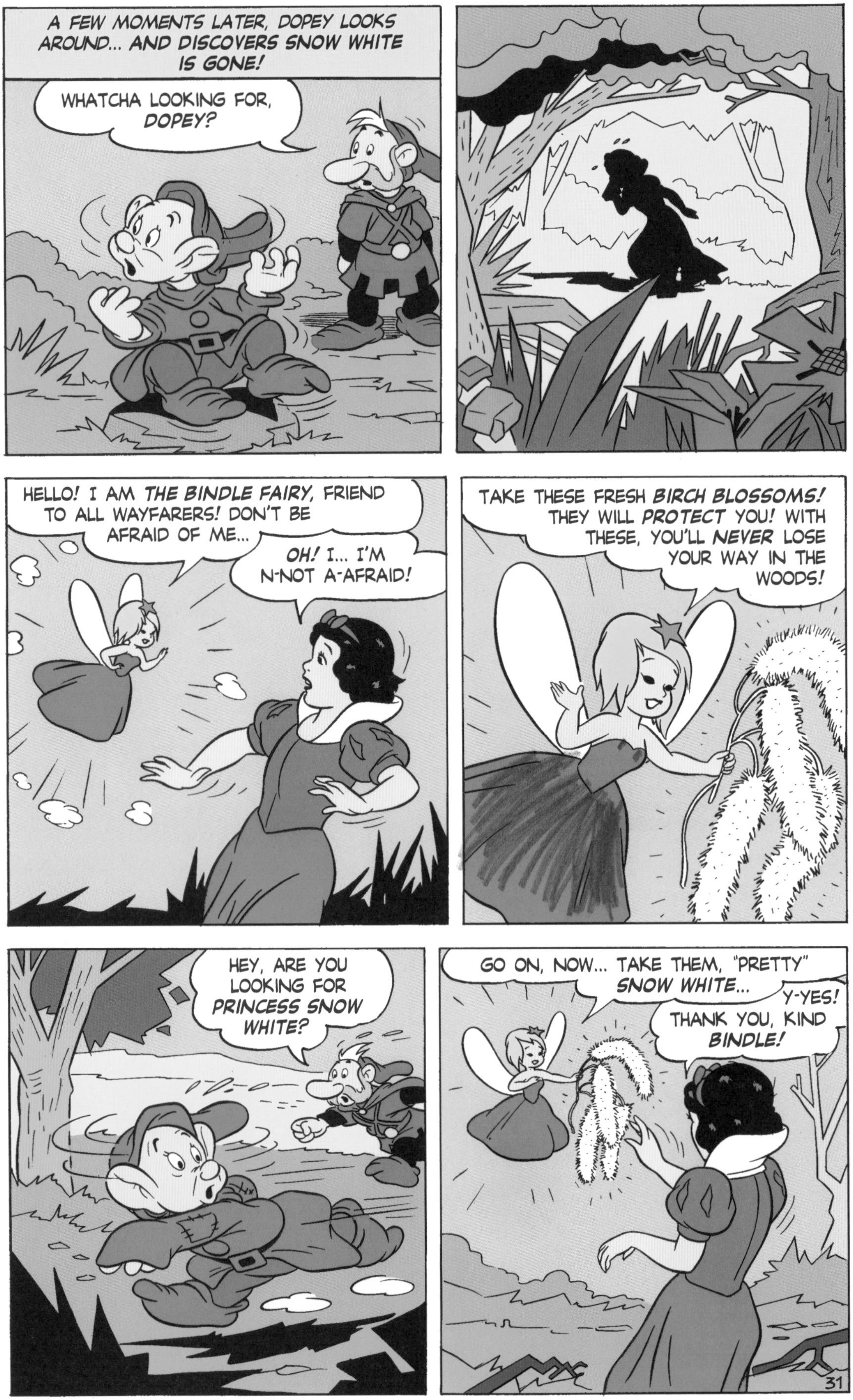
A FEW MOMENTS LATER, DOPEY LOOKS AROUND... AND DISCOVERS SNOW WHITE IS GONE!
WHATCHA LOOKING FOR, DOPEY?
HELLO! I AM THE BINDLE FAIRY, FRIEND TO ALL WAYFARERS! DON'T BE AFRAID OF ME...
OH! I... I'M N-NOT A-AFRAID!
TAKE THESE FRESH BIRCH BLOSSOMS! THEY WILL PROTECT YOU! WITH THESE, YOU'LL NEVER LOSE YOUR WAY IN THE WOODS!
HEY, ARE YOU LOOKING FOR PRINCESS SNOW WHITE?
GO ON, NOW... TAKE THEM, "PRETTY" SNOW WHITE...
Y-YES! THANK YOU, KIND BINDLE!
31

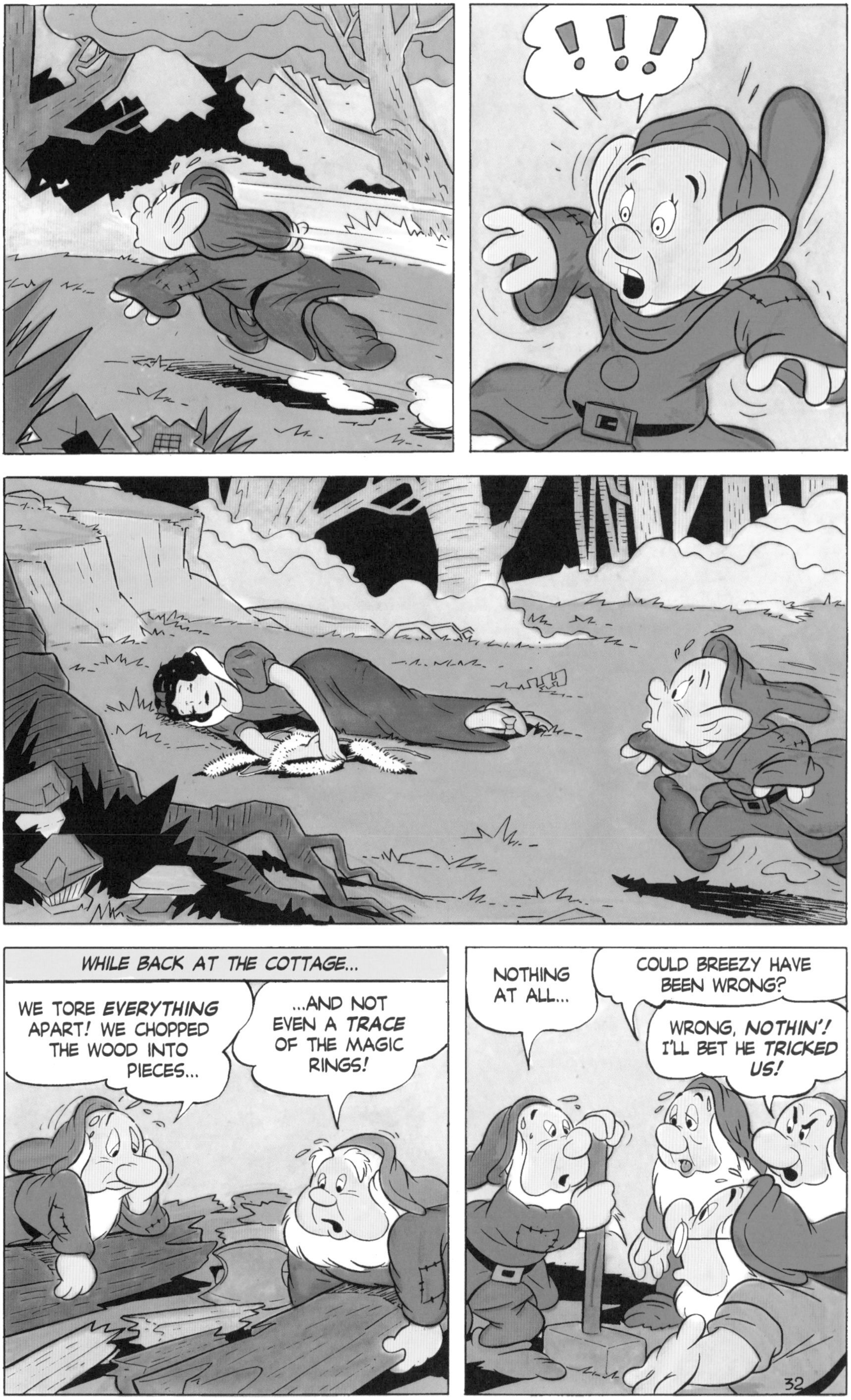
!!!
WHILE BACK AT THE COTTAGE...
WE TORE EVERYTHING APART! WE CHOPPED THE WOOD INTO PIECES...
...AND NOT EVEN A TRACE OF THE MAGIC RINGS!
NOTHING AT ALL...
COULD BREEZY HAVE BEEN WRONG?
WRONG, NOTHIN'! I'LL BET HE TRICKED US!
32

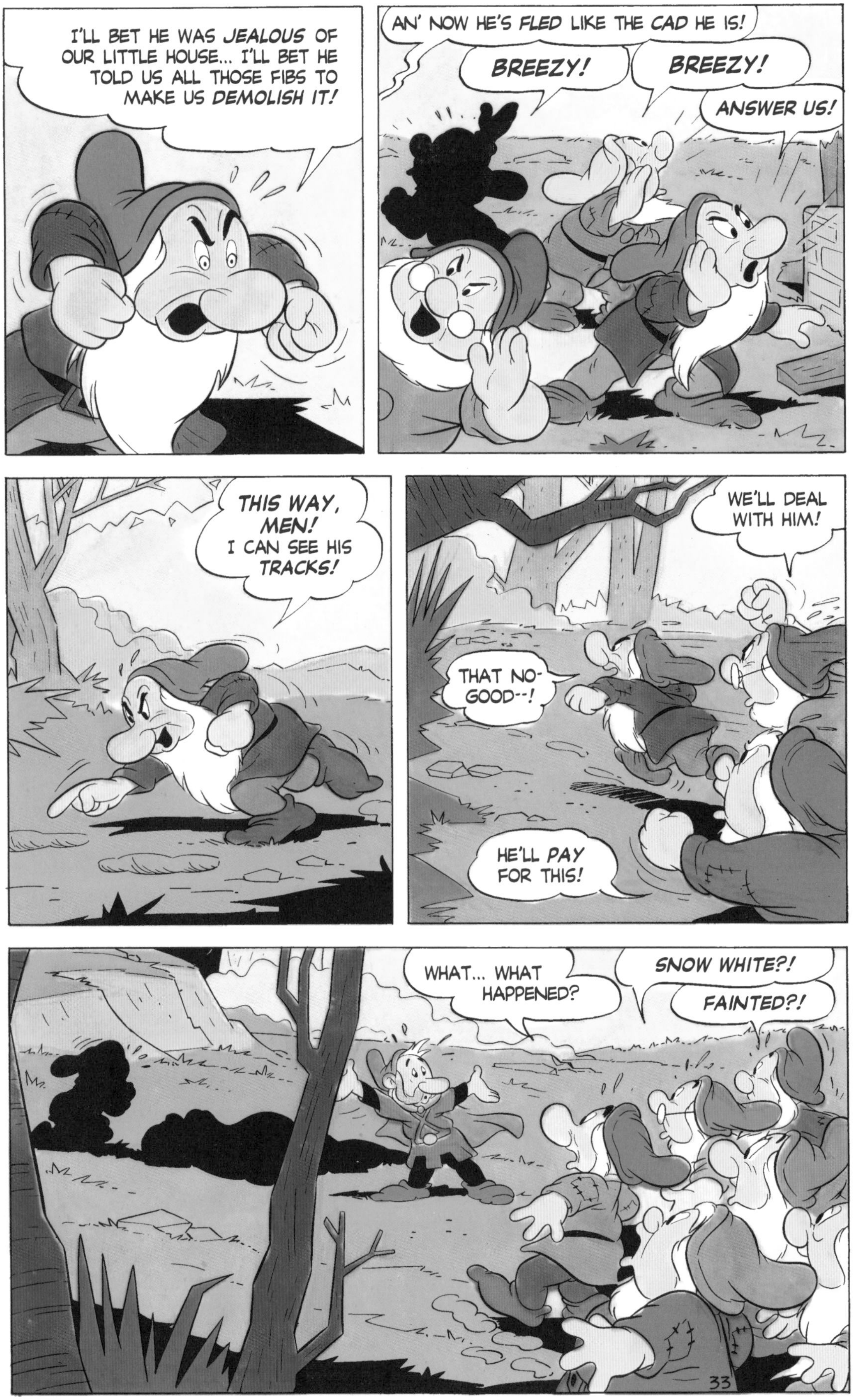
I'LL BET HE WAS JEALOUS OF OUR LITTLE HOUSE... I'LL BET HE TOLD US ALL THOSE FIBS TO MAKE US DEMOLISH IT!
AN' NOW HE'S FLED LIKE THE CAD HE IS!
BREEZY!
BREEZY!
ANSWER US!
THIS WAY, MEN! I CAN SEE HIS TRACKS!
WE'LL DEAL WITH HIM!
THAT NO-GOOD--!
HE'LL PAY FOR THIS!
WHAT... WHAT HAPPENED?
SNOW WHITE?!
FAINTED?!
33

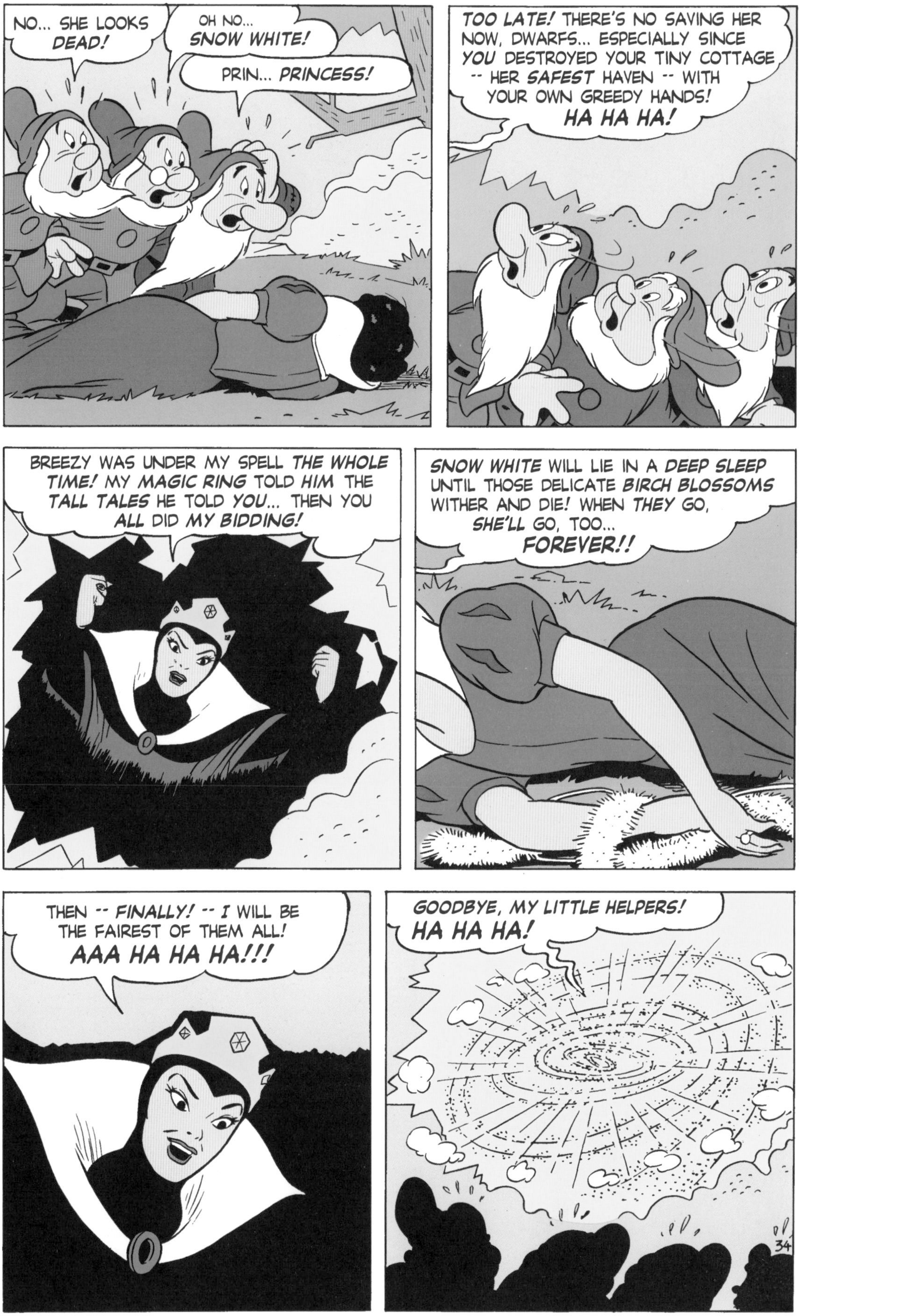
NO... SHE LOOKS DEAD!
OH NO... SNOW WHITE!
PRIN... PRINCESS!
TOO LATE! THERE'S NO SAVING HER NOW, DWARFS... ESPECIALLY SINCE YOU DESTROYED YOUR TINY COTTAGE -- HER SAFEST HAVEN -- WITH YOUR OWN GREEDY HANDS! HA HA HA!
BREEZY WAS UNDER MY SPELL THE WHOLE TIME! MY MAGIC RING TOLD HIM THE TALL TALES HE TOLD YOU... THEN YOU ALL DID MY BIDDING!
SNOW WHITE WILL LIE IN A DEEP SLEEP UNTIL THOSE DELICATE BIRCH BLOSSOMS WITHER AND DIE! WHEN THEY GO, SHE'LL GO, TOO... FOREVER!!
THEN -- FINALLY! -- I WILL BE THE FAIREST OF THEM ALL! AAA HA HA HA!!!
GOODBYE, MY LITTLE HELPERS! HA HA HA!
34

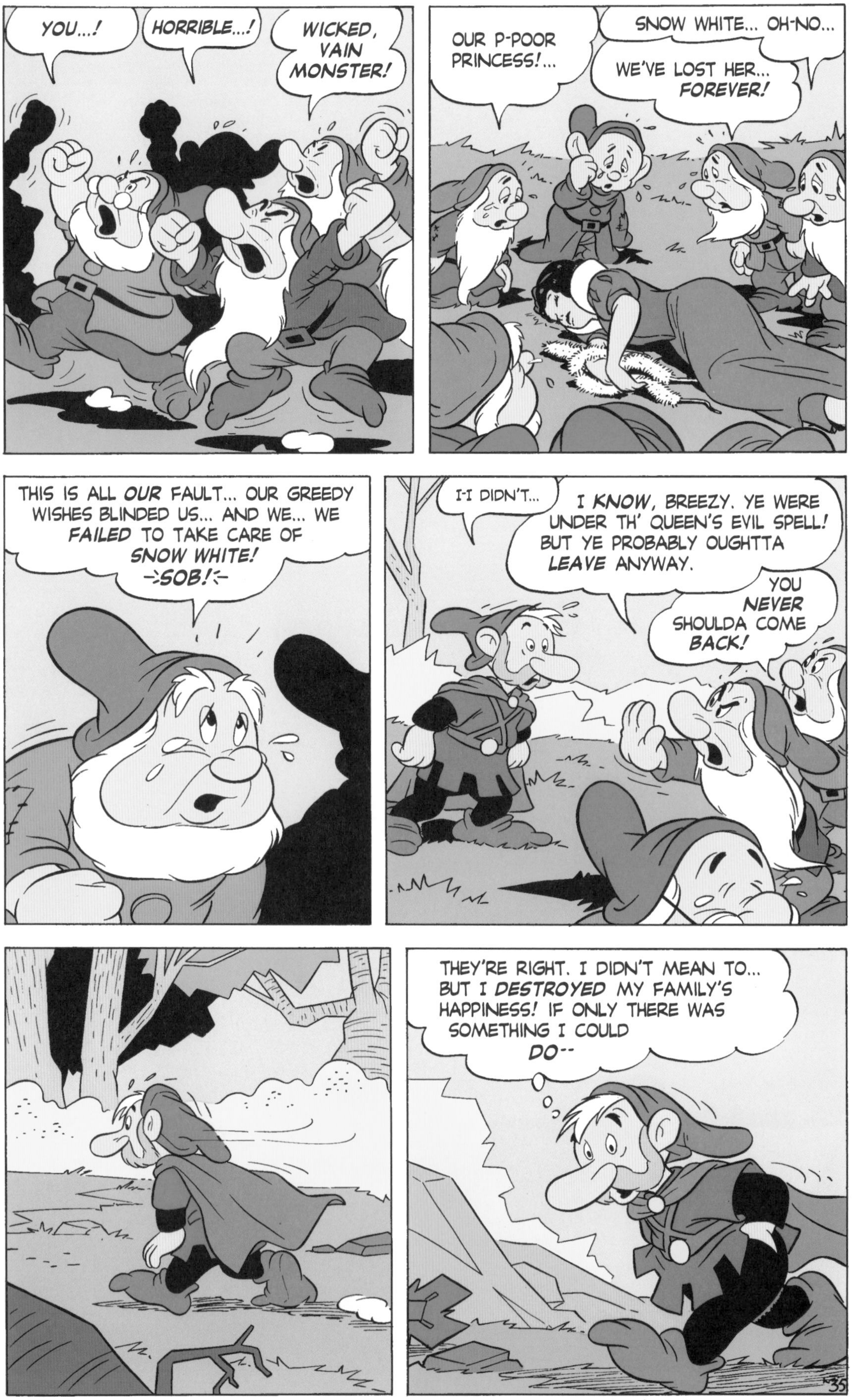
YOU...!
HORRIBLE...!
WICKED, VAIN MONSTER!
OUR P-POOR PRINCESS!...
SNOW WHITE... OH-NO...
WE'VE LOST HER... FOREVER!
THIS IS ALL OUR FAULT... OUR GREEDY WISHES BLINDED US... AND WE... WE FAILED TO TAKE CARE OF SNOW WHITE! -SOB!-
I-I DIDN'T...
I KNOW, BREEZY. YE WERE UNDER TH' QUEEN'S EVIL SPELL! BUT YE PROBABLY OUGHTTA LEAVE ANYWAY.
YOU NEVER SHOULDA COME BACK!
THEY'RE RIGHT. I DIDN'T MEAN TO... BUT I DESTROYED MY FAMILY'S HAPPINESS! IF ONLY THERE WAS SOMETHING I COULD DO--
35

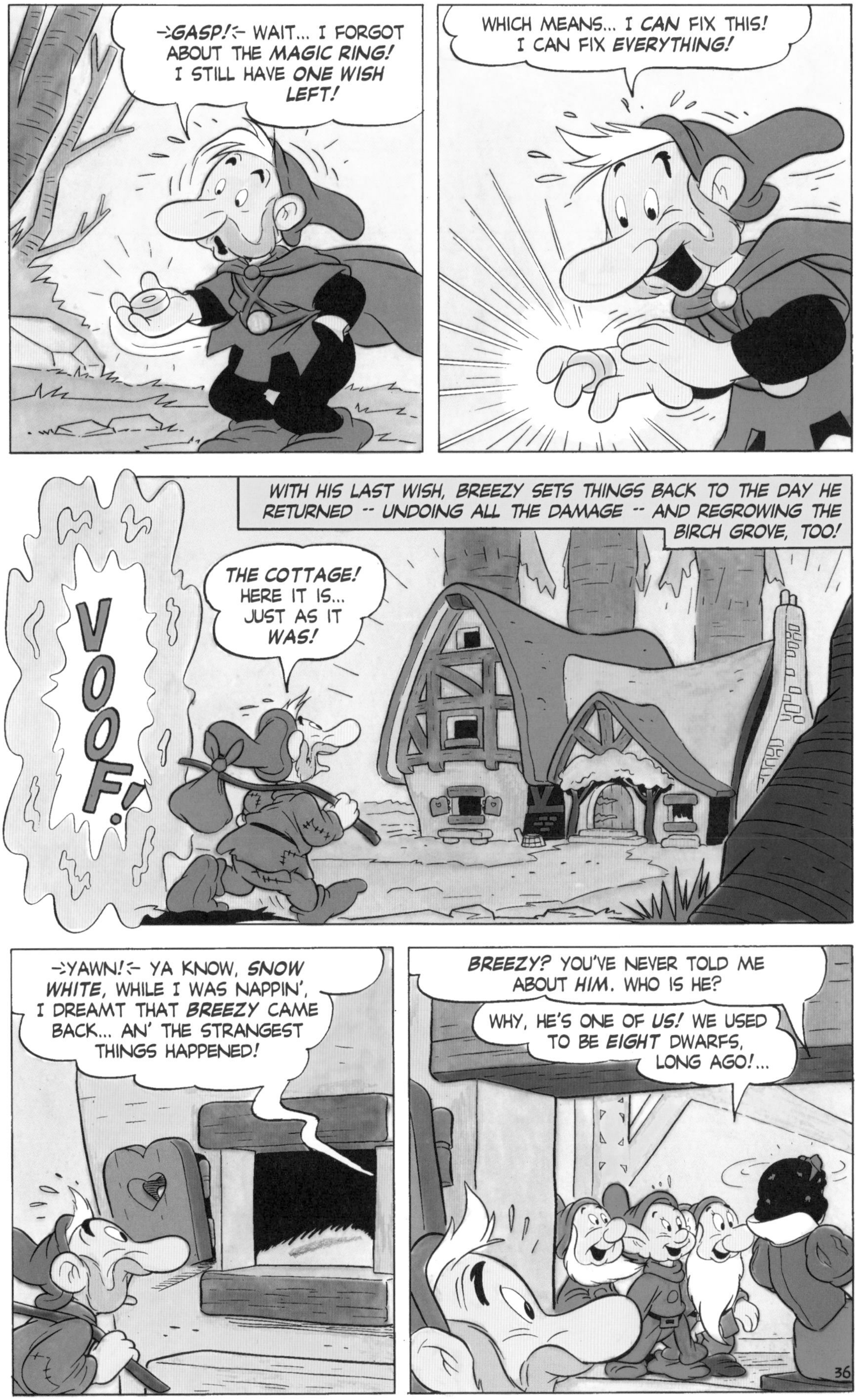

–GASP!– WAIT... I FORGOT ABOUT THE MAGIC RING! I STILL HAVE ONE WISH LEFT!
WHICH MEANS... I CAN FIX THIS! I CAN FIX EVERYTHING!
WITH HIS LAST WISH, BREEZY SETS THINGS BACK TO THE DAY HE RETURNED -- UNDOING ALL THE DAMAGE -- AND REGROWING THE BIRCH GROVE, TOO!
VOOF!
THE COTTAGE! HERE IT IS... JUST AS IT WAS!
–YAWN!– YA KNOW, SNOW WHITE, WHILE I WAS NAPPIN', I DREAMT THAT BREEZY CAME BACK... AN' THE STRANGEST THINGS HAPPENED!
BREEZY? YOU'VE NEVER TOLD ME ABOUT HIM. WHO IS HE?
WHY, HE'S ONE OF US! WE USED TO BE EIGHT DWARFS, LONG AGO!...
36

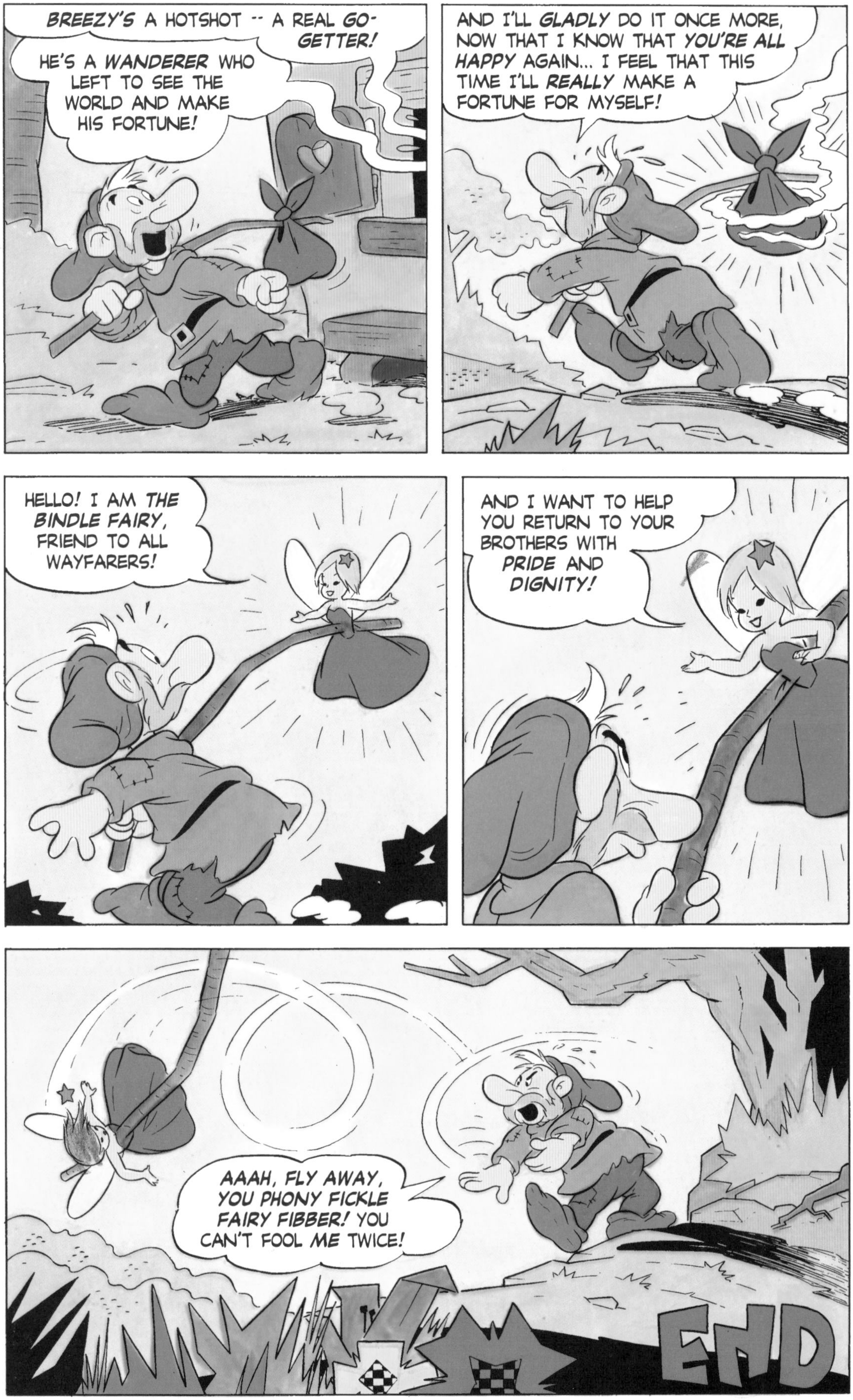
BREEZY'S A HOTSHOT -- A REAL GO-GETTER!
HE'S A WANDERER WHO LEFT TO SEE THE WORLD AND MAKE HIS FORTUNE!
AND I'LL GLADLY DO IT ONCE MORE, NOW THAT I KNOW THAT YOU'RE ALL HAPPY AGAIN... I FEEL THAT THIS TIME I'LL REALLY MAKE A FORTUNE FOR MYSELF!
HELLO! I AM THE BINDLE FAIRY, FRIEND TO ALL WAYFARERS!
AND I WANT TO HELP YOU RETURN TO YOUR BROTHERS WITH PRIDE AND DIGNITY!
AAAH, FLY AWAY, YOU PHONY FICKLE FAIRY FIBBER! YOU CAN'T FOOL ME TWICE!
END